Justice Comes to Jean Ville Through

SISSY

Madelyn Bennett Edwards

D1595591

Printers Amazon KDP and IngramSpark
Book design by Mark Reid and Lorna Reid at AuthorPackages.com

Library of Congress Cataloging-in-Publication Data
Names: Edwards, Madelyn Bennett, author
ISBN: 978-0-9994027-8-8

Subjects: Mystery, crime, coming of age, romance, race relations, Louisiana, Cajun

Manufactured in the United States of America

Other Books by Madelyn Bennett Edwards

Catfish
A Novel

Lilly
Sequel to Catfish

Contents

Reading Group

Discussion Questions

Biography

Dedication

For Billy
A brother and supporter like no other

Prologue

～

1984

I t was the wedding that should never have happened—at least not in Jean Ville, Louisiana in 1984. More than four hundred guests responded to the two hundred invitations sent to announce the nuptials of Susanna Burton and Rodney Thibault at St. Alphonse's Catholic Church on June 30. Most of the people in the congregation were natives of Toussaint Parish and had never seen a mixed-race couple, especially one so blatantly willing to expose their relationship in public.

Whispers filtered through the crowd as Senator Robert James Burton escorted his daughter down the aisle, then shook hands with Major Thibault, who'd recently retired from the US Army JAG Corps after ten years of service. The retired state senator took his seat behind his estranged wife, Anne Baylor Burton, who sat on the first pew with her escort from Houston.

Normally an article about such a high-profile wedding would include a description of the bride's gown, which was a white, floor-length, full-skirted, and full-sleeved version of Lara's attire in *Dr. Zhivago*, a popular movie from the 1960s. This narrative should also mention that the bridesmaids were the couple's daughter, Lilly Franklin, sixteen, the bride's half-sister, Marianne Massey, and full sister, Abigail Burton who all wore floor-length fuchsia taffeta gowns, also with full sleeves, *a la* Lara. Miss Franklin was unescorted. Miss Massey was escorted by Thibault's brother, Jeffrey, a local attorney, and Ms. Burton by Joseph Franklin, Miss Franklin's adoptive father who resides in New York City.

The names of those in the wedding party, and the abundance of lilies that filled the air with a sweet perfume would be important details in a high-profile wedding such as this one, but that's not the case here.

It's what happened after the couple said, "I do," and kissed, in front of a mostly white crowd, that is the real story.

When Major Thibault and the daughter of Senator Burton walked through the double doors of the church into the hot and humid sunny day just after 1:00 in the afternoon, shots rang out. Two shots, to be exact, according to those who witnessed an old, blue, pickup truck speed away with two men allegedly in the cab.

Interviews with those willing to discuss the shooting indicate that both shots hit the major as he fell on top of Susie Burton-Thibault in an effort to protect her from the bullets.

"It was as though he had a premonition," said Jeffrey Thibault, who was just behind Lilly Franklin as the wedding party marched out of the church. Miss Franklin was too disturbed to answer questions.

Confusion was the order of the day as Miss Massey, a registered nurse who works at Jean Ville Hospital, summoned Dr. David Switzer from the church to attend the victims. Blood poured from Thibault onto his wife in such a way that no one could tell who was bleeding, or whether they both were, as Susie's long, red hair matted to the concrete.

The bride seemed to gasp for air, then made an effort at slow, easy breaths to calm herself. The groom lay very still on top of his wife. Not a muscle moved, but in those first few minutes, witnesses said they knew he was alive because there was a slight rise and fall of his back. It was not evident whether Susie was breathing until the two groomsmen rolled the major off his wife and she gasped, taking in a deep breath.

Senator Burton and Mrs. Anne Burton, who'd stood over the couple like immovable statues, inhaled deeply when their daughter took that breath, then began to retch and vomit on the concrete.

Sirens, piercing and loud, burned through the air outside the church as anxious guests strained to see what was happening. Gurneys appeared and the victims were strapped on and transported to the two waiting emergency vehicles parked in front of the church.

Dr. Switzer climbed into the back of one of the ambulances with Major Thibault while Marianne Massey and Lilly Franklin accompanied Susanna Burton-Thibault in the second unit. City and parish police officers and firemen were at the scene and milled around talking to the attendees, asking questions, taking notes.

One of the two ambulances took Burton-Thibault to Jean Ville Hospital. Major Thibault was driven to Alexandria Regional Hospital; however, due to the serious nature of his condition, he was airlifted to Ochsner Medical Center in New Orleans.

There are no reports as to the condition of either of the victims.

Part 1

The Crime

～ Chapter One ～

Abigail

I WISH I DIDN'T have to tell this part of the story.

Susie was in an ambulance, being whizzed off to the nearest emergency room, her head cracked open and bleeding all over her white wedding gown. Marianne might have been a logical choice as storyteller because she and Susie go back further than Susie and I do, but Marianne was awfully busy trying to save our sister's life.

So it falls to me to tell what happened.

I'm Susie's younger sister, Abigail Burton, but everyone calls me *Sissy*.

*

This is what I witnessed that day, and in the months that followed the wedding.

The sanctuary was filled with guests. On the groom's side were all the brown and black folks, and mulattoes, like Rodney. On Susie's side were the white class who curried favor from our dad, Bob Burton, ex-mayor and former senator who still wielded power and influence throughout Toussaint Parish.

Daddy showed up at the last minute and walked Susie down the aisle, which shocked everyone because he had been against the relationship between Susie and Rodney from the beginning. In fact he had organized an old-fashioned posse of guys with guns and ropes to hunt Rodney down in the early 70s when he attempted to move to

New York to marry Susie.

Daddy wore a black tuxedo, and since I was one of the bridesmaids, I was close enough to see him fur his brow and sneer when he shook hands with Rodney at the altar. Marianne was also a bridesmaid, and her face turned scarlet because she was embarrassed by Daddy's presence so close to her. She is our half-sister whom Daddy fathered with Tootsie, our help. Lilly was the third bridesmaid and she didn't notice anything amiss. She just stared lovingly at her parents, so proud that they were getting married to each other.

Susie looked confused, since she never expected Daddy to show up. He dropped her arm and didn't lift her veil to kiss her, like fathers-of-brides are supposed to do. He hadn't attended the rehearsal, so maybe he didn't know how to act, but I could tell Susie was upset, and even a bit sad. Rodney later lifted her veil and kissed her in front of the entire world.

Daddy plopped down in the pew behind my mother and her Mafia boyfriend from Houston, and crossed his arms over his chest. He remained like that for the entire mass, communion, and vow exchange.

Marianne and Susie are the same age and they have a strong sisterly bond. I am almost a decade younger, and they pulled me into their reationship when they told me that Lilly was Susie's daughter. Lilly was born in New York when Susie was an eighteen-year-old sophomore at Sarah Lawrence University. Susie chose a mixed-race couple, Emalene and Joe Franklin, to adopt Lilly, and never told a soul about the baby. Susie revealed her big secret to Lilly at age twelve, and to Rodney when Lilly was almost fifteen. Lilly and Rodney became very close over the last year as they got to know each other as father and daughter.

Rodney is a great guy, plain and simple.

The aroma of fresh lilies filled the air and the organist played *Pachelbel's Canon in D* as Susie and Rodney walked down the aisle and out of the church after their vows. Lilly was right behind them, then

Marianne and Jeffrey, Rodney's brother; then me, with Joe Franklin.

As I walked through the double church doors into the sunshine, I heard two gunshots and saw an old, blue, pickup truck peel-out and spray gravel and dirt behind the tires as it sped towards town. Susie lay on her back on the concrete landing that spanned the entire front of the church, with Rodney face down on top of her, blood drenching her red hair and wedding gown. Lilly screamed and I grabbed her arm while Marianne ran back into the church calling for Dr. David Switzer, a family friend and wedding guest.

Dr. Switzer directed Jeffrey and Joe to roll Rodney off Susie and shouted, "Someone call for ambulances." My brother Robby, number four of us six Burton kids, ran towards the priest's house next door and left our other three brothers and their girlfriends standing around like dummies, the girls in mini skirts and tube tops looking as though they'd shopped together for their inappropriate wedding outfits.

When they rolled Rodney onto the concrete, Susie's chest swelled as though she'd been holding her breath while underneath him, and was finally able to draw the damp summer air into her lungs. I knelt on one side of her in my fuchsia, taffeta bridesmaid dress and tried to block out the sounds of human voices murmuring like a huge swarm of bees.

Blood covered Rodney's face, and his right arm looked broken and was blood-coated. More red liquid collected under his torso while his stiff and still body lay prone on the concrete. Lilly hung onto me, shouting, "Oh, God, please!" over and over.

Susie's head was in a huge pool of blood, and her eyes were closed. After that initial intake of breath, her chest didn't rise and fall again. I thought she was dead and began to shake.

Marianne, who is a nurse at Jean Ville Hospital, knelt on the other side of Susie and put her ear on Susie's chest. It seemed like a very long time before Mari lifted her head and nodded at me as if to say, "She's breathing."

I inhaled hot tar and burned rubber from the pavement where the truck had peeled-out, and got a whiff of something like soured milk in the close space around Susie. That's when I noticed her retching, but she was on her back and couldn't get it up. Marianne and I rolled Susie onto her side so the vomit could spill out on the concrete. It soaked her thick hair that I tried to lift and hold out of the way. Lilly still hung on my back and screamed, "Oh, God, please."

It all happened in slow motion, so I can't say how long it took before I heard the beautiful sound of sirens and clanging bells. Finally, I saw a reflection of blue lights bounce off the church's stained glass windows. Two ambulances, three police units, and a fire truck pulled up in front of the church. The responders got out of their vehicles and stood in the street as though the parking lot—filled with Lincoln Continentals, 98 Oldsmobiles, and GTOs—was a barricade. I felt helpless, shocked, and totally out of my element as I knelt on the concrete between the unconscious bodies of my sister and her new husband.

I counted ten uniformed men, who walked around each other on Jefferson Street when they should have been tending to the injured. Marianne ran past the cars in the parking lot and snagged hold of the shoulder of one of the EMTs. I sat back on my heels and chewed my fingernails while Lilly leaned against my back, screaming, "Oh, God, please!"

"Get over here and help me, Gary." Marianne hollered, and one of the EMTs grabbed a bag and followed her as she weaved between a Ford LTD and a Cutlass to get to Susie. Dr. Switzer seemed to hover over Rodney's lifeless body, holding one eye open for a few seconds, then the other eye. Someone handed Dr. Switzer his bag, and he grabbed a stethoscope and began to poke it around on Rodney's chest.

Once Marianne got Gary to follow her, the other responders began to move, and soon two paramedics knelt beside Susie, and two beside Rodney. The three police officers stood around as though they had never been near a church. Four volunteer firemen emerged from their truck wearing fireproof get-ups and milled around with some of the wedding guests as they exited the church onto the concrete landing.

Gurneys magically appeared, and the paramedics hauled Susie and Rodney through the gravel, potholes, and rows of cars, and slid them into separate ambulances. Marianne got into the front of the unit that held Susie and Dr. Switzer in the one with Rodney.

Lilly screamed, broke loose from my arms, and ran after the men who pushed Susie's stretcher, and before I could stop her, she jumped in the back of the ambulance with her mom. The doors closed and the two emergency units took off up Jefferson Street, heading north towards the hospital.

I ran after Lilly and stood on the street with my hands in the air as sirens blared, bells clanged, and the police units twirled their blue lights and followed the two ambulances in parade-like fashion.

It was a few moments before I realized I'd been left behind. I took off walking, holding the hem of my floor-length bridesmaids dress in one hand, my high heels in the other. The hospital was only a half-mile away.

After I'd walked a little more than a block and was in front of the Fox Theatre, Warren Morrow pulled up beside me in his black Ford pickup and said, "Get in." I stared at him as though I didn't know him, although we'd dated through high school and had restarted our stagnant relationship when I dropped out of college and moved back home a couple of years back.

Warren was a Cajun with questionable friends, a dead-end job assisting a surveyor, barely a high school education, and the manners of a prison refugee. I don't know why I continued to date him, except that there were no alternatives in the small town of Jean Ville where I was imprisoned by my own lack of education and ambition.

I climbed into the front seat of Warren's truck and it was rolling before I closed the door.

"Did you see what happened?" I didn't look at him, just stared out the front windshield.

"No. When I came out of the church, everyone was gathered around Susie and the black guy. I couldn't see nothing."

"Maybe you could ask around. Your 'friends' might know something." I pouted when I thought of Warren's friends and the things they were capable of.

"Yea. Sure." He dropped me off at the emergency entrance to Jean Ville Hospital and said he was going to park his vehicle.

"Don't come in, Warren." I held the door ajar and stood on my tiptoes because his damn truck was jacked up in the air. "I'll call you later."

"But..." Warren stammered and I slammed the door because I had more important things to do than to argue with a dumbass like him.

Two paramedics pushed an empty gurney out the double glass doors as I walked into the emergency department at the small hospital, which was abuzz with activity. The paramedics who'd rolled the gurney out the door returned and joined the three police officers who hung around the nurses' station like stooges. I presumed they were waiting for news as to the fate of Susie and Rodney.

No mixed-race couple had ever been brave enough to show themselves in public in Jean Ville. I told Susie it was a mistake to have their wedding in this town. She'd lived in New York since she was seventeen and she refused to believe that bigotry still existed in the Deep South to the extent it did.

I didn't have to look far to find Lilly. She stood in the middle of the bustling emergency room between the patient cubicles and the nurses' station. I grabbed her and found a corner where we'd be out of the way. She sobbed on my taffeta-covered shoulder.

"What will I do without Susie?" Lilly called her mother "Susie" because they met when Lilly was four, and she thought Susie was Emalene's friend. When Lilly was almost six, Emma became very sick and had brain damage from her disease, causing severe dementia. She no longer recognized Lilly, Susie, or Joe, who went off the deep end and gave custody of Lilly to Susie, but he remained in Lilly's life. Susie married a plastic surgeon named Josh Ryan who died in a helicopter crash six years later. His death was almost the end of Susie. If she hadn't had Lilly, I don't think my sister would have survived.

Two years after Josh's death, Susie heard from Rodney. They got together in New York and discovered they were still in love. That's when Susie finally fessed up about Lilly. She told Rodney first, then she was free to tell everyone else. Of course, she had already told Marianne and me, but we had kept that info among us three sisters.

We all adore Lilly. She's an amazing teenager who has been through a lot: the loss of Josh, her mom's dementia, her parents' divorce. Losing Susie would be catastrophic for her—for all of us. Susie's the rock of our sisterhood, of which I tend to include Lilly, since she's only ten years my junior.

Lilly couldn't be consoled at the hospital. I asked someone at the nurses' station where they'd taken Susie, and the nurse said, "She's in the trauma room with Dr. Cappell." I asked about Rodney, and the nurse said he was not a patient at Jean Ville Hospital; that they might have taken him to Alexandria if his injuries were serious.

I held Lilly and assured her that I would take care of her if anything happened to her mother, but in my mind, I wondered how I would handle a sixteen-year-old?

Give me a break.

I'm single, no real job, no real home. Susie built a garage apartment for me at the house she bought on Gravier Road in Jean Ville where she and Lilly stay when they come for visits. Susie refused to spend even one night in our family home with our dad, where I lived until Susie built my apartment.

I guess I still harbor some resentment towards Susie for leaving me when I was only eight. She rarely came home for visits in all the years she went to college and grad school in New York. I was stuck with four brothers and parents who hated each other.

I'm number five of the six Burton kids, and spoiled rotten by my dad. It's funny, Susie and I have completely different relationships with him. Daddy acts as though he hates her, but he dotes on me. As for Marianne, Daddy has never recognized her as his child and ignores her altogether.

I teach piano and voice lessons to kids whose parents can afford such luxuries. My income pays for gas in the Camaro my dad bought me, as well as cosmetics, and wine. That's all I really need. I don't have to pay rent and I have my dad's credit card for food, clothing, and other essentials.

*

Marianne came out of one of the cubicles and saw Lilly and me standing in a corner wrapped in each other's arms. She said that the doctor had stitched Susie's head and inserted a drain.

"He's concerned about fluid buildup." Marianne washed her hands in the sink that hung on the wall outside the trauma room. "It's a nasty gash. Looks like her head split open when she hit the pavement."

"Was she shot?" I squeezed Lilly's shoulder. Her eyes were as big as watermelons.

"We didn't find a gunshot wound. She has a sprained wrist and a gash on her ankle that took a few stitches, but it's the head wound that's concerning." Marianne whispered in my ear, "It's serious," then walked towards the nurses' station.

"What about Rodney?" Lilly followed closely behind Marianne and I was hot on their tails.

Marianne called central dispatch, who patched her by radio to the ambulance transporting Rodney. The driver told her they had just gotten to Alexandria Regional Hospital, but Dr. Switzer mentioned they might have to airlift Rodney to New Orleans.

Mari took us to a small conference room where Lilly sat down and finally ran out of hysteria. Mari said she didn't want to lie to Lilly; there were so many things that could happen with a head injury and that she wasn't sure, herself, whether Susie would make it. As for Rodney...?

We were in the conference room when Rodney's parents found us. Mari hugged her aunt and uncle and told them Rod was probably in Alexandria. My mother came into the conference room with her boyfriend and hugged me, then Lilly, but ignored Mr. Ray and Mrs. Bessie. *Whew.*

Mama asked about Susie, and Marianne said she would go to ICU to see how she was holding up. Mrs. Thibault had her arms around Lilly, and Mr. Thibault stood behind the two chairs with his hands on Lilly's shoulders. He was pale, which says a lot about Ray Thibault. Both his grandfathers were white, so his skin tone is not really brown; it's more the color of walnuts, like Rodney's.

I left the conference room with Marianne and waded through the antiseptic smell and eerily quiet activity of nurses coming and going without speaking. A glass door led into the ICU where a nurse with a name tag that read, "Martha Chenevert, RN" sat behind a desk watching monitors. Their constant beeping and pulsing gave me hope that Susie's condition was stable for now. Mari slid open the glass door between the room with the monitors and Susie's room. There was a window above the monitors through which I watched Marianne feel Susie's pulse and place a stethoscope on her chest. Mari bent forward and placed her mouth beside Susie's ear, and it appeared Marianne whispered to Susie, but I saw no reaction from my white sister, who looked like sleeping beauty, her long reddish hair spread out, her left ear pressed against a pillow.

When we walked out of ICU, I ran into Daddy, who seemed lost.

"How is she?" He actually seemed concerned, which surprised me since his relationship with Susie was tenuous, at best.

"She's alive, but not out of the woods." I hugged him and took his hand to lead him to the conference room where our family and Rodney's had gathered. When I opened the door and he saw my mother and Rodney's parents, he turned and marched back down the hall and, I guess, out of the hospital.

*

It was a long night. Lilly insisted on staying at the hospital, so Marianne found a gurney and placed it in the little conference room, and I tried to doze off and on in a chair. The Thibaults went home to wait until we discovered where Rodney had been taken. When Marianne called them at midnight to say he was in New Orleans, they agreed to drive the four hours to Ochsner Medical Center in the morning.

Mama peeked in on Susie once, then said she was going to her hotel in Alexandria, would I call her with any news? "Of course," I said, but she didn't seem overly concerned.

Warren showed up, and I sent him home. Suddenly I couldn't look at him without thinking about some of the things I'd witnessed with him and his friends off-and-on over the past ten years. I wondered whether the shooting had shaken me up so that those actions I'd been able to justify in the past, now seemed to bother me, even eat at me; especially when I saw Warren or heard his voice.

After he left, I went to a payphone outside the emergency room and called my dad.

"She's still hanging on," I said when he answered.

"Is your mother there?"

"No, she's gone for now." We hung up, and about fifteen minutes later, Daddy appeared in the conference room. He hugged me and sat in the other chair, but we didn't speak. I wasn't sure whether he was there to keep me company or to be close to Susie in case things took a turn. As hard as he was on Susie, I knew he must love her. After all, she was his daughter. Daddy left about midnight, and I drifted off to sleep.

Marianne and I took turns going to check on Susie during the early morning hours. Although we never said the words to each other, Mari and I were worried Susie would die during the night, and we didn't want her to be alone. She was unconscious, but she fluttered her eyelashes a couple of times when I talked directly into her ear.

Dr. Switzer came in at about six o'clock on Sunday morning and said that Rodney was still hanging on. The surgeons in New Orleans had removed the bullet from his head but weren't sure how much brain damage there was. Rodney's arm was torn up pretty badly by the second bullet that went all the way through his arm and re-entered his back, under his shoulder blade.

"Thank God it didn't reach his lung," Dr. Switzer told us. "They got that bullet out, too, but he has a long road ahead, if he makes it." Lilly cried, and Marianne asked Dr. Switzer a bunch of medical questions I didn't understand.

I thought about the strong friendship Rodney and I had formed since he and Susie decided to get married. I hadn't known him all the years before, but he had become an important part of my life over the past year. He had questioned me about Warren.

"You can do better, Sissy." Rodney was direct but kind. He looked me in the eye when he spoke to me, as though I were his equal. "You are smart and talented, and he's... well, he's a zero."

"I know, Rod. I guess it's just habit."

"Habits can be hard to break, but think about it. He's bad news. His friends are really bad guys. They've done things that would put them in jail if they lived anywhere but Jean Ville." Rodney shook his head, and I knew he meant that discrimination was still prevalent in our little town and parish in South Louisiana. I knew some of the things Warren and his friends did to black guys.

It's funny how I stopped seeing race once Lilly, Marianne, and Rodney came into my life.

I thought a lot about what Rodney had said to me as I waited in the hospital that entire weekend. My disgust for Warren grew, and I began to have flashbacks about some of the things I'd witnessed. I felt embarrassed and disgusted with myself for being a part of those horrible actions, even if I didn't participate.

*

Dr. Switzer went into Susie's room, checked her vitals, read the monitors, and spoke with the nurses.

"It depends on whether there's brain damage." He removed his glasses and rubbed his eyes with his thumb and forefinger. "It's possible there is only tissue swelling, but I'm concerned that she's still unconscious. The sooner she comes out of this coma, the better her chances of survival without long-term problems."

Dr. David Switzer was a kind, gentle man who had delivered all six of us Burton kids. He lived across the street from our antebellum home on South Jefferson Street and had doctored Susie when she had "accidents," which he later discovered were beatings by our dad. Susie and Daddy had sort of patched things up over the past ten years, but neither of us had expected him at the wedding.

And Daddy was a sick man—liver disease from drinking; plus he could be as mean as a rabid wolf.

*

Lilly, Marianne, and I slept in shifts in the conference room and checked on Susie throughout the weekend. She remained in a coma, and Dr. Switzer said that wasn't a good sign.

We three girls were in the cafeteria having sandwiches for lunch on Monday when one of the nurses came running over to our table.

"She's awake." Martha Chenevert said. "She's asking for someone named Rod." All three of our chairs scraped the linoleum floor, and mine almost fell over backwards as we pushed away from the table and pace-walked towards ICU as though escaping a burning house.

"You and Lilly stay in the hall." Marianne stopped us just before we got to the ICU door. "Let me examine her first." Lilly wanted to go in, but I held onto her in the monitor room where we could see Susie in her bed through the glass above the screens. A nurse had a stethoscope on Susie's chest.

Marianne walked into the room, and it was obvious that Susie recognized her.

"Thank you, Rebecca. I'll take it from here." Marianne went to Susie's bedside, and the nurse left the room. Susie's eyes were opened and followed Mari.

24

"You're awake. That's good. How are you feeling?" Marianne shined a penlight in Susie's eyes. Susie stared at Mari, her glare wide and questioning, but her lips didn't move. "Can you talk?" A frightened look crossed Susie's face. Her lips parted as though she were about to say something, then she pressed them together and closed her eyes.

"It's okay. It might be a while before your brain can tell your mouth how to get words out," Marianne spoke softly while she examined Susie, bending her arms one at a time at the elbow and running a silver instrument on the bottoms of Susie's feet. "You're worried about Rodney, right?"

Susie opened and closed her eyes rapidly. "He's hanging in there," Marianne whispered and continued to examine Susie. "They took him to New Orleans. He needed surgery that we don't perform here. His parents are with him."

Susie blinked again.

"Lilly? She's right through that window with Sissy. Worried about you, but she's fine." Marianne sat in the chair next to the bed. "I'd like to call Dr. Cappell and let him check you out before Lilly and Sissy come in." Mari looked through the glass and nodded at the two nurses who sat behind the monitors. One of them picked up the telephone and paged Dr. Cappell. Susie moved her hand over the bed as though she wanted to reach Marianne.

"I know, sweetie." Marianne stood up and bent over Susie. "You have lots of questions. Let's take this a little at a time. Right now all you need to know is that you will be okay, Rodney is still alive, and Lilly is right through that window with Sissy."

Dr. Cappell barreled into the room. He filled the space with his large frame, wild hair that stuck up as though he'd been electrocuted. He had dark, recessed Jewish eyes that were concerned and professional at the same time. Marianne moved aside so he could get close to Susie.

After he examined her and tried to get her to talk he motioned to

Marianne to follow him into the nurses' station where Lilly and I stood waiting impatiently.

"I think she's out of the woods." His voice was deep and easy with a northern accent. "It's not unusual that she can't form words, yet. There's still a lot of swelling, but the fact that she is awake is a good sign. It means that the inflammation is receding."

"Can Lilly and Sissy see her?" Marianne put her arm around Lilly's shoulder. We were crammed into the small chamber between the hall and Susie's room with the two nurses.

"Yes. But only for short periods." He glanced at Lilly, then at me, directing his words to both of us. "Susie needs rest, and any stress could cause a setback." He patted Mari on the shoulder and went back into Susie's room. Lilly, Marianne, and I followed him. Mari caught Lilly by her arm as she walked through the doorway.

"Be calm around her, Lilly," Marianne whispered. "Talk softly. Don't cry. No excitement, just love. You got that?"

"Yes." Lilly looked at Mari, then at me, her big, almond-shaped green eyes glazed with tears. Marianne stood next to Dr. Cappell on one side of Susie's bed. Lilly stood on the other side but couldn't see Susie's face because she was turned on her side, facing Mari and the doctor. I stood at the foot of the bed with a feeling of utter horror. Susie looked awful and smelled worse. Her hair was matted with blood and vomit. She was pale as a ghost, and her hand shook like she had Parkinson's when she tried to lift it.

"Whew. You need a bath." I couldn't hold it back. Susie looked at me standing at the foot of her bed and tried to laugh. She was happy to see us and attempted to look over her shoulder at Lilly, who bent over and kissed Susie on the cheek. Two tears crept out of the corner of Susie's eye and dripped down the side of her nose. Silent tears ran down Lilly's face, but Susie couldn't see that.

"It's okay. Don't try to talk." Marianne put a straw to Susie's lips and told her to take a couple of small sips of water, which she did. "Just blink if you hear me."

Susie blinked once.

"That's good. Now blink twice if you know who I am." Mari squeezed Susie's hand.

She blinked twice and shifted her eyes towards Lilly, who leaned over Susie from the other side of my bed, her tears dripping on Susie's cheek.

"Do you know Lilly?" Marianne motioned towards Lilly, who walked around the bed and stood next to Mari and Dr. Cappell.

Susie blinked twice.

"This is Doctor Cappell. He stitched you up." Marianne motioned across Lilly to the doctor. Susie shifted her eyes towards him.

"You have a pretty nasty gash in the back of your head, Mrs. Thibault." His use of Susie's new name jarred all of us. "I placed a small drain in the wound in case there is fluid buildup, so you'll have to remain on your side."

The drain he inserted was a good move. Blood and yellow fluid filled the tube, and Dr. Cappell called the lab and instructed them to examine the contents to determine what was in the fluid.

"Head traumas are scary," Dr. Cappell said the next time he came into Susie's room. He pointed a light in one of her eyes, then the other. "You don't know if the injured brain is bruised, swollen, or fluid-filled, so we need to watch you closely over the next seventy-two hours."

Susie dozed off and on. There was a constant beeping and the whishing of air, plus a sort of buzzing sound that came from a vent in the ceiling.

Marianne had a stethoscope around her neck and looked beautiful, as always. Her thick mahogany-colored hair was pulled back into a bun at the nape of her neck, tendrils popped out around her face, her huge, round eyes glinted their greenish cast and amber glow. None of us look alike. Susie has red hair, alabaster skin, and eyes the color of a bluish-grey sky after a rain. She's tall and slim like Marianne, and carries herself like a model. I am only five feet two inches, and that's stretching it. I have dirty blonde hair that I highlight—well, I don't do it—I use Daddy's credit card and go to a hairdresser in Alexandria every month. My eyes are the color of artichokes, and my skin tone leans towards olive.

Even though we look different, and I'm nine years younger than Mari and Susie, we share similarities that point to our shared genetics. And we love each other unconditionally.

*

I was only four years old when Susie and Mari met. They were twelve, almost thirteen. That was the summer Marianne's grandfather, Catfish, retired from his job at the slaughterhouse and stopped walking in front of our house on South Jefferson Street where he and Susie would have long conversations. Susie started sneaking off to the Quarters to see him, and he told her stories about his granddad and dad, and some of the folks who had been slaves, then sharecroppers at Shadowland Plantation.

Susie adored Catfish. He died just before she completed her master's program in writing at St. John's University in New York. She was devastated and used her grief to write a book, *The Catfish Chronicles*—a compilation of the tales he'd shared with her over a period of more than ten years. It was published after Josh died.

"I know you have lots of questions, but you can't talk yet." Marianne took Susie's hand and held it in both of hers. "That's normal, for now. Once the swelling in your head subsides, your speech and motor skills will return. Be patient. Meanwhile, let me try to answer some of the questions I know are plaguing you most." Mari sat in a chair she'd pulled up close to Susie's bed and spoke softly, as though trying not to awaken a sleeping baby.

"Today is Monday. You've been here since Saturday afternoon. It's been a long weekend for everyone. Lilly and Sissy will be leaving in a little while to go home and get some rest. I'll stay with you tonight. Right here. In your room. If you need anything, just move your arm, and I'll be here. Do you understand?"

Susie blinked.

"Good." Marianne took a deep breath. "You want to know about Rodney?"

Susie blinked twice, and tears began to pour from her eyes.

"Rodney's still alive. He was shot. Twice. One bullet in the side of his head above his right ear, the other went through his right arm, came out, and reentered his back under the shoulder blade. It missed his lung, thank God." Susie's eyes looked like Frisbees, wide-opened, unblinking. "They've removed both bullets. He's in ICU in a coma, but he's still alive. Doctors say that every day he holds on is a good sign."

She closed her eyes as though trying to absorb the information.

I stood there and, for the first time, wondered: *Who shot him. Were they aiming for Susie too? Why would someone want to shoot Rodney and Susie?*

*

I took Lilly to the Shadowland Quarters to stay with Tootsie so I could do some recognizance.

First stop, my dad's house. I was in a stew and hollered for him as soon as I entered the back door.

"Daddy! Where are you?" My steps on the tiled kitchen floor sounded louder than usual. I was on a mission and stomped through his bedroom to the office he'd built when he enclosed the side porch. We called it the *Lion's Den*, because we were all afraid to enter it; and if we were summoned, we knew it meant trouble.

Daddy wasn't in his bedroom or his office. I went back into the hall that ran from the front door to the back door in the antebellum house. My shoes slapped against the hardwood floor, announcing my presence as I paraded towards the huge, wooden door that led to the long porch across the entire front of the house.

I let the screen door slam behind me and stood staring at my dad, who sat, nonchalantly, in one of the rocking chairs, staring at Dr. David Switzer's house across South Jefferson Street.

"Here you are." I stood with my hands on my hips, unaware that my anger was reflected in my tone of voice.

"What's the matter with you?" He glanced at me then back at the street.

"Are the police looking for the people who shot Rodney?" I spoke softer, calmer, trying to entice Daddy into a conversation that I was sure he didn't want to have.

"I don't know." He scowled at me then looked back at the street.

"Daddy. He's Susie's husband. He might not make it. They flew him to New Orleans."

"I heard."

"He was shot twice. Once in the head, once in the arm, and that bullet lodged in his back. They aren't sure whether he'll survive, and if he does, he might have brain damage. Don't you care?"

"Of course I care, but I can't be involved." He rocked harder and gripped the arms of the chair so tightly, his knuckles were white.

"Will you call Sheriff Desiré and ask him if he has any leads?"

"Why would I do that?"

I stared at the side of his face for a while. I'm not sure whether I was shocked, disgusted, angry, or frustrated. Maybe all of the above. Finally, I walked down the steps from the porch to the front yard and traipsed across the thick St. Augustine grass towards my car that I'd parked around back.

That night I called my brother, James. He's the oldest of the six of us, a prominent attorney in Jean Ville. I asked him if he would help me find out who shot Rodney, and he told me he would ask around.

"Do you know whether a police report was filed?" I gripped the receiver in my hand and stared out my kitchen window at the shadows of the pecan trees that crisscrossed the backyard.

"I'm not sure. Do you want me to look into it?"

"Yes, please find out and let me know." I took a deep breath and felt relieved that James would help me. "We have to find out who shot Rodney and make sure they are charged with a crime."

"Of course, Sissy." James hung up without elaborating, but I felt as though I had a partner in my quest.

*

By Wednesday, the fourth of July, Susie could speak a little and was moved to a regular hospital room where she could have visitors. Tootsie came, as did Jeffrey and Sarah Thibault. Tootsie's sister, Jesse and her husband, Bo, who was Ray Thibault's brother, also came along with Marianne's uncles Tom and Sam, and their wives Gloria and Josie. Mari's younger sisters and some of her cousins streamed in and out of Susie's room during visiting hours when only two people could visit at a time. They had all known Susie since she was twelve years old, and I guess Susie was more like family to the Massey clan than to us Burtons.

For days there was a constant flow of visitors. Lilly sat in the chair beside Susie's bed and slept there at night. She took it upon herself to make sure every visitor stayed for short periods and didn't create excitement.

On Friday afternoon, Marianne and I were in the cafeteria having a cup of tea. I was pensive and stirred my tea over and over without thinking.

"Have you noticed that, like, other than my mother and my dad, I'm the only white visitor Susie has had all week?" I didn't look up from my tea.

"Hmm. I hadn't really noticed, but I'm not surprised." Mari took a sip and put her cup back on the table. "Susie hasn't lived here for more than fifteen years, and has lost touch with all her white friends. As for my family, Susie's been close to all of us for twenty years."

Marianne looked over my head as though in a trance. "I remembered the first time I met Susie. She was sitting on my grandfather's porch one afternoon when I walked out of my house next door with a book I was going to read to him. There was this beautiful, redheaded white girl in the extra chair on his porch, and they were talking as though they had been friends forever. Come to find out, they had been, since she was six or seven. He would walk down South Jefferson Street every afternoon and stop to visit with her if she was in y'all's front yard. After he retired and no longer saw her every day, she started to come to the Quarters to see him.

"I was put off by her at first, but she was so genuine and looked at me as though I was just like her—no difference." Marianne's eyes were wet, but no tears flowed out of them. "That was Susie. She never saw color or race or gender or any deviation as different from her. She accepts and loves everyone, which makes it easy to love her.

"I remember how she listened and squeezed my hand when I talked about tragic things that had happened to me. I always knew we were half-sisters because I had figured out long ago that your dad was my biological. I never say biological *father* because the word *father* sticks in my throat; so in my mind, he's simply my *biological.*

"Susie was in her twenties before she realized your dad had been screwing my mother all those years... decades, in fact. Since before Susie was born, for sure, because I'm a few months older than Susie." Marianne paused as though remembering something she didn't want to talk about. I took the opportunity to ask the question on my mind.

"On another subject, is there any talk about who did this?" I looked up from my cup of tea. "I mean, are the police looking for the shooter or shooters?"

"I haven't heard." Marianne looked at me with a questioning brow. "I don't know if there's a case."

"A crime was committed." I was surprised that this was the first time we'd discussed who shot Rodney. "I mean, someone shot an innocent person. Rodney could die, in which case it's murder."

"Sissy, this is Jean Ville, Louisiana. Do you think these people care that a black man was shot?" Marianne's eyebrows lifted, and she stared at me as though I could answer such a nebulous question.

"I would hope so. This is 1984, not 1964 for God's sake. A black woman became Miss America last year."

"Yeah. And there's talk they want to oust Vanessa Williams.

Something about posing nude for a magazine." Marianne seemed agitated, and I wondered, for the first time, what it must feel like to be black in this whitewashed world.

"Well, you have to admit, it's against the Miss America rules to pose nude."

"If she had been white, they'd have given her a slap on the wrist."

I glared at my tea, then at Mari. "Well, all that aside, someone needs to talk to Sheriff Desiré. Maybe my dad?"

"Has he mentioned it?"

"No, in fact, I talked to him about it, and he said he couldn't be involved." I watched Marianne's expression, which was one of disgust. "He says he cares, but he doesn't act like he does."

"Since he was never a dad to me, I suppose I don't expect him to be one to Susie, either." She got up from the table and headed towards ICU. I watched her and thought about what she said, then my mind automatically returned to finding out who shot Rodney.

⌇ Chapter Two ⌇

⌇

Sleuthing

I'D KNOWN THE DISTRICT attorney, Reggie Borders, since I was little. His daughter Bonnie and I had been best friends from kindergarten through high school, and we were still friends. She'd married Danny Goudeaux, a guy who was a year ahead of us in school, and they had two boys, about two and three years old.

I drove to the Borders' home after Mass on Sunday. I knew the entire family would be gathered there for dinner and an afternoon around the pool. That's how they'd spent every summer Sunday since I was a child. I'd often been there for sleepovers on Saturday nights, then I'd attend Mass with the family the next morning. All of their kids and lots of friends would gather for a big noon meal and a leisurely afternoon of croquet, tetherball, badminton, and swimming.

I felt like one of the Borders kids, especially after Mama left Daddy and moved to Houston when I was fifteen. I think Mrs. Phyllis Borders felt sorry for me and pulled me in like a mother hen.

No one was surprised to see me when I walked through the back gate with my swim bag over my shoulder.

"Hey, Sissy!" Each one yelled "Hi" at me, and Bonnie came running over to hug me. Her older brothers Jules and Frank were there with their wives and children, although I didn't know which kids belonged to which parents. Bonnie's younger sister, Emily, and a couple of girls she'd brought home from college were sunbathing on lounge chairs near the pool. The youngest brother, Stephen, who was still in high school, sulked on a stool at the far side of the pool. I felt a heart-tug for him because I knew he'd rather be anywhere else, and I could remember feeling that way when I was his age and had been forced to be with my family.

Now I wished I had a family.

I changed into my swimsuit and accepted a beer from Mr. Reggie. Bonnie and Danny got into the pool and were trying to teach the little boys to float. The bigger kids were in the deep end, jumping off the diving board, competing to create the largest splash.

I sat at the oval table with an umbrella stuck through the center hole. Mrs. Phyllis and Mr. Reggie sat in two of the chairs, with Jules and his wife, Lisa across from them. I was on one end, and no one sat in the sixth chair.

"How's Susie?" Mrs. Phyllis patted my hand and looked directly at me. She was the type who made you feel as though the whole world stopped when you talked because she listened so intently. She nodded and squeezed my hand, and tilted her head sideways as though I were the only person at the table.

"She's better. It's been touch-and-go. Dr. Switzer moved her out of ICU Wednesday, and she's starting to say a few words." I spoke loud enough for everyone at the table to hear.

"I'm glad, honey. We've been so worried." Mrs. Phyllis patted my hand and ran her other hand through her short, brown hair, cut like Dorothy Hamill. I wanted to ask her why she hadn't visited Susie, if she was so worried, but I held my tongue. I had a more important mission to accomplish.

"We're still worried about brain damage." I looked around the table and everyone had concerned expressions. "We are very worried about Rodney. He might not make it." I stared directly at Mr. Reggie. He nodded but didn't respond. We were all quiet for a while and sipped our beer. Mrs. Phyllis was drinking wine, as usual.

"Do you know who did it?" I stared at Reggie Borders, Toussaint Parish district attorney. Everyone looked at him. He couldn't hold my stare and lowered his eyes, but didn't answer my question. "Is anyone interested in finding out?" Still no response. Jules began to shift in his seat, and his wife got up to dig around in the ice chest for a beer. Mrs. Phyllis called to one of her granddaughters who was walking towards the diving board. The girl, about eight years old, came running over and sat on her grandmother's lap. Mrs. Phyllis jumped up because now her shorts and shirt were wet and she needed a towel. Jules got up to help his wife.

That left only Mr. Reggie and me at the table.

"Are you going to pursue it, Mr. Reggie?" I stared at him while he looked at the tabletop.

"That's up to the sheriff, Sissy." He pushed his chair away from the table and walked off.

I got in the pool and played with Bonnie and her kids for a while, then I changed back into my jeans and blouse, told everyone goodbye and went home to my apartment on Gravier Road.

*

I loved my little place above Susie's detached garage. It had one bedroom, a study that could serve as a small spare bedroom, a living room and kitchen combination, a fairly nice-sized master bedroom with an en suite bathroom and, my favorite room, a deck off the kitchen that faced the huge park-like backyard. I had a swing and two rocking chairs on the porch, which was about fifteen feet above the ground.

I sat on the swing with a glass of lemonade and thought about how to find out who shot Rodney in a town that was run by privileged white men who would prefer if all the black and brown people moved away. There was still a faction of the Ku Klux Klan in town, although I had no idea who the members were.

The next morning I went to the Toussaint Parish Sheriff's Department. I tapped on the glass window where a woman with large glasses and hair teased like a rat's nest was turned sideways to the window typing on a manual typewriter. She told me I needed to file a complaint and gave me a clipboard with six pages of forms to fill out.

"But someone was shot. That's a crime, not a complaint." I stood at the window and thumped my fingernails on the counter.

"If it was a crime inside the city limits, there should be a police report. Check with the city police department." She closed the sliding glass across the window and returned to the typewriter.

I went to the police department, and a woman who could have been the twin of the one at the sheriff's office sat with her back to the same type of sliding window and gave me the same runaround.

"Why isn't there a police report? There were three city police units at the scene." I glared at her as though she could manufacture a piece of paper that didn't exist. She got up and walked to the copy machine, and all I saw was the back of her gaudy red blouse with frilly sleeves that got caught with the paper on the machine when she closed the top.

I went to the hospital. Susie looked better and was able to say a few words that I understood, although she was frustrated that she couldn't get an actual sentence to come out of her mouth.

"I talked to Mama last night. I think she's coming to see you tomorrow." I stood on the side of Susie's bed, holding her hand.

She smiled and tried to move her head, then winced.

"Are you in pain?" I fluffed her pillow and fitted it around her neck to keep her head wound from touching the bed.

"Nooooo, I'm. Ohhh. Kay." Susie never complained. I could remember her with black eyes, stitches across her cheek or under her chin, a sprained wrist or ankle, and other injuries my dad had inflicted on her. She would act as though nothing was wrong.

"I don't guess you'd tell me if you were hurting, would you?" I smiled at her, and she giggled and shook her head a little, then winced again. "I'll leave you alone. I think I'm making you hurt."

She winked at me when I left. I walked down the hall towards the cafeteria and ran into Marianne.

"I was going to check on Susie." Marianne stopped to hug me.

"I just left her. I think she needs some rest." I hugged Mari and took a step back. "Hey, do you have a minute to chat?"

"Sure." Marianne led the way to the cafeteria where we got cups of coffee and sat at a table in the far corner. I told her about my attempts with Reggie Borders, the sheriff's department, and the city police. She wasn't surprised that I'd hit dead ends everywhere.

"What else can I do? Surely there's a police report." I stirred my coffee and added some cream.

"They've buried it. Maybe you should give up."

"There has to be someone who can help." I thumped my fingers on the table as though I were playing the piano.

*

I drove to James's office and walked past his secretary into his inner sanctum. There was a client in the chair facing James, who sat behind his desk.

"I need to talk to you." I had my hands on my hips and stood with my legs spread.

"Sissy, I'm busy. Can you come back later?" He lifted his eyes to look at me, his chin still pointing towards his desk.

"No. I have to talk to you now."

James apologized to his client, got out of this chair, and took me by the elbow. He practically pushed me out the door, down the hall, and into the library. "What can be so important that you interrupt me when I'm with a client?"

"You said you'd help me find out who shot Rodney. I've been to the sheriff's office and the city police department, and neither has a report. They aren't even looking for the shooter." I stared at my brother who was at least a foot taller than me. "I need your help."

"Okay, I'll call the sheriff. Go home. I'll call you when I know something." He turned and left me in the library. I stood there not thinking about anything specific, then I noticed a file on the table that said, "June 30, 1984." I picked up the manila folder and flipped through some of the pages. There were names I recognized: Tucker

Thevenot and Keith Rousseau. They were a couple of Warren's renegade friends. I shivered when I thought of some of the things I'd seen them do to black people.

There were some figures on one of the pages: $500, and $1000. There were other things I didn't understand: bank statements, copies of drivers' licenses, and other numbers such as '37L402', which didn't mean anything to me, but I memorized it anyway, by playing a mind game where I attached the number '37' to my brother, James, who was thirty-seven years old. The 'L', of course, stood for Louisiana; and '4-0-2', well, that was like saying 2-4-6-8-10, only without the 6 or the 8, and backwards. 4-2 with the 0 from the 10 in the middle.

Sometimes I worried about how my mind worked.

*

Mama arrived from Houston on Tuesday. She was dressed in a green, silk dress with a suede jacket and huge, diamond earrings. There were so many bracelets on her arms that she jingled as she walked down the hall. Her high heels clicked on the tiled floor and turned heads as she waltzed by. I stayed with her in Susie's room most of the afternoon while Mama read from a book of Shakespeare, then from *Gone With The Wind*. When she left she mentioned she'd be staying at a hotel in Alexandria and would return the next day.

The next afternoon, I peeked through the glass on the door to Susie's room and watched Mama kiss Susie on the forehead, say a few words, then walk out. Mama threw the door open and walked into the hall. She stopped to kiss me on the cheek and told me she'd be returning to Houston, and to please keep her informed about Susie's condition. She didn't speak to anyone as she strutted down the long corridor and out the front door of the hospital. I laughed at the metamorphosis from the plain Jane, cowering wife of my dad, to the now wealthy Houston socialite kept-woman who was our mother.

"Hi. How was the visit, Mom?" I stood at the foot of Susie's bed and pinched her toes through the sheets. Marianne walked in behind me.

"Nice." She spread the word out like soft butter on a soft, baked biscuit, and she had a frown across her brow.

"She's worried about you," I said.

Marianne walked around to the side of Susie's bed and shined her penlight in Susie's eyes. "You're getting better every day. How's the pain?"

"Ohhhh. Kay." She closed her eyes for a few seconds, then she looked up at me, then at Mari, her brow wrinkled and eyebrows lifted as though she had a huge question to ask.

"You want to know about Rodney?" Marianne sat in the chair near Susie's bed, and I stood at the foot of the bed, my hands holding Susie's feet through the sheet and blanket.

"Yes."

"He's hanging in there. There's not much more I can tell you." Marianne held Susie's hand. "I was thinking about driving to New Orleans tomorrow on my day off, if it's okay with you that I leave?"

Susie opened her eyes with a jerk and blinked rapidly, then turned her head to look at Mari. She winced as though the movement caused a great deal of pain.

"I take it that means you want me to go. Blink once for yes."

"Yes." She blinked, then looked at me.

"Okay, but when I come back, I'm going to tell you the truth." Marianne squeezed Susie's hand. "You've been through more than most thirty-three year olds, so I trust you can handle whatever the truth is."

Susie blinked once, closed her eyes, turned her head, and stared at the ceiling through her eyelids. Mari didn't talk anymore, and I hoped Susie was going to sleep.

Lilly came into the room and Marianne asked us to step into the hall. She told Lilly she was going to New Orleans to see Rodney. Lilly begged Mari to take her. They both looked at me.

"You two go on and see about Rod. I'll hold down the fort." I laughed as their expressions broke into smiles, which I knew had as

40

much to do with their amusement at the way I talked as with their happiness with my answer.

*

"If you've never seen a man on life support, with tubes in every orifice, cylinders next to the bed, some pumping oxygen, blood, and medicines in; some taking urine, drainage, and air out; you have been spared," Marianne told me on the phone from New Orleans. "As a nurse, I've seen lots of people on life support, but never someone I loved."

Rodney was two years older than Marianne, and he was more like a big brother than a cousin. Mari told me that since she'd never had a brother, Rodney was the one who had protected her, taught her how to cut cane, shuck corn, and play ball. He'd made her into a tomboy because she'd wanted to impress him and hated it when he called her a silly girl.

"The sounds of beeping and gurgling flooded the ICU room where my big, tall, handsome cousin lies comatose with tubes and machines surrounding him." Marianne choked down a sob and said that if Lilly had not been there, she might have fallen apart.

"I spoke with the nurse who manages the monitors. She told me that they took him off the medication to induce a coma, but he hadn't come around. She said they'd removed the bullets, but there might be fragments in his brain that are causing him to remain unconscious.

"I walked into the room with Lilly so close behind me I could feel her breath on the back of my neck," Mari said. "I found Rodney's hand under the sheet and pulled it out. There was an IV line in the side of his wrist. I stroked the top of his hand and whispered to him.

"'Hi, Rod. It's me, Marianne. If you can hear me, blink your eyes.' I waited, but there was no movement. I told him Susie was fine and would come to visit him as soon as the doctor allowed her to travel. 'She's fine. Do you understand?' I thought I saw a slight movement of his eyelashes.

"Then I said, 'Lilly is with me.' His eyelashes lifted ever so slightly, then fell. I pulled Lilly around to the front of me, held her shoulders from behind, and told her to hold his hand and talk to him."

"'Dad. Rodney. It's me. Lilly.' Her voice caught in her throat. 'I want you to wake up. I'm worried.'

"Sissy, you won't believe what happened next. I watched Rodney over Lilly's shoulder and his eyelashes raised and lowered twice. Lilly said, 'Rodney. I love you. Susie loves you. We want you to come home.' Lilly started to cry softly and squeezed Rodney's hand. He turned his head towards her, ever so slightly. It was a small movement, but was so significant that the nurse burst through the door and stood at the foot of the bed. His eyelashes lifted so that we could see a sliver of the whites of both eyes, then they lowered to his cheeks.

"'I think he squeezed my hand,' Lilly looked at me sideways over her shoulder. 'Rodney. Dad. Please squeeze my hand again. She looked down at their hands entwined on top of the sheet, and I watched as his long fingers encircled her hand and gripped it; not tightly, but his hand encompassed all of hers, and his eyelashes fluttered several times. Lilly couldn't hold her emotions any longer, and she laid her head on top of their hands and cried.

"Sissy, the most miraculous thing happened. Rodney lifted his other hand, pulled it out from under the sheet and reached over to stroke Lilly's hair. I felt tears stream down my face, but I couldn't move." Marianne had tears in her voice. I gripped the phone receiver and held my breath.

"Rodney's lips turned upward on the corners, and the edges of his eyes lifted as he rested his fingers on Lilly's hair. I squeezed her shoulders to keep myself from collapsing. I'm not sure how long we stayed there before Rodney fell asleep and his hand became heavy on Lilly's head. I lifted the long, strong fingers and put his palm on his stomach on top of the sheet and pulled Lilly away from the bed.

Lilly became hysterical.

"'Is he dead? What's wrong?' She grabbed Rodney's hand with both of hers and began to shake it. I told her he'd fallen asleep because what he had done took a lot of energy. I moved her away from the bed so the nurse could get close to Rodney to check his pulse and listen to his heart rate.

"'He's fine.' The nurse turned and looked at Lilly and me. 'Just sleeping for now. Let's let him rest, okay? He knew you. That's a great sign. I want to call his doctor. Would you mind stepping out for a while?'

"Lilly and I went down to the cafeteria and got cold drinks. We sat in a booth in the corner of the room and were quiet for a long time. I asked her whether she'd like to stay overnight so she could see Rodney in the morning. She looked up at me through those thick lashes and reminded me so much of Rodney in that moment.

"'I'd like that, Aunt Mari. Thank you.' She looked back down, and I realized it was the first time she'd called me, 'Aunt.' I wondered if today had been the first time she'd called Rodney, 'Dad.'

"We got a room at the Brenthouse." Marianne sounded as though she wanted my permission to stay in New Orleans another day. "It's the hotel connected to Ochsner Medical Center for patients and visitors. What do you think?"

"I think that's a great idea." I turned to look at Susie, whose eyes were as large as grapefruits. "I'll tell Susie everything you told me, and I won't leave her."

"Can you put the phone near Susie's ear?" Marianne said Lilly wanted to talk to her mom.

I whispered to Susie that Lilly wanted to speak to her, and I put the phone near Susie's ear.

"Ho." Susie's voice was weak, but I could hear the excitement in her small word. I don't know what Lilly said, but Susie whispered, "Yes."

I put my ear next to the phone, so I could listen in.

"Mom? I mean, Susie?" Lilly was close to tears, and I heard Marianne say something to her. "Mom. Dad woke up, sort of. I mean, he knew me." Lilly's voice cracked, but she held it together. "I mean, Rodney. He squeezed my hand. He put his hand on my head. He blinked his eyes when I talked to him."

"That's won-der-fullll." Susie had tears the size of golf balls running down her cheeks.

"I told you he'd be alright." I took the phone away from her ear so I could talk to Marianne.

"Sounds like good news, right?" I spoke softly, afraid of the answer. Marianne said the doctor would check on Rod the next day, but in her opinion, it was a good sign. I spent the next two hours telling Susie what Marianne had described, and answering Susie's repeated questions over and over to reassure her.

*

Marianne called the next day to tell me that she and Lilly had met Rodney's doctor.

"We were in the ICU waiting room fifteen minutes before visiting time, and a doctor came in and asked if there were family members for Rodney Thibault." Marianne's voice was soft and slow. "Lilly and I followed him into a small glassed-in room, and he introduced himself as Doctor Warner, the neurosurgeon who'd operated on Rodney and removed the bullet from his brain. I told him that I was Rod's cousin and introduced him to Lilly.

"You would have been so proud of her." Mari's voice raised an octave. "She stepped forward and reached out to shake the doctor's hand, like a grown up."

"'Well, Lilly, you are a miracle worker.' Dr. Warner shook Lilly's hand and held it while he talked to her. 'Your dad must love you very much. We've done everything we could to get him to wake up, but he's been unresponsive until now. I'd like to observe you with him, if that's okay?'

"'Okay,' she said and looked directly into Dr. Warner's eyes. 'When can I see him?'

"'How about now?' He led the way to Rodney's room. The doctor and I stood at the foot of the bed and watched Lilly go to Rodney's bedside and reach under the sheet for his hand. She began to talk to him, and he turned his head towards her, ever so slightly, and fluttered his eyelashes, a small smile turned up the corners of his mouth and the edges of his eyes. Lilly pulled Rod's hand out from under the sheet, and Dr. Warner and I watched Rodney wrap his fingers around her hand and squeeze.

"'I love you, Dad. I mean, Rodney. Sometimes I don't know what to call you, but Dad feels best to me, if that's okay with you?' Lilly had her mouth close to his ear, and his grin spread across the bottom of his face, the corners of his eyes raised a bit more, and his cheekbones lifted. I looked at Dr. Warner and, Sissy, his expression was one of amazement."

I stood in Susie's room, pressing the telephone to my ear so hard it began to burn. Susie looked at me with those big blue-gray eyes, worry lines across her forehead, so I put the receiver near her ear and bent down so both of us could hear Marianne.

"Rodney opened his eyes about halfway and looked directly at Lilly." Marianne's voice was filled with excitement. "His lips moved as though he wanted to say something, so Lilly put her ear right next to his mouth, then she nodded. I couldn't hear what he said, but he must have said something because she said, 'Okay, then it's Dad.'

"Lilly couldn't hold it together any longer and burst out crying. When she put her head on the side of his bed, he reached his other hand over his chest and stroked her hair as he had the day before, only this time his hand actually moved back and forth a little." Marianne took a deep breath, and I could tell she was choking back tears, too. "The doctor went to the other side of Rodney's bed and listened to his heart, felt his pulse, shined a light on his pupils, and tapped on Rodney's elbows and knees, then he motioned for me to follow him out of the room.

"'He has a long way to go.' Warner is tall and very handsome, although I shouldn't notice things like that." Marianne laughed, and Susie grinned and winked at me.

"'We don't know how extensive the damage is,' Dr. Warner told me. He showed a great deal of compassion towards Rodney. 'My greatest concern has to do with his cognizance, but if he knows his daughter, that's the best sign that he does not have memory loss.'

"I told him that I'm a nurse and that Susie had also been injured and was in ICU in Jean Ville. I said that if she and Lilly were both here with Rodney, he would make significant progress." Marianne took a deep breath, and Susie smiled. "He agreed with me and asked that I not take Lilly back to Jean Ville just yet. He said it might be disturbing for Rodney if Lilly disappeared, that patients with brain injuries think all sorts of things that can cause stress on their brains and obscure recovery.

"I told him I had to get back to Jean Ville, but maybe I could arrange something so Lilly could stay. I asked him if Susie could be transferred to Ochsner, and he said that if she has a brain injury, he would take her as a patient, but only if Dr. Switzer would make the referral." Marianne took another deep breath, and I could hear exhaustion in her exhale.

"I'll call Rodney's folks and ask them to drive to New Orleans to be with Lilly so you can come home." I took the receiver from Susie's ear, and she closed her eyes, a huge grin across her face.

*

"She's making progress here; why should we put her in a vehicle and transport her almost four hours?" Dr. Switzer pinched the bridge of his nose with the fingers of his left hand and removed his glasses with his right. He looked tired and stressed. Marianne and I had confronted him in the doctors' lounge.

"It's more for Rodney than Susie." Marianne got a cup of coffee from the coffee maker on the counter and sat across from him at the square table. I stood behind her chair.

"What's your opinion of Rodney's condition?" He slumped in his chair and put his glasses back on.

"Dr. Warner thought that the way Rod responded to Lilly was nothing short of miraculous." Marianne paused and took a sip of her coffee. "We believe having Susie there would help to speed Rodney's progress even more, and I think it would be good for Susie. She's worried sick about Rodney and doesn't think we're telling her the truth. She needs to see him for herself."

"You make a good case." Dr. David winked at me over Marianne's head. "I'll call Warner and make the referral." He pushed his chair back from the table.

"Before you go Dr. David, I have a question." I leaned forward on the back of Marianne's chair and spoke softly.

"What is it?" His brow wrinkled, and he placed his hands on the table as though he were about to lift himself up.

"Have they found out who did it?"

"Did what?" He looked confused.

"Shot Rodney. Who shot him?" I felt agitated. I wanted to shout at him that someone should be pressing forward to try to catch the person or people who shot an innocent man.

"I'm sorry, Sissy." Switzer leaned back in his chair. "I've been so intent on caring for the injured that I haven't thought about how it happened."

"I didn't see who it was, but I saw a blue pickup truck speed away from the church after the shots were fired." I stared at him, and Marianne glanced over her shoulder at me. "Isn't that what you saw, Mari?"

"Exactly." She turned back towards Dr. David.

"Hmm. I'll talk to the DA" Switzer had a puzzled expression. "He's one of my patients, and a friend."

"Would you call me if you learn anything?" I wrote my phone number on the back of one of Marianne's business cards and handed it to him.

*

"Hi, sunshine. How are you today?" I stood on the foot of Susie's bed. Mari had followed me through the door and stood on the side of the bed.

"Worrrrrr -eeeed," Susie said the word slowly, trying to pronounce each syllable correctly so we could understand.

"Wow! Speech therapy must be working." Mari sat on the side of Susie's bed. "What are you worried about?"

"Lilly?" Susie spoke slowly, but pronounced her daughter's name clearly. "Rod...?"

"Well, Lilly is with Rodney because she's his best medicine right now." Marianne told her about Rodney's improvement, and tears rolled down Susie's face; especially when Mari said Rodney said something to Lilly, and she said, "Then it's Dad."

"The good news is, I'm going to take you to New Orleans to see your husband for yourself." Marianne was smiling, and it took Susie a minute to digest what she said.

"Huh? Whhhhh-nnn?" She spoke too quickly and her words were jumbled, but Marianne and I both understood Susie. That's the good thing about sisters.

"Yes, really." Marianne squeezed Susie's hand and smiled a confident smile. "Rodney's doctor, Warner, has agreed to take you as a patient, and Dr. Switzer is making the referral. As soon as that's done, we'll schedule an ambulance to transport you."

"Oh! Hahhhhh-peeee." Susie's smile was broad and it was the first time I'd seen her dimples since the shooting.

"The two of you will be good medicine for each other. And you'll like Dr. Warner." Marianne grinned, and I stared at her intently, trying to read whether there was something beneath those words. Susie must have sensed it too.

"You? Like Warrrr-ner?" Susie laughed.

"Don't jump to conclusions." Marianne laughed too, but I could tell Susie had struck a chord. "He's a good neurosurgeon and seems genuinely interested in Rodney."

"Heeee? Likes. You?" Susie started to laugh, which made Marianne laugh. None of us had been very happy since we'd walked out of the church on Susie's wedding day almost two weeks before, so it was quite a relief to laugh like sisters and feel a bit lighthearted.

Then I thought: *If Susie, Marianne, Rodney, and Lilly are all going to be in New Orleans, it falls to me to find out who did this, and bring them to justice. Me, twenty-five-year-old Sissy Burton.*

~ Chapter Three ~

New Orleans

MARIANNE TOOK A WEEK off from work and rode in the back of the ambulance with Susie, which was a smart move because the trip was grueling and painful for her. Mari had to sedate Susie about thirty minutes outside of Jean Ville. I followed the ambulance with our luggage and more things for Lilly, since she'd hadn't packed much when she'd gone to New Orleans the week before.

Susie was admitted to the step-down unit at Ochsner, where patients went directly from ICU before they were transferred to a medical floor. Dr. Warner said he wanted to assess her and monitor her brain function and nervous system.

Warner was a good-looking guy—tall, well-built, masculine, and with a hint of mischievousness about him. I watched the way he looked at Marianne and how he found reasons to ask her to go out to the hall with him to discuss things. I tried to read Marianne's reaction to the handsome doctor, but it was difficult. I don't think she knew how to act. She'd never been attracted to a man, but it seemed to me this one had her attention.

It was a slow, grueling pace for Susie because she was eager to see Rodney, but Warner had other plans. Lilly stayed with Susie whenever the nurses allowed, and with Rodney for ten minutes every two hours, as per the ICU rules. Marianne kept reminding Susie to be patient, but she wanted to see her husband in person.

I got to see Rodney twice during the two days I was in New Orleans. He didn't respond to me, but I sat near his bed and talked to him as though he understood everything I said. I told him he was right about Warren. That I would get the creep out of my life. I told him I was going to make sure we got justice for what happened to him. I thanked him for saving Susie's life, because I was sure that he'd either seen something or had a premonition, and that's why he'd wrapped his body around her—to protect her, taking both bullets himself.

I loved my brother-in-law and wanted him to recover fully. He'd made me feel important and taught me to look at myself in a way I'd never done. The way he treated me encouraged me to be a better person, and that new, better person was determined to find out who did this to him.

A couple of days after arriving at Ochsner, Dr. Warner moved Susie to a room on the brain injury floor, called Neurology.

Warner agreed that Susie could visit Rodney once she was able to sit up in a wheelchair and be transported to his room in ICU. Lilly told Susie about every inch of progress Rodney made. Lilly would climb into bed with Susie and turn on the television that was mounted near the ceiling. I'd sit in the chair in the corner of the room, and we'd all laugh at cartoons as though we were three-year-olds.

Susie worked hard with the team of physical, speech, and occupational therapists who taught her how to hold her head up when she sat on the side of the bed or in the chair in her room; but her neck would give way to the weight and the excruciating pain that she never complained about. Dr. Warner suggested a soft neck brace, which helped, but she said she wouldn't let Rodney see her in it because he would worry that she might not be recovering.

"Look, Suse. I need to get back home." I sat beside her bed.

"Why? I neeeee you." Her lips turned downward, and her brow crinkled.

"I feel like it's up to me to find out who did this." I watched her as she closed her eyes for a few seconds, and when she reopened them, there was a look of rage in them. I'd never seen Susie angry and, at first, I feared it was directed at me.

"Yes! Pleeeeese. Fiiine them."

I took a deep breath, more like a sigh of relief, and said, "I don't have any clues yet, but James said he'd help me. And Dr. Switzer, too. I need to go back to follow up."

"Oh kaay." She seemed angry and edgy. "Fiiine whoooo shu Rod." She took a deep breath as though the anger and sentences took all of her energy.

"Don't worry about it. I'll find them." I squeezed her hand and she closed her eyes. "You worry about getting better so you can see your husband. Let me do the sleuthing!"

She opened her eyes and grinned at me. I winked at her and remembered how I had felt when I was seven or eight and saw her get into a car with a boy I now know was Rodney. They were in Dr. Switzer's driveway, and my dad was standing near the street, yelling at Rodney. My mother was holding onto me because I wanted to run across the street and ask Susie to take me with her. Instead, she slammed her door and Rodney got in the car and drove off. I didn't see her again for three years, and I hated her for leaving me.

She came home a few times, once when Catfish died, then again when I was a teenager. I went to New York with Marianne twice after Josh died. That's when I saw Susie as a vulnerable person, not the princess who had everything, lived in a fancy city, and forgot that she had a younger sister. That was when I realized she had not lived the fairy tale I'd invented. That was when I forgave her, even though she never knew I harbored all that resentment for almost twenty years.

*

Around noon on Monday, I found Dr. Switzer walking through the parking lot from his office to the hospital. I was perplexed about how to stir up the local politicians to open a case on the shooting, and Dr. Switzer had told me he would talk to Reggie Borders.

"Hi. Hey, Doc. Wait up!" I ran across the pavement and tried to get Dr. Switzer's attention before he went through the back door that could only be unlocked with a code.

"Hi, Sissy." He turned around and stopped with his hand on the door's silver handle. "What are you doing here?"

"I'm looking for you, actually. Got a sec?" I was a little out of breath and looked up at the reflection of sunlight that bounced off his glasses. I couldn't see his expression because of the glare. "Could we get a cup of coffee?"

"Follow me. We'll go to the doctors' lounge." He punched some numbers into the code box and I watched: 4863. I thought about how to memorize the code, in case I should ever need to sneak in the back door of the hospital. I told myself that it was 1984, so the first two numbers, 48, were the reverse of 84. The number 63 was easy. I was born in 1960. All I had to do was remember what it was like to be three years old when, on my birthday, Mama had a bakery make me a Tinker Bell cake. Easy-peasy: 48-63.

I followed Dr. David into the hallway, past the nurses' station, and through a wooden door just before Administration. There was no one in the room. A coffee maker was set on a counter with a tray of sandwiches covered in plastic wrap next to it. There was a large, clear plastic bowl filled with soft drinks and crushed ice and a stack of plastic glasses and paper coffee cups next to that. Napkins and plastic forks were in the corner.

"Want a sandwich? I'm having one." He got a clear plastic plate near the flatware and piled several sandwich halves on it. "Help yourself."

I took a Sprite from the bowl, put some ice in one of the plastic glasses, and sat across from Dr. David.

"I spent the last few days in New Orleans." I took a swig of my Sprite. "Susie was moved to neurology. She's doing remarkably well."

"Yes, I talked to Dr. Warner. He calls me almost every day." He took a couple large bites of his sandwich and drank about half his Coke.

"So I guess you know Rodney is still in ICU." I wrapped both my hands around the can of Sprite and bent forward towards the table a little.

"Yes. Not out of the woods." He finished off his first sandwich and started on the second one.

"I want to talk to you about the shooting." I stared at him, but he was busy with his sandwich.

"Oh, yes. I said I would talk to Borders. It slipped my mind." He gulped the rest of his Coke and got up to get another one.

"I went to see Mr. Borders. He brushed me off. Told me to see the sheriff." I told Dr. David about the dead ends I hit at the sheriff and police departments. He sat down and opened his Coke and stared at me.

"Surely there's a police report. The city cops were at the church. I know they talked to people." He sat back in his chair with a thoughtful expression on his face.

"That's what I thought, but I'm getting the runaround." I watched him fold his arms across his chest and close his eyes as though deep in thought. He pushed his chair away from the table, the sound of the legs scraping on the linoleum floor startled me and I stood up.

"Come with me." He headed out the door, and I had a difficult time keeping up with his long strides as he marched past Administration and out the front door of the hospital. My short legs had to run to keep up as I attempted to count the cracks in the sidewalk, a habit I couldn't break any more than I could quit biting my nails. My purse strap slipped from my shoulder, and I almost dragged it along the pavement as we crossed the street thirty-one sidewalk cracks later. Dr. David turned left and marched two blocks on another sidewalk, twenty-two cracks, to the courthouse, which stood on a full square block of grass and pavement in the middle of town.

*

We climbed two flights of concrete steps on the outside of the building, ten in the first flight, ten in the next, with a landing between that took seven extra steps. The four-story parish building looked like most small-town courthouses built in the 1920s.

We entered double glass doors that led into the second floor of the building and walked on tiled floors that smelled of Clorox and disinfectant. That gave me a peaceful feeling, like maybe I wouldn't have to wash my hands every five minutes if the place was clean.

Dr. Switzer seemed to know exactly where he was going as he turned and started up an internal flight of stairs, ten up, then a landing, another ten, and we were on the third floor facing a huge door with a sign above it that said, "Courtroom of Judge Edward DeYoung."

Switzer opened the door and stuck his head in, then he closed it and started down the hallway that was really a balcony overlooking the floor below. At the first door on the right, he pressed a black button, and a few seconds later there was a clicking sound. He opened the door and held it for me to enter ahead of him.

A pretty lady, about forty years old, sat behind a desk with headphones in her ears. She pulled them out and stood up.

"Dr. Switzer. What a pleasant surprise." She walked around the desk and hugged him. "The Judge will be happy to see you. Let me tell him you're here."

The door to an inner office opened, and a big man with sandy hair turning grey around the temples came out with his hand extended.

"David. This is a nice surprise. To what do I owe the honor of you coming all the way up here?" He shook hands with Switzer and grabbed the doctor's elbow with his other hand.

"Ed, I need to talk to you about something." Dr. David smiled at the Judge, who wore a shirt and tie and black slacks, no robe. He turned and led us through the door. Inside his office was a hall tree with two black judges' robes hanging on coat hangers. He had a large desk with a tall, leather chair behind it facing the door we'd entered.

In front of the desk were two shorter leather chairs. He pointed to them.

"This is Abigail Burton. The senator's youngest daughter." Dr. David turned towards me, and the judge extended his hand to shake mine.

"Most people call me Sissy. Nice to meet you, Judge." I shook his hand and smiled my most charming smile.

"So, Miss Burton. I take it your sister is the one who…" He didn't complete his sentence, but I knew what he meant.

"Yes, Your Honor. She married Rodney Thibault, who was shot when they walked out of the church." I looked him dead in the eye. He dropped my hand and walked behind his desk.

"Have a seat." He sat in his tall chair, folded his hands together on his desk, and leaned forward.

"Look, Ed." Switzer didn't waste time. He propped one leg across the other, sat back in his chair, and stared at the judge. "Sissy has been to see Borders. She's been to the sheriff's department and the city police. They all say there's no police report."

"Did the police show up at the scene?" The judge looked at Switzer then at me.

"There were three city police units there, along with two ambulances and the fire truck." I sat on the edge of my seat and looked from the judge to the doctor.

"Were you there, David?" Judge DeYoung looked at Dr. Switzer.

"Yes. I didn't see what happened. I rushed out of church to help Thibault. He was shot twice. One bullet went through his arm, exited, reentered under his shoulder blade, and lodged near his lung. The other bullet entered the side of his head above his right ear."

"What did you see, Miss Burton?" The Judge looked at me. His glare was intense, and I could almost see the wheels turning inside.

"I heard the shots and saw a blue truck take off, spewing gravel and tar from its tires." I didn't want to say much. Both men seemed like no-nonsense types who would be put off by a girl rambling on about helping her sister and all the blood, and Lilly screaming.

The judge picked up his phone.

"Lydia. Get Chief Marchand on the phone for me." He turned and looked at me. "What was the date?"

"June thirtieth."

"June thirtieth, Lydia. Thanks." Judge DeYoung kept his stare on me. "What have you been told, so far?"

I explained that I had spoken to Mr. Reggie, although I didn't reveal my relationship with the Borders, or say that I went to his house on a Sunday afternoon.

"He told me it was up to the sheriff." I paused because I didn't want to ramble.

"Did you see Sheriff Desiré?"

"No, sir. The receptionist said he was busy and gave me a bunch of papers to fill out. She said I needed to file a claim. I told her it wasn't a *claim*, it was a *crime*. She told me she didn't have a police report."

"Did you talk to the mayor or the chief of police?"

"No, sir. I went to the police department and got the same thing. The receptionist said there was no police report."

Judge DeYoung turned towards Dr. Switzer. "What do you think is going on, David?"

"I think a black man was shot by some vigilantes who think they are above the law. That's what I think." Switzer's face was red, his arms folded across his chest. "It seems as though no one feels it's important, but someone knows something. They just aren't sharing the information."

I thought about that. Why would anyone want to hide a crime by a couple of vigilantes?

"I don't put up with that kind of behavior. This is the 1980s, not the 1880s." His phone buzzed, and he picked it up. "Yes. Thanks. Put him through.

"Winn. What do you have on the Thibault shooting?" He listened for a few seconds. "Have you opened an investigation?" There was

another pause. "Well, get on it and keep me posted on what you find."
He hung up.

"The police chief says he doesn't think there's an investigation, but I figure he'll get one started pretty soon." DeYoung stood up, which was our cue to leave. I stood too, and Dr. Switzer slowly rose from his chair.

"Look, David, I'll let you know what I find out. Thanks for coming up here with this." He came around the desk and squeezed my shoulder. "I hope your sister and her husband survive this. Give Lydia a phone number where I can reach you."

"Thank you, Judge. Thank you very much." I stuttered and felt flushed.

"Please give my best to your dad. I hear he's not well. And let me know how things go with your sister and Mr. Thibault."

"Her name is Susie. Susanna. His name is Rodney. He's Ray Thibault's son." I had to bend my head back to look at him because he was very tall and was standing close to me.

"I know Ray. Good man. I get my gas as his station. And I know Jeffrey, too. He's been in my courtroom, a good lawyer. I didn't know Ray had two boys."

"Yes, sir. Rodney was in the army for ten years. He was a JAG officer, a major. He's a really good guy." I knew I was prejudiced when it came to Rodney, but I was telling the truth.

"Hmm. I didn't realize it was Ray's boy. Another lawyer, huh? JAG? Major? Impressive." Judge DeYoung opened the door to his secretary's office, and I walked through it. He and Dr. David said a few words to each other, and the doctor and I left. We didn't say much as we walked back to the hospital, but when we sat back down at the table where Dr. Switzer's uneaten sandwiches and Coke remained as though he'd never left, he looked at me with a serious expression.

"If you are going to pursue this thing, you need to be careful." He picked up his Coke, and I noticed the condensation ring it left on the table. "If there is a cover-up, it's by powerful people who won't take kindly to someone snooping around."

"I'm not afraid of *powerful* people," I emphasized the word 'powerful.'

"You should be." He put his Coke down and leaned forward. His expression was fatherly, kind. "Be careful, Sissy."

～ Chapter Four ～

Small Steps

USIE HAD BEEN ON the neurology floor for a week when she could finally hold her head up on her own, although not for long. She wore the neck brace when Marianne rolled her down the hall in a wheelchair, onto the elevators, to ICU. I walked alongside, and Susie took the brace off her neck and handed it to me just before we all entered Rodney's room.

Marianne explained to Susie that Rodney was partially unresponsive, had lots of tubes and machines around his bed, and his head was wrapped like a mummy. Lilly was sitting in the chair on the side of his bed when Marianne rolled the wheelchair to the other side. Susie reached up to find Rod's hand under the sheet that covered him to the top of his chest.

There was a clear tube in both his nostrils, an IV line in his right hand, and a catheter that led to a bag of yellow fluid on the underside of the bed; but Susie didn't notice of any of that, nor the gauze wrapped around his head and the cylinders that made whooshing sounds beside the bed.

She picked up his hand, and before she spoke, he turned his head slightly towards her and opened his eyes halfway. Susie winked at him, and a grin started slowly at the corners of his lips. His mouth lifted slightly, then his half-mast eyes began to turn up on the outer edges, and his nose rose and widened. Finally, I saw the bottoms of his upper teeth, white and straight as his top lip spread across his face.

Rodney reached his left hand across his chest and held Susie's hand in both of his. She dropped her head to his bed and kissed his fingers, one at a time. She cried sweet, soundless tears.

Before I realized what Susie was doing, she had lifted herself out of the wheelchair, her hands on the armrests, and stood up. I froze while Marianne rushed to stand behind her in case she fell. But Susie had something else in mind. She bent at the waist and laid her head and torso over Rodney's chest, her long, red ponytail flipped across him, her head turned so that her mouth was in the bend of his neck under his chin. His right hand was trapped under her, but he lifted his left hand and wrapped it over her back and pulled her closer to him. Her hands went around his neck.

He smiled broadly, eyes opened, his hand stroking her back.

Dr. Warner walked in and stood beside me, smelling of antiseptic, shaving cream, and coffee. We all watched as though viewing a beautiful sunset, sole witnesses of something unspeakable.

Rodney mouthed, "I love you," and tears streamed down my face and pooled under my chin in the folds of my neck. I could hear Susie murmur something to Rodney, and he nodded slightly, just a small movement, but it was important, and Warner walked around me and gently pushed Marianne aside so he could get closer to Rodney. The doctor didn't try to move Susie away, but shined a light in Rodney's eyes to look at his pupils. Lilly stood on the other side of the bed, watching, her mouth opened, her auburn curls askew from sleeping in the chair.

Warner nodded and grinned. He backed away and motioned for Marianne to follow him through the nurses' station and into the hall. I stood at the foot of the bed and felt as though I was watching a movie.

*

Later, Marianne told me that Warner believed Rodney's reaction to Susie was miraculous progress. "He looked down at me and I realized how tall he is, and beautiful, almost seductive." Marianne leaned against the wall in the hall outside Rodney's room.

"Who?" I faced her and shuffled my feet on the mint-green linoleum floor.

"Warner. The doctor." Marianne looked at me as though I should know whom she was talking about. "He said he didn't believe me when I said Susie would be good medicine for Rodney. I told him I've known them both for a very long time; that their bond is stronger than any I'd ever witnessed. While we talked, he held one of my hands between us, like we were connected.

"I found myself looking at his hands for a wedding ring." She took a deep breath and looked at me with a questioning expression. "Then he said, 'You know what I really think? I think you are a good nurse.' He smiled at me, and I noticed so many things about him at once. The way his hair curls above his collar, dark with a few lighter streaks. His features are sharp, and I can't distinguish whether he's Jewish, Italian, or French; maybe a combination. His smile isn't wide, but it's sincere, and his eyes are a deep blue, topped by thick, dark eyebrows and lashes."

I took Marianne's hand, and she smiled at me as though she remembered something pleasant.

"I wanted to laugh at myself for such a pointed observation, but I was mesmerized by his aura and stood dumbfounded." She laughed aloud at herself. "Then he asked me, 'Aren't you going to say something?' and he started to laugh. It caught me off-guard, but I said, 'Thank you,' and laughed, too.

"He asked if we could grab a cup of coffee or glass of wine this evening after he's done with rounds. He said he wants to talk to me about working for Ochsner." Marianne sighed.

"What did you say?" I couldn't believe Marianne was attracted to a man. She had been raped by white Klansmen when she was twelve, and the way she'd coped was to hate men and say she was attracted to women.

"Do you think it's okay?" She scrunched her nose and lowered her eyebrows like someone deep in thought. "I mean. Well, I don't know what I mean."

"Of course it's okay. I'll be here with Lilly and Susie." I laughed out loud.

*

"It makes me so angry that no one will tell me anything." I was in Susie's room, getting her tucked into her bed. "Most of the politicians in Jean Ville are bigots." I told Susie about my discussion with Daddy, the DA, and the receptionists at the sheriff and city police departments.

"Dr. Switzer took me to see Judge DeYoung." I felt agitated and realized I needed to get back home to find out about that report. "He doesn't seem like a bigot. He told me he'd get someone to produce a police report."

"Rodney is friends with, uh, umm..." She closed her eyes as though trying to remember something she should not have forgotten. "The A-gee... uh."

"You mean Louisiana's Attorney General? Robert Morris?"

"Yeah... friends... law school. The, uh, bar exam together."

"How can I get in touch with him?"

"My suit... house."

"Are you saying it would be in your suitcase at your house in Jean Ville?"

"Yeah."

"Oh, my, does that mean the luggage you packed for your honeymoon is still at your house? Do you want me to bring it when I come back?

"Yeah Pleeeeees."

"Sure, no problem." I pulled her sheet and blanket up to her neck, and she closed her eyes. "So you don't mind if I go through your suitcase to find your address book?"

"Don't mine..." She opened her eyes and stared at me. "Gov-Bro. Rod knows."

"Governor Breaux?" I felt a surge of optimism. "Do you mean Rodney knows the governor, too?"

"Uh, huh, worked for him…"

"Would his contact information be in your address book, too?"

"Uh, huh." She nodded a couple of times. "Call them. Pleeesss. They luv Rod. Will help."

"Well, I'd better get going. I have a long drive and lots to do." I kissed her on the forehead. "Get some rest."

She winked at me and shut her eyes. I hurried out of the room, down the hall, to the parking garage and set off towards Jean Ville with a new sense of purpose.

I'm going to get those SOBs who did this to Rodney and Susie, I thought as I barreled North on I-10 West.

*

"I happen to know that the Klan still exists in this parish." I sat across from Judge DeYoung in his office. It wasn't quite eight o'clock in the morning, but I'd parked near the place he usually parked his car, as I'd learned from sleuthing around over the past few days. I didn't have to wait long when he slid his car into his regular spot, got out, and crossed the street from the Bailey Theatre to the back of the courthouse.

"Hey. Judge. Wait up." I ran to catch up with him. He didn't seem put off by my intrusion and led me through a series of doors and hallways, up a tiny elevator, to the third floor. Lydia wasn't at her desk, yet.

"How would you know that?" He squinted his grey eyes, partially hidden behind glasses that sat on the end of his nose.

"I just know. In fact, I think I know who some of the members are." I had been busy since I'd gotten home, talking to people, following up on leads. I felt pretty confident that my information was correct.

"So what does the Klan have to do with the shooting?" He rocked in his chair a couple times then leaned forward, his hands folded on his desk.

"I think the Klan was behind it." I crossed my arms and leaned back.

"Do you have proof? Names? Motive?" He talked like a lawyer, which he was before he became a judge.

"No, sir. It's a gut-thing. That's what investigators do, right? Find proof and motive?"

"Yes. But I don't have anything to do with that." He pulled on his earlobe. "The police, who investigate a crime, turn over a case file to the district attorney, who will review it and make a decision to bring charges. My job is to try people who are charged either by a bill of information filed by the district attorney or a bill of indictment filed by the grand jury."

"I understand. But you have some leverage over Reggie Borders."

"Maybe."

"If the police don't investigate, there won't be a case file. And even if a case file is developed, I don't see Mr. Borders filing a bill of information or taking the case to the grand jury. He wants to see it evaporate." I took a deep breath and dropped my hands to my lap, trying to hold the judge's gaze without looking away. "How can we get him to recuse himself so the attorney general can take over the case?"

"Actually, Borders can make the decision, himself, for recusal. If he doesn't recuse, the victims, in this case your sister or her husband, or perhaps you, in their stead, can file a motion for recusation—considering that you have valid grounds."

"Okay, I can do that. What happens next?"

"There will be a hearing, and the judge, in this case, I will decide whether or not the district attorney should be recused. If I find he should be, I will appoint an attorney or notify the state attorney general, and he can appoint a member of his staff or an attorney from another parish to prosecute." He pushed back in his chair.

"Then I'll talk to Mr. Borders and explain it to him." I stood, ready to leave.

"He knows the rules. I don't think you need to explain them to him."

"Then, I guess I need to convince him."

"That makes more sense. Let me know what he says." Judge DeYoung smiled at me and stood up.

*

I walked across the street to the DA's building.

It was still not eight o'clock when I walked into Reggie Border's building. No one was at the receptionist's desk, so I strolled past it as though I belonged there. I went directly to the door marked, "Private."

Mr. Reggie stood behind his desk, gathering files and putting them in a briefcase. I slammed the door behind me. He straightened up and looked at me with a huge surprise across his face.

"How'd you get in here?"

"Just walked in." I went to his desk and stood about two feet from him. "I want you to recuse yourself from the case."

"We don't have a case." He didn't look at me, just kept stuffing things in his briefcase.

"Do you have a police report?" I looked at the pile of papers on his desk, on the floor, on every surface. It was chaotic.

"Yes, I have one somewhere. It doesn't say much." He looked around at all the stacks as though he were looking for the report.

"It says a shooting occurred, right?"

"Yes. But no details. No suspects. I closed the case."

"Look, Mr. Reggie. You know me. Bonnie is my best friend." I tried to appeal to his *daddy* side, and his expression made me think it might work. "I've spent more nights at your house than at my own. This is me, Sissy Burton. Help me out here."

"You think you've got an ace in the hole, because Thibault knows the AG, huh?" He started to laugh.

"No, but I've been told that the state attorney general, Mr. Morris, can reopen the case if a family member makes a request and the state investigators turn up evidence." I stared at him, not blinking.

"Don't threaten me, young lady. The AG can't do anything without a police report. Anyway, I've done the investigation. The case is closed." He pulled his hand out and snapped his briefcase shut. "I have to be in court. Goodbye, Sissy."

"Make sure this is your last word." I talked to his back, and he stopped at the door and turned around. "I'm giving you a chance to be in control of this case."

"You can't do anything. I'm the DA." He walked out the door and left it opened. I was about to leave when I had a thought. I shut the door and started rooting around in the filing cabinet, but I didn't find anything there, so I began shuffling papers and manila folders on his desk and around the office.

There it was—a file marked, *Thibault,* mixed in with a bunch of files on a coffee table. In the file was a simple police report with the date, place, and victim: "Rodney Thibault, Negro." I read it several times and memorized the names of the three police officers who'd been at the scene. I knew one of them, a loser named Joey LeBlanc. I didn't remember seeing him at the church, and I would have recognized him had he been there. Red flags appeared behind my eyes.

Also in the file were a few quotes from wedding guests who said they didn't see anything. Of course they didn't. They were all still in the church during the shooting. I put the file back on the table and left.

*

I went back to the courthouse and climbed the stairs to the third floor. Judge DeYoung was headed down the hall to the back entrance to his courtroom.

"Judge. I just need one second." I tapped him on the shoulder and he turned around. He was wearing a long black robe, a red-and-blue striped tie, and a starched white shirt. His wing-tipped shoes peeked out from the hem of the robe.

"Miss Burton." He turned around and looked surprised.

"Sissy, Judge." I was out of breath from the twenty steps on the outside of the courthouse and the additional twenty steps inside. I put my hand on my chest. "I just left Borders. He said he did an investigation and closed the case."

"If you can get a copy of the police report to the AG, he has the authority to order the state police to investigate." He started to walk down the hall.

"I'm on it, Judge." I stopped in the middle of the hall. He turned around and smiled at me, then went through the door to his courtroom. I almost ran down the staircase to the second floor and picked up a copy of the Free Advertiser, a newspaper that promoted businesses in Toussaint Parish. I stuck it under my arm and flung my purse strap over my shoulder.

I skipped down the outside steps and crossed the street to the DA's office—only thirteen sidewalk cracks. I was moving fast, and told the girl at the front desk that I'd left my drivers license in Mr. Borders's Borders' office.

"I'll get it for you." She started to get out of her chair.

"No, that's okay. I know exactly where I left it. I'll run in and get it myself and will be out of your way in less than a minute." I was already through the door before she could stop me. I went directly to the table and grabbed the file I'd just put back in the stack. The police report was still there and I wrapped in the Advertiser and put it back under my arm. I pulled my drivers license out of my wallet and waved it at the girl as I walked past her desk on my way out the front door.

"Just as I remembered. I left it on the table. Thanks." The door slammed behind me before I could hear a response.

*

I drove home to pack, and stopped to see my dad. He was in the wing-backed chair in his bedroom with a book on his lap.

"Hi, Daddy. How are you feeling today?" I kissed him on the forehead and sat on the edge of his bed.

"I feel okay. I'm bored, though. I wish I could go back to work." He scratched his head but didn't look at me. Daddy was the type to feel sorry for himself, but he didn't have empathy for anyone else.

"Sorry. Maybe you could do some part-time accounting work at home."

"Maybe." His expression didn't change.

"I'm going to Baton Rouge, then to New Orleans to see about Susie." I wanted to set a basis for the use of his credit card. He didn't like surprises.

"Yea. There were charges on my latest bill for a hotel called the Brenthouse in New Orleans." He didn't seem angry, which surprised me. "How is she? I'd like to go to see her, but I'm not allowed to drive."

"Maybe James can take you one weekend."

"Why can't I go with you?" He looked sad, and I almost thought he was serious about going to New Orleans to see Susie.

"Well, I'm going to Baton Rouge, first, for a couple of days, to meet with the attorney general."

"Why are you doing that?" His brow furred, eyes darting.

"I'm going to ask him to take the case away from Mr. Borders."

"What case?"

"The shooting. Someone shot Rodney. That's a crime. He could die."

"Oh, yes. The shooting." The color started to rise on his neck, an indication he was getting angry.

"Look, I'm trying to get someone to pursue this case." I was pissed and could feel the color rise on my own cheeks.

"No one cares about that shooting." He crossed one leg over the other and leaned back in his chair.

"I care. Susie cares."

"I think you should let it go, sweetie." His face turned red, my cue to skedaddle.

"I'm not going to let it go. I'm going to find out who shot Rodney and tried to shoot Susie." I kissed him on the forehead and walked out of the house. Sometimes Daddy could be so obstinate. Well, maybe all the time.

*

I found a parking spot on North Third Street, directly across from the attorney general's office Monday morning. Susie was right, my phone call to Robert Morris's home the night before was well received. He said he had a full day but could see me before 8:00 AM, so I walked briskly across the street in my low-heeled pumps and tried the front door of the building. It was locked. There was a buzzer next to the door, so I pressed the beige button and heard a crackling.

"Yes, can I help you?"

"I'm Abigail Burton, here to see Mr. Morris."

"I'll be right there." He opened the door himself. I peeked into offices along the hallway as I followed his grey suit to a door at the end of the corridor. No one appeared to be in the building but the two of us.

"Miss Burton, it's a pleasure." He extended his hand and shook mine as though we were equal, not like I was some young, air-headed girl. I liked him even before he stared directly into my eyes as though I held his interest, somewhere behind my panicked look.

"Sissy, Mr. Morris. My name is Abigail, but everyone calls me Sissy." I faced him inside the office door.

"Then Sissy it is." He pointed to a round table with four chairs. "Have a seat. How's Rodney? And Susie? I think the world of both of them, you know."

I'd already told his wife, Brenda, about the shooting, so I figured Morris knew that part. What he didn't know was why I wanted to meet with him.

"Rodney was moved out of ICU to a step-down unit this weekend, which is progress." I sat in one of the chairs and crossed my ankles on the side. "He still can't speak, and there's no feeling in his feet and lower legs, but he seems to have survived, although barely."

"Ever since Brenda told me about the shooting, I've wondered why I didn't know." He sat across from me and leaned on the table. "How could I have missed it in the newspapers?"

"It hasn't been in the news." I folded my hands together on the table and leaned forward. "That's one of the reasons I'm here." I told him about the case, at least what little there was. I explained that there had been no police report and how I'd gotten the runaround in Jean Ville.

"Judge DeYoung pressured someone at City Hall to produce a police report, but the DA closed the case. The judge would like to see the case reopened and thinks you are the one to do it." I didn't blink, and he was totally engaged.

"Did the police show up at the scene?" He got up and went behind his desk, picked up an ink pen, and scribbled something on a legal size pad with yellow lined paper.

"Yes, there were three police units, plus two ambulances, and the volunteer fire department at the church." I leaned my back against the chair and folded my hands on top of my purse that sat in my lap. I felt fidgety and deliberately held my hands together to keep them steady. I didn't know whether I could trust this man with my secret theft.

"This is how the process works." He sat in the chair behind his desk, still holding the pen, poised to write something else on the yellow pad. "I can take the case if I have proof it should be reopened, or if the DA recuses himself. Would he do that?"

"I don't think he would recuse himself, no." I stared at him, and he didn't blink. "I believe Mr. Borders wants to sweep this under the rug."

"Why?" He sat back in the large, tan leather chair, and it creaked.

"Rodney's black. He married a white girl." I looked at him as though he should understand how politicians in Toussaint Parish operated. "Poetic justice is what I believe they are thinking."

"They?"

"I don't think Borders is alone in trying to downplay this crime."

"Do you have any idea who else might be behind this?" He was poised to write something on the pad, then changed his mind and put the pen down.

"I have my guesses—the mayor, maybe the sheriff. The Klan, for sure, but I don't know who, specifically."

"I forgot there are still factions of the Klan in some rural areas of Louisiana." He picked up his pen and jotted something down. "I'll give Borders a call and see what I can find out. Give your contact information to Millie at the front desk so I can reach you." He stood up, my cue to leave. Meeting over. "I'm sorry, but I have to be at a meeting at the Capitol in a few minutes. Please give my best to Rod and Susie. I'll be in New Orleans next week and will go by to see them. Would you leave their room information with Millie, too?" He pushed the knot on his tie up closer to his collar.

"Sure. And thanks." I walked towards the door then turned around. "Mr. Morris…"

"Robert, or Rob. That's what your sister calls me." He grinned and reached for his briefcase.

"We can't let this go away. Louisiana is better than this." I stared at his reaction.

"You're right. I'll stay on top of it." He started to walk towards the door. "If you can get a police report, though, that would speed things up."

"I'm all over that!" I walked down the hall and noticed all the offices now had people in them, busy working, steaming Styrofoam cups of coffee on their desks. Robert Morris must have taken a rear exit because he didn't appear in the waiting room when I got there.

Millie was a middle-aged woman with mousey-brown hair coiffed like a helmet. I almost laughed at her shirtwaist dress, thick shoes with rubber soles, and embroidered cardigan buttoned at the top, but thought better of it.

"Hi, I'm Abigail Burton. Everyone calls me, Sissy." I reached my hand out. She looked at it and back up at me. "Mr. Morris asked me to give you some contact information."

Millie picked up a pen and stared at the white paper in front of her. I spelled my name and gave her my address and phone number. I gave her Rodney and Susie's information, too and the phone and room numbers at Ochsner.

"Anything else?" She looked up at me over her cat-eyed glasses.

"There is one more thing. May I use your copy machine?" I smiled at her, and she nodded her head towards the machine that was behind her. I made a copy of the police report and put the original and copy in my purse. I was out the door before Miss Millie could question what I'd done.

*

I checked into the Capitol House Hotel downtown and used my dad's credit card for the room. I spent the afternoon sunbathing by the pool and dressed for dinner at six o'clock.

Nikole Breaux had given me the address of their personal residence in a subdivision called Country Club of Louisiana. She said that since they were new to the governorship, they wanted to start out by having personal gatherings at their home rather than the Governor's Mansion, which was being renovated. When I arrived, she met me at my car, introduced herself with a welcoming smile, looped her arm through mine, and walked me through the double front doors under a portico of stone and plaster.

"We are terribly disturbed about Rodney and Susie." She patted my arm with her free hand as we walked on the marble floors. "What happened?"

"They walked out of the church after their wedding, and someone shot Rod twice," I spoke softly and tried to sound as sophisticated as Nikole.

"Who would do a thing like that?" We were in a kitchen the size of a basketball court with marble countertops, tall dark-stained cabinets, and black appliances.

"We don't know, and it doesn't seem that the authorities in Toussaint Parish are interested in finding out." I was guided to a bar stool on one side of a huge island made of stone and topped with marble. There was so much marble in the house that I wondered whether they had a quarry out back.

"Greg will be so upset when he hears this, Sissy." She picked up two crystal wine goblets off a glass and silver tray that sat on the counter with an opened bottle of white wine in a silver chiller. "Greg and Rod have been friends since Rodney was in law school. He worked for Greg, who was the clerk of court for Baton Rouge Parish back then. Greg thinks the world of Rodney. They even exchanged letters when Rod was in the army."

"Oh, I didn't know the connection. Susie just asked that I meet you and the governor. She isn't speaking very well, yet, so she wasn't able to explain the friendship."

"We adore Susie, too." Nikole asked whether I'd like a glass of Maçon Village.

"Sure. Thanks." I didn't know what Maçon Village was, but I crossed my ankles that dangled from the bar stool and acted sophisticated while she poured two glasses of white wine and set one before me. The governor came in through a back entrance, kissed his wife on the cheek, and walked towards me.

"You must be Abigail." He extended his hand and stood in front of me.

"Sissy, Governor." I shook his hand like a man. "Everyone calls me Sissy."

"And you can call me Greg, just like Susie and Rodney do." His Cajun accent was thick and appealing, and bled into his laugh. He was tall, with dark curly hair, dark eyes, and skin that looked permanently suntanned. He asked me about the shooting. I described what I knew and told him about the attitude of the political leaders in Jean Ville.

"Everyone but Judge DeYoung." I took a sip of wine, and Nikole handed Greg a highball she'd mixed while we'd been chatting. "He seems intent on finding justice, although I think his hands are tied, to some extent. Although he did pressure on a few people, like Borders, Desiré, and Wallace."

"Remind me who they are." He took a sip of his drink and sat on the stool next to mine, facing me.

"Borders in the DA, Desiré is sheriff, and Wallace is the Mayor of

Jean Ville." I turned to face him. "The chief of police and fire chief might also be involved in ignoring this crime—Marchand and Brazille."

"Have you given those names to Rob Morris?" He stood up and motioned to Nikole that he wanted to move our conversation to the patio. It was a balmy evening, and we stayed outside about thirty minutes, until a pretty older lady in a black dress with a white apron came out and said dinner was on the table. Nikole took my arm again, and Greg followed us to the dining room that was set with beautiful, but casual, white china and silver.

We all sat on one end, Greg at the head and Nikole and I on either side of him, and we ate crawfish étouffée over rice with French bread and a salad. An older gentleman came in and poured wine in our glasses and made sure our water was replenished. Greg thanked him and spoke with him as though he was an old friend, but he never introduced us.

We talked about their kids, who had both graduated from LSU. The older, a boy, was in New York pursuing a career in finance while their daughter lived in Baton Rouge, was married, and had a new baby. I told them about Lilly, whom they said they'd met before Susie and Rod were married. I said that she would be at LSU in the fall. They mentioned how impressed they were with Lilly, and how they wanted her to call them when she was in Baton Rouge so they could have her over for dinner.

"She was planning to attend Columbia, and had been accepted, but the shooting happened, and she doesn't want to leave Susie and Rodney to go back to New York." I folded my napkin and put it on the table, beside my plate.

"Understandable," Greg said. "How are they? Rod and Susie?"

"It seems like slow, small steps, but their doctor is happy with their progress," I told them about how far Susie and Rodney had come in the six weeks since their wedding.

The conversation ultimately turned to who did it, why it wasn't on the news, and the way the politicians swept the crime under the rug. Greg talked about bigotry and discrimination. The governor reiterated how much he cared about and admired Rodney, "Not only for his brain and determination, but also for his ethics and character. He's quite a guy."

"I couldn't agree with you more. He's the best, and you'd really be impressed with him if you could witness how hard he's worked to learn simple things, like how to lift his arms and use his hands." I sat back in my chair, and Greg motioned for the gentleman to refill our wine glasses.

"Let's go to the den." Nikole stood up, and we carried our wine to a huge glassed-in room with two sectional sofas and a baby grand piano.

"Oh, you have a Steinway baby grand." I ran my hand over the shiny black ebony as though caressing a baby's behind. "Do you mind?"

"Please." Greg pulled the bench out, and I sat on it. The couple sat on the sofa behind me, and I started to play a slow waltz, feeling the ivory keys under my fingertips as though I were rubbing pearls. I worked my way to a boogie-woogie, and soon Greg and Nikole were standing on either side of the piano singing along with, *When the Saints Go Marching In*, and *Kansas City,* then I slipped into *When a Man Loves a Woman* and *Unchained Melody*. They danced to the final number.

We drank more wine; I got loose and told some jokes, like a stand-up comedienne, which were really true stories about things that had happened in our family— Mama living with a Mafia guy in Houston, and Daddy nursing his sick liver with Cutty Sark. They were in stitches and said I could get a job as a stand up at the Roadhouse in Baton Rouge, or as a piano player at Pat O'Brien's in New Orleans.

Greg insisted that his gentleman drive me back to the hotel in my Camaro and get a cab home. It was probably a good idea because I'd had lots more wine than I was accustomed to drinking.

The next day when I called Susie, she said Greg had called her. She was laughing. "Greh say you, uh, um, good time."

"They are a great couple." I yawned because I hadn't slept well. "They love you and Rod."

"Luh-Key. Grey friends." I could almost see her smile because her joy seeped through her words and made me happy that she felt lucky.

"I met with Robert Morris yesterday morning. Another good friend, I'd say." I sat on the side of my bed and rubbed my forehead.

"Yea. I, uhm… him, too." She was saying more words, although some of her choices were not clear. Marianne told me that Dr. Warner said that her speech would return in time.

"I'm working on things, trying to get someone to reopen the case." I yawned.

"Than you, Sis."

*

When we hung up, I called Marianne. She told me that Susie had visited with Rodney twice.

"She's impatient about her progress and bothers Lilly and me all day to take her to visit Rod. She doesn't understand the visiting restrictions for patients in ICU." Marianne sighed, and I could tell the stress was getting to her.

"Look, I'm in Baton Rouge. I can drive down there tomorrow and take some of the pressure off of you."

"That would be great. We need to discuss a long-range plan." Marianne's voice raised an octave.

~ Chapter Five ~

~

Jules Avenue

"SUSIE WILL GET OUT of the hospital long before Rodney, maybe in a couple of weeks," Marianne whispered to me in the hall outside Susie's room as doctors, nurses, and other medical personnel walked up and down the hall, some pushing gurneys or wheelchairs, some rushing in and out of rooms, some talking with each other outside of doors.

"Are you suggesting that they live here in New Orleans?" I was caught off-guard.

"Susie won't leave Rodney." Marianne shook her head, indicating it was something we couldn't change. "Even after he gets out of the hospital, he'll be in outpatient rehab for months. His recovery could take as long as a year."

Marianne and Lilly had been staying at the Brenthouse Hotel, which was expensive, plus Marianne needed some privacy if she was going to remain in New Orleans long term.

"I'll be coming back and forth." I had already decided my role was to keep things stirred up in Jean Ville until we found the shooters. Marianne said we should talk to Susie about how to manage housing for the immediate and not-so-immediate future. We went to Susie's room to discuss our plan to find an apartment in New Orleans.

"Close." Susie's eyes were wide as she formed the word that meant she wanted whatever living arrangements we made to be located close to the hospital.

Jefferson, Louisiana was a small community of about 7,000 residents in 1984, around twice the size of Jean Ville. It was located North of the Mississippi River from downtown New Orleans.

After two days of apartment hunting, we realized that rental units were cramped, lacked privacy, and had stairs that we weren't sure Susie would be able to handle for some time, and Rodney, maybe never.

Susie agreed we should get a realtor and look at rental houses, or even a house she could purchase near the hospital. We found a three-bedroom bungalow for rent on Jules Avenue, about a mile from the medical center.

"On good days we can walk back and forth." Marianne stood at the foot of Susie's bed, and I sat in a chair. Lilly, who refused to leave the hospital, was piled up in bed with Susie.

"You'll need a car in New Orleans," I said to Marianne. I'd driven down in my Camaro, but Marianne had ridden to New Orleans in the ambulance with Susie. Mari said she planned to ride back with me in a couple days and return in her Datsun station wagon.

Money was not an issue because when Josh Ryan died, he left his entire estate to Susie and Lilly, and it was sizable. Susie hadn't told Marianne or me how much it was, but it was probably more money than she could spend in her lifetime, even if she purchased a mansion in New Orleans.

"We need to think about the present." I looked at Marianne, then at Susie. "With both you and Rodney in the hospital, Lilly doesn't have a place to live or an adult in charge of her unless Marianne stays here."

"Mari?" Susie looked at her, and an expression of surprise crossed Marianne's face.

"I hadn't thought about it." Marianne looked at Lilly, then back at me. "I mean. What would you do if I went back to Jean Ville?"

"Lilly... stay Jean Ville? You and Toot." Susie was speaking a lot better, although not forming complete sentences. She was holding Lilly's hand.

"No! I'm not leaving you and Dad!" Lilly sat straight up in the bed and looked as though she'd been slapped.

"I can stay as long as you need me." Marianne laughed at Lilly's reaction. It was probably my place to stay with Susie because I didn't have a job or a reason to live in Jean Ville, other than the case, which wasn't really a case, yet; but I wasn't very nurse-y, and I reasoned with myself, Susie needed Marianne as a nurse as much as a sister.

"When I, uhm, out... I take care, uh, my family." Susie's eyes filled with tears. "But now, Mari?"

"I have a lot of paid vacation and sick leave accrued." Marianne took Susie's hand and smiled. "It'll be like a holiday for me, and I'll be with my favorite people."

"You staying wouldn't have anything to do with a handsome neurosurgeon, would it?" I laughed aloud, and Marianne shot her eyes at me as if to say "Shut it!" I did.

"Susie, we need to know how to pay for everything," I looked at Susie, who was still staring at Marianne. She shifted her eyes and stared at me. "We need to put a deposit on the house. We need furniture. I think Marianne has been paying for the hotel rooms and meals these past three weeks. She should be reimbursed." I hated to be the voice of reason, but I knew Marianne would never ask Susie for money.

"Oh, God, Mari. Sorry. I didn't..." Susie stuttered, which meant she was upset, tired, or both. "Milton. Vernon Milton. My attorney. His business—my wallet."

"I'm impressed that you remembered Milton's name so easily." I reached for Susie's purse and gave it to her. "I remember him. He came to your house after Josh died."

I called Mr. Milton that evening. He was disturbed to hear about the shooting and said he wanted to fly to New Orleans to see Susie and help us set up something so we'd have cash flow for expenses. I think Susie was touched that he cared so much.

*

"He asked me whether I was attached." Marianne took a long sip of coffee. We were sitting in a booth in the hospital cafeteria. "I didn't know how to answer him. And I couldn't take my eyes off his; I mean, he's gorgeous."

"Do you mean Warner? What did you tell him?" I was surprised that Marianne seemed interested in a man, especially a real He-man like Dr. Warner.

"Yes, Warner. I told him, no." She blushed, and it made me laugh. "He said his name is Donato and that his parents are from Florence, Italy but he was born in New Jersey." Marianne was eager to tell me about her date with the dreamy doctor. "We went to a place called Jacques, a cafe about a mile from the hospital in his two-seater sports car that I learned later was an Audi, a German brand I'd never heard of, which made me feel like a small-town girl in a big city."

"Do you like him?"

"It's way too early to say yes or no to that, but I think he's interesting." She took a sip of coffee and put her cup down. "He might be a bit self-absorbed, because he ordered red wine without asking me what I liked. I prefer white. He asked me about Susie and Rodney being a mixed-race couple, which he said was not unusual in New Jersey."

"What did you tell him?" I stirred more cream into my coffee.

"I told him it was very unusual in Toussaint Parish and that I thought that was why Rodney had been shot." Marianne paused and looked past me as though thinking of something confusing. "He asked me whether they'd caught the people who shot Rodney and I said I wasn't sure whether anyone was looking."

"I'm looking!" I was serious, but Mari burst out laughing.

*

Marianne and I met Mr. Milton at the New Orleans airport on Wednesday afternoon. He was fifty-ish, with grey hair at his temples and over his ears. He wore a fedora, which he removed when he shook our hands and introduced himself.

"It's such a pleasure to see you both again. I think the world of

Susie, you know." He smelled of Old Spice aftershave and fresh toothpaste, as though he'd brushed his teeth in the men's room as soon as he got off the plane. He winked in a fatherly manner, and we made our way to my car in the parking garage.

Mr. Milton was genuinely concerned about Susie and Rodney, almost like a dad or favorite uncle, and it made me wonder about my own dad, who didn't seem as worried about Susie. Mr. Milton flew from New York City for two days, visited Susie, Rod, and Lilly, and helped Marianne and me make financial decisions. He told us we could call him anytime if we had questions or needed advice.

Milton drew up papers that Susie signed, giving Marianne power of attorney in the state of Louisiana, which meant that she could manage Susie's funds and make purchases for her family. Susie was especially concerned that Marianne should take care of Lilly, who would enter LSU in a few weeks.

Lilly said she wasn't going off to college as long as her parents were invalids, but we all knew her life had to move forward, regardless. Marianne and I talked to Susie about it and agreed Lilly would be ready when the time came.

Marianne and I took Mr. Milton to see the house we'd found, and he approved. He told Marianne where to send all the receipts for purchases, and she didn't seem put-off at the subliminal suggestion that she might not be honest with Susie's money.

"I'll keep her honest, Mr. Milton," I laughed and pushed my elbow into Marianne's side.

Marianne didn't ride back to Jean Ville with me on Saturday after Milton returned to New York, because she wanted to stay with Susie and Lilly, and Lilly refused to go anywhere. We arranged for Rodney's dad and mom to drive Marianne's Datsun to New Orleans that week.

I headed home and stopped in Baton Rouge Sunday night.

*

Miss Millie sneered at me as I stood in front of her sliding glass window Monday afternoon. She buzzed Robert Morris.

"He's busy right now. Do you want to wait, or leave a message?" She put the phone receiver on the hook and looked up through the window that she slid open a crack.

"I'll wait. Thank you." I found a magazine and sat down. I thumbed through the pages, not thinking about what I saw. The copy of the police report was folded in my purse, which I put on the chair next to me.

I'd had a helluva time returning the original report to the file in Mr. Borders's office. I'd sat in my car across the street from the DA's office and waited several hours, watching the front door. At about two o'clock, the receptionist I'd tricked about my drivers license walked out of the door with a file under her arm. She crossed the street and climbed the steps on the outside of the courthouse. That told me two things: she wasn't at her desk, and Borders must be in court and needed a file.

I walked as quickly as my short legs would take me, trying not to count my steps, which would divert my focus from the mission I was on. There was no one behind the front desk, and I walked past it and through the door that read "Private", as though I belonged there. The file was in the same stack on the table, untouched, which told me Borders hadn't given the case another thought. I slipped the original police report into the file and walked back out of Borders's office.

I thought about how close I came to getting caught when I got in my car and saw the receptionist walk back across the street to the door I'd just walked out of.

*

I waited about twenty minutes in the AG's waiting room, trying not to stare at Miss Millie's beehive hairdo that had a barrette with a butterfly sitting precariously over one ear.

"Hi, Abigail." Robert Morris came into the waiting room with his hand extended, a typical politician.

"Please, call me Sissy." I shook his hand and smiled.

"That's right, Sissy. What can I do for you?" He put one hand in the pocket of his slacks. He wore a light blue Oxford shirt with and pink-and-purple tie, the knot loosened, the top button of his shirt unbuttoned.

"I have the police report." I put my purse strap over my shoulder and tucked the bag under my arm.

"Follow me." He led me down the hall to his office. We sat at a small, round table that had four chairs. "How'd you get the report? I've gotten the runaround from the Toussaint DA's office. They said the case was closed."

"I know. Frustrating, huh?" I pulled the copy of the report from my purse, unfolded it and tried to iron out the creases. I pushed it across the table to Morris. "It's a copy. I hope that's okay."

"Where'd you... never mind. I probably don't need to know, right?"

"Probably not." I smiled my most charming smile and sat back in my chair. "Judge DeYoung said that if you had the report, you could reopen the case and have the state police investigate."

"That's right." He glared at me as though he couldn't figure me out.

"So, what else do you need?" I glared back at him.

"A list of witnesses would help." He reached for a legal pad on the table and took an ink pen from his shirt pocket. "A place for the investigators to start."

"Oh, I have that list." I pulled another sheet of paper from my purse with the list I'd made of the people who might have seen something: Rodney, Susie, Marianne, Lilly, Jeffrey, and Joe Franklin. I had their addresses and phone numbers beside their names. Also on the list were the names of the paramedics and the volunteer firemen who were at the scene. I'd gotten their names from the emergency room supervisor who was on duty that day, who had graduated from high school with Susie. The names of the police officers were on the report, and I'd written their contact information on my sheet of paper.

"This is perfect." He read the list and made notes beside some of the names.

"I also thought you might want the names of Rodney and Susie's doctors." I handed him Dr. Warner's business card and a slip of paper with the names, Bernie Cappel, MD and David Switzer, MD, and the phone number for Jean Ville Hospital.

"Yes, this is good." Morris got up from the table and went behind his desk. He picked up the phone and punched a number. "Have Detective Sherman step in my office for a minute, would you, Millie?" He sat back down at the table.

"How are they? Susie and Rodney? I'm going to try to get down there to see them this week."

"They are improving. There's a lot going on in New Orleans. Marianne is getting Lilly ready to come up here to attend LSU. We rented a house near the hospital." I filled him in on the salient facts while we killed time waiting for the man named Sherman.

"Lilly's coming up here to school?"

"Yes. In a couple of weeks. She'll be a freshman." I watched his eyes dart around as though he were trying to process something.

"Who's Marianne?"

"She's our half-sister—my dad's daughter with another woman. Marianne's a nurse, a good one. She's been with Susie since the shooting. First in Jean Ville, now in New Orleans."

There was a knock on the door, and a man entered wearing a grey suit. He was mostly bald with a rim of hair around the sides of his head, and he wore glasses. He sat in one of the chairs at the table. Robert Morris introduced him as Detective Sherman then delved into the case. He gave Sherman the police report and went over the witnesses.

"Can you tell me anything about what these witnesses might know?" The detective looked at me then down at the paper. I told him what Lilly and Marianne had told me and he took notes.

"There's something strange on that report." I pointed to the names of the city cops who were listed as being at the scene. "Joey LeBlanc. I know him. He wasn't at the church."

"That's strange." Detective Sherman made a note on his notepad. "What about the victims, uh, Mr. and Mrs. Thibault?"

"You should interview them." I folded my hands on the table and smiled. "Maybe you can help them remember. Both are recovering from brain injuries, so their memories are sketchy. Rodney can't talk, and although Susie is improving, she still struggles to make sentences."

When I left the AG's office I felt I had accomplished something. At least there would be an investigation.

*

Maple trees were turning gold and red as I drove into Jean Ville after a week in New Orleans and decided to take Shortcut Road from Highway One to Jefferson Extension. James lived in a nice brick house in a beautiful pecan grove that few people knew about; in fact, I didn't know about Shortcut Road until he moved there and told me how to get to his house.

I was driving slowly because it was a winding, narrow road. I thought that if James's car was home, I'd stop to say 'Hi' and tell him how things were going with Susie and Rodney's recoveries, and ask whether he'd made progress on the case. Parked in the driveway of James's house was an old blue pickup truck that seemed familiar to me. I crept by, and just before I passed his house the front door opened and someone walked out. I stopped my car in front of the house next door and watched as a familiar looking guy with scraggly dirty blonde hair that hung in strings past his ears, walked out of the house and turned back towards the front door to speak to James, who was standing in the doorway, holding the screen door open.

I looked at the truck again. There was someone with dark curly hair sitting behind the wheel, and I could tell the engine was running because there was smoke coming from the exhaust. The license number was 37L402. I knew that number—I'd seen it on one of the papers in the folder in James's library. I tried to remember what else was in the file: the names of Tucker Thevenot and Keith Rousseau, and some other numbers that had dollar signs.

I didn't want to be seen, so I drove on and made a circle, turned on Smith Street, and doubled back. The truck went by, going towards Jefferson Street as I returned to James's house. I saw the driver more clearly, and I realized it was Keith Rousseau. The scraggly guy was Tucker Thevenot. I knew them. They were Warren's friends, the ones who'd done lots of questionable things that I didn't want to remember.

I drove up in James's driveway and got out of the car. The front door was closed, so I knocked and said, "Yoo-hoo, James. It's Sissy. You home?" I opened the door a crack and hollered again. I heard footsteps coming towards me from the back of the house, and James appeared in the living room just as I opened the door fully.

"Hey, what are you doing here?" He seemed surprised, almost like I'd caught him zipping up his pants.

"I'm just getting back from a week in New Orleans and thought I'd stop by and give you some news." I walked through the door and let it shut behind me. It was dark in the house, and we stood staring at each other as though he couldn't understand why I was there. "I mean, what's so strange about a sister dropping in to see her brother. I saw your car in the driveway, so on impulse, I pulled in."

He just stared at me as though trying to figure out what planet I was from.

"Long drive. Can I use your bathroom?" I didn't wait for an answer and went directly to the bathroom in the hall off the living room. When I got back, he was sitting on the back porch drinking a soda.

"Want something to drink?" He pointed to an ice chest between the two chairs, and I grabbed a Coca Cola from the dense ice.

"You always keep drinks iced in a cooler on your back porch? Don't you have a refrigerator?" I wiped dirt off the chair with a Kleenex from my purse and sat down, then used another tissue to wipe the top of my Coke can.

Fall had dissipated the extreme Louisiana summer heat and

replaced it with cool, brisk air. I took a deep breath and exhaled slowly.

"I'm having a party tonight, that's why the ice chest." He didn't elaborate, nor did he invite me to his festivities.

"So. Do you want to know about Susie and Rodney?"

"I guess you're going to tell me, whether I care or not." He stared straight ahead as though talking to the tree in front of him.

"She's your sister."

"Yeah. Well. We aren't close." He took a long sip of his soda that smelled like it had whiskey in it.

"Okay. Then I won't tell you that she's doing better. She's been moved to the rehab floor and is walking with a walker, talking better, and actually forming sentences."

"Good." He lit a cigarette and took a huge amount of smoke into his lungs.

"When did you start smoking?" I had never seen any of my brothers smoke. I'd seen them drink beer, but that was about all. Of course, three of the four were older than me, and probably hid things since they thought I was a *Squirt,* their nickname for me growing up.

"A couple years. I don't smoke often." He took another puff.

"Rodney was moved to the neurology floor; no longer in ICU. And he's forming some words. Susie is his number-one therapist and is teaching him how to feed himself. They are amazing together."

*

I thought about what I'd witnessed in New Orleans the week before. I'd walked into Susie's room and she was pushing a walker, a physical therapist holding a strap around her waist.

"Bravo!" I clapped my hands, and Susie smiled.

"I want to get out of here," she told me. "That way...can be a reg-lar visit-or and sit with Rod long...er." Her speech was a little slow, and some of her words slurred, but she sounded much better. The physical therapist was funny. He said, "Not so fast, Mrs. Thibault. Dr. Warner said you have to remain on the Rehab floor for another couple weeks." He was a small Asian guy in his late twenties with eyes that almost closed when he smiled, which he did when he spoke.

Susie said, "I know. But...sooner I...walk, sooner I'll be out," and she took a few steps towards me. "I tried, uhm, convince Andy...let me walk, uhm, hall. Maybe you can help...sense into him." She smiled at Andy, and he laughed at her.

"Maybe tomorrow, huh?" Andy patted Susie on the back as he helped her into her chair on the side of her bed.

"I'm glad to see that spunk back," I was happy that my sister's determination and tenacity were intact.

*

I took a sip of my Coke and watched the side of James's face. He looked strange to me. "Rodney can't speak, and he has no feeling in his legs and feet. Did I tell you Susie rented a house in New Orleans?"

"Probably a good thing. She doesn't need to live here. Unhealthy." He drank three big gulps from his soda can, then belched. It was strange watching my brilliant older brother, an esteemed attorney, vice president of a bank, act so weird—drinking and smoking, pensive, almost guilty about something.

"Did you know that the state police are going to investigate the shooting? The attorney general said he would reopen the case." I stared at the side of his head.

"No. I didn't know that." He turned towards me with a jerk. "You need to stay out of that, Sissy."

"I'm only trying to find out who shot Rodney and injured Susie. Don't you want to know? You said you'd help me. What have you found out?"

"Nothing. And you need to leave it alone." He got up and walked quickly down the steps into the backyard. He just kept walking towards the back fence, as though on a mission.

"But you said... Well, if you aren't going to invite me to your party, I'll leave you to get ready." I spoke loud enough that he could hear me, even though I was yelling at his back. I let myself out the front door, got in my car, and drove to my dad's house.

*

"I just had the strangest conversation with James." I was sitting on the front porch with Dad, he was in a rocking chair and I was on the swing.

"Why was it strange?" Daddy rocked and let his eyes drift side-to-side.

"Because I mentioned that the state police were investigating the shooting and it seemed to disturb him."

"Stay out of it, Sissy." Daddy turned and stared at me with an even, angry expression.

"That's exactly what James said." I stood up and looked down at Daddy. I felt like I had missed something important that both James and Daddy were trying to clue me in on "I'm not involved. The attorney general has taken over the investigation because Mr. Reggie closed the case without even trying to find the culprit."

"The attorney general? When did that happen?"

"Recently. They'll probably come around to interview you. They are going to talk to anyone who might have seen something."

"I didn't see anything."

"You were one of the first ones out of the church, behind me. I remember."

"I told you, I didn't see anything." He made a sound in his throat as though clearing it, but it sounded hoarse and mealy.

"So you didn't see the blue truck speed off?" A light went off in my head—that's where I'd seen that blue truck, the one parked at James's house. It looked like the one that sped off from the church, tires squealing against the hot pavement, 37L402.

"No. I told you. I didn't see anything." He glared at me as though he could chew me up and spit me out. I glared back then left without another word.

*

I drove to the Burger Barn to pick up dinner, and on my way home I saw a young, colored boy who looked about fifteen or sixteen walking down Main Street. He was wearing a hoodie pulled over his head, but I thought I recognized him as one of Marianne's cousins, Sam Massey's son. I slowed down as a red pickup truck went by, going in the opposite direction. On impulse, I looked in my rearview mirror and saw the truck make a U-turn in the middle of the road and speed up, heading back towards my car that was barely moving.

The truck pulled up on the sidewalk behind Sam's son and started blowing the horn. The boy was frightened half to death and took off running, the truck chasing him down the sidewalk past my car. Sam's son ran off the sidewalk, made his way between two houses, then jumped a fence. The red truck got back on the road, in front of my car, drove a block, and turned right. I knew the driver was going to try to head the boy off as he came out on the back road, which was really an alley. I followed the truck.

We arrived in the alley at about the same time. Sam's son stopped running and stared at both our vehicles, mine behind the truck, penning it in. I rolled down my window and yelled, "Hey, Massey. Come on. Get in my car. I'll take you home."

The boy looked from my car to the truck and back again. I guess he decided I was a better option. He ran to the back door and climbed in behind me.

"Remember me? I'm Susie's sister, Sissy." I put my arm across the back of the front seat and looked behind me to back up. Once we were back on the main road, I turned towards Main Street. My tires screeched as I made the turn and slowed down to the speed limit. "You okay?" Of course he wasn't okay. He was petrified.

He didn't answer.

"What's your name?"

"Jacob."

"Well, Jacob. I don't know what to say about those idiots who were chasing you. Does that happen often?"

"Yes, ma'am."

"Oh, God! Please don't call me, 'ma'am.' You make me feel old."
I was laughing, but he wasn't. "Just Sissy will do." Jacob told me he
was eighteen and he had an older brother, Brandon, who was twenty.
"Don't you have a younger sister, Chrissy?"

"Yes. She's sixteen."

"Yep. She's my niece's best friend. Do you know Lilly?"

"Yes, ma'am. I'm sorry." He corrected himself and tried to call me
Sissy. "Yes, I know Lilly."

"I know your parents. Good people." I tried to make small talk,
hoping to calm him. "I'm not sure if you know it, but Marianne is my
half-sister."

"Yes. I knew that." He was starting to relax a little. Maybe it
helped to know that I had a niece and a sister who were African
American.

I drove down South Jefferson Street and saw James on the porch
with Daddy. I'm sure they saw my car go by; there aren't many white
1977 Camaros in Jean Ville.

I'll never forget the look on Jacob Massey's mother, Josie's face
when we pulled into the Quarters. I wondered if, every time Jacob or
Brandon left the house, she worried whether they would come home.
That thought made me so angry I almost screamed.

*

When I left the Quarters, I thought about James and Daddy on the
porch. I parked my car in the garage under my apartment on Gravier
Road and walked behind the houses that were on the east side of South
Jefferson, stopping at the fence that surrounded Dr. Switzer's
backyard. I sleuthed my way to the Switzers' front yard and stood
behind a huge oak tree, laden with Spanish moss, and peeked around
it to see that my dad and James were still on the porch, having a serious
conversation.

I backtracked a few houses south then crossed the street and
sneaked behind neighbors' houses until I came up behind my dad's
house. I slithered around the side of the house, its foundation as tall

as me, and positioned myself beside the front porch where I could overhear what Daddy and James discussed.

"I'm not sure how that happened," James said.

"If your sister had anything to do with it, she'll be in big trouble." Daddy was rocking hard back and forth.

"Sissy can't do anything. She's a dumbass and can't possibly know the attorney general."

"No, but she knows Borders. I need to have a talk with him, see what he might have told her." Daddy took a long swig of something and kept rocking.

"I'll see him tomorrow and find out whether he's the one who turned the case over to the AG." James must have stood up because I heard feet stomp on the wood planks.

"You tell Borders he'd better not be the one, if he knows what's good for him." I heard the screen door slam and figured James had gone through the house to his car parked out back. I waited and watched the street until I saw him drive by, then I made my way back home, again walking low behind the houses down Jefferson to where it met Gravier Road.

*

That night, sitting on my deck overlooking Susie's backyard, I tried to understand the conversation between my Dad and James. Although there was something that should have turned a light on in my brain, my mind felt blocked against allowing the information to seep in.

I thought about Jacob Massey and how nothing had really changed with respect to how white people in Jean Ville treated Negroes. It made me sick, but I remembered when I had been just as guilty, when I didn't think that colored people were equals, either. Until Marianne, Lilly, and Rodney became family, and it dawned on me that the color of a person's skin had nothing to do with his or her soul.

I heard a vehicle pull up in the driveway in front of my garage apartment. A minute later, a door slammed, and the sound of boots hit the stairs on the outside of the garage. The staircase ended at a deck where the door to the apartment was located. The deck wrapped around the back of the apartment, and I was sitting on the swing, staring at the gorgeous sunset over the trees.

"Hey. How long you been back in town?" Warren came around the corner, walked over to the swing, and kissed me on the cheek. He sat in one of the rockers.

"Just got home. I stopped to see James, then went by Daddy's and the Burger Barn first. Want to split a burger?"

"No, thanks. But I'll have a beer if you've got a cold one." He got up and walked through the sliding glass doors into my apartment. I heard the refrigerator door open and shut, then the sound of the tab popping off the aluminum can. He walked back onto the deck and sat in a rocker. "Did you miss me?"

"Not really. Too busy." I looked at the side of his face and couldn't believe I was still dating this loser. We'd gone steady in high school. He was a football player, I was a cheerleader. Then I went off to college for a couple years, but when I dropped out of school and came home, there was Warren, waiting for me as though no time had ever passed. He'd never left Jean Ville—took a job as a flunky for a surveyor after high school graduation. He and his friends got together on weekends and relived every touchdown, tackle, and interception of every high school football game they'd ever played. It was as though they'd never moved on. I guess, in essence, they hadn't.

Had I? Or was I stuck, too?

"That's not a nice thing to say to your boyfriend." He took a long swig of his beer. "You got plans tonight?"

"Not really. I'm tired. Going to eat my burger and hit the sack."

"You want to see my new truck? It's out front."

"Not tonight, Warren. I told you. I'm tired." My voice was laced with anger and aggravation.

"Can I stay with you?"

"No."

"Just like that? No?"

"Just like that. No." I got up, walked into the apartment, pulled the doors together and locked them, then closed the drapes. About five minutes later, I heard his boots clop down the stairs and his truck start up. I looked out the front window and noticed he was driving a new, red pickup. I could have sworn it was the same truck that had chased down Jacob Massey that afternoon.

What was I doing? Living in Jean Ville, dating a loser who chased and assaulted black people? I'm not an introspective person, but I felt it was time I considered my life and made some changes, or I would end up married to Warren Morrow, have a passel of children, and be penniless, uneducated, and miserable.

~ Chapter Six ~

≈

Moving On

MISS MILLIE WAS SURPRISED to see me when I walked up to her sliding glass window just before 5:00 PM on Wednesday afternoon. I was on my way to New Orleans and had called Robert Morris before leaving Jean Ville to ask if I could drop by for a few minutes.

"Is Mr. Morris expecting you?" She looked at me over the top of her cat-eye glasses and frowned.

"Yes, he is." I smiled a broad smile and winked at her, which caught her off-guard. She picked up the telephone and punched a couple of numbers.

"Miss Burton, sir." She put the phone down and told me to have a seat, then pushed the window sideways to shut it. Her pouting bottom lip said she was upset. She probably thought she'd have to work late because Robert Morris had an after-five appointment with me. I certainly didn't want to mess up her social life.

I waited about ten minutes, and Morris walked into the waiting room.

"Sissy. Nice to see you. Come on back." He held the door opened, and I walked in front of him. "You can go home, Millie. No need to stay." He followed me back to his office, which, by now, I knew how to get to.

We sat at the round table.

"What can I do for you?" Morris leaned back, stretched his legs out and loosened his tie.

"I was wondering how the investigation is going." I put my purse on the table and folded my hands in my lap.

"Well, I don't really know. I don't keep up with every investigation on a daily basis." He went to his desk and picked up the phone. "Chris, can you come to my office before you leave? Thanks." Morris sat back down.

"Whew. Long day. I could use a drink." He took a deep breath and folded his hands across his chest.

The same detective I'd met on my last visit to the AG's office came in without knocking. I remembered his name, Detective Sherman.

"You remember Chris Sherman, right, Sissy? Detective, this is Abigail Burton."

"Please. Call me Sissy." I stood and shook hands with the detective and we all sat at the round table. He told us that he'd been to Jean Ville several times and, so far, hadn't gotten very far with the people who were at the wedding. He talked to Doctor Cappel and Doctor Switzer, and both were helpful in explaining the injuries Rodney and Susie had incurred, but they had no idea who'd shot the two bullets that hit Rodney.

"Have you spoken with my dad or any of my brothers? They were all there." Although James and Daddy both warned me to say out of it, I'd been feeling rebellious and off-center after overhearing their conversation. "Also, Rodney's family, especially those who live in the Quarters near Shadowland Plantation. And Rod's brother, Jeffrey, was best man. He walked out of the church before I did."

"What did you see, Miss Burton? I mean, Sissy?" Chris Sherman had a small spiral-bound pad he'd pulled from his shirt pocket. He flipped a few pages and clicked the top of a ballpoint pen.

"All I saw was Lilly screaming and a blue truck speeding away. The tires screeched, and rocks flew."

"A blue truck. This is the first I've heard about the vehicle involved. What makes you think there's a connection?"

"I'm not sure. Instinct? It was sitting still, shots rang out, then it peeled out on the pavement."

"How many people were in the truck?"

"I only saw the one sitting shotgun, and I really didn't see his face. There had to be someone driving. So at least two people."

"Did you recognize anyone?"

"No. It was too far away. I barely saw the side of the guy's head." I thought about Tucker Thevenot standing on James's porch, and wondered whether he was the one, but I couldn't, honestly, make that connection. "Have you spoken with Susie and Rodney?"

"Where can I reach them?" He looked down, ready to write what I said.

"They are both in the hospital in New Orleans. I gave Mr. Morris that list of contacts with addresses and phone numbers." I stared at him as though he were some idiot who couldn't read.

"That file is in my office. I'm handling a number of cases." He seemed apologetic, and I felt bad for my snide remark. I gave him Susie and Rodney's room numbers at Ochsner. I mentioned he should talk to Lilly and Marianne, and suggested Jeffrey, again.

"And Joe. Joe Franklin. Lilly's dad. He walked out with me, a groomsman. He lives in New York City, but his contact information is in your file."

"I'll get right on those interviews." He looked weird, as though he was frightened of something. His eyes darted from me to Robert and back to his writing pad.

"Is something wrong, Chris?" Robert must have noticed it, too.

"I haven't wanted to bother you, but we've had some threats." He stared at Robert a couple of seconds then looked down at the table.

"What kind of threats?"

"Notes left on the windshield, slashed tires, red paint on one of our cars. Stuff like that." He stared at Robert without blinking.

"Where?"

"Jean Ville. Both times we were up there." His feet shuffled under the table and beads of perspiration gathered on his forehead.

"I'll tell you what. You go to New Orleans and follow up with the victims and their family members." Robert Morris stood up, which made Detective Sherman stand, too. "I'll take Lieutenant Schiller and Sergeant Montgomery and go to Jean Ville myself. I'd like to visit with Senator Burton and talk to his son, the lawyer. They don't intimidate me." He sat back down, and Sherman left the room. "Sorry, Sissy. I don't mean to talk about your family in front of you."

"Look, that's okay. I'm just glad you're going to try to get to the bottom of this." I leaned back in my chair and crossed my ankles. "I figured something happened to stall things, or I would have heard from you."

"Yeah, well. I have a number of cases, and I haven't followed up on this one as I should have. I want to visit Borders. And DeYoung. Yep. I need to go up to Jean Ville and shake the bushes. And I have a team of state policemen who won't be put off by bullies and threats." He rubbed his forehead and shut his eyes. It was dead silent for a minute or so.

"Look, I'm beat." He opened his eyes and looked at me. It was as though he'd had an attitude adjustment behind his closed lids, and was back to normal. "What do you say you follow me to my house? Brenda is dying to meet you."

"Sure. If you think it's okay." I stood up. He went to the back of his desk, picked up the phone, and dialed a number.

"Hi. Susie's sister, Sissy, is here. The one I told you about." He paused and listened for a few seconds. "Yep. Right here in my office. What about I bring her over for a drink, and you can meet her." He paused again. "Okay. See you in a few." He hung up, picked up his suit coat from the back of his chair, and grabbed his briefcase. "I'm parked out back, a black Saab. I'll pull out on Third Street and you can follow me."

His house was in Spanish Town, on the other side of the state Capitol, maybe five minutes away, but with traffic, it took us ten. The house was an older, frame house that Robert and Brenda had renovated a few years before, and it was beautiful. We sat outside in a fenced-in courtyard made of cobblestones and bricks that reminded me of New Orleans. I could smell the Mississippi River just over the levee, and every now and then a foghorn sounded in the far-off distance.

Brenda made a pitcher of something with rum and juice, similar to the famous Pat O'Brien's hurricanes, and the three of us chit-chatted about their two children who were in high school, and about Rodney and Susie's progress.

"So, Sissy, I feel as though there's another reason for your visit, although you don't need one." Robert looked at me and winked at Brenda.

"Actually, I need a job. I want to move out of Jean Ville and thought maybe you could help me." I put my drink down and tried to be serious.

"What can you do? Besides sleuthing?" He laughed and took a sip of his drink.

"Mostly, I'm a musician. You have a piano?" I guess I caught them off-guard, but Brenda rose to the occasion and led me inside where a baby grand sat next to the huge glass opening between the family room to the courtyard. Robert stayed in his lounge chair outside, and I hit the keys. First I played some boogie-woogie, then I slipped into, *When the Saints Go Marching In,* then a version of *Beethoven's Fifth.* Finally, I played *Time After Time,* and sang the entire song.

I stood up, took a bow, and returned to the patio.

"Wow! I'm impressed." Brenda had been standing next to the piano the entire time I played and sang. She followed me out and refilled my glass.

"Thanks. I teach piano and voice to kids in Jean Ville. But, really, I want to move away, maybe to Baton Rouge." I sat in one of the iron chairs under an umbrella stuck in the center of a black iron table. We talked a while longer, then their two kids came in.

The Morrises' seventeen-year-old boy, Robert, Jr. whom they called Bobby, looked just like his dad—over six feet tall, brown wavy hair and the build of a football player. He had dark, thick eyebrows, long, curly eyelashes and a regal nose, similar to Michelangelo's fourteenth-century sculpture of David that I'd studied in art history at Centenary College in Shreveport. His lips were full, his bottom lip sort of pouty, and he had a dimple in his cleft chin. When he smiled, two huge dimples, one in each cheek, indented into deep holes and made his cheekbones lift and become even more pronounced.

Their daughter, Jessica, who was fifteen, had blonde hair like her mother and blue eyes that were shaped like sideways teardrops. When she smiled, her nose wrinkled, and her eyes turned to slivers, like wings on a bluebird. Her hair was in a ponytail that hung halfway down her back, tied with a wide navy bow. She was a couple of inches taller than me—everyone was taller than me—and she was very slim and flat-chested, like an athlete. I asked her if she was into sports, and she said she ran track and played softball. But she was feminine and had dainty features, small hands, and a chiseled nose.

I liked both of the Morris kids right away and thought about how much Lilly would like them.

"Have you guys met my niece, Lilly, yet?" I looked at the teenagers, who shrugged their shoulders and eyed their dad.

"No, not yet, but we should have her over one evening. She's at LSU, right?" Robert looked at Brenda, who smiled and nodded.

"Yes, she's a freshman. She graduated from high school a year early, though, so she's your age, Bobby."

"You wouldn't be matchmaking, now would you, Sissy?" Robert laughed at me.

"Nope. I'm just saying...!" I smiled, and everyone started to laugh. I stayed for dinner of lasagna, salad, and hot rolls, plus a bottle of red wine. By the time I left, I was a bit tipsy, and was glad I didn't have but a few blocks to drive to the Capitol House Hotel downtown. Of course, I used my dad's credit card to pay for the room.

101

Sissy

*

The rector at the front desk of Lilly's dorm buzzed her room, then told me I could go down the hall to #142. She was on her bed crying, and jumped into my arms as soon as I walked through the door.

"What is it, baby girl?" I held her and whispered words of encouragement, but she just cried and cried. When the sobs finally died down, I got her to wash her face and go with me to get lunch at a local seafood restaurant a couple miles off-campus. We stirred sugar into our iced tea and waited for shrimp poor-boys.

"I hate it here." She stared at her tea as she squeezed lemon into it.

"It's only been a week. What do you hate?" I tried to reach for her hand, but she pulled it away.

"I hate everything except my classes. I like them. I like going to school. I like studying. I like my professors. But I hate living in the dorm with giddy girls who only care about dates and drinking and going out every night." She finally looked at me, her eyes narrowed to slits, her forehead wrinkled.

"Tell me about it."

"Well, to begin with, none of the girls in my suite ever study. They rarely go to class. They stay up late talking on the phone, giggling, trying out different make-up. Stuff like that. Our phone rings at all hours." She took a breath and a sip of tea. I listened. "When I get back from class, they are just waking up. I can't study in my room. I have to go to the library way across campus, and I'm afraid to walk back alone at night."

"Have you told your mom, I mean Susie, about this?"

"No. I've told Marianne a little, but I don't want to bother Susie. She has her hands full with Dad and her own recovery." She took another sip of tea. Our waitress brought lunch, and we inhaled the smell of fresh-baked bread and fried gulf shrimp. I didn't say anything because I wanted her to talk.

"I want to be a doctor. I'm serious about college." She took a bite

102

of her sandwich and stared at me as though I should understand her dilemma.

"Of course you are. And you should be."

"Look. I'm younger than everyone here. I can't get in bars, even if I want to." She put both her hands on the table, leaned forward, and spoke in a low voice so no one would hear. "I don't want to date fraternity boys who think you should have sex with them. That's not what I want. I want to go to my classes, learn, study, and make good grades. My roommates think I'm a geek."

"Do you want to transfer to another college?"

"I don't think it would be different anywhere else." She sat back in her chair and looked deflated. "I mean. I like school. I just don't like living in the dorm."

A light went off in my head. What if I were to get an apartment in Baton Rouge and Lilly could live with me. Susie would probably pay the rent, and I could take some classes at LSU. I didn't mention it to Lilly because I didn't want her to be disappointed if I couldn't make it happen. Meanwhile, I needed to introduce her to some other people; kids who were serious about school; kids like Bobby and Jessica Morris.

We chit-chatted for a couple hours. I mentioned that there were probably other serious students on campus, and she should be on the lookout for them. "Pay attention to those in your classes who stay late and don't rush out of the classroom. Also, in the library. Those who spend a lot of time there are probably serious."

"Good idea. I hadn't thought about looking outside of my dorm."

"My mother used to say girls went to college to get an MRS Degree." I laughed.

"That's about right. Sounds like my roommates."

"Yeah. I think that's why my mother went to college." I wiped the catsup off my mouth and took a sip of tea. Lilly was laughing hard, and I thought how much better she seemed from a few hours before. "Are you coming to New Orleans this weekend?"

"Yes. Will you be there?" She beamed at me.

"Yes, but I'll be in Baton Rouge another couple days. Maybe we can get together again?"

"Okay, yes. I'd like that, Sissy."

The next afternoon, I picked Lilly up at her dorm and we drove to Spanish Town. I parked across from the gated home I'd been to Monday night.

"Is this where Mr. Morris lives?"

"Yep. Do you remember meeting him last year?" I turned the ignition off and reached for my purse.

"Yes, and his wife, Miss Brenda. Very pretty."

"They love your parents, and they've been wanting to get together with you, but didn't know how to get in touch." I opened my car door and stepped into the street. Lilly came around, and we held hands as we crossed. I rang the doorbell and Jessica opened the door.

"Miss Burton. It's nice to see you again." Jessica smiled and swung the door wide so we could walk in.

"Please, Jessica, call me Sissy."

"Okay. If you'll call me Jessie." She laughed and was charming in her fifteen-year-old way.

"This is Lilly. She's my niece." I put my arm on Lilly's shoulder and pulled her into the room.

"Hi. So are you Susie's daughter?" Jessica closed the door and stood facing Lilly.

"Yes, and Rodney's."

"Awesome. We love your parents." Jessica took Lilly's hand, and I walked behind them through the living room and dining room and into the kitchen. Brenda was behind the island with a cooktop in it. There were stools all around, and after we exchanged greetings, we sat around the island while Brenda prepared supper.

Beyond the kitchen was the solarium where the baby grand piano sat in front of the sliding doors that spanned the entire back of the house. When Brenda declared everything was done and she could put things on warm until dinnertime, we walked through the opened glass doors into the courtyard. Lilly and Jessie sat at the round table with the umbrella, and Brenda pointed to a lounge chair where I sat. She sat in one next to it and put a bottle of wine on the small table between our chairs.

We talked about Susie and Rodney, and Brenda said she would come to New Orleans in the next couple of weeks to visit the patients. I told her to let me know when, and I would make it my business to be there, too. "Maybe we could have lunch."

"That would be great!" Brenda took out her calendar and started to flip pages.

"Would you be bringing the kids with you?" I took a sip of my wine and put the glass down on the table.

"If they want to come. Once they are teenagers, they pretty much decide what they want to do on weekends." She grinned at me as though I should know what she meant, but I was probably closer in age to the teenagers than I was to Brenda. I told her how miserable Lilly was in the dorm, and that I was going to talk to Sissy about renting an apartment so I could get her out of there.

"Lilly's a serious student," I spoke softly so Lilly didn't hear me. "There's too much disruption and partying going on in the dorm."

"Oh. She should stay here." She sat up in her chair as though a thought had just occurred to her. "We have plenty of room, and I'll bet Jessie would love to have her."

"You need to talk to Susie about that." I was a bit surprised at Brenda's immediate invitation for Lilly to stay with them.

Robert and Bobby came into the courtyard at about six o'clock. Robert said he'd gone to Bobby's football practice and drove him home. Robert hugged Lilly and introduced Bobby, who joined Lilly and Jessie at the table where they were playing dominoes. Robert kissed Brenda, and she poured him a glass of wine. The three of us went inside and sat around the kitchen island. After a few minutes, I got up and went to the piano. I couldn't resist playing a baby grand.

I played, *Billie Jean,* then *Beat It,* both by Michael Jackson. The three kids came inside and stood around the piano while I finished the second song. They asked me if I could play certain songs, and we all sang, *Total Eclipse of the Heart,* and *Never Gonna Let You Go.* I banged out, *What's Love Got To Do With It,* but didn't know all the words, yet I sang every word to *Time After Time,* and *Girls Just Want to Have Fun,* by Cyndi Lauper.

Lilly, Jessie, and Bobby loved the music, and all laughed and tried to sing along. Brenda broke up the party by calling us to the table she'd set in the courtyard. We ate shrimp in a cream sauce mixed with pasta. I was impressed with how adult-like the Morris kids were; very much like Lilly. And the three seemed to hit it off famously.

On the way back to campus after such a fun evening, Lilly was happy and talkative. She said she really liked Bobby and Jessie, and felt comfortable at their house.

"What did y'all talk about while you were playing dominoes?" I stared out the front windshield and tried to remember what it felt like to be sixteen.

"We talked about school. Bobby is taking two college classes at his high school." Lilly sat sideways on her seat, staring at the side of my face. Her voice was upbeat, and she seemed excited. "He says he's going to be a lawyer like his dad. He's very serious about school. Jessie is, too. She wants to be a journalist. She says she might go to law school, too, because journalists who have law degrees have an edge."

"So you liked them?" I was close to her dorm and began to look for a parking spot.

"Oh, yes. I like them a lot—more than any of these snobbish college kids. I wish I was still in high school." Her voice fell flat, as though she were remembering something that made her sad.

"Do you miss New York?"

"I miss Daddy." She became pensive and sat with her head bent, her hands folded in her lap. "And I'd like to visit Mama, even if she doesn't know me. But I'm very happy with Susie and Rodney."

"It must be great to have two moms and two dads." I parked the car, put it in park, and kept the engine running.

"It is, but when I'm with one, I miss the others." Her voice was riddled with tears that she held in check, and I was amazed at how quickly she could go from happiness to depression in a few minutes.

"I'll take you to New York when you want to go. We can talk to Susie about it this weekend, okay?" I turned the motor off and reached for the handle of my door.

"Yes. Let's do that." She turned towards me and had a small smile. "Maybe we could go during the Thanksgiving holidays?"

"Sure. Let's see what Susie says." I started to open the door.

"You don't need to come in with me." She put her hand on my shoulder, and I turned towards her. "And, Sissy. Thanks. You're an awesome aunt." She bent over and kissed me on the cheek, and before I could say anything, she was out the door and across the street. I watched her walk into her dorm. She had more of a lilt to her step than she'd had over the past couple of days, and I hoped she could stay positive until we worked things out.

*

Susie's room seemed like Grand Central Station when I arrived at the end of the week. Miss Bessie and Mr. Ray had been there for a few days and had driven Marianne's Datsun wagon down to New Orleans. Lilly was excited about everything: having her grandparents and her aunts with her, moving into a house near the hospital, and seeing Rodney get better every day. She went from Susie's room to Rodney's to the house on Jules Avenue all day.

I heard the jangle of bracelets and the clicking of stilettos when Mama emerged from the elevator and started down the hall to Susie's room on Tuesday. John Maceo, her live-in beau, was with her. He stood in the corner of Susie's room while Mama acted like mother-of-the-year. She kissed and hugged me, then hovered over Susie, gave her sips of Sprite, and read a poem from the small book by Emily Dickinson that she'd pulled from her leather Gucci handbag.

"We're staying at the Roosevelt Hotel in the city. Here's the phone number if you should need me." She handed a card to me, kissed Susie on the forehead and me on the cheek. "I'll be back tomorrow, and we'll have a wonderful visit." The next day I wasn't there when she returned without John. Susie told me that Mama sat in the tall chair next to her bed and read from Walt Whitman's *Leaves of Grass.* Thankfully she only stayed an hour or so, then jingled her way back to John and some fancy dinner at some fancy restaurant downtown.

"I was immediately off to visit Rodney." Susie laughed, and I couldn't help but laugh with her.

Susie was ready to be free to go to Rodney's room on her own, without someone pushing her in a wheelchair, which Marianne, Lilly, and I took turns doing—back and forth. She had devised her own therapy for Rodney: a particular speech therapy, a sit-up-straight therapy, a let me pump your legs that you don't feel therapy, and the all-important how to hold a spoon therapy. She was convinced he would get well sooner if she were with him more.

Susie's determination to be normal and to make Rodney recover was the talk of the medical center. Doctors and nurses stopped to speak to her when one of us rolled her wheelchair down the halls.

I walked into her room Thursday, and she was waiting, dressed in slacks, a silk blouse, and sneakers. She had even applied a little lipgloss and mascara, and was sitting in the tall chair in the corner of her room.

"I'm ready. What kept you?" Susie laughed and pulled the walker towards her. "I'm done with that wheelchair. Too confining, and no one looks down at me." She started towards the door to the hall just as Marianne walked in. Susie strolled right past Mari, who looked at me, her shoulders lifted. I was stuck to the floor, dumbfounded.

"Did Dr. Warner give you permission to amble around this huge medical center on your own two feet, missy?" Marianne tried to catch up to Susie in the hall. I went after Marianne and heard Susie's reply.

"I don't need permission." She turned her head sideways to talk to Mari over her shoulder as we headed down the hall like the follow-the-leader game. When we passed in front of the nurses' station, everyone stood up: the therapists, the nurses, two doctors, and several housekeepers. Susie knew all of them by name and waved at them and smiled as she walked by. They were surprised to see her walk down the hall, even with the support of the walker. I shrugged my shoulders at them as I went by.

When we got to the elevators, I heard a roar of applauds behind us. All three of us turned to see that everyone had filed out from behind the desk and stood in the hall watching us, clapping, whistling, and cheering. Susie was touched, but she acted like it was all in a day's work, and waved at them as Marianne and I followed her into the elevator.

"Okay," Susie said when we walked into Rodney's room. "It's time for you to try to sit up." He was still flat on his back with oxygen in his nostrils, a catheter, and an IV line. He smiled at her and winked. Lilly got up from her chair and rushed to Susie's walker to help.

"Lil, please lift the head of Rodney's bed." She pointed to the crank at the foot of the bed, and Lilly hesitated. "Tell her it's alright, baby." Susie looked at Rodney, and he nodded at Lilly. Lilly started turning the crank, and the head of the bed began to rise. When it lifted about six inches, Susie told Lilly to stop. "Okay. That's good for today. Every day another six inches or so until you can sit up straight. Okay?"

Rodney smiled so wide his straight white teeth gleamed. He nodded again.

"Now, for speech therapy." Susie pushed her way to the side of his bed and asked Marianne to lower it so she could sit next to him. Susie planted her butt at his waist and put one hand on each side of his head, bent forward and kissed him for a long time. He closed his eyes and kissed her back.

When she lifted her head, and their faces were a few inches apart she said, "Say, 'Love.'"

I watched his tongue touch the back of his upper teeth, his lips parted about an inch, as he tried to form the word.

"Push air through your mouth from your throat," Susie spoke softly and was close enough to his mouth to kiss him.

"Luhhhhhh." Rodney's voice was raspy and deep, but the sound was loud and clear.

"Great job!" She kissed him again and sat straight up. "Now. Try again. Louder."

"Luhhhhhh-bbbbb." He smiled at her then looked at Lilly, who was still standing at the foot of the bed. "Luhhhhhh-bbbb."

"I love you, too, Dad." Lilly held onto the bed to steady herself. Rodney smiled at her and said it again, "Luhhhhh-bbbb. Liiiiiiiii."

"Great. You've got the L's!" Susie laughed aloud. "And that's the most important letter of the alphabet." She kissed him again and pulled her body into his bed so she could lie down next to him, her head on his shoulder, her arm across his chest. Rodney simply smiled and shut his eyes, savoring the deliciousness like chocolate pie.

Dr. Warner walked into the room and gasped. I wasn't sure how much of it he saw and heard, but it was enough to impress him.

"It looks like someone is hampering to get out of ICU and into a regular room." He smiled and walked past Marianne and Lilly, who stood at the foot of the bed. He squeezed Marianne's elbow as he went by, a little gesture I noticed but didn't comment on.

"Let me examine my patient, Susie." He tried to help her out of the bed, but she insisted on doing it herself. "I hear you ran a marathon this morning. You're the talk of the Rehab Unit, young lady." She smiled and shrugged.

"So, Rodney, I see your bed is raised a bit. How does that feel? Does your head hurt in this position? Just blink once for yes, twice for no." Warner shined his penlight into Rodney's eyes.

"Oooooh." Rodney's mouth formed an 'O' as he pushed the sound out. Warner backed up and stared at him, then turned to look at Susie.

"He said, 'No,'" she laughed at Dr. Warner. "We were having speech therapy. You interrupted us, but I'll forgive you this one time." Warner looked from Susie to Rodney and back and forth a few times, then at Marianne. She shrugged as if to say, "I have no control over this pair."

"Okay. I can see where I'm not needed around here. When you can sit up at forty-five degrees for thirty minutes or more without additional pain and no medical problems, I'll move you to the Neurology floor where you can have visitors all day." Warner knew this was important to Susie, Rodney, and Lilly. Susie was only allowed to see Rodney four times a day for ten to fifteen minutes each time; although she often convinced the nurses to let her stay longer. Lilly was considered his attendant and could sit quietly in his cubicle for two hours at a time, then the staff had to empty drains, take blood, and do all the medical things Rodney needed several times a day. That's when Lilly went to Susie's room.

"Yahhhhhh." Rodney seemed to enjoy pushing air over his vocal cords. Marianne contends, to this day, that his determination was spirited by Susie's positive attitude. Susie didn't buy into that compliment. She believed that if she could get better, he could, too.

Twice a day, Susie insisted on raising the head of Rodney's bed a few more inches and leaving him upright as long as he could stand it. Nurses came in and out, pointing their penlights on his pupils, and agreed he was able to tolerate the new positions. By the end of the week, he was sitting at forty-five degrees for thirty minutes, several times a day and pushing out sounds that almost made words.

*

Marianne and I were at the house on Jules Avenue most of the next day, unpacking boxes, hanging art, putting dishes in cabinets, making beds, all the things you do when you move into a house. Marianne was quiet, and when I tried to chat with her she gave one-word answers.

"I can tell something is bothering you, and I'm wondering when you might spill it." I smiled at her. We were in the kitchen, filling the cabinets with things the interior designer had sent over and stuff I'd brought from Jean Ville. I pointed to the round table in the center of the room, and she sat down. She told me that she'd had an awkward encounter with Dr. Warner at a sports bar on Deckbar Avenue, and that she'd been avoiding him since.

"What happened?" I put water and coffee grounds in the Mr. Coffee and pulled two coffee mugs out of a box.

"He got fresh with me." She had her hands folded on the table in front of her and stared at her fingers as she formed a church steeple, then folded her fingers back into a double-handed fist.

"What's the problem. He seems attracted to you." I rinsed the mugs in the sink and pulled a dishtowel out of a drawer, surprised I remembered where they were. "No one could blame him. You are stunningly beautiful, smart, talented, kind."

"Sissy. You know my history. I've never been with a man." She continued to stare at her hands, fisted so tightly I could see the veins across the tops. "I think he tried to kiss me, and it scared me out of my skin."

"Well, how did it feel?" I stood with my back resting against the cabinet in front of the coffee maker and stared at her, but she didn't look up.

"I felt his breath on the side of my face, and he said that he wanted to kiss me every time he saw me."

"Hmm. Have you thought about telling him?" I turned when the coffee pot sputtered and spat the last of the water through the grounds.

"Oh, no! I couldn't." She started to cry, and I went to the table and put my arms around her from behind, laying my head on top of hers.

"Mari, you need to be honest with him."

"He'll hate me." She whimpered.

"He might." I patted her shoulder. "But it's best to find out rather than keep secrets. They will come out eventually, and the longer you wait, the more invested you will be in the relationship, and harder it will be to lose him. If you're going to run him off, do it now before things go any further."

She didn't respond, and I could feel her whimpers get smaller and further apart.

*

The next day, we were in ICU and Susie had Rodney's bed at forty-five degrees when Dr. Warner rushed in with two nurses behind him.

"I heard you are trying to get out of bed!" He stopped at the foot of Rodney's bed. Marianne was sitting in the corner reading a magazine and looked up over it. His eyes met hers, and she immediately looked down and hid behind the book. Warner looked at Rodney. "What are you trying to do, get me off your payroll?"

Rodney laughed. Susie was in bed with him, reading aloud Robert Frost's *The Road Not Taken*, very slowly. She'd stop to ask if he understood, and required him to say certain words, like "wood," "fair," and "way." He pushed sounds out that mimicked the words, and she would pat him on the leg and smile at him each time. Lilly would clap her hands when he made sounds, which were deep, throaty, and sometimes sounded, to me, like a foghorn.

Watching Susie and Rodney was enchanting, and I sneaked a peek at Dr. Warner, who was grinning at them. Marianne also watched Susie and Rodney, and Warner caught Mari's glance, winked at her and lifted his chin, pointing it towards the door as if asking her to meet him in the hall. She looked back down at the magazine. I stood next to her chair and pinched her shoulder. She shrugged me off.

"Marianne told me Susie would be the best medicine for you. She was right." Warner looked at Marianne, and she looked up when she heard her name. He winked at no one in particular, and I had to agree with Marianne that he looked pretty sexy. She blushed. He examined Rodney, shined the light in his eyes, ran a sharp object on the underside of his feet, then pulled the sheet back over them.

"Okay, I'm convinced. I'll spring you out of ICU. You're taking up too much of my staff's time." He laughed, went to the side of Rodney's bed, and shook his hand, man-to-man. "Congratulations. If I were a writer, I'd write an article about you two for the Journal of the American Medical Association."

Rodney pointed to Susie and grinned. "Sheeeeeeee. Riiiiiiiiiiii."

"He's trying to tell you that Susie is a writer." Lilly stood on the other side of the bed, watching, smiling.

"Oh, really. What do you write?" Dr. Warner shifted his attention to Susie.

"I only have one published book, *The Catfish Chronicles.* My second, a sequel, is with the editor." Susie was holding Rodney's hand. "Will you really transfer him to a regular room?"

"Yes. But if there are problems, he's coming back here." Warner shook Rodney's hand again. "Congratulations. Next graduation will be to Rehab. Susie can tell you all about that."

"By the way, when are you going to discharge me? I'm doing fine." Susie got out of the bed and stood facing Warner.

"Well, let me get the reports from your therapists. I'm concerned about where you will go when you leave here." Warner looked at Marianne again, then back at Susie.

"Marianne moved us into a house not far from here. But I'll stay in Rodney's room most of the time."

"That's what I'm afraid of. He needs his rest." Warner looked at Rodney, who was grinning. Susie acted as though she didn't hear Warner.

"It doesn't matter. After you move him to a room, I'll start staying with him as much as I want to, anyway. Whether you discharge me or not." She laughed, and I knew she was pulling his leg, but only a little. She would stay with her husband as long as the nursing staff would allow, and then some. She was not going to be shooed off easily.

"I'll talk to Marianne about this house and make sure you can handle living there." He looked at Mari and motioned with his chin again. "Can I speak with you in the hall?"

I started to laugh, because Marianne was cornered and had to get up and follow him out of the room. That night she told me that he'd apologized for coming on to her and asked for another chance. "He said he wanted to prove he's not a scumbag." We laughed, and she told me that she'd agreed to go out with him again.

～ Chapter Seven ～

Investigation

"OKAY, NOW HOLD THIS spoon in your left hand." Susie stood next to Rodney's bed and helped him grip a spoon from the breakfast tray. He held onto the spoon and smiled after she let go. The muscles around his jaw tightened. "Good. Now put it in the applesauce and bring it to your mouth." She held the plastic container close to him, and he dipped his spoon in the applesauce. He was able to get some on the spoon and slowly brought it to his mouth.

He swallowed and put the spoon back into the container and did it again. He smiled at her, and repeated his new trick. I was so happy for them, I wanted to cry.

"I think you've been sandbagging me." Susie cut his omelet into pieces and handed him the fork. "Now, try this."

He held the fork as though it were a butcher knife used to stab someone. Once he got the eggs on the fork he couldn't figure out how to turn it around to get it to his mouth. Susie took the fork from his hand and readjusted it.

"Like this, baby, remember?" They got through breakfast with Rodney sitting up in bed at a ninety-degree angle. She put the head back a little.

"How's it going, you two?" I stood next to the door to the hall. Susie hadn't seen me, so she was startled.

"Oh, Sissy, I didn't hear you come in." She turned around to look at me.

"I've been watching your therapy session." I walked over and hugged her. "Pretty impressive, brother-in-law." I squeezed Rodney's arm, and he smiled at me. "I don't want to disturb your lessons, so I'll be off to Jules Avenue. If you need anything, call me." I kissed Susie on the cheek, and she hugged me for several seconds longer than usual. I kissed Rod on the forehead, told them both I loved them and that I'd come back soon.

As I walked towards the door, I heard Susie say to Rodney, "Are you ready for speech therapy? I have a novel I think you'll enjoy. The title is *A Confederacy of Dunces* by John Kennedy Toole and, it's set in New Orleans." She paused, and I turned around to see her pull a book from her bag. "Can you say, "New Orleans?"

"Noo Ore Lins."

"Hey, that was good. Say it again."

"Noo Ore Lins."

"Where do we live now?"

"Noo Ore Lins."

I walked down the hall, laughing at the absurdity of it all, how they could be so happy after almost being killed, simply because they were finally together.

*

Marianne came into the house on Jules Avenue at around five o'clock and headed to the kitchen.

"How about a glass of wine." She talked as she walked, and I followed her. "I'm beat."

"Sure." I grabbed one of her arms when I caught up with her and steered her to the table. "I'll get the wine, you sit down."

We sat at the kitchen table with two glasses and one bottle of Chardonnay, and Marianne began to tell me about everything that happened.

"First off, the governor came to visit Rodney and Susie at the hospital earlier this week. Don arranged it all and sneaked Governor Breaux in through the doctors' entrance and up the exit staircase."

"Don?" I looked at her with my eyes squinted and eyebrows lowered.

"Warner. That's his name." She took a sip of wine and smiled.

"You call him Don?"

"Actually, I usually call him Warner, but his friends around here call him Don. His family calls him Donato." She grinned and drank the rest of the wine in her glass.

"Seems you've gotten to know a lot more about Dr. Warner." I looked at her over my glass.

"He took me to a fancy restaurant last night, called Antoine's. It's in the French Quarters." She poured more wine into her glass. "He said he'd been married once, but things didn't work out. He's been in New Orleans almost six years and thinks he'll stay here."

"So what else did you talk about?"

"He said after his divorce he was a 'rogue.' That was his word for dating lots of girls and leaving them heartbroken. He told me he started meeting with his priest a year ago and quit dating altogether, trying to find his 'authentic self,' again, his words." She rubbed her closed eyes with her thumb and forefinger. "He said, after what happened last week at the restaurant on Deckbar, he went to see his priest, for an 'attitude adjustment.'"

"His words?"

"Yep." She took a long sip of wine and turned to look at me. "He said his priest told him that he'd reacted like he did because I rejected him, and women have never rejected him. He said he admitted to his priest that he wants what Rodney and Susie have."

"Wow. That's pretty honest. How did that make you feel?"

"It scares me because it feels like his honesty requires me to be honest, too." She grabbed my hand on top of the table and looked directly at me. "I told him I'd never had a boyfriend."

"Is that all you told him?"

"Yeah. I just couldn't make myself tell him the rest."

"It's a start, Mari. Give yourself some credit." I squeezed her hand,

and we sat there in silence for a long time.

She put her head down, and for a minute I thought she was crying, then she looked up at me and grinned. "By the way, my mom and Rodney's parents are coming this weekend to see the house. We're going to have a barbecue, and they are staying over. Rodney's sisters might come, too."

"Then I'm going to shimmy out of here. Too many people, not enough beds." I got up from the table and rinsed my glass. "Anyway, I got a call from Robert Morris today. He asked whether I could meet with him tomorrow afternoon."

"If that's what you want to do, but you can always stay at the Brenthouse. It's walking distance."

"Listen, I love Tootsie, Miss Bessie, Mr. Ray, and all the others, but I'm going to Baton Rouge tomorrow, then back to Jean Ville to make sure things are still moving forward on the case."

*

I arrived at the attorney general's office at about four thirty Friday afternoon. Miss Millie met me with her snake-eyed stare, as though I were about to wreck her very busy weekend. Robert ushered me down the hall and told Millie she could go home whenever she was done, and he'd see her Monday. We turned into a doorway before we got to Robert's office. His was the last one at the end of the hall next to the back door that said, "No Exit." I had to laugh, because I knew it was the door he went through to and from the parking lot.

We entered a conference room where four other men were seated. They all stood when we came in. Two were wearing state police uniforms, two were in suits. I recognized Detective Sherman as one of the suits. Robert sat at one end of the long table and pointed to the chair catty-corner from his. When I sat, the men took their seats, too.

For the next hour, I heard reports about the investigation that I wasn't sure I should be privy to, but I listened and took notes.

Lieutenant Thomas Schiller started off the meeting. He reported on a trip he'd taken to Jean Ville with Robert Morris, Sgt. Lee

Montgomery—who was the other officer in uniform—and two other state troopers. He said they drove into Jean Ville in three state "units" and parked on the concrete pad on the grounds of the courthouse that was cordoned off for official use only. The five men went to Judge DeYoung's office and met with him for over an hour.

"We were impressed with the Judge." Schiller's expression didn't change, nor the cadence of his voice shift as he relayed the information he'd recorded. "A straightforward guy who is opposed to discrimination and bigotry and is appalled that his parish still has factions of the Klan who continue to impose violence on black people." He said DeYoung didn't have any information about the actual crime, but asked that he be kept in the loop. They discussed how to issue warrants when the time came to make arrests, which Schiller felt they were close to doing.

"Next we went to see your friend, the DA." Robert looked at me and emphasized, "Your friend." I wanted to say, "He's not my friend," but decided to keep my mouth shut and listen. "He's quite a trip. I guess we should have expected him to be defensive and combative." Robert said Reggie Borders didn't understand why they wanted to investigate the incident. He said it wasn't a crime.

"'Someone's gun went off, and that Thibault boy happened to be hit,' he told us." Robert laughed along with the others, who must have witnessed the idiocy of the Toussaint Parish DA. "He said that even if it had been done on purpose, 'which, I guarantee you, it wasn't. And I should know, I investigated it myself,' he said that we should just 'leave it be.'"

Robert said that Borders was insistent that they would never turn up any evidence to the contrary and that, if they did, they would never find the person or people who did it. "That made me more determined to turn over every stone and empty every can until we find the guys who did this."

"We know there were two of them—a driver and a shooter." Sgt. Montgomery stood up and walked to a whiteboard, and used a black marker to diagram where the truck was with respect to the front of the church. He drew red lines to show the trajectory of the bullets.

"We just got the ballistics report on the projectiles that entered Major Thibault." Montgomery sat back down at the end of the table. "Looks like they came from a 45-caliber handgun. Thank God it wasn't a rifle like those deer hunters use or Thibault would be dead, for sure."

I took a deep breath when I thought about how lucky Susie and Rodney were to be alive.

"The blue truck. I'd like to talk to you about that, Miss Burton." Detective Sherman sat directly across from me and met my stare. "Several people saw it, including Rodney, Susie, and Marianne Massey. Jeffrey Thibault said he thought he recognized the guy riding shotgun because he'd been part of a Klan attack on him ten years ago."

"Jeffrey knows who did it?" I sat up straight in my chair.

"Yes, he gave us a name, Tucker Thevenot. Do you know him?" Sherman looked at me as though I were guilty of something.

"Yes. I'm embarrassed to say he's friends with my ex-boyfriend." In my mind, I could see that scroungy-looking guy standing on James's front porch and the blue truck idling in the driveway.

"Sandy blonde hair, scraggly, longish, past his ears; a goatee and mustache. Skinny, lanky, dirty. Those are the adjectives Jeffrey used." Sherman never took his eyes off me.

"I saw him a few weeks ago in Jean Ville. He got in an old blue truck that was driven by a Cajun guy with dark curly hair who used to work for Sheriff Guidry." I looked at each of the men around the table and spoke slowly.

"Who's Sheriff Guidry?" Sherman wrote something on his pad and looked up.

"He was Sheriff before Desiré was elected. He ran a suspicious crew. There was talk he and some of his deputies were members of the Klan." I took a deep breath. "I might know the license plate number."

"Of the blue truck?" Sherman poised his pen over his paper.

"Yes. I mean, I didn't see the license plate at the church. But when I saw Thevenot and Rousseau in the truck a few weeks ago, I memorized the plate number." I inhaled and felt afraid they'd ask me where I saw the truck. "It's 37-L-402, if I remember correctly."

"Do you remember if the plate said, 'Sportsman's Paradise,' or 'Bayou State'?" Sherman wrote something down.

"Bayou State." I crossed my ankles under the table and put my hands in my lap to keep from twisting my hair.

"Where did you see the truck?" Robert looked at me and I realized I wasn't in that room to receive information. I was there to give it.

"It was on a road in Jean Ville called, Shortcut Road. Sometimes I take it from Highway One to Jefferson Street." I watched Sherman write everything I said on his pad. I prayed they wouldn't find out that James lived on Shortcut Road. Then I realized they were bound to find out, so I'd better tell them, as though it were meaningless information. "My brother lives on that road, and I sometimes stop by to visit him if he's home."

"Which brother?" Robert was direct, not very friendly.

"James. My oldest brother. He's a..."

"I know. A lawyer and vice president of Confederate Bank and Trust." Robert nodded at Sherman, who wrote something on his pad. "I spoke with James when we were in Jean Ville."

"How'd that go?" I was curious about how James reacted to having the attorney general drop in on him.

"Let's just say he was evasive." Robert looked at Lt. Schiller, and they laughed. "I tried to be friendly, said I'd heard good things about him, wanted to know whether he'd support me for reelection in three years. I intimated I was there on a campaign stop, but he's a smart one." Robert said he left the four uniformed officers outside in the parking lot, but thought James saw them through his window. "He said he didn't know Tucker Thevenot, had never heard of him, had never seen an old blue truck like the one I described. Although I didn't describe it; I just said, 'blue truck.'" Robert laughed.

"Why didn't you tell us about the license plate number before this?" Lt. Schiller looked at me from across the table.

"I'm not sure it's the same truck that was at the church, but it looked similar, which is why I memorized the plate." I tried to speak with confidence so they wouldn't think I was hiding anything. Was I? Hiding something? I felt like I was, but I couldn't figure out what it might be. I think I felt uncomfortable with the discussion about James in the same vein as Tucker Thevenot and the blue truck; as though James had something to do with the shooting. I knew James would never be involved in anything like that, but why would he tell Robert he didn't know Tucker Thevenot? I saw them talking on James's front porch.

"Do you think Tucker Thevenot shot Rodney Thibault?" Lt. Schiller was still staring at me.

"I couldn't make that connection even if I wanted to." I took a breath and sat back in my chair, my legs stretched out in front of me under the table. "I didn't see the shooter, only the blue truck. Months later I see a blue truck that looked similar to the one I saw at the church, and you describe a scroungy-looking dude named Tucker Thevenot. The description reminded me of the truck I saw a couple weeks ago. That's what I know."

"We spoke with the police officers who were at the scene: Mike Richard, Joey LeBlanc, and Grady Baudin." Sgt. Montgomery looked at me with a kind expression. "Do you know any of them?"

"I went to school with Joey. He was a couple years ahead of me, but I knew him." I thought about the one date I had with Joey LeBlanc and how he tried to grope me. I slapped him, and he slapped me back. Hard. The blow bruised my cheek for weeks. I remember getting out of his car to walk home. He followed alongside me saying awful things about my figure and how every boy at Jean Ville High School wanted to get in my pants. I eventually got in the back seat and let him take me home, but I never went out with him again.

I'd heard things about Joey LeBlanc in the years since high school.

I'd heard he joined the Klan and that he terrorized young black girls. There was talk that he'd raped a fourteen-year-old girl near the Indian Park. I wasn't sure if it was true. The thing that bothered me most as I sat in that conference room with Robert and the four investigators was that Joey and Warren were good friends, maybe best friends. They'd played football together and went in the woods to hunt squirrels and deer, and other critters. Warren always had stories about Joey, but I would never agree to go to parties if he would be there. I didn't want to be alone with Joey LeBlanc again.

The other thing that bothered me was that I would have noticed if Joey LeBlanc had been one of the cops that showed up at the church. I was sure he wasn't one of them.

"What can you tell us about him?" Sgt. Montgomery asked.

"About Joey?"

"Yes. Joey LeBlanc."

"Well, I had one date with him in high school, but I never went out with him again. He's a creep." I shuddered when I thought of that night.

"Do you know any of his friends?" Sgt. Montgomery looked at me as though he knew that I knew that he knew. I sat still like a cat cornered by a bulldog and thought about how to answer that question.

"Yes, of course. Jean Ville is a small town. Everyone knows everyone. One of his best friends is Warren Morrow, the guy I used to date." I took a deep breath and thought about how they would interrogate Warren, and that made me sad, as though I were ratting him out. But I couldn't lie. Montgomery knew.

"And your relationship with Warren Morrow?" He glared at me.

"I told you, I use to date him. But he's a loser." I stared back at Montgomery, and he started laughing. Everyone around the table joined in, and soon we were all laughing—at me! The atmosphere relaxed after that, and the discussion was more about sharing information and less about interrogation. I wanted to let out a huge sigh of relief, but I was afraid to break the spell and have things turn on me again, so I didn't tell them that Joey wasn't one of the cops at the church.

"Sissy," Robert touched my shoulder, and I turned to look at him. "We believe that Tucker Thevenot did the shooting and that the driver was Keith Rousseau. What do you know about Rousseau?"

"He was the one driving the blue truck the day I saw it on Shortcut Road. Keith used to be Sheriff Guidry's deputy." I felt as though I'd already explained that, and he must have forgotten.

"You told us you recognized the driver as one of Guidry's deputies. You didn't tell us his name." Robert looked at me, then at Detective Sherman, then back at me.

"If I recall our conversation half an hour ago, when I told you about Guidry's deputy, you changed the subject to the license plate number. I didn't mean to withhold his name." I felt my blood start to rise. My chest was hot, and I knew a red rash would begin to climb up my neck onto my face.

"I'm sorry, Sissy. I didn't mean to sound accusatory." Robert's expression became much friendlier.

"Y'all keep jumping from one thing to another. First it's Tucker Thevenot, whom I barely know. Then you talk about my brother, James; then Joey LeBlanc, then Warren, now Keith Rousseau. I'm just trying to keep up." I took a deep breath and folded my arms across my chest.

"You're right. You must feel like we've ganged up on you."

"Look, I'm the one who asked for this investigation." I raised my voice louder and louder as I talked and realized I was almost screaming at the end. "Why are you making me feel like I did something wrong. I can't help who I know. It doesn't mean I'm aware of what they do in their spare time."

"Not even your brother?" Robert still had a friendly expression, but the others didn't look so amicable.

"Not even my brother."

"Not even your boyfriend?"

"He's not my boyfriend. I told you. He's a loser." I didn't smile, even though the others tried to stifle laughs.

"Not even your dad?" Robert spoke very softly and tried to use his most brotherly expression.

"What's my dad got to do with this?"

"Probably nothing. I was just wondering whether you might know if he's ever been engaged in any behaviors against black folks that could be construed as unlawful and bigoted?" Robert was searching my face for clues that I knew something about my dad that was far from my understanding about who he was.

"If he has, I'd be shocked. My dad raised us to be nondiscriminatory." I sat up in my chair and folded my hands together on the table. My face was inches from Robert's. "I can't believe he'd ever do anything to hurt another person, black or white."

"I believe you." Robert sat back in his chair, indicating that he was finished with his questions.

The suit who had never said a word the entire time identified himself as Detective Craig Comeau, and said he was more interested in discovering why there was a cover-up.

"We know who did it, and they will be arrested soon." Comeau sat forward in his chair and looked around the table to indicate he was not singling me out. "What we don't know is why? And why is everyone in Jean Ville trying to cover up this crime? Everyone but Judge DeYoung seems determined that we hit a dead end. Why? Is there one big cheese behind this? Why would someone want to kill Rodney Thibault unless it was a contract by a big cheese? Was Thibault a threat to one of the politicians? Those are the questions I want answered. Can you help us?"

"Geez. I hadn't thought that someone might be behind it. I mean, I believe Tucker Thevenot is just a mean-ass s-o-b who would want to take down a black guy who had the audacity to marry a white girl." I was still leaning forward on the table; the detective was across from me, but almost at the other end.

"Not just any white girl." He glared at me.

"What does that mean?" I looked from Detective Comeau to Schiller, to Montgomery, to Sherman, then my eyes landed on Robert Morris.

"Certainly you can read between the lines, Sissy," Robert reached forward and patted my hands, which were still folded on the table in front of me. I looked at all the men around the table, questioning: *what were they getting at?*

Maybe I have a blind spot when it comes to James. But my mind couldn't wrap itself around the insinuations being made. I blew them off, and we all sat in silence for the longest time. I had the distinct feeling they were waiting for me to say something, for a light to go on in my head. But that didn't happen, and eventually, Robert disbanded the meeting.

After everyone left the room but Robert, he reached out and took one of my hands.

"I'm sorry if that was difficult, Sissy. You helped us a lot. You have a great deal of information that you don't realize is important." He was kind and understanding, but I was angry because I'd been ambushed. "That's not uncommon, which is why it takes skilled detectives who ask the right questions, to get you to remember things you stored away."

Robert invited me to go home with him and have dinner with his family, but I declined. He almost begged me and told me Brenda would be livid if I didn't show up, but I stood my ground and drove to the Capital House Hotel. I'd originally planned to drive to Jean Ville after my meeting, but it was seven thirty, and dark, and I was tired and angry.

I went straight to the bar without checking into my room first. I ordered a Martini. I'd never had one, but it was my mom's drink of choice, and it seemed appropriate.

Two Martinis later, I made my way to my room and flopped out on the bed. I wanted to cry, but I was still too angry, and a bit drunk.

The phone started ringing, and I ignored it. Who would know where I was, anyway? It had to be a wrong number. I went to the bathroom and when I got back in the room, the red light was blinking on the phone. I punched '0' and listened to the prompts until it played the message. It was Brenda.

"Sissy. Please come over for dinner. Call me." She left her number, but I didn't return the call. I couldn't remember ever being so angry.

The next morning I checked out of the hotel with a headache. When I got to my car in the parking lot across the street, there was a white slip of paper under the windshield wiper. I thought, *Geez. All I need is a parking ticket.*

I took the ticket off the windshield and stuffed it in my purse, which I slung on the other front seat. I started the car and let it run a minute so the motor could warm up. I reached over and pulled the ticket out of my purse so I could stuff it in my glove compartment. The folded paper opened and I saw bold, red print: *Stay out of this investigation, or you'll end up like your sister!*

Now, I was really angry!

*

When I got to Jean Ville, I called Marianne to find out how the family barbecue went.

"Warner sort of invited himself over to meet everyone." She sounded tired, and it was only noon. "Lilly followed me to the door when the doorbell rang, and when she saw Don Warner standing there, she thought he'd come to give us bad news, and she became hysterical. Once we explained that he had come as a friend to meet our family, things calmed down.

"What else?" I took a long swallow of water.

"They all loved him, and he seemed to enjoy himself."

"Is that all? I have a feeling you aren't telling me something." I took another long swallow of water and refilled my glass.

"Well, I spent the night at his house."

"You what?" I stood up, and the phone cord got all tangled around me, but I held onto the receiver.

"Well, there were so many people at the house on Jules Avenue, and he said he needed to convince me he wasn't a scumbag." She took a deep breath, and I heard her take a sip of something, probably coffee. I needed some caffeine. "We started talking, and he asked me why I'd never had a boyfriend. I told him that I'd been abused when I was young."

"Is that all you told him?"

"Yes, because I started to cry and couldn't stop, and ended up falling asleep in his arms." She took a deep breath and sounded like she was about to cry again. "I woke up this morning in the guest room. He didn't touch me."

"That means a lot."

"Are you sure? I'm confused."

"You're confused because you aren't being totally honest with him, and it seems like he's been transparent with you."

~ Chapter Eight ~

Arrested

S USIE WAS DISCHARGED FROM the hospital at the end of the week, and we girls went out to dinner to celebrate. We called it "Girls' Night Out," and Marianne said Dr. Warner was jealous. Susie said Rodney was, too. Lilly and I looked at each other as if to say, "Maybe we're lucky not to have men who want to control our lives," but neither of us said anything until we got home later that night, and we sat up and giggled for an hour.

I told the girls about my experience at the attorney general's office, but I didn't mention the note on my car because I didn't want to worry Susie. She said Rodney thought he recognized Tucker Thevenot the day of the shooting because he remembered that Tucker had been one of the members of the posse who had chased Rodney in Jackson, Mississippi in the '70s when he tried to take a train to DC to marry Susie.

"He said Tucker Thevenot was on the train to Memphis," Susie told us. "The one Rodney jumped from because he recognized four white men from Jean Ville and knew they were there to get him."

The whole plan had been for Rodney and Susie to get married in DC in 1974, but that plan went down the tubes because of the posse. He and Susie gave up on their dream to be together—too dangerous—and Rodney returned to Jean Ville.

Fast forward ten years and lots of water had flowed upstream: Rodney went to Vietnam, got married and divorced, and spent ten years in the Army. Susie found Lilly when she was four years old but didn't tell Rodney—or anyone, for that matter—about the baby Susie had at eighteen. She eventually married the doctor who had delivered Lilly.

Both Susie and Rodney had been through a lot, and they'd finally come back together with Lilly as the crown on their relationship. Their biggest mistake was having their wedding in Jean Ville, Louisiana. They were paying the price for that.

Rodney tried to tell the detectives from Robert Morris's Morris' office that Tucker Thevenot had also been part of the group of men he called a "posse" who'd hung Jeffrey in a tree in Jean Ville. This had been a few days before they tracked Rodney to Jackson, Mississippi.

Susie said that Rodney still couldn't speak clearly and struggled with consonants, so the Detectives didn't understand everything he tried to tell them. Susie said she tried to help fill in the blanks, but lots of what Rodney knew, he'd never told Susie.

"I sat there and listened while the Detectives asked him questions," Susie told us when we four girls sat at a table in a restaurant called, Brennan's on Royal Street in the French Quarters. "The detectives asked Rod why all those men wanted to kill him. Rodney said it was because he had the nerve to love a white girl. 'Not any white girl,' he said, struggling to get the sounds out so that they understood. 'Senator Bob Burton's daughter.'"

"What are you saying, Susie?" I watched Susie's face, and the look on it made me think that something important had been implied.

"Well, I'm pretty sure Daddy was behind what happened to Rodney ten years ago. And that makes me wonder…" She didn't elaborate.

Daddy would never do anything like that. The bullets that hit Rodney were inches from Susie's head. If Rod hadn't shielded her and pulled her to the ground, taking the bullets himself, she could have been killed, something my daddy would never be a part of.

We didn't talk about the shooting any more. We talked about

Marianne and her relationship with Dr. Warner. Marianne told us that it was getting serious.

"At least on his part." She laughed and blushed. "I mean, he says he's crazy about me."

"Have you told him how you feel?" I looked at the grin on her face and could tell she was ate up with the man.

"I'm not sure how I feel." She blushed.

"How will you know?" Lilly stared at Marianne as though she were trying to figure out how a person might know if she's in love with someone.

"I'm not sure. They say you just know." Marianne laughed, which made us all laugh.

"Well, I'll say this: if I ever think I love a guy, I'm just going to tell him. Playing games is too stressful." I giggled, but I meant what I said.

*

Dr. Warner was examining Rod when I walked into his room at Ochsner Monday afternoon. His head was no longer wrapped in gauze; instead, there was a big white pad taped on the side of his shaved head, above his ear.

"Another week in here and we'll have you off all these tubes and IVs," Warner said as he pulled the sheet off Rodney's legs. "Then we can talk about moving you to Rehab."

Warner ran a pin up and down the soles of Rod's feet. I didn't see a reaction and looked at Susie, who knew exactly what was wrong. She shrugged as if to say, "At least he's alive." I agreed, but I wouldn't be the one married to a man who couldn't walk.

Warner turned around and saw Marianne standing with Lilly and me in the doorway. A smile spread across his face as though he'd opened a Christmas present with his dream toy inside. I pushed my elbow into Marianne's side and laughed under my breath.

"Hi." Warner walked up to Marianne and ignored the rest of us. "Want to grab a glass of wine?"

"I have to get Susie and Lilly home…"

"I'll take care of them, Mari." I patted her shoulder and winked.

"I can take Susie home in my new car." Lilly dangled the keys to her Mustang in front of Marianne.

"Lilly and Sissy are right, Mari." Susie slid off Rodney's bed and walked without help to the wall where her walker was parked. We'll be fine. Go on."

Lilly smiled at me as though she knew some secret I didn't.

"It's settled, then." Dr. Warner took Marianne's hand and pulled her out of the room. I looked over my shoulder at Susie, and she and Lilly were laughing, so was Rodney. I obviously had a lot to catch up on.

*

I retrieved the *Times Picayune* from the front yard Sunday morning and was sorting through the sections, looking for the comics, when I saw the headline on the front page of Section D. "Two Arrested in Wedding Shooting."

Pictures of Keith Rousseau and the scraggly-looking dude, Thevenot, whom I'd seen on James's front porch, were plastered across the top of the page. They wore orange jumpsuits, and neither had shaved in days. The article said that the state police had been looking for the pair for several days and the accused had eluded the officers by going into the woods north of the Guillot Community on a four-wheeled all terrain vehicle. It said state troopers went up Red River in two speedboats while several other cops scaled the woods on the four-wheelers and in jeeps until they flushed out Thevenot and Rousseau.

They'd been charged with resisting arrest, aggravated flight from an officer, and two counts of attempted first degree murder.

"Investigators say the attorney general's office will prosecute the case and has asked the Judge for six weeks to prepare evidence, which District Judge Edward DeYoung granted," the article stated. "Should the attorney general charge the accused through a bill of information, they will stand trial sometime next year." I kept reading the article, which mentioned Susie and Rodney's names and said that Susie was the daughter of retired State Senator, Bob Burton.

The end of the article said that more charges were pending against Thevenot and Rousseau related to other cases as far back as the 1970s.

I stared at the newspaper as though it had appeared out of nowhere. I wanted to pick up the phone and call Robert Morris, but I figured if I were supposed to be *in-the-know* he'd have told me that the arrests would be made this weekend. As I thought about it, I realized they must have had warrants for the men before they grilled me, which made me angry all over again. I wondered why they felt they had to put me through the wringer when they had all the information they needed for the arrests.

Susie staggered into the kitchen, rubbing her eyes, her hair in tangles as though she'd slept upside down. She sat at the table, and I poured her a cup of coffee and put the newspaper in front of her. She sipped her coffee and thumbed through the paper. When I was sure she was awake, I slid Section D over the part she was reading.

"Oh. My. God!" She looked up at me and back at the paper. I sat still while she read it. "What happens next?"

"I'm not sure. I think I'll go to Baton Rouge tomorrow and speak with Robert Morris." I twisted my hair and stared straight ahead at nothing in particular.

"I can call Rob Morris." She kept staring at the newspaper as if it could magically erase itself and create a new story.

"Brenda is coming to New Orleans to see you and Rodney today. Let's see what she has to say first, okay?" I reached for Susie's hand to get her attention.

"Okay. But I'm going to show this article to Rodney when I get to the hospital this morning." Susie's brow was furrowed, and her eyes squinted.

Lilly skipped into the kitchen dressed in jeans and a T-shirt, her hair brushed and lip gloss on her mouth.

"I'm going with you to see Dad this morning. I'll bet he missed us last night." Lilly was bright-eyed and bushy-tailed. She kissed her mom on the top of her head, hugged me, and poured herself a glass of orange juice. "I don't see how you can drink that awful black liquid. It looks like muddy water from Bayou Noir."

"When you drink too many glasses of wine one night, you're glad to have bayou water in the morning." I hugged her and laughed. She sat at the table with Susie, who was still staring at the newspaper.

"What is it, Susie?" Lilly watched her mom's eyes go back and forth across the page, reading it for the umpteenth time.

"They arrested the guys they think shot Rodney." Susie held the paper so tightly that it wrinkled in her hands.

"Let me see." Lilly tried to take the paper from Susie, but it began to tear. "Susie. Can I read the article?"

"I'll read it to you." Susie was acting strange, and Lilly looked at me with a questioning expression. I shrugged my shoulders and smiled.

"Two Arrested in Wedding Shooting." Susie started to read, stuttered, then continued. "After a chase of almost three days on the Red River and through the wooded area north of the Guillot Community of Jean Ville, police finally captured two suspects in the June 30 shooting of Rodney Thibault which occurred in front of St. Alphonse's Catholic Church on Jefferson Street. Captain Roger Lamoré served Tucker Thevenot and Keith Rousseau with arrest warrants that had been signed by Judge Edward DeYoung Friday morning. Louisiana law states that, to obtain an arrest warrant, police must provide the judge with information that establishes probable cause, by the named person(s) who committed a particular crime.

"Thevenot and Rousseau have been charged with resisting arrest, aggravated flight from an officer, and two counts of attempted first degree murder.

"Investigators say the attorney general's office will prosecute the case and has asked the Judge for six weeks to prepare evidence, which District Judge Edward DeYoung granted. Should the attorney general charge the accused through a bill of information, they will stand trial sometime next year.

"Thibault is a retired army major and JAG officer who graduated valedictorian from Adams High School in 1967. He walked out of the church with his bride, Susanna Burton, and was shot twice with a 45-caliber pistol. Doctors removed two projectiles from Thibault; one from his head, the other near his right lung. He remains in Ochsner Medical Center in New Orleans where he has been a patient since the incident. Burton-Thibault is the daughter of former mayor and retired State Senator, Robert Burton.

"Thevenot and Rousseau were booked into the Toussaint Parish jail where they will remain pending a bond hearing on Monday morning and arraignment sometime Tuesday. No information about which attorney or attorneys will represent the accused has been released."

Susie looked up at Lilly, whose eyes were as wide as dinner plates. They stared at each other but didn't speak.

"Look. You girls run off to the hospital. I'm going to straighten up around here before Brenda Morris arrives. I'll bring her to the hospital so she can visit with you and Rodney. It'll probably be after lunch."

"Are Jessie and Bobby coming with her?" Lilly pushed her chair back from the table and stood up.

"I'm not sure. If they do, would you like for me to call you at the hospital?" I picked up plates and cups from the table and took them to the sink.

"Yes, please. I'll come back here, and the three of us can go to the lake or something while you adults visit." Lilly was sort of bouncing up and down, excited, happy.

"I hope she brings them, Lilly. But when I asked her, she said it was up to them, that they stay pretty busy on weekends." I didn't want Lilly to be disappointed.

"Oh, if she gives them a choice, they'll come." Lilly walked out of the kitchen, her shoulders squared in a confident manner.

"I think she's kind of sweet on Robert's son." Susie looked at me and winked.

"Really? I thought she and Jessica really hit it off." I was at the sink with my back to Susie. "I didn't notice any chemistry with Bobby."

"You know Lilly." Susie got up from the table and joined me at the sink. She put her coffee cup and plate in the sudsy water and flopped her arm over my shoulder. "She'd never let on that she liked a boy. I just picked up on it in a couple of our conversations. Let's see if he shows up with Brenda. That will be telling."

I sat at the kitchen table after they left, and thought about the arrests. I wondered whether Thevenot and Rousseau had hired lawyers or would use public defenders. I also wondered how much their bail would be and whether they would be able to bond out while they awaited trial.

*

Brenda Morris arrived just before noon with Bobby, who was driving a black Volvo sedan that looked brand new. He got out and went around to open the door for his mother. She stepped out of the car dressed in jeans, a lavender silk blouse, and low-heeled pumps. She carried a Coach handbag and pulled her Prada sunglasses off and put them on top of her head, pulling her hair back from her face. Her hoop earrings almost touched her shoulders, and her golden Breck hair hung in waves down her back. She was a gorgeous woman, who walked with the confidence of a corporate executive. I stood on the front porch and watched her strut up the sidewalk with Bobby behind her.

"Hi, Sissy." Brenda extended both arms and folded me into a bear hug when she got to the porch.

"I'm so glad you're here. Rodney and Susie are excited to see you." I hugged her and reached for Bobby. "Hi, big boy." I grabbed his shoulders and embarrassed him by planting a big kiss on his cheek.

"Lilly asked me to call her if you came with your mom. Come on in, you two."

We went into the living room, and Brenda asked for the bathroom, which I pointed to, then I headed to the phone on the table behind the sofa.

"Have a seat, Bobby." I picked up the receiver.

"I've been sitting for over an hour. I think I'll stand if you don't mind." He put his hands behind his back and stood in front of the unlit fireplace as though warming his tush.

"Lilly's at the hospital with her dad and will come right over." I dialed the number and asked for Rodney's room. Lilly answered the phone.

"Hi. Bobby's here." I spoke in a normal tone because he could hear what I said.

"Just Bobby? Or did Jessie come, too." Lilly sounded breathless, as though she'd been running.

"Yes." I didn't want to say, "Just Bobby," because he was standing there and would know she asked.

"Yes, what?" She was confused.

"Yes, you should come home. I'm sure the two of you can find something to do this afternoon." I hoped she understood my hint that it was just Bobby.

"I'll be right there." She hung up.

"She'll be here in a few. She drove her mom to the hospital this morning." I asked Bobby if he'd like something to drink, and he declined. Brenda walked into the room, and I showed her around the house. Bobby said he'd stay in the living room and wait for Lilly.

"Brenda, it's a small house. We rented it so Susie has a place to live while Rodney is still in the hospital." I showed her the three bedrooms and two bathrooms, the dining room and kitchen, and we ended up on the back porch that Susie had paid to have enlarged. It now spanned the entire back of the house, complete with a swing and four rocking chairs. She'd also had a landscape company spruce up the yard so that it resembled a park, with thick, green grass and dogwood and magnolia trees that Susie said made her place "feel southern." Brenda pronounced the house, "charming," and we both laughed.

We returned to the living room just as Lilly and Bobby were saying hello to each other, shyly, but it was obvious there was something special between them. Lilly hugged Brenda and asked whether it would be okay if she took Bobby to see Lake Pontchartrain.

"Sure. That sounds like fun." Brenda had her arm around Lilly's waist. "Bobby hasn't had lunch, have you?"

"No, ma'am. We can grab something at one of the marinas if that's okay with you." Lilly looked at Bobby, and he nodded.

"Sounds good. Sure." Bobby kissed his mom on the cheek, told me goodbye, and took Lilly's hand. The last I saw of them, they were walking towards her Mustang, hand-in-hand, talking a mile a minute.

"Well, I guess you haven't had lunch, either?" I turned towards Brenda, who was staring out the front door as Lilly backed out the driveway and drove down Jules Avenue.

"I'm sorry. What did you say, Sissy?" She turned towards me then looked back at the front door with a look of confusion. "I'm really sorry. It's just that I've never seen Bobby so, well, so... I'm not sure what."

"It looks like he and Lilly like each other. I mean, as friends, of course." I couldn't get her attention; she was creeped out about something.

"Bobby has never had a girlfriend." She stared at the front door as though viewing an apparition. "I mean, he's never been interested in girls. They like him, but he's always said girls are stupid."

"Lilly's not stupid. That's for sure." I started to pace a little, uncomfortable for some reason.

"Well. I'm glad." She finally turned to look at me. "I'm famished. Want to have lunch before we go to the hospital?"

"Sure. There's a great little seafood place about a mile from here." I grabbed my purse, and we drove to the restaurant in Brenda's new car.

*

"Rod. Susie. I'm so happy to see you both." Brenda strolled into the hospital room on the Rehab floor like an angel floating down from heaven. They all hugged and sat around to talk. Susie brought up the article in the newspaper almost immediately. Rodney seemed a bit agitated, although he tried to hide his emotions. I stood near the door and watched the three of them.

"Robert told me they arrested a couple of suspects." Brenda held Susie's hand, and Rodney sat in his wheelchair, facing the two girls.

"Rodney told the detective that Thevenot shot him," Susie said. Everyone looked at Rodney. His brow was furrowed, and he rubbed it with his thumb and forefinger. "I hope he was right. He's worried he might have been wrong and, well you know how Rod is. He wouldn't want to make someone suffer unduly."

"I believe the detectives have evidence to back up your testimony, Rodney." Brenda reached over and patted his knee. "They wouldn't arrest someone with only one person's supposition."

"I guess not," Susie said. "We just hope he didn't go to all this trouble and they both get off. Or worse. That they aren't the ones who did it."

"You can't worry about it, Rod." Brenda patted Rodney's hand, and he stopped rubbing his brow.

"That's right, baby," Susie looked at Rodney, then winked at Brenda. "Our job is to get you well and out of here. Can you believe how good he looks, Brenda?"

"I'm amazed at both of you." She winked at Susie. "I remember how dire it was in the beginning. Robert came to see you a few days after Greg was here because Greg was so upset about the state you both were in. But look at you now."

"Better," Rodney stuttered. "Suse. Ty-rant." He winked at Susie, who blushed. I was amazed that he could still make her turn pink around the gills. "Won't let me out—hos-tal... walk."

"I'm not the one keeping you in here. Talk to Dr. Warner." She laughed at him. "Rodney still doesn't have all the feeling in his legs and feet, but it's returning, and every day there's a little more reflex, right Rod?"

"Riiiii. Wahh." Rodney put both hands under his his right knee, lifted his leg, and put his foot back down on the wheelchair footrest. He repeated his new trick, several times. Next, he did it with his left knee.

"He doesn't feel the bottoms of his feet, yet," Susie said. "But he's learning to recognize the pressure when he puts weight on them." Susie patted his knee. "He'll walk out of here. I'm sure of it."

"I'm sure of it, too." Brenda patted his other knee. Rodney seemed a bit put-off by the two women patronizing him.

"Let's get out of here so he can get some rest." Susie got up, pushed Rodney's wheelchair towards the bed, and pressed the nurse's call button for an orderly to help Rod into bed.

Brenda kissed him on both cheeks and walked over to where I stood by the door. Susie kissed Rodney on the lips, and we girls went to the cafeteria for a couple hours.

Brenda told Susie that she and Robert would be happy to have Lilly stay with them.

"We have lots of room, and our kids love Lilly." Brenda got a shadowed look on her face for a few seconds.

"Sissy is looking for an apartment in Baton Rouge, and I think that's the best thing for Lilly. I don't want to impose on you and Robert." Susie fiddled with her tea bag, as though not sure about her decision.

"Whenever Sissy is out of town or busy, Lilly can stay with us." Brenda looked at me and grinned.

"That's a good plan." I looked at Susie. "How do you feel about that arrangement? Lilly will live with me but can stay with the Morrises if I have to be away?"

"If it's not too much to ask of you, Brenda." Susie looked from me to Brenda, and back at me.

"Look." Brenda grabbed Susie's hand. "We adore Lilly. We'd love to have her, full-time or part-time. Just consider our home her second home. Okay?"

"Okay. If you insist." Susie squeezed Brenda's hand. "And thank you. You're such a dear friend. You and Robert, both."

"Well, I probably need to go." Brenda stood and gathered her purse and sunglasses. "I told Bobby we'd leave here about four, so he'll be back at your house looking for me soon."

"Thank you for coming, Bren." Susie got up, and they hugged. "It means the world to Rodney and me."

"I'll come back. And I'm looking forward to having Lilly whenever she wants to stay with us." Brenda kissed Susie again. I hugged Susie and told her I'd be back later to get her.

When we got in her car, I told Brenda I would be in Baton Rouge for a few days the following week to look for an apartment.

"Lilly will probably stay with me at the Capitol House." I buckled my seatbelt and breathed the scent of new leather as I sank into the plush black seat. "I'm going to try to make an appointment with Robert for tomorrow afternoon or Tuesday morning."

"I think he'll be in court all day tomorrow, maybe Tuesday, too." Brenda drove the car out of the garage and onto the street. "Why don't you and Lilly come over for dinner tomorrow night? You can talk to him then."

"Are you sure it's not an imposition?" I looked at her profile. She was a beauty, yet she was gracious and down-to-earth.

"We'd love to have you, but only if you agree to play the piano." She laughed and glanced at me, then back at the road.

*

We got to the house on Jules Avenue, and Lilly's car was not in the driveway. Brenda seemed a bit peeved, but it was only three fifty, so Bobby wasn't late, yet. We went inside and split off to separate bathrooms. When I came back into the living room, the phone was ringing.

"Hello."

"Sissy, It's Lilly. I've been trying to reach someone for over an hour."

"Are you okay?"

"Yes. We're fine. I talked to Dad several times, but he said you and Susie and Miss Benda left and he had no way of reaching y'all."

"What do you need? Are you sure you're okay?" I looked at Brenda, who had just come into the living room. "It's Lilly."

"Are they okay? Where are they?" Brenda looked worried and reached for the phone.

"Is Miss Brenda there? Bobby wants to talk to her." Lilly sounded excited, not worried.

"Okay." I handed the phone to Brenda. "Bobby wants to talk to you."

"Hi, Son. Where are you? I'm ready to leave." She held the receiver to her ear and listened for what seemed a long time. "Okay. I guess that's alright. Please be home by dark or I'll worry about you and Lilly on the highway." She paused, and a smile crossed her face. "I love you too, Son. See you in a few hours." She handed me the phone.

"Sissy. We're going to a movie, then we'll come home so I can get my things and tell Susie goodbye." Lilly talked quickly, with lots of breaths. "Bobby is riding back to Baton Rouge with me tonight."

"That sounds fine. But if you're going to be in Baton Rouge before dark, you'll have to leave here by six thirty, or seven."

"I know. I love you. See you later."

"Have fun. Be careful."

"You sound like my mother!" She laughed loudly, and it made me laugh. We hung up, and I looked at Brenda. "Are you alright with this?"

"Sure. In fact, I'm happy about it." She smiled at me, and I felt like there was something she wanted to say but didn't know how. "Well, I think I'll get going so I can be home in time to make dinner for Robert tonight. Bobby won't be there, and neither will Jessie. It's rare we have an evening at home, alone."

"Well, get going, girl. Your man is waiting." I hugged her, and she left.

*

I picked Susie up at the hospital at six o'clock that evening. It was typically Marianne's job to transport Susie when Lilly wasn't available, but Dr. Warner had come by before nine o'clock that morning to take Marianne to the World's Fair, which was being held on the New Orleans riverfront in the Warehouse District. I explained to Susie that Lilly would be home to get her things at about six thirty and wanted to tell her mom goodbye before she went back to LSU for the week.

"Lilly and Bobby have been together all afternoon and called to say they were going to a movie," I told Susie when we got in the car. "Brenda went back to Baton Rouge alone, and Bobby is going to ride back with Lilly."

"That's good. I always worry about her on the highway alone, especially at night." Susie put her seatbelt on and admonished me until I did, too, even though we were only driving one mile.

"I think Brenda expects them back in Baton Rouge before dark." I started the car and drove out of the parking garage.

"Was Brenda okay with Bobby staying and driving back with Lilly?" Susie turned sideways so she could look at me.

"I think she was thrilled." I turned onto Jules Avenue. "But she acted strange, like she was surprised that Bobby and Lilly liked each other."

"Oh, that's funny." Susie started to laugh.

"What's so funny?" I drove slowly in case a child or dog ran out in the street. It was a quiet neighborhood with lots of families who treated Jules Avenue as though it were a park where they could throw Frisbees and footballs.

"That Brenda!" Susie laughed louder. "She's been worried that Bobby might be gay because he didn't like girls. Robert kept telling her she was crazy, but Brenda has been frantic about it."

"That explains why she acted like she just couldn't believe her son was holding hands with a girl." I turned into our driveway.

"Oh? They were holding hands?" Susie stopped laughing and sounded serious.

"You should ask Lilly. It looked pretty innocent to me." I turned off the car, and Susie grabbed my arm to keep me from getting out.

"They were holding hands? Where? When?"

"Really Susie. It was nothing. They walked to the car holding hands. No big deal." I reached for the door handle.

"It's a big deal because Lilly has avoided boys. She says none of them are smart enough or serious enough. She must think Bobby is pretty special." Susie was still holding my arm, and I was ready to get out of the car. I didn't like talking about Lilly, or anyone else, for that matter. It felt like gossip.

"Lilly's the special one, if you ask me." I opened my car door, broke free for Susie's stronghold, and got out.

Lilly and Bobby pulled up at about six forty-five. He jumped out of the passenger door and ran around to open Lilly's car door and helped her out by pulling on her hands. They both had red cheeks, as though they were wind burned.

"Sorry we're late, but we went by the hospital to see Dad." Lilly left Bobby standing in the living room while she went to her bedroom to get her book bag and suitcase. I followed her and told her that I'd washed her clothes that afternoon after Brenda left, and had repacked everything because I knew she'd be in a hurry.

"You're the best Sissy." She hugged me. "I had the best time ever today."

"I'm glad, sweetheart." I hugged her and kissed her on the cheek. "He's a great guy, isn't he?"

"The best. I can't believe there's a boy out there who's smart, serious about his future, funny, and fun to be with." She beamed, red wind-burned cheeks all aglow.

"Did you know that his mother invited you to stay at their house whenever you want to." I squeezed her shoulder. "I hope you don't mind, but I told Brenda how miserable you were in the dorm."

"Wow. What did Susie say about that?" Lilly had her book bag over one shoulder, her purse on the other, and her suitcase in her hand.

"She thought it was an imposition at first, but Brenda convinced Susie that her family loves you and they want you to stay with them."

"Thanks, Sissy." She kissed me again and headed out of the bedroom. Bobby met Lilly in the hall and took her book bag and suitcase, told Susie and me goodbye, and walked out the front door. Lilly kissed her mom and said she'd call during the week and would be home Friday afternoon. Then she skipped out of the house and Susie and I listened to her engine start up and turn onto Jules Avenue. I heard Susie let out a huge sigh.

"She's only sixteen, you know," Susie said it aloud, but I think she was talking to herself. I thought Lilly had turned seventeen in August, but Susie said, "No, sixteen."

"How'd she graduate from high school so early?" I sat on the sofa across from Susie, who was sitting in the chair next to the fireplace.

"She's very smart, Sissy." She scratched her eyebrow and put her chin in her hand. "She started school a month before she turned five. Then she skipped third grade. When she got into high school, she was so far ahead that she finished in three years."

"So she just turned sixteen in August?"

"Yes. But she's really mature for her age, don't you think?" Susie looked as though she needed someone to agree with her.

"If level-headed means mature, yes." I wondered why Susie was so insistent that Lilly go off to college when she was so young. No wonder the child was miserable in the dorm with girls more than two years older. Lilly was like an alligator on land. "I think she will be very happy staying with the Morrises. Both their kids are mature, more like Lilly. And closer in age."

"Yes, I agree. I don't want to impose. Will you keep a close eye on that? I mean, make sure Lilly doesn't wear out her welcome?"

"Of course." I got up, squeezed Susie's shoulder, and headed towards my bedroom. I turned towards her before I got to the hallway. "In fact, I'll be in Baton Rouge tomorrow and plan to stay a couple days. Lilly can stay with me."

Susie nodded, but didn't respond, as though she had something serious on her mind and was a million miles away.

~ Chapter Nine ~

Arraigned

LILLY AND I ARRIVED at the Morrises' at about five thirty Monday. Jessie met us at the front door, and the two girls started up the stairs. I heard Jessie say that Bobby was at football practice and Lilly asked if they could go watch him.

"He's usually done by five thirty, so it's too late." Jessie stopped about halfway up the stairs and turned to look at Lilly. I watched from the foyer. "But we can go another day. He practices every afternoon except Fridays. That's game day. You should come to his games with us."

"I go to New Orleans every weekend." Lilly looked down at me, then back at Jessie. "I usually leave right after my last class on Friday, but maybe I could wait and go Saturday morning. I'll have to ask my mom." She glanced back at me, and I winked and gave her a thumbs-up.

I followed the aroma of sautéed onions into the kitchen, where Brenda stood behind the island wearing an apron over her black dress. She looked like a million bucks.

"Hi. Robert went to get Bobby at practice." She waved the spoon she was using. "They should be home about six. Want a glass of wine?"

"Sure." I went around the island to the fridge and pulled out a bottle of wine that had been opened and had a plug in the top. "What can I do to help?"

"You can set the table." She pointed to the stack of plates, silverware, and napkins on the end of the bar. "The weather is mild tonight, so we'll eat in the courtyard. Setting the table is usually Jessie's job, but I guess she's with Lilly, right?"

"Yep. They took off upstairs as soon as we walked in the door," I said.

"Everything's done and in the oven on warm. Let's go outside." She led the way, and I followed her through the kitchen doors with the stack of dishes in my arms. The back of the house was an L-shape, with the kitchen on the short side of the L, and a huge den with the baby grand piano on the long side. There were wide sliding glass doors from both rooms, which made the outdoors and indoors seamless.

After I set the table, I joined Brenda, who was sitting in one of the lounge chairs. We talked about the weather and the kids, mostly; just chit-chat. Brenda seemed relaxed and happy.

"How was your evening with Robert last night?" I remembered she was going to get home to have an intimate dinner with her husband.

"Divine." She exhaled, and it almost sounded like a whistle. "He's amazing. When I got home, he had dinner started. The kids didn't get back until after eight o'clock. Robert and I were enjoying our evening so much that we didn't realize it was past dark when Bobby came home."

"Wow. I hope I have someone, someday, who makes me feel like Robert makes you feel." I breathed in and out, and didn't realize I'd said those words aloud until Brenda answered.

"Oh, Sissy. Don't you have a boyfriend?" She turned towards me with a jerk.

"Not really." I laughed to lighten the conversation. "I used to date this loser named Warren, but I outgrew him a long time ago. There's not much to choose from in Jean Ville."

"Well, you'll be moving to Baton Rouge soon, and that will change." She leaned against the back of her lounge chair and stared at the stars that blinked and accumulated into groups resembling clouds.

The sky was so clear you could count parts of the galaxies like Christmas tree lights. "In fact, we can fix you up when you're ready. There are lots of young attorneys at the AG's office. I'm sure some of them are single. I'll talk to Robert about it."

I didn't respond because I wasn't sure I wanted to be set up on a blind date. I was too old for that, but too young not to be. I thought about Warren, and I was disgusted with myself for wasting so much time on him.

Robert and Bobby walked into the courtyard a little after six o'clock. I told Bobby I thought Lilly was upstairs with Jessie and he headed into the house.

"Get the girls and y'all come down, okay son?" Robert called after Bobby, who seemed in a hurry to get upstairs.

"Yes, sir." He turned around and faced his dad when he spoke, then continued on his mission.

After dinner, I played the piano—at the request of everyone. They gathered around the baby grand, and I took requests. We all tried to sing along, and Robert and Brenda danced to *Don't Stop Believing* by Journey.

The kids disappeared into the house, and I sat in the courtyard with Robert while Brenda finished up in the kitchen.

"What happened today?" I had been eager to ask him about the case.

"Judge DeYoung went to the parish jail in Jean Ville this morning and held a bond hearing." Robert sat in a lounge chair, and I was at the iron table in a straight chair, facing him. "He set bail at $500,000 for each of the accused."

"Do you think they'll bond out?" I was worried about what Thevenot and Rousseau might do to get back at Susie, Rodney, and me if they were out on the street.

"I don't think either of them can come up with ten percent, do you?" He crossed his ankles and folded his arms behind his head.

"I hope not." I didn't tell him my fears. "What happens next?"

"We filed a bill of information, and they'll be arraigned Wednesday." He took a sip of his drink and stretched. "They will plead guilty or not guilty, and we'll find out whether they've hired their own lawyers or accepted public defenders," Robert said. "There will be motions filed and, eventually, a trial date will be set. It's a process. We'll know more after Wednesday."

*

I drove to the Toussaint Parish courthouse early Wednesday morning. I heard an announcement on the car radio that said a special bank account had been set up at the Confederate Bank and Trust in the name of "People for the Rights of Men," to help pay the legal expenses for Tucker Thevenot and Keith Rousseau. The announcer said that donations should be made in person or mailed directly to the bank. I wondered why the defendants were soliciting donations, but I discovered the answer when I was in court and saw that both of the accused had hired private attorneys to represent them.

Keith Rousseau was represented by Steven Regard, a young lawyer who had recently opened a law practice in Jean Ville. It was well known that Reggie Borders helped Regard financially, both with college and law school expenses as well as setting up his practice.

Tucker Thevenot showed up at the arraignment with John Perkins, an attorney from James's law firm. I found both of these affiliations odd.

The lawyers entered pleas of "Not Guilty." Rousseau's attorney, Regard, asked the judge to consider the letter requesting a motion to sever. The state had no objection, and the judge ruled that Rousseau and Thevenot would be tried separately. DeYoung set a trial date for six months out and gave the defense fifteen days to file pre-trial motions.

The defense attorneys argued that the defendants should be released on their own recognizance. DeYoung told the defense attorneys they should file a formal motion to reduce bond, and he would schedule a hearing to decide.

*

James pulled into his driveway just as I drove up to his house. I followed his car and parked outside the garage while he parked inside. When he got out of his vehicle, he turned around and saw me getting out of mine.

"What are you doing here?" He turned and walked through his garage to a door that led to his kitchen. I followed him in a half-run and made it inside just before he shut the garage door.

"I came to see you." I put my purse on the counter in his kitchen and looked around. It was a new house he'd lived in less than a year. The kitchen was spotless, as though he'd never cooked in it or had guests over. "Do you have a maid? It's so clean in here."

"Once or twice a week. Yeah." He hung his keys on a hook near the door to the garage and loosened his tie. "Want a beer?"

"No thanks. You go ahead." I walked around the kitchen and admired the tiled countertops and white appliances with stainless-steel trim. James opened a beer, removed his suit coat, and hung it on a large hook near the back door. He led the way to the back porch, and we sat and studied the pecan and pear trees for a while.

"Are you representing Tucker Thevenot?" I didn't look at him, just kept studying the landscape.

"No. One of my partners is." He took a sip of his beer.

"Isn't that the same thing?"

"No. Not really." He put his beer down and started to roll up his shirtsleeves.

"Did you set up the defense fund at the Confederate Bank?"

"Look, Sissy. I told you none of this is your business."

"Why is it yours?" I stood up and stared at him.

"I'm a lawyer. I take cases that can pay my fees. In this case, I'm helping those goons raise money so they can pay me." He continued to roll up his sleeves.

"I thought you said you weren't representing them." I took a deep breath to stop the bile I felt rise in my throat. "You are going to bring suspicion on yourself, you know."

"How's that? Someone has to represent these guys. Just because my firm is involved doesn't mean any of us had anything to do with what happened." He seemed defensive, and it made me think that maybe he protested too much.

"Be careful. The investigators with the AG's office are really smart." I kissed the top of his head and went into the kitchen, where I retrieved my purse. I let myself out of the front door and went to my garage apartment on Gravier Road.

I spent the weekend in Jean Ville, so I could attend the preliminary hearing the following week. I pulled into my dad's driveway Saturday afternoon, and James's car was parked in the carport. When I went in the back door, he came out. He'd probably seen me drive up and decided to leave before I could find out why he was there.

"What are you doing here?" I grabbed his arm as he tried to walk by me.

"Same reason you're here. I came to see about Dad." He shook my hand off his arm. "I come by almost every day." He walked out the back door, and I heard him take the steps two at a time.

*

I was one of the first people in the courtroom Wednesday morning for the pre-trial motions. The defense filed motions of discovery and inspection, bill of particulars, and other stuff I didn't understand; although it all seemed to ensure the defense attorneys knew what evidence The State had against Rousseau and Thevenot.

I sat on the first pew, behind the AG's table. I didn't know any of the lawyers or paralegals who represented The State, but I recognized Detective Sherman and Lieutenant Schiller. They both nodded at me before they took their seats.

Thevenot and Rousseau wore orange jumpsuits, and their wrists were handcuffed in front when they entered the courtroom. A sheriff's deputy took the handcuffs off before the two sat at the table with their lawyers.

The hearing included testimony by The State's detectives Sherman and Schiller. They said that they had eye-witness testimony from some of the people who lived around the church and were on their porches on June 30, and that one of the neighbors identified Keith Rousseau as the driver of the blue truck. A woman described a man who resembled Tucker Thevenot as the person, "riding shotgun." It was damning testimony, and the judge agreed there was enough evidence to go to trial.

Judge DeYoung sat behind a raised desk and wore his black robe, a white shirt, and a blue striped tie. He saw me sitting in the gallery and nodded at me. Defense attorney Steven Regard once again asked the judge to consider his motion to reduce bond, to which DeYoung replied, "I'll set a hearing date for your motion. For now, the accused will remain in jail until they can produce bond."

The following week, the judge held the hearing and denied motions by both defendants for bond reduction. The bail remained at $500,000 each.

I let out a sigh of relief when I read in a newspaper article that the "People for the Rights of Men" had only raised $10,000. The article said the identity of the donors was confidential.

I packed my car and headed for New Orleans, with a stop in Baton Rouge.

*

Miss Millie was at her desk when I arrived at the AG's office at two o'clock. She opened her window and told me that Robert was not in the office.

"He's in court all day, probably all week." She grinned at me as though she'd won some contest. "Can someone else help you?"

"Is Detective Schiller in?" I smiled back at her as our match continued.

"Let me check." She picked up the phone and stared at me while she spoke. "Detective, Miss Burton would like to see you." She put the phone down and reached for the handle on her window. "He'll be right with you." She slid her window shut and went back to her typewriter.

Schiller came into the waiting room and shook my hand. He held the door to the hall open for me, and I walked past him. We went into the second door on the right. There was a young man in a grey suit sitting at a round table in the corner. He stood when we entered the office, and I recognized him as one of the lawyers who'd presented testimony at the preliminary hearing.

"Luke, this is Sissy Burton. Miss Burton, Lucas McMath." He shook my hand and smiled, which produced a dimple in his right cheek. He had the bluest eyes I'd ever seen, sky blue on a clear day, and his sandy blonde hair swept across his forehead like Ryan O'Neal in *Love Story.* I couldn't take my eyes off him, and he continued to hold my hand until I finally spoke.

"Nice to meet you, Luke." My hand felt limp and damp. I had to bend my head backwards to look at him, which made my long hair hang down my back, almost to my butt.

"Luke is the lead attorney on the Thevenot case." Schiller pulled a chair out and indicated I was supposed to sit in it. First, I had to detach my hand from the smoking-hot hunk who held it, as well as my attention. "We've separated the cases because they're different. Maybe you should explain, Luke."

I let go of his hand and hovered over the chair that Schiller pushed in as I lowered myself into it.

"Yes, well, Thevenot was the shooter." Lucas McMath sat in the chair next to mine, a stack of file folders and a yellow legal pad in front of him. Schiller sat across from me. He had his little notepad and ballpoint pen on the table. "There's more culpability for Thevenot. Rousseau was the driver. We aren't sure whether the charge of first degree attempted murder will hold up against Rousseau because his defense is that he was just driving the truck."

"Oh. Is it possible that Rousseau will get off?" I took a tissue from my purse and dabbed at my chin, in case I was drooling. Guys didn't typically have that effect on me, but this one named Luke certainly did. I tried to concentrate on what he said, not on his full lips, which moved in perfect cadence.

"We have to wait and see. Either way, we're going to ask the judge to try Thevenot first." His hands were folded on the table, and he looked at me when he talked. He didn't blink or shift his eyes to Schiller or anywhere else. I listened to Schiller and Lucas McMath talk about the case and some of the witnesses. I was tongue-tied for about ten minutes, then I finally remembered why I'd come.

"Did you know about the defense fund someone set up at the Confederate Bank?" I looked from Lucas McMath to Schiller.

"No. I don't, do you, Luke?" Schiller looked at Luke then back at me.

"No. What's that about?" Luke stared at me as though I were the most interesting person on earth. I loved it. I told them about the fund, and that the donors were confidential. I said the last I'd heard the fund had grown to almost $40,000. "I wonder if this has something to do with the cover-up that Robert, I mean Mr. Morris, is concerned about."

"This is interesting. I'll tell Mr. Morris about it." Schiller made a note on his pad. "I wonder whether we can get the judge to sign a subpoena for us to review the list of donors."

"I'll draw up a request." Luke wrote something on his legal pad and nodded at Schiller. "Do you know the officers at the bank, Sissy?"

"The president is Mr. Tom Preston. My brother, James is vice president. He's also an attorney, has the largest practice in the parish." I spoke slowly. I didn't want to implicate James, but if I acted like I didn't know he was an officer, it would seem and though I was trying to hide something.

"James?" Luke put his pen down and leaned back in his chair. "James Burton? He's your brother?"

"Yes. He's twelve years older. I was an afterthought, I think." I laughed at my own joke, but the two men were serious and didn't catch my quip.

"Isn't his firm representing Thevenot?" Luke leaned forward and wrote on his pad. I could read James's name upside down.

"Yes. One of his partners, I think." I didn't like the way the conversation was going. I wanted to steer it somewhere else, but while I considered how to do that, they fired more questions at me about James, his partners, his affiliation with the bank, his interest in the defense fund.

"Do you think your brother is a donor?" Schiller asked that question, then looked at Luke.

"That doesn't seem likely." I sat up straight in my chair, ready to spring out of it and run. "He told me he wanted the fund to work so that his firm could be paid. I don't know why he would put money into something that would go back to him."

"You talked to him about the fund?" Schiller looked incredulous.

"Yes, I asked him about it after I heard the announcement on the radio and read about it in the newspaper." I shifted in my seat, uncomfortably. "He told me he just wanted to be paid."

"Did he say anything else?" Schiller asked.

"About the fund?" I exhaled and realized I'd been holding my breath.

"Yes."

"No. That's all he said. He's not very talkative." I held my purse in my lap and felt my palms sweat against the leather. Suddenly it was very quiet. "Well, I'd better go. I just thought Mr. Morris might want to know about the fund."

"Is there anything else you can tell us?"

"I don't think so." I stood up, and Luke did, too.

"I'll walk you out." He took his suit coat off the back of his chair and put it on. Schiller stood up and shook my hand.

When we got to the front door, Luke said he'd walk me to my car, which was parked across the street. We didn't talk until we got to my Camaro and he made a comment about how he'd never have guessed I'd be driving an almost seven-year-old sports car.

"My dad gave it to me when I graduated from high school." I had my hand on the door handle. "He picked it out, never asked me what I liked."

"That's unusual." He grinned, and his dimple caved into the side of his face.

"Yep. My dad's unusual. That's for sure." I turned towards the car and started to open the door. He reached around and put his hand on top of mine.

"Let me get that for you." His hand covered mine, and it felt like a hot iron on my skin. I slid it out from under his, and he opened the car door. "Look. Sissy. Is that your real name?"

"Abigail. But I prefer Sissy."

"Okay. Look. I don't mean to be forward. But... uhm... Are you seeing anyone?"

"What does that mean, like dating someone or going steady?" I started to laugh, and his grin widened.

"Yes." His blue eyes glistened in the sunlight.

"No. I'm not. Are you?" I didn't mean to ask that question, and I felt embarrassed when I heard the words come out of my mouth. Heat spread across my face and knew I was blushing.

"You're really cute when you blush." He blocked the opening to my car so I couldn't get in without stepping over him. "No. I'm not seeing anyone. Would you go out with me?"

"When?" I was tongue-tied, and the word just popped out of my mouth.

"When I call you." He laughed hard, and his teeth were so white and straight that I stared at them.

"Do you have my phone number?" I laughed, too, at him laughing.

"No. That was my next question."

I gave him my phone number in Jean Ville, and the one at the house in New Orleans. I didn't tell him I was looking for an apartment in Baton Rouge.

"I'm staying at the Capitol House Hotel until Saturday." I told him I didn't have that phone number, and he said he could look it up. "I'm actually going to a high school football game Friday night. Catholic High."

"Really?"

"Yes, long story." I didn't elaborate because I felt my friendship with the Morrises was not something I should share with one of Robert's employees.

"Are you busy tomorrow night?" He looked a bit shy, as though worried I'd reject him.

"Not really."

"Can I pick you up after I get off work? About five thirty, or six?"

"I guess so." I shifted the weight from my right to my left leg and put the strap of my purse over my shoulder. He finally moved aside so I could get in the car. I slid behind the wheel and reached for the door handle to pull the door shut, but he was still holding it open.

"I don't want to come on too strong, but could we have a drink tonight after I get off? We can go to the bar in your hotel."

"I think so. I have to make arrangements because my niece who goes to LSU is staying with me. Can I call you after I talk to her." I had to look up into the sun to see him. He moved in front of the direct light when he saw me squint and took out a business card. He handed it to me and told me he'd written his extension number on the back of the card.

"Well, I'll see you later, I hope." He handed the card to me, and I noticed that he'd also written his home phone number on it.

"Okay. I'll call you before five." I pulled on the door handle, and he let me shut it. I rolled down the window after I started the car.

"Okay. See you." He watched me drive off, and I watched him in my rearview mirror until I could no longer see him standing in the spot where my car had been.

*

Lilly was waiting for me in the lobby of her dorm when I pulled up about twenty minutes later. She ran into my arms as though she hadn't seen me in a year. She followed me to the hotel in her own car so she could drive to her class at eight o'clock the next morning.

When we got in our hotel room, she sat on the side of her bed and talked like a chatterbox. She told me how the past few nights in the dorm had been miserable and that she almost called Brenda Morris, but decided it would be an imposition. She said her classes were getting harder, and that she had a paper due the next day and a math test on Friday. She complained about how the girls in her dorm were loud and that boys threw rocks at their window during the night and one of her roommates snuck out and didn't come back all night.

Lilly finally stopped talking, and I told her about meeting Luke, and that he wanted to come over and have a drink with me.

"I have homework, so that's just fine." She started to unpack her book bag, putting the contents on the desk. "It'll be nice and quiet in here with you gone."

"Well, don't try so hard to make me feel loved and wanted." I laughed, and she giggled.

"Is he cute?" She turned around and looked at me, hard.

"Who?"

"The guy you met today. The one you're going to have a drink with." She put her hands on her hips as though she couldn't believe she had to explain her question.

"Yes. Very." I smiled and knew I probably looked ridiculous. "You can come down to meet him and see for yourself."

"Okay, but then I'm coming back to the room to study, and I hope you'll stay downstairs a long time." She stacked her books on the desk, and I picked up the phone and pulled Luke's business card out of my pocket. A robot answered the phone and said if I knew the party's extension to dial it now. I hit 3-2-3, and he picked up after two rings.

"Lucas McMath." His voice was deep and raspy.

"Do you prefer Lucas or Luke?"

"Oh. Hi." He paused and took a deep breath. "Luke is fine."

"I can meet you downstairs when you get off work today." I felt nervous, like a silly schoolgirl. "My niece needs to study and wants me out of the room."

"Great. I'll be there about five thirty." He sounded excited, and that made me less jittery. "Want me to call your room?"

"No. I'll either be in the bar waiting for you or will be down soon after you arrive."

"Okay. Good." His voice was breathy, and I heard him inhale. "See you then."

"Okay. See you." I held the phone until I heard the dial tone. Lilly stared at me as though I'd just grown a large wart on the end of my nose.

"What?" I put the receiver back on the hook.

"You look funny, Sissy." She started to laugh. "Your face is red, and your hands are shaking."

"Oh." I went to the bathroom and looked at myself in the mirror. Lilly was right. I was beet red. I had to get hold of myself before five thirty. I changed into jeans and a long-sleeved pink blouse that buttoned up the front. I pulled the sides of my hair back and clasped it in a barrette and added a little lip-gloss.

*

He was sitting at the bar facing the door when Lilly and I walked in. A huge grin spread across the bottom of his face and his cheekbones lifted. He ran his hand through his hair, pushing it sideways and away from his face, but it fell back across his forehead within a few seconds. I introduced him to Lilly, and they talked a little about LSU. He said he was an alumnus of the university and the law school.

"I just finished law school a few years ago, so I'm not that far ahead of you." His manner with Lilly was smooth. He treated her like an equal, not like a child, and I could tell she liked him.

"Well, I've got to study, and anyway, I'm too young to drink." She laughed, shook Luke's hand, and kissed me on the cheek. "Keep her down here as long as you like, Luke. I need the quiet time."

"I'll try. Maybe she'll agree to have dinner with me. Can we send something up for you?" He looked at me and winked. I felt goosebumps crawl up my arms.

"Thanks, I'll get room service." She squeezed my shoulder and left.

We sat at a table near the window that looked onto Lafayette Street. We watched people walk in front of the bar on their way to the Convention Center next door. Luke told me there was a Van Halen concert there that night and that he'd almost bought a ticket but didn't feel like going alone. We chatted about music we liked, and he said he loved Halen's newest release, *Jump.* I told him I especially liked *Pretty Woman* and *Dance the Night Away.*

He had a cocktail, and I had a glass of wine. We never stopped talking, and at eight o'clock he looked at his watch and said he was hungry, and asked whether I wanted to get something to eat? We walked a few blocks to the Pastime Restaurant, a casual poor-boy and pizza place that had been around for decades and was popular with college students. It was a nice evening, and when we walked back to my hotel, he held my hand and we talked and talked, and never ran out of things to say.

He rode on the elevator with me and kissed me on the cheek outside my hotel room door.

"Are we still on for tomorrow night?" He held both my hands between us and faced me.

"Sure." I smiled at him, and he grinned.

"I promise to take you to a decent place tomorrow night." He squeezed my hands.

"And I promise to wear something other than blue jeans." I stood on tiptoes and kissed his cheek. "I had a really good time with you tonight. Thank you."

"Yeah. I enjoyed it, too." He bent down and kissed me on the mouth. I was so surprised I didn't have time to kiss him back. I felt my face flush and knew I was blushing. Dang, I hated it that I blushed so easily. He acted as though he didn't notice.

When I walked into the room, Lilly was sitting up in her bed reading. She took one look at me and started laughing.

"You're all red again."

"I know. I hate it that I get so flushed." I went to the bathroom and washed my face, brushed my teeth, and put my pajamas on. When I came out, Lilly was under the covers.

"Did you have a good time?" She whispered as though we might awaken someone.

"The best." I crawled in the other bed and turned on my side so I could face her.

"He's really handsome." She was lying on her back facing the ceiling.

"I know." I felt myself start to blush again.

"You like him, don't you?"

"Yes. And you like Bobby Morris, don't you?"

"A lot. He's awesome." I could feel her grin in her words.

"Does he like you?"

"I think so. I mean we talk on the phone every night. I've gone to some of his practices, and we have a Coke or ice cream before I take him home. I had dinner with the Morrises twice this week and two or three times last week. I love being with Bobby. It seems like we never run out of things to talk about. And we laugh. A lot!" Her voice got softer as she talked.

The room got very quiet, and soon I could hear her breathing and knew she was asleep. I lay there and relived the entire evening, and could barely sleep because I was excited about the next night.

∼ Chapter Ten ∼

∾

Romance

WHEN I WOKE UP, Lilly was gone. I ordered coffee and called Brenda to see if she'd like to have lunch.

"Oh, I just love the Capitol Grille," she said. "I'll come down there a little after noon. Will you get us a table?"

Brenda was wearing a red dress that hugged her perfect figure. She glided across the room as though her heels weren't three inches high, and I thought how I wished I were graceful and ladylike rather than a tomboy.

I picked at my salad, and Brenda talked about her kids and the upcoming football game. I told her Lilly and I were excited about it and thanked her again for inviting us.

"Lilly should spend the night with us Friday because the kids are going to a party after the game." She took a sip of her water then looked at me funny. "Oh, Sissy. I didn't mean to leave you out. You are welcome to stay with us, too."

"That's okay. You and Robert deserve some time alone." I pushed the lettuce around my plate and wondered how to tell her about Luke. "Anyway. I met someone. I was wondering whether I could invite him to the game."

"Oh, do tell. Who is he? Last week we talked about blind dates."

"I know. When I tell you who he is, you might not want me to bring him to the game."

"Why not? He's not a convict, is he?" She laughed at her own joke and took a bite of a tomato.

"No, actually he works for Robert." I lifted my eyes from my plate and looked at her shyly.

"Oh, who?"

"His name is Lucas McMath. He's an Attorney in the AG's office."

"I don't know him. I'll ask Robert about him and let him decide if it would be uncomfortable to have him at a family function." She peered at me over her glass of water.

"I didn't tell him I know you and Robert." I sat up straight and crossed my ankles under my chair.

"How well do you know him?" Her glare made me feel uncomfortable, but I didn't know why.

"Not well. We've only had one date. It was last night. We're going out to dinner tonight." My hands were folded in my lap. I'd quit trying to eat my lunch. I couldn't swallow.

"Do you like him?" She put her fork down and gave me her undivided attention.

"Yes, but I'm trying not to. I'd like you to ask Robert about him." I felt hot tears gather behind my eyelids and pulled a tissue from my purse. "I mean, I want to know if he's a creep or if he's for real. I don't know who else to ask."

"I'll find out and let you know." She reached for my hand and patted it. We talked about Luke a little more, and she asked me what he looked like, what we talked about, how much we had in common. Then we talked about the case, and I told her I'd met Luke the day before when I went to the AG's office to tell Robert about the defense fund someone had set up for Thevenot and Rousseau.

"Robert was in court, so I met with Detective Schiller." I patted my eye with the tissue. "Luke was in Schiller's office. That's how I met him. He's handling the case against Thevenot."

"He must be a smart lawyer if Robert trusts him with such a high-profile case." The tenor of her voice was kind and supportive, and I started to feel better about telling her.

We talked about the football game and about how much the Morris kids loved Lilly.

"If I didn't know better, I'd say Bobby likes Lilly more like a girlfriend than a friend. How does she feel about him?" Brenda looked directly into my eyes when she spoke.

"I'm not sure. I know she loves both your kids." I wasn't going to tell Brenda that Lilly was crazy about Bobby. I had a philosophy not to share another person's business, especially family.

"Oh, well. I hope Bobby doesn't get hurt. This is the first time he's shown interest in a girl." She looked at her salad. I changed the subject to what I should wear on my dinner date. Brenda said she would take me to her favorite dress shop near the campus.

Shopping with Brenda was like taking a bath in a tub full of bubbles. She floated above all the merchandise until she found the perfect thing that seemed to appear from nowhere. She had me try on a couple of dresses and declared the black Chanel sleeveless sheath perfect for any occasion. She insisted I buy a gold, black, and red pashmina shawl and made me promise I had a pair of black pumps with at least two-inch heels.

"No matter where he takes you to dinner, you'll be dressed perfectly." She watched the sales clerk hang the dress and put it in a black travel bag with "Chanel" stamped in gold on the front. "You can't go wrong with a little black dress."

I paid with my dad's credit card and knew he'd scream when he got the bill. I didn't care.

*

That evening, I put my long hair up in a ponytail and applied a little make-up, some mascara, and lip-gloss. Lilly said I looked glamorous, and that she was happy I was going out because she had a big math test the next morning.

Luke called my room from the house phone in the lobby and was standing just outside the elevator when the doors opened on the first floor. The look on his face told me that no matter how much my dad yelled at me, my Chanel dress was worth it.

Gino's Italian Restaurant was located on Bennington Avenue, off College Drive. Luke said that Grace Marino and her family had opened the intimate eatery in 1966 about fifteen years after they emigrated from Sicily.

"It was on Perkins Road back then," Luke told me while we waited for the maître d' to seat us. "They moved to this location in 1975." The restaurant had low lighting, white linen tablecloths, and dark wood accents. The traditional southern Italian food was supposedly prepared according to Mrs. Marino's personal recipes. Our waiter said he'd worked for Gino's since it first opened in '66. His Cajun drawl had not been affected by the Italianese of the chef and her team. Raphael was as Cajun-French as they came, and was the best server I'd ever had.

Luke and I talked about his college and law school days, and I asked him how he could be twenty-eight years old and unattached. He told me that he dated a girl all through college and she was killed in a car accident on graduation night.

"We weren't together that night." He swirled his drink around in his glass and stared at the golden-brown liquid as he spoke. "I'd graduated the year before and was studying for law school finals at the end of my first year. She went out with her girlfriends, and the car went off the highway and wrapped around a street light. The other three girls were hurt, the driver, pretty badly. Sheila was the only one who died. It's taken me a long time to work through the guilt."

"I'm so sorry, Luke." I squeezed his arm and let my hand linger on the fabric of his suit coat. He wore a purple, white, and yellow bow tie and looked gorgeous in the table's candlelight in the corner of the restaurant. He didn't look at me for the longest time. Finally, he looked up and smiled.

"It's funny. Just when I think I've healed and moved on, a memory washes over me." He winked at me. "Sorry."

"That's perfectly understandable." I patted his arm and stared at him. He looked directly into my eyes as though he could see my soul. "My sister lost her husband three years ago, remarried this past June, but still has waves of grief wash over her at times."

"Yes. Well. It's been six years. You'd think..." His voice drifted off, and he took a sip of his drink. I let go of his arm and drank some wine. "So tell me about this football game you and Lilly are going to tomorrow night."

"Oh, Lilly is sort of sweet on this boy who's a senior at Catholic High. He's the quarterback." I liked that he changed the subject to something lighter. I told him about Bobby but didn't say his last name or mention that he was Robert's son. I hadn't heard from Brenda, so I evaded the subject, unsure of how Robert felt about me inviting Luke to the football game. I explained that Lilly and I would be going to New Orleans Saturday for the weekend.

"When will you be back in Baton Rouge?" He asked it off-handedly.

"I'm not sure." The waiter arrived with our salads, and we didn't talk until he left. "I'm looking for an apartment or a rental house for Lilly and me."

"You're getting a place in Baton Rouge?" He put his fork down and stared at me.

"Yep. I promised Susie I'd find a place so Lilly can move out of the dorm." I took a bite of lettuce and pretended I didn't know he was staring at me.

"Really? When?"

"As soon as I find something. I've looked at all the flyers and followed up on some of the ads in the paper, but nothing feels right. I don't want a place where college students live. I'm too old for that."

He told me about the neighborhood where he lived and said it had a number of rental houses. He gave me the name and phone number of his landlord.

"He might have something come up." Luke finally started to eat his salad. "He doesn't advertise because he usually has a waiting list. I'll put in a good word for you, and maybe he'll move you to the top of the list."

"That's nice of you. Thanks." I put my fork down and took a sip of wine. "This is good wine. Thank you."

"Thanks for going out with me." He put his fork down, took the napkin off his lap, and put it on the table. He turned in his chair so his knees were almost touching the side of my leg. "I haven't dated anyone seriously these past six years. Oh, a little here and there, but no one interested me." He took my hand off my lap and held it. Then he pulled it to his mouth and kissed my fingertips. "I guess what I'm saying is that I really like you and I'd like to see you again."

If I had tried to talk, I would have stuttered, because he had me all twisted up inside, so I didn't say a word. We call it being "fâchéd" in Cajun French. It's pronounced: fah-shade. The literal French translation is, angry; but Cajuns use the word to mean embarrassed or all messed up and tongue-tied.

During dinner, he asked me whether I had a job. I guess it seemed unusual that I could live in Jean Ville, move to Baton Rouge, and spend most weekends in New Orleans. I told him I taught private piano and voice lessons, and he seemed enamored that I was a musician. He asked whether I would play something for him, and I told him I needed a piano.

After dinner, we went into the bar for after-dinner drinks, and there was a guy playing an upright piano in the corner of the dimly lit room. Luke went to talk to him and put some bills in the tip jar. When the guy took his break, Luke said I could play the piano. He laughed and said he had cleared it with authorities. He took my hand and led me to the black, ebony Yamaha and sat next to me on the bench.

I played a piece by Beethoven, then broke into some boogie-woogie. The people sitting at the bar and tables all stopped talking, and soon, about ten of them were gathered around the piano. I took requests for a while and played *Staying Alive, Dancing Queen,* and

American Pie. Everyone sang along, and I didn't look at Luke until I returned the piano to the guy who was paid to play it.

Luke's mouth hung open, and I used my hand to push his chin up to shut it. We both laughed and left the bar. He held my hand while we waited for the valet parking attendant to drive under the portico. He hadn't said anything to me since I'd played the piano, and I wondered whether the ruckus I had caused had changed his mind about me.

Before he drove off from the restaurant, he turned to me and took both my hands in his.

"Now I'm really smitten." He bent towards me and kissed me on the cheek. "Beauty and talent, too. My, my. And how is it that you are still unattached?" He put the car in gear and drove off.

"Let's just say I dated this guy from high school for a long time and came to my senses," I whispered as though I didn't want to admit I'd ever known Warren Morrow.

"I'm glad you did, then." He smiled at me sideways and drove me back to the hotel in silence. He parked in the lot behind the hotel and turned the car off. "I don't want to scare you off, but I'm not one to play games. Will you go out with me again?"

I felt myself blush, the rash hot on my neck was climbing up fast. "Look. I don't have much experience. I mean, I had this one boyfriend in high school, and we just kept seeing each other. I don't think you could say we really 'dated'; we just went out, or he came to my house. I don't know how to date. Not really."

"You're doing very well for not having had any experience." He took my hands and faced me. "Tell me if I crowd you. You're just so different from any girl I've ever known. You're so . . . let's see, how do I say this. You're natural. There's nothing fake or pretentious about you. If you think something, you say it. You don't try to impress others, and I don't think you would know how to tell a lie if you wanted to. You're very transparent."

"Is that good?"

"Very." He smiled. "And the way you blush and get that red rash on your neck is totally charming. I know what you're thinking and feeling without you saying a word."

I put my hand around my neck and rubbed it as though I could make it disappear. He laughed at me and pulled my hands off my neck and kissed my fingers.

Lilly was asleep when I crept into the room. I undressed slowly and hung my dress and pashmina in the closet, then washed my face. I looked in the mirror and saw that the rash on my neck was slowly disappearing. When I thought about Luke, it started to come back.

*

Brenda told me it would be fine to invite Luke to the football game, but I decided it would complicate things. I needed a break from him to filter through my thoughts and feelings. I was conflicted about whether I should formally break up with Warren before dating someone else. It was all sudden and confusing.

At halftime, Robert sat next to me and said Brenda had told him I was seeing Luke McMath.

"He's a great guy. Not that you need my approval." Robert offered me some of his popcorn, and I said "no", because I didn't like getting the kernels in my teeth. "I don't mind if you tell him we're friends. It shouldn't make a difference."

"Thanks. I like him, but I don't really know him." I watched the band on the field, and tuned out the music.

"He's a very smart guy, a brilliant lawyer. As a person, I think what you see is what you get."

"That's good to know." I shifted in my stadium seat. "By the way, how's the case against Thevenot and Rousseau coming along?"

"Luke would know more about the case than I do." He put a handful of popcorn in his mouth as Brenda got back from the bathroom and sat next to him. "They brief me at our weekly staff meetings. I think we're waiting for a trial date." He took Brenda's hand and held it.

"Did they tell you about the defense fund someone set up at the Confederate Bank?"

"Yes. Interesting. We're going to try to subpoena the bank records to find out who's funding it."

"What would that tell you?" I didn't understand Robert's insinuation.

"It could give us an understanding of who might not want the defendants to sing." He tilted his popcorn towards Brenda, and she took a few pieces. "We are sure there are bigger fish behind the two yo-yos who went after Rodney. If we can't get Thevenot and Rousseau to rat them out, maybe we can find out another way. Schiller is on it."

I thought about what Robert said about there being people behind the shooting. Maybe ex-Sheriff Guidry. It was well known that he'd been head of the Klan in years past. I mentioned his name to Robert, and he told me to tell Luke about my suspicions.

*

I arrived at the house on Ryan Avenue at about four o'clock on Saturday. No one was home, so I let myself in and put my things in Lilly's room. Marianne had taken a job with a cardiology practice at Ochsner Clinic so she could work days and have weekends off. Susie spent every day with Rodney in the rehab unit, but she had to leave by seven at night, and she was free in the middle of the day when Rod was in therapy.

By the time I unpacked my things and poured myself a glass of tea, I heard a key in the front door.

"Hey. Sissy. You here? I see your car out front." Marianne hollered from the living room, and I met her in the dining room. We hugged, and she looked at my glass of iced tea. "That looks good, but I'm thinking something a little stronger."

We went to the kitchen, and she opened a bottle of white wine. We took our glasses onto the back porch and sat in facing chairs.

"How was your week," I took a sip of my wine and stared at Marianne. She looked tired and stressed.

"Fine. I like my job. I'm usually off on Saturdays, but I went in this afternoon to get my charts done." She smiled at me and took a sip of wine.

"How are Susie and Rodney?"

"Better every day. I usually go to the hospital to see Rodney at about seven, and bring Susie home for the night. Soon she'll be able to walk here from the hospital." She slouched in her chair as though overly tired.

"I'll go get her tonight. You look tired." I sat on the edge of my seat as though I were about to stand up.

"She eats dinner with Rodney, and I fend for myself. What would you like for supper?" Marianne seemed preoccupied, her eyes at half-mast.

"What about your boyfriend, Dr. Warner? Are you still seeing him?"

"Yes. In fact, we have a date tonight." Marianne rolled her wine glass back and forth between her hands.

"Well, you go get a shower and dress for your date. I'll go to the hospital, visit with Rodney, and bring Susie home. Where's Lilly?"

"Her boyfriend came from Baton Rouge, and they went down to the World's Fair. Have you been, yet? It's really sensational" Marianne took a sip of her wine and leaned back in her chair.

"No, I haven't had time, but I'll put it on my 'to-do' list." I smiled at her and thought I should tell her about Luke. "I met someone."

"Oh, Do tell!" She sat straight up in her chair. "Someone special?"

"It's hard to know. I've only been out with him twice, but I like him." I smiled when I thought about Luke. I told her about our dates, and how Robert said that Luke was a great guy.

"When will you see him again?" She reached over and took my hand, almost motherly.

"He'll be in Jean Ville next week for a hearing on the case. I'm going to invite him to my apartment for dinner."

"The case? What does he have to do with the case?"

"He's a prosecutor with the attorney general's office, and is in charge of the case against Thevenot and Rousseau."

"He must be smart." She looked serious. I thought about Luke and all the things he had going for him: intelligence, talent, looks, manners, pretty much everything a girl would want in a guy. The opposite of Warren Morrow. I felt my neck start to burn, and soon the warmth spread to my cheeks, and that damn blushing thing happened. Marianne started to laugh, and we both ended up in stitches.

*

Rodney looked better than I'd seen him in months. He was in a wheelchair, and I sat next to him and told him about how the case was proceeding. Then I told him about Luke. Susie was all ears, asking questions as though she were my mother and needed to screen my dates. I reminded them both that I was almost twenty-six years old, and that meant I was an adult.

"But I do appreciate that you both care so much." I looked from Susie to Rodney and smiled. "You make me feel loved."

"You... are..." Rodney said in a stutter.

"I appreciate that, brother." I hugged his neck, and he put his left arm over my shoulder and squeezed. "I want a man just like you."

Rodney and Susie both grinned.

"When are you planning to move to Baton Rouge?" Susie finally had followed me into the hall and stood facing me.

"I can move any time, but I'll need some financial help. I mean, I can't really afford an apartment."

"I'll pay for an apartment for the two of you." Susie leaned against the wall. "That sounds like the best idea."

"I've been looking, and I have a few leads. Meanwhile, if Brenda offers, and Lilly wants to stay there, she could stay with the Morrises until I find a place, buy some furniture, and get settled."

"You can have the furniture from the house on Gravier Road. Hire a mover to take it to Baton Rouge. If you move out of the garage apartment, I think I'll either sell or rent that place. Rodney and I will never live in Jean Ville." Susie looked from me to Rodney.

"I'd like to keep the apartment through the trial, so I have a place to stay." I looked at Susie and she nodded.

We chatted for another fifteen minutes, and I told her I'd like to take Lilly to New York during the Thanksgiving holidays.

"I think she misses Joe. She also mentioned going to see Emma." I watched Susie's face darken.

"It would be good for her to go to New York," Susie looked up, and her expression changed to something that resembled understanding. "I only wish I could take her. She's never been up there without me."

"She'll be fine. Really, Susie, she's old enough to go alone, but I'm happy to go with her. You were close to her age when you went off to Sarah Lawrence all by yourself."

Susie didn't respond, only looked off into the distance as though remembering something unpleasant.

*

The next morning, Marianne told me that Warner had kissed her. She blushed when she said she liked it, which made me laugh.

"He took me to a restaurant in the French Quarters called Galatoire's. It was fancy, expensive, romantic." Marianne had a faraway look in her eyes.

"How was the restaurant?"

"It was fabulous. He told me the fish was always fresh, and I told him about Catfish and how he loved to catch fish and cook them fresh. We talked about how much I miss my grandfather, and he said he'd lost his grandfather, too." She looked at me intently. "I wonder what Catfish would think of Donato Warner." She paused and looked at the ceiling with a faraway expression.

"Anyway, I was sort of confused by everything: the menu selections were complicated—so many different kinds of fish, sauces, sides; so he ordered for us both." Marianne laughed at herself and continued talking as though I weren't in the room. "I was also confused by him: his presence, his hands, his kindness. He held my hand on the corner of the table, and I couldn't think.

"He apologized for being a scumbag. I told him I don't have enough experience to know what a scumbag is, and I felt myself blush. 'A scumbag is someone who comes on too strong. Who takes you to dives instead of nice restaurants. Who expects you to put-out. Who moves too fast.' He squeezed my hand, and I finally looked at him.

"'Then I guess you're a scumbag,' I said and started to laugh. He sat back in his chair and laughed, too. I guess it broke through the curtain of distrust that hung between us because we actually had a great conversation after that. We talked about him, a lot. About his background, his parents, his three siblings. We talked about his ex-wife and New York and medical school. We talked about Rodney and Susie, and the unusual medical progress they are making.

"'I want what they have,' he said and looked at me intently. 'I see the way you watch them. You want that, too, right?'

"'Who doesn't? Who wouldn't want what they have?' I said. Then I told him how difficult Susie and Rodney's journey had been, and that mixed-race relationships aren't accepted down here. I wanted him to know upfront that I was afraid of what might happen if he and I dated.

"'I don't know how to say this without insulting you and your race,' he said 'But you don't look African American.' Just then, the waiter brought our food, which gave me a chance to think. I told him that I was proud of my heritage and that maybe no one would know I was black in New Orleans, but that at home, in Jean Ville, everyone knows my family and my background.

"'Okay, let's just stay out of Jean Ville,' he said and laughed, as if the solution was so simple. I said, 'My family is there. My life. My career.' I started to think about what I had in Jean Ville that would coax me back: my mom, my four sisters, my two nieces, my uncles and aunt, and their spouses and kids. Then he said, 'I don't mean to sound trite. I'm sorry. Tell me about your family. I already know and love your mom.' He put his fork down and listened, giving me his undivided attention. I told him about my aunts, uncles, and cousins, and explained how we all lived with our back porches almost touching and were in and out of each other's cabins day and night.

"'What about your love life?' he asked me. 'Do you have someone in Jean Ville you miss?'

"'No. I haven't...' I started to stutter, got hold of myself, and told him that I'd never had a boyfriend and had never been kissed by a guy. I looked at my plate and blushed with embarrassment. He sat back in his chair so hard it was as though he'd been punched in the gut with a cannon. Then he started to laugh and said, 'I don't want to sound like I don't believe you; but, really. I find it hard to...' His expression turned from mistrust to concern to sympathy, as though I'd missed out on something vital. Then he said, 'I mean, you're so beautiful.'

"I was embarrassed. I hung my head and dropped my chin to my chest. I heard his chair scrape the floor as he turned it towards me and said, 'You ready to go?' 'I asked, Do you mind?' I looked at him and felt hopeful, like we needed to get out of there, out of the public. I wanted some privacy. I said, 'I mean the food is wonderful, so is the wine,' but he said, 'I'll have it packaged,' and he motioned to the waiter who silently took everything off the table and returned a few minutes later with a shopping bag. Donato paid the bill, and when we stepped outside the car was waiting. He handed the valet parker a wad of cash and opened the door, put his hand on the small of my back, and helped me into his sports car.

"We didn't talk as he drove towards Metairie. He turned down a narrow road near Jules Avenue, and before long, we were on the levee, watching tugboats push barges up and down the wide Mississippi River. He reached in the bag and pulled out the bottle of wine and two clear plastic glasses the waiter had packed. He handed me a glass and filled it, then filled his own. 'Here's to honesty,' he said, and tipped his glass against mine and took a sip. He never took his eyes off me. 'I'll go first,' he took another sip. 'I want to kiss you. I've never kissed someone who hasn't been kissed, so I guess I'll teach you how to kiss, you can teach me how slow to go.' He laughed and touched the side of my face.

"I said, 'Now? I mean, are you going to me kiss now?' I felt afraid and pressured. He started to laugh and said, 'This may be more difficult than I thought. First, you don't announce that there will be kissing. It just happens because you both want it to happen.' He was still laughing. I felt like I was twelve years old again, having feelings stirring inside but not knowing what to do with them.

"He took my hand and pulled it to his lips and kissed my palm. It sent chills up my arms to my neck, and I felt heat start on my chest and climb upward onto my face. Then he let go of my hand and got out of the car. At first, I just sat there and wondered what he was doing, then he opened the door on my side and reached for my hand. He pulled me out of the car, and I stood facing him. I could taste his breath and smell the starch in his dress shirt. He put his arms around me, over my shoulders, and when he pulled me to him, my arms went around his waist under his sports coat. At first, I gasped, then tried to relax. I could hear his heartbeat, tha-thump, tha-thump. He rested his face on the top of my head, and we stood there for a long time, wrapped in each other's arms. When I felt him lift his head off mine, I looked up, and my chin was under his. He bent his head and kissed me.

"'You're a natural,' he said, and whispered into my mouth. I felt his hardness against the lower part of my belly, and it frightened me. I pulled away and took a breath. 'I'm sorry,' he said. 'I can't help my reaction. I'm really attracted to you. I felt tears gather behind my eyelids because I remembered the only other time I'd felt a man's genitals press against me. I started to shake, and he pulled me close to him in a way that I couldn't feel his crotch. He pushed my head against his chest and stroked my hair with one hand. I was crying, I must have been heaving, because he tightened his grip and rubbed my back and said, 'It's okay. Whatever happened to you in the past is over. I'll protect you.'"

"He pulled a handkerchief from his back pocket and handed it to me, but didn't release me when he said, 'We can take it as slow as you like. I'm in no hurry.'

"He helped me clean the mascara off my face, then we tried to get the spots off his shirt and laughed at the mess I'd caused. We got back in the car and finished our wine, talked about Susie and Rodney, and laughed a little." Marianne took a deep breath and sat back in her chair. She finally looked at me, and her expression said that she'd forgotten I was there.

"Susie said that's what Josh Ryan told her, 'We can take it slow, I'm in no hurry.' She said you can trust a man who has that kind of patience." I put my hand on Marianne's, and she smiled as though those words answered her questions about Dr. Warner.

~ Chapter Eleven ~

Revenge

I T WAS A BUSY weekend in New Orleans. Rodney was moved to the inpatient Rehab floor so that he could focus on speech, occupational, and physical therapy. He still had trouble forming words, and he couldn't walk, at all. He was finally able to feed himself, although it took him an hour to eat a meal. Susie's patience was endless, as she would eat her meals with him and take slow, small bites so that they finished at the same time.

Susie insisted on being with Rodney every minute during the weekend, because the staff was off, and that's when she could be his personal therapist, working with him on his speech by giving him reading assignments that increased his ability to say words and identify sentences. She also worked with him on eye-hand coordination, throwing a beach ball to him, helping him to hold a pencil and make scribbles on paper, setting a table with plates and utensils, and insisting that he identify the fork, knife, and spoon, then reach out to grab one of them, and hold them correctly in his left hand. We were all glad Rodney was left-handed since his right arm was still stiff and weak from the bullet that went all the way through it and tore muscles, ligaments, and nerves.

I took Lilly shopping for winter clothes suitable for a college girl, and I spoke to Luke's landlord about a rental house in Baton Rouge. He told me he had one that would be available the first of December and I could see it the next time I was in town.

I left for Jean Ville at about ten o'clock Monday morning and stopped to see my dad before I got to my garage apartment. He was in the kitchen making a sandwich, and he looked better than I'd seen him in a long time.

"You're up and moving around, Daddy. That's good." I kissed him on the cheek and poured myself a glass of tea from the pitcher on the counter. We sat at the kitchen table and talked while he ate his sandwich. I didn't bring up the case, nor did he.

Daddy said that his physical therapist had been coming three times a week and took him outside to walk around the block.

"I feel like I'm getting my strength back." His tone was upbeat and positive, and it made me happy. "His name is Lyle. He explained that the more I move, the more energy I'll have. The less I move, the less energy. I'd never thought about it that way."

"I'm glad to see you doing so well, Daddy."

"Where have you been, little girl?" He had called me 'little girl' since I was a baby, and he called Susie, 'pretty girl.' Neither she nor I cared what he called us as long as he didn't get violent. He'd been physically abusive with Susie from as far back as I could remember, but he'd never hit me.

When I left my dad's house, I drove by James's office on my way to the bank to cash a check. I could have sworn the old blue truck I'd seen at the church and again at James's house was parked in his parking lot. I backed up and pulled in so I could read the license plate: 37L402. Wow. I wondered who might be driving it, since Rousseau and Thevenot were in jail.

*

Luke called Monday afternoon and said that he'd be in Jean Ville the next evening because the judge had scheduled a hearing for Wednesday morning. "I was wondering whether you'd be free for dinner, although I'm not familiar with the restaurant scene in Jean Ville."

"There are one or two worth trying, but why don't you come to my place and we can grill steaks." I didn't tell him that I was afraid to be seen in public with him. Small-town gossip and Warren on the loose, so to speak.

"That would be great. Can I bring anything?" He sounded excited.

"Just yourself," I said, and laughed.

After we hung up, I drove to the grocery store to buy steaks and potatoes to cook the next night, and I picked up the local newspaper, called the *Toussaint Journal*. When I got home, I unpacked my car, stored the groceries, and put a load of clothes to wash. I poured myself a glass of tea and sat down with the newspaper.

The mug shots of Thevenot and Rousseau were plastered across the front page. The caption read: *Shooting suspects released from jail.* The article said that the defense fund at the Confederate Bank had raised more than $100,000—enough to post their bail. I read and re-read the article. Then I picked up the phone and called the attorney general's office in Baton Rouge.

When the robot answered, I dialed 3-2-3. The phone rang five times, and I was about to hang up when Luke answered.

"Did you know Thevenot and Rousseau were bailed out?" I was angry.

"Yes. I heard about it this morning." He was out of breath.

"Aren't you afraid of what they might do to get back at me, at you, and maybe others?"

"I hadn't thought about that." He let out a heavy breath, and I heard his chair creak. "We took it as a positive thing because we can follow them and see who their contacts are."

"I hope you have them followed 24-7. They are in Jean Ville. So am I!" I hoped he understood that I was afraid of them, but since I hadn't told him about the note on my windshield, he probably hadn't put two-and-two together.

I didn't mention that I'd seen the blue truck at James's office, but it occurred to me that if investigators were tailing Rousseau and

Thevenot, they'd see it there. I felt I needed to warn James, but I was torn between my loyalty to my brother and my feelings for Luke.

"Okay. See you tomorrow night." I hung up and paced my living room and kitchen, and tried to figure out how to handle the fact that I had insider's knowledge that could affect my brother. What was his affiliation with the two guys who shot Rodney? Then I remembered that one of James's partners represented Thevenot, so it would be logical for the truck to be at his office. I breathed a sigh of relief and decided to treat the investigation the way I treated gossip: zip the lips.

*

I spent Tuesday cleaning my apartment. I marinated the steaks, washed the potatoes, made the salad, and put it in a Tupperware container. I washed wine glasses, scrubbed the toilet, cleaned my barbecue grill, swept the deck, and dusted the swing and rockers. Then I took a long bath, washed my hair and dried it, brushed my teeth twice, and put on a little make-up. I dressed in jeans, a short-sleeved polo shirt and sandals. Then I paced and waited. I'd bought candles, so I stacked them, then placed them in various places around the room, then gathered them up again.

My phone rang at four o'clock. It was Luke, who said he'd arrived in Jean Ville before the others and had already checked into his motel. He wanted to know if it was too early to come over.

"What about your meeting?" I held the phone to my ear and looked around my apartment, trying to visualize what he might see when he got here.

"We met before I left Baton Rouge." I loved the sound of his deep, raspy voice. It had just enough Southern drawl to be sexy and enough straight talk to sound intelligent. "We'll have a briefing at breakfast, before we head to the courthouse."

"Sure. You can come over." I checked to make sure everything was ready and was actually glad I didn't have to obsess for another two or three hours.

"See you in a few minutes."

After we hung up, I looked out of the front windows at Gravier Road in case his car might already be there. I washed my hands and made another pass through the apartment to make sure everything was in place. I spread the candles out again, all seven of them. I washed my hands and reminded myself that I had cold beer, red and white wine, sodas, and I'd bought a bottle of Crown Royal because that's what Luke had ordered at Gino's.

I washed my hands again and took out the tortilla chips and spinach dip I'd bought at the store, and poured some salsa in a bowl. I set the food on the island and tried not to wash my hands again. Then I paced. I walked out on the deck, then came back in. I left the sliding glass doors opened since it was pleasant outside, and I liked the way it made my place feel big and spacious.

I heard his car drive up, and I stepped onto the landing. He looked up and saw me smiling down at him, and he took the stairs two at a time. When he reached me, he folded me in his arms and kissed me. When he pulled away, he was out of breath. I heard another vehicle pull in my driveway and saw Warren's new red truck stop, idle for a minute, then back out onto Gravier Road. I'd been caught red-handed, but didn't care.

Luke followed me through the side door into the kitchen and looked around my apartment.

"It looks like you, Sissy." He smiled at me and walked slowly around the living room and kitchen that was one big room from the front of the garage to the back. The garage itself held two cars and had room for lawn equipment, so the living area was over half of the garage, the other half, which comprised a large bedroom, a bathroom, and a study, was over the other half.

"Do you want something to drink?" I moved towards the refrigerator. The bottle of Crown Royal was on the island next to the dip and chips. He sat on a stool and asked for a glass of ice. He poured some Crown over the ice and dipped a chip in the salsa. I poured myself a glass of Chardonnay and asked if he'd like to sit on the deck.

184

We walked through the opened glass doors, and he stood at the railing and looked out at the acre of land with its rows of trees: pecan, pear, fig, oaks, and magnolias.

"What a view." He didn't turn around.

"My favorite room in the house." I walked up to the railing and stood next to him. He put an arm over my shoulder, and we just stood there and breathed the fall air, stared at the sun that hovered above the trees, and listened to the birds calling to each other. My shoulder was tucked under his arm, and I got a whiff of his aftershave. He set his drink on the top of the railing, turned to face me, put his arms around me, and pulled me to him. I let him. He just held me and rested his chin on the top of my head. I could feel his heartbeat against my neck as though the rhythm was trying to talk to me. I listened intently and felt a sense of sadness or impending pain, like something that was just beginning, might have to end.

I tried to shake off the feeling.

The rest of the evening went off without a hitch. Luke grilled the steaks, and I put the potatoes in the oven. I had a loaf of French bread that I buttered and wrapped in foil and put in the oven with the potatoes. I dressed the salad, and we ate at the island on the bar stools. It was about ten o'clock when he left. I took a quick shower, checked to make sure the doors were locked, and went to bed.

*

My digital clock said 2:03 AM when I awoke to a clinking sound, followed by crunching. Before I was completely awake, someone appeared next to my bed and pulled a cloth, like a sack, over my head, tied my arms behind my back, and dragged me to the floor. I kicked and screamed, but it didn't stop the person from pounding my head with a fist and kicking me. I felt like I'd fallen into a deep, dark well, where there were people with clubs taking turns whacking me. There was a coarse, wet laugh, a belch, the smell of beer or whiskey, cigarette breath, and strong body odor.

I fell deeper, and in my dream, I smelled burning rubber and gasoline creep under the doors and through the cracks in the windows and fill the room. I heard the sound of an eighteen-wheeler come through my apartment, blowing the air horn and grinding the gears. The sound got louder and louder, and I could smell diesel fuel and grease, then I was enveloped in a cloud.

The roar got louder, the smells got stronger, and I tasted bile and salt. Then I couldn't swallow.

A searing pain shot into my belly from between my legs and I felt myself try to scream, but there was no sound other than the roaring in my ears and a loud grunt from somewhere above me. It felt like a hot branding iron had been poked inside me, and there was a weight on my chest that I could have sworn was a load of bricks. I couldn't breathe and gasped for air. The cloth around my head clogged my nose, and I began to suffocate. When I tried to breathe through my mouth, I tasted bile and blood.

Then everything went black.

*

There was an incessant ringing. It would stop for a few seconds then start again. I tried to wake up so I could identify where the ringing came from. My hands were tied behind my back, but I began to twist them around and was able to pull one through the loop in the rope. I reached up and yanked on the fabric that covered my head, and saw that it was a bloody pillowcase. I freed my other hand and sat on the floor, propped against my bed. I was totally naked.

The digital clock said 8:42 AM. The ringing started again, and I realized it was the telephone. I tried to stand up, but my legs were so weak they folded under me. There was blood all over the floor, and I tracked it as I crawled to the bathroom on hands and knees and pulled myself up by hanging on the lavatory. What I saw in the mirror made my stomach turn over. I started to vomit and held my head over the toilet.

When I finally stopped retching, I made my way to the kitchen and tried to pick up the receiver on the telephone. I needed to call someone for help, but who could I call? Daddy didn't drive. James would be at work, maybe in court. Warren? He worked on the highway and couldn't be reached during the day. My only option seemed 9-1-1, but I didn't want the publicity that would create. I hung up the phone.

What had happened? I tried to remember. I was asleep.

I looked at the kitchen door that led to the outside landing. One of the panes was broken, and there were shards of glass on the floor. I remembered the clinking, crunching sounds that woke me.

I got a ziplock bag from the drawer and filled it with ice. I laid on the sofa and put the ice on my face. My eyes were black, my nose felt like it was broken, and one of my teeth was chipped. I felt a burning between my legs, hot and searing, like a curling iron had been inserted in my vagina.

The phone started to ring again, and I slowly made my way back to the kitchen. It hung on the wall next to the door to the landing, and just when I got to it, the ringing stopped. I started to make my way back to the sofa when the ringing started again.

"Hello." I didn't recognize my own voice, it was almost a whisper, and riddled with something like mucus or blood.

"Sissy? Is that you?" His voice was deep and raspy, and I recognized it, but couldn't place it.

"Yes. Who's this?"

"It's Luke. Are you alright?"

"Luke?" I tried to remember. Yes, Luke had been at my place the night before. Had he done this to me? Suddenly I was afraid of him. I hung up the phone. It rang again. I was afraid to pick it up. I made my way back to the sofa and put the ice on my face. I heard a car pull up in my driveway, but I was helpless. If someone were going to beat me up again, they'd have to kill me, because I couldn't defend myself. I couldn't even yell or talk or beg.

I heard the kitchen door open, and I lay paralyzed, waiting for whoever was there to finish me off.

"Sissy!" I thought I recognized Luke's voice, and it scared me, but

I lay there and waited for the blows. "Oh, my God. What happened?" He knelt beside the sofa and lifted the ice pack. He picked me up like a bride and carried me out of the apartment, down the stairs, and put me in the back seat of his car. I couldn't move.

I must have fallen asleep, then I felt a bevy of humans hovering over me. The air was cold and smelled of antiseptic, rubbing alcohol, and Lysol. A familiar fatherly voice came through the chatter.

"Sissy. It's me, Dr. David." I could smell the cigar smoke on his clothing, and I tried to open my eyes to look at him, but they were swollen shut. "Nancy, get the police here. NOW!"

"Sissy. Can you hear me?" He bent towards me, and his breath smelled like coffee and bacon. I could hear him, but I couldn't talk. My mouth was swollen inside, and I tasted blood and salt. "Do you know who did this to you?"

I shook my head side-to-side in very tiny movements to indicate, "No."

"Who's the man who brought you here?" Dr. David hovered over me. I shook my head side-to-side again to indicate I didn't know.

"I'm Lucas McMath, Doctor. I'm with the attorney general's office in Baton Rouge." His voice started to make sense to me, and I listened to his explanation. "I'm here for a hearing in Judge DeYoung's Courtroom in the Thevenot-Rousseau case. I'm Sissy's friend. We had dinner at her place last night. I left about ten and tried to call her at least a dozen times this morning to thank her, but she didn't answer her phone, so I went to her place and found her like this." He took a deep breath and choked back tears. "Will she be okay? Should I contact someone?"

"I'll call her dad. We're neighbors. Do you have any idea who did this?" Dr. Switzer pointed a light in my eyes. He had to pry them open to do it, and it hurt.

"No, sir. I couldn't guess." It sounded like Luke was standing at the foot of my gurney. I figured I was in the Emergency Room.

Someone started an IV, and I heard Dr. Switzer say I was going to feel more relaxed soon. Within seconds, I drifted off. When I awoke, I was in a hospital room. There was a hissing sound, and something was clicking like a clock, and the smell was less antiseptic, more like cleaning supplies. I could feel someone's presence and tried to open my eyes. One of them opened a slit, and I saw my dad in a rocker in the corner of the room. I must have grunted because he appeared at the side of my bed and asked if I wanted water. I nodded, and he put a straw to my lips.

"Who did this to you, Sissy?" He put the glass on the side table and took one of my hands out from under the sheet. I shook my head side-to-side. "The police have been to your apartment. They say it looked like someone broke the glass in your door to enter and that there was a bloody pillowcase and a rope on the floor next to your bed. Blood everywhere. They took samples, and by the looks of you, I'm guessing it will be your blood."

I couldn't talk, but I tried to piece together what had happened. Daddy bent his head to my mouth so he could hear. I told him that I had heard a clinking, crunching sound, and looked at my clock. "It was two o'clock in the morning, and someone put the pillowcase over my head and tied my hands. Then they beat me, kicked me, and God knows what else. At some point, I blacked out." The swelling inside my mouth made my words slur.

I'm not sure how much Daddy understood, but he nodded his head and told me I should get some rest. I heard him mutter, "Cowardly sons-of-bitches. They cover her head while they beat and rape her. Damn them. When I catch those bastards..." He walked out of my room, and I heard him talking to someone in the hall.

I dozed off and on all day, and Daddy mostly sat in the rocker and would give me sips of water every now and again. I heard him use the phone a few times. It sounded like he talked to Susie once, and James.

Luke came to my room at some point. I heard him talk to Daddy, who left. Luke stood beside my bed and held my hand and tried to talk to me. When I attempted to answer his questions, he put his ear to my mouth and listened.

"Don't try to talk unless you can give me an idea of who might have done this." He bent his head, and I tried to tell him whoever did it covered my head and never said a word. I said it felt like more than one person, but that I wasn't sure. I had my suspicions. I'd been worried that if Thevenot and Rousseau got out of jail, they would want to take revenge on me for stirring things up and getting the attorney general to take the case. But I didn't say that to anyone, nor did I mention that Warren had pulled up in my driveway and saw me kissing Luke, nor did I tell anyone about the warning note on my windshield.

*

It was a long week, but every day I was a little better. By Wednesday, the swelling inside my mouth was much less, and I could form some sounds. One of my eyes was halfway opened, and I could manage to open the other one a slit if I strained. My left wrist was broken and was in a cast, and I had stitches in various places on my neck, legs, arms, and back. The burning between my legs disappeared, but I felt a heaviness down there.

Daddy spent most days in the rocking chair in my room and was diligent about giving me sips of water, then 7-Up, which tasted really good. I guess someone called Mama, because she sauntered into my room Wednesday evening, jingling her bracelets and swishing her skirts. She was civil to Daddy, who left the room while she stayed with me. She read to me from some of her poetry books, and I felt as though she had me confused with Susie, the English major who loved that stuff; but it was comforting to hear Mama's voice. She came back Thursday morning and stayed until about noon. She told me she was going back to Houston and would come back to help me when I went home if I needed her.

By Thursday afternoon, I was able to get up and walk to the bathroom, so they removed the catheter. That was a relief. Friday, I ate some Jell-O and soup broth, so they took the IV out.

Luke came back Friday evening. He spent the night in the chair in my room even though I begged him to go to my apartment and get a good night's sleep. I'd never seen anyone so worried.

Saturday morning, they finally brought me real food: scrambled eggs, grits, and best of all, coffee. Luke stirred sugar and cream into my coffee and helped me take sips of it. I swallowed it, even though it burned the inside of my mouth. It made me feel like I was heading back to normality.

Luke sat on the side of my bed and put his hands on either side of my face. He whispered that he wanted to kiss me, but he knew it would hurt. He said he'd never been so scared and worried in his life. He said he thought, at first, that I was going to die, and that he'd relived Sheila's death a million times over.

"What do you remember about what happened?" He was so close to my face that I could taste the coffee on his breath. I told him what I remembered. He asked me if I suspected anyone. I said, "No."

"Did you smell anything?" Luke's voice was so comforting. I remember I'd initially thought it might have been him, but I knew now that he could never hurt me, or anyone, for that matter. "I mean, did you recognize someone's odor or anything? Did he grunt or make any sounds that you remember? Try to think of any little thing, something you heard, or tasted, or smelled, or felt."

I concentrated and could remember some things: a strong body odor, like someone who hadn't taken a bath for a week. Cigarette breath. Grease. Diesel fuel. Beer. Grunts, like a hog being butchered. A wet, throaty laugh. I realized there had been two different laughs, one higher pitched. But I didn't tell Luke any of those things, I just held onto the thoughts and wondered whose penis had been inside me. I wanted to vomit when I thought about it.

Luke agreed to stay at my apartment Saturday evening to get some rest, and I thought about the rape all night. By Sunday morning, I was pretty sure I knew who did it. Luke was right: I had recognized some sounds and smells.

*

Dr. David let me go home Sunday afternoon, and Luke took me in his car, carried me up the stairs, and put me in my bed. He said he had washed the sheets after he'd slept on them. He spent the night in my study on the pullout sofa bed and left early the next morning to drive to Baton Rouge. Mama showed up as if by magic on Monday at noon and stayed until Wednesday when Tootsie came to replace her. She cleaned my apartment and stayed with me until Friday.

When Luke returned, I could hear him talking to Tootsie in the kitchen. I put on my robe and slippers and shuffled in. They both looked at me as though I were an apparition.

"See. I can take care of myself now. Y'all don't have to feel like I can't be left alone." I smiled, both my eyes were opened, although one was still pretty black and the other was turning yellow. Luke and Tootsie looked at each other with peculiar expressions. "Okay. What is it? Don't keep anything from me."

"Aren't you afraid the person who did this will come back?" Luke walked towards me and put his arm over my shoulder. He walked with me to the sofa and eased me down in a sitting position. "That's why we won't leave you alone."

"Oh. No, I hadn't thought of that." I believed that the person who beat me had accomplished what he'd set out to do, so why did he need to do it again?

After Tootsie left, I asked Luke about the hearing. It had been almost two weeks, but I hadn't thought much about the case since the beating.

"We got true bills on both defendants." He sat next to me on the sofa and held my hand. "First degree attempted murder and the other charges. We were afraid they would bring a lesser indictment on Rousseau, but they didn't."

"Has the judge set trial dates?"

"We got the dates today." He held my hand and turned towards me, with one leg bent on the sofa between us. "That's why I'm here early. I had to be in DeYoung's court this morning at ten."

Luke stayed over the weekend and bought take-out food for our meals. He walked into my bedroom with two mugs of coffee at about seven o'clock Monday morning, and I asked him why he wasn't in Baton Rouge, at work.

"I'm going to take you to Dr. Switzer to have your arm X-rayed, and I'm going to convince him to let me take you to New Orleans to stay at Susie's house." He asked me if he could help me get dressed, and when I shook my head 'No,' he laughed and left me in my room to dress and pack a bag.

Dr. David was amazed at how well I was healing. He looked at my X-ray, cut the cast off my arm, and replaced it with a removable splint that I could take off when I showered. "Only when you shower. Otherwise, wear it all the time, day and night. Dr. David agreed I could go to New Orleans. It seemed everyone was worried that the guys who'd accosted me would come back and finish me off.

I wasn't worried or afraid. I figured I had been warned and punished. They were done with me, unless I stirred up more trouble.

*

Luke took me to New Orleans Monday afternoon and drove back to Baton Rouge that evening. Susie and Marianne hovered over me. They worked out a schedule for the week: Susie would stay with me in the mornings, and Marianne would take off from her job early and care for me in the afternoons. I told them I didn't need all the attention. I could walk around, get myself coffee or tea, go to the bathroom. By Wednesday, they realized I was self-sufficient and went back to their regular routines of being gone all day: Susie with Rodney, Marianne at her job with the cardiologists. Susie came home for a couple of hours during the middle of the day and rested while Rodney was in therapy.

Thursday, Susie didn't come home for lunch. When Marianne came in at four o'clock, I asked whether she'd talked to Susie and she said she hadn't. She changed clothes and went to the hospital to make sure Susie was okay. I tried calling Rodney's room, but there was no answer. I called Luke twice to vent, and he was reassuring and said, "If you need me to come to New Orleans, say the word." Of course, I couldn't ask him to drive seventy miles simply because I was nervous.

I was pacing from the living room to the kitchen when Susie and Marianne came home after ten o'clock. Susie looked horrible. She'd been crying, her hair was in tangles, she limped; Marianne was holding her around the waist, and they crept across the floor.

"Oh my God! What happened?" I rushed to help Marianne get Susie to her bed. We pulled off her jeans and got a nightgown over her head.

"Donato gave her a sedative. She should drift off in a minute." Marianne pulled the covers up to Susie's chest and kissed her on the forehead. We backed out of the room as soon as we heard Susie's even breathing and knew she was asleep.

"Rodney had an accident. He's back in ICU." Marianne sat down hard at the kitchen table.

"Accident?" I got a bottle of wine and two glasses and put them on the table.

"I could use something stronger. Do we have any bourbon?" Marianne was pale, and her hands were shaking. I got the Jack Daniels from the cabinet, poured it over ice, then added some Coke.

"Okay, tell me what happened. From the beginning." I put the glass of bourbon in front of Marianne, and she took a long swallow of it.

"He was trying to use a walker. He fell and hit his head against the foot of his bed. He blacked out and couldn't be revived." Marianne took another swallow of her drink. "They worked on him for an hour. I called Donato myself.

"When I left the hospital, he was still out cold. Donato calls it a coma, and is staying with Rod all night. It's serious." Marianne finished her drink and said she really needed to go to bed. We went to our separate rooms, and I couldn't sleep. I thought about how to tell Lilly.

The next morning I called Luke and told him what happened,

then I called Brenda. She said she would go to Lilly's dorm that afternoon and tell her. I knew Brenda would handle things well and keep Lilly from total hysteria. Brenda said she would take Lilly back to her house for the rest of the week.

Marianne took a couple of days off from work because she said she needed to take care of Susie and me. She took Susie back and forth to the hospital to see Rodney for ten-minute visits, four times a day. She said Susie would hold his hand and talk to him as though he could understand everything she said. Dr. Warner said that there was swelling on Rodney's brain and that he would come out of his coma when the swelling receded—or not.

Lilly arrived Friday afternoon and went directly to the hospital with Susie. Marianne said she was going to have dinner with Dr. Warner, but would be in early. Luke surprised me when he arrived at about seven o'clock. I was alone and afraid to answer the door until I was sure it was him. Then I unbolted and unlocked it and threw myself into his arms before he could cross the threshold.

We sat on the sofa, and he rubbed my back. I felt sad for Rodney's setback, and for Susie and Lilly and their anguish. I felt sorry for myself, too; but I didn't admit it. Luke held me, my head on his chest, his arm over my shoulder, the other hand holding mine in his lap. I felt protected and cared for in a way I'd never felt in my life.

Marianne came home at about ten o'clock and Luke and I were sitting at the kitchen table eating ham sandwiches he'd pulled together when we realized we were famished.

"So this is the handsome prosecutor I've heard so much about. I'm Marianne." She stood with her hands on her hips, Dr. Warner standing behind her. "And this is Donato Warner."

"Lucas McMath." Luke stood and shook Marianne's hand, then Dr. Warner's. Marianne hugged him like a brother, and they both laughed. We all sat around the kitchen table, and Warner explained that Rodney was still in a coma, but he was showing signs of coming around.

"We'll have to start at ground zero when he wakes up." Warner seemed concerned and worried, which worried me.

Luke was going to drive home, but it was late, and Dr. Warner suggested that he had a guest room where Luke could stay. Come to find out, Warner lived only three blocks from the house on Jules Avenue. "Marianne won't stay at my house, yet. I think she's afraid of me." Warner reached over and squeezed Marianne's hand.

"No, I'm afraid of me." She laughed, and they looked at each other with something that resembled how Susie and Rodney looked at each other.

Susie and Lilly came home a few minutes later. I introduced Luke to Susie, and she excused herself, saying she was exhausted and needed to go to bed. Lilly followed her to the master bedroom after hugging Luke as though they were old friends.

By the end of the next week, I was feeling almost normal, except for the splint on my wrist. Luke called on Friday and asked whether I felt well enough to go out to dinner in New Orleans on Saturday night.

"Yes!" I shouted into the phone. "That's just what I need. This week has been grueling, but I feel fine; it's just all the stress surrounding Rodney's fall."

"How is Rodney?" The sound of Luke's voice calmed me.

"He came out of the coma yesterday. He recognized Susie and Lilly, but he can't speak at all. Susie said she'll have him talking again soon, and I don't doubt her."

"I know this is self-serving, but I hope he gets well enough to be at the trial next month. He's our star witness and without him…"

*

That night, Marianne didn't come home. When she stumbled in at around noon on Saturday, she looked as though she hadn't slept all night.

"What happened to you?" I took her hand and led her to the kitchen.

"Oh, Sissy. It's been a long night." She sat down heavily at the table. I went to the counter and started a pot of coffee. "Donato took me to his yacht club on Lake Pontchartrain. He actually has a cruiser, a thirty-six-foot sailboat with a couple of bedrooms below deck. We sat on the back deck, and I told him."

"Told him? What?" I put a cup of coffee in front of her and sat down.

"About being raped by those two white men with the Klan when I was twelve."

"Oh, God. Mari. What did he say?" I leaned forward so I could hear her because she was speaking in a whisper. "By the time I finished my story, he was on his knees in front of me holding my hands. He put his head on my lap and cried." She took a swig of her coffee. "After what seemed like a long time, he stood up and pulled me out of my chair. We stood on the deck of his boat wrapped in each others' arms, both crying.

"Finally I whispered into his ear, 'There's more,' and he pulled his head back to look at me. I told him that I'd dated women, that I hated men, especially white men, 'Like you,' I said. He stared at me as though I'd grown two heads and I knew the news about me being with women had finally turned him away, but you and Susie both told me I had to tell him the truth."

"Mari, I'm so sorry." I took one of her hands in both of mine and realized I hadn't taken a breath until that moment.

"He said, 'Mari, look at me.' He lifted my chin, and I met his eyes." Marianne put her mug down and looked at me for the first time. "I stared at him, unblinking. I figured I could take it, whatever criticism he had. I had prepared myself for that moment. Then he said, 'I wouldn't expect you to react any differently.' I was so shocked; I sat back down in the deck chair.

"'Aren't you repulsed?' I asked him. This is what he said: 'You were twelve years old.' He knelt in front of me on the deck and took both my hands in his. I looked him straight in the eye, and he said: 'White men did unspeakable things to you. Of course you should hate them and blame all white men for what they did. Of course when you wanted companionship, you felt more comfortable with women.' I started to cry and couldn't stop. I was heaving, shaking. He pulled me out of my chair and held me.

"I was hysterical. I couldn't control all the grief that had built up inside of me for twenty years."

Marianne and I sat in silence, both absorbing her story. I was proud of her for being honest, and I was equally shocked that Dr. Warner proved he was a man of character. I had him pegged as a player. She told me that he took her to his house and put her to bed in his guest room, and that he'd been the perfect gentleman.

*

The next night, Luke took me to dinner at K-Paul's on Chartres Street in the French Quarter, which was owned by Paul Prudhomme, the famous French and Creole chef who invented blackened dishes. After dinner we walked down to Jackson Square, where Luke talked me into letting an artist sketch me.

When I asked him whether the detectives on Rodney's case had talked to ex-Sheriff Guidry, Luke said he had given Guidry's name to Detective Schiller but didn't know whether he had spoken to the former sheriff.

"Should we talk to anyone else?" Luke squeezed my hand while we walked from Jackson Square to the bar at the Royal Orleans Hotel. "I mean, do Thevenot and Rousseau have any friends who are high up either in politics or finance?" He squeezed my hand while we walked.

"I wouldn't know." I thought about seeing Thevenot and Rousseau at James's house, but I didn't think they were friends. "It's just that Rousseau was one of Guidry's deputies, and when Desiré was elected, Rousseau quit his job, and I think he went to work for Guidry, who has a plumbing business."

I asked Luke about Thevenot's trial, which would be held in a few weeks. Luke said that the prosecution really needed Rodney's eye-witness testimony or Thevenot might get off Scot-free.

He took me back to Susie's house at about ten o'clock and said he was driving back to Baton Rouge. We'd had several drinks, and I didn't think it was a good idea for him to drive to Baton Rouge, so I persuaded him to stay over, and I put him in Marianne's room since she said she would be staying at Don Warner's house that night.

Susie and Lilly were asleep when we crept into the house, and I showed him to Marianne's room, which had its own bathroom and a queen size bed. I shared a bedroom with Lilly, but she slept with Susie, so I had the room to myself. Luke brought his gym bag into the house, and I shut him up in Marianne's room. I wrote a note to the girls that said a man was sleeping in that room and taped it to the outside of Marianne's bedroom door.

*

I slipped into a pair of shorts and a T-shirt and stumbled into the kitchen the next morning. Luke was sitting at the table with Susie and Lilly, and they were laughing and drinking coffee and juice. I filled a mug with coffee and sat in the only available chair, across from Luke, between Susie and Lilly.

"What's so funny this early in the morning?" I took a sip of coffee and burned my lip. "Ouch. It's hot."

"Well, sunshine." Susie teased me in the mornings because it took me a while to wake up. "You are your regular morning bundle of joy, aren't you?"

"Don't tell Luke. Maybe he won't notice." I took another sip of coffee and grinned at him over the top of my cup.

"You are ravishing this morning." He winked at me and smiled.

"How do you start the day so chipper?" I put my cup down and my chin in my hand, elbow on the table.

"A hundred sit-ups and fifty push-ups." He bent his arms to show his biceps, like Popeye the Sailor Man." We all laughed. "Then a pot of coffee and a two-mile run."

"No. You're pulling my leg." I sat up straight and put both my hands around my mug.

"Maybe just a little. I did go for a run this morning, then took a shower." He got up and went to the counter to refill his cup. "Anyone need a refill?"

I put my mug in the air but didn't look at him. Everyone laughed at me.

"She'll be fine in about an hour." Susie poked me in the ribs. "By the way, Sissy, where'd you find this dreamboat?"

"Don't give him a big head." I watched him fill my mug, and he poked out his bottom lip as though I'd hurt his feelings.

"Do you want to have lunch before I head back to Baton Rouge?" He winked at me.

"I usually go to Mass at St. Agnes at eleven." I looked at Susie and Lilly. "Did y'all go yesterday afternoon?"

"Yep. We went to the four o'clock vigil so we could spend the day with Rodney today." Susie stood up slowly, and I could tell she was still in pain. "We're heading to the hospital in a few minutes."

"I thought you could only see him ten minutes at a time." I tried to wake myself up so I could understand the confusion around me.

"Dr. Warner moved Rodney to the Neurology floor yesterday." Susie pushed her chair from the table and stood up.

"Wow, that's good news. He must be doing better." I swallowed as much coffee as would fit in my mouth, and grinned.

"Yep, now we can get back to therapy. We need to have him talking in the next few weeks so he can testify at the trial."

"Do you think that's possible?" Luke leaned against the counter and looked at Susie.

"It's a long shot, but we're going to work hard to make it happen." Susie and Lilly hugged Luke, kissed me on the cheek, and left for the hospital.

"Do you want to go to Mass with me, Luke?" I looked at him as he leaned against the counter, looking sexy as hell. "We can grab lunch afterwards."

"I guess you could drag me back to church. I've been lax ever since..." He dropped his guard for a split second, then recovered. I figured it had something to do with Sheila. "Well, sure. It would do me some good."

We went to St. Agnes Catholic Church, which was just a few blocks up Jefferson Highway from Ochsner Medical Center. We had lunch at Jefferson Seafood Shack and sat around drinking iced tea and laughing until almost three o'clock. Luke drove me back to Susie's house, and we went inside. I stood in the living room and waited while he got his leather bag from Marianne's room.

We stood next to his car, and he kissed me so passionately, it left me out of breath. I stared at his license plate. The number was 36H989, easy: 36—one year younger than James; H—for Heart, mine—the one beating so hard it felt as though it would burst from my chest; 9—the last number before10; 89—the last two numbers before 10. I had it memorized before the taillights on his Beemer were out of sight.

Part 2

The Fallout

⌒ Chapter Twelve ⌒

 ⌒

Jury Selection

1985

THE HOUSE IN BATON Rouge was perfect. It was located in a residential neighborhood off Lee Drive near Robert E. Lee High School. Luke's house was about eight blocks away and had the same floor plan, but after I took Susie to see the house, she gave me a credit card and a list of things she wanted to have done to make it more comfortable. When I told the property owner all the things I wanted to do to the house, he thought I expected him to pay for the renovations, so he suggested we buy it. Susie agreed, and she returned to Baton Rouge in the middle of January to sign the papers.

It was a busy spring.

Luke filed several motions, and the judge heard arguments as to why The State should be allowed to present evidence that the defendant, Thevenot, had a history of tormenting and attacking black folks. I went to the hearing and listened as Luke argued that the behavior showed a pattern which was consistent with the shooting at the church. John Perkins, Thevenot's attorney, argued that past acts were not relevant and would sway the jury against his client. In the end, the judge decided to allow the testimony by people who were actual victims of Thevenot's abuse, "within reason," something the judge referred to as, "other crimes evidence."

Lilly had a full load of classes and studied when she wasn't with

Bobby, who'd become a fixture around our house. The Baton Rouge house was larger than the one in New Orleans: four bedrooms, three baths and a powder room, and a large kitchen with separate dining and living rooms.

Carpenters arrived and took down the walls separating the kitchen, dining, and living rooms, making it one huge, open space. The kitchen was across the back of the house with an island that partially separated it from the living and dining areas. Two of the bedrooms were fine for guests, but we replaced the paneling with sheetrock in the master and Lilly's bedroom. Susie said we'd do the other two rooms later. All of the bathrooms needed new fixtures, and Susie wanted new appliances and plumbing fixtures in the kitchen. We added French doors off the master, the kitchen, and Lilly's room onto the back porch that spanned the entire rear of the house. In front, we rebuilt a long porch with columns. We had everything painted, inside and out.

It was a major overhaul, but when it was done, it was beautiful, spacious, and comfortable; similar to the house Susie had renovated on Gravier Road in Jean Ville.

*

We had a housewarming party the last weekend in March. Marianne and Dr. Warner brought Susie and Rodney, who had been released to Outpatient Rehab. Rodney was in good humor, but still in a wheelchair and could he only say a few words. Susie was back to her old, spunky self, which made us all happy. Lilly invited Bobby and Jessie, I invited Robert and Brenda, and Susie invited Governor Breaux and First Lady, Nikole.

The afternoon of the party, a moving truck pulled up in front of the house, and several men unloaded a baby grand piano that they set it in the front corner of the living room, facing the dining and kitchen areas. I was stymied and asked the men where it came from, just as Susie and Rodney arrived and told me it was a gift from them for my sleuthing work. They laughed at their explanation, but I was so enamored with the black, ebony piano that I had to put my hands on the keys. I sat and played all my favorite pieces until Luke arrived, and everyone agreed I should stop playing and start helping get ready for the party.

After everyone arrived and had eaten, I sat in a chair in the corner of the living room and watched Luke move through the crowd with ease. Every now and then he'd wink at me or come by and squeeze my hand. I didn't know how I felt about him, yet. I hadn't had time to think about Luke as a partner or boyfriend; he was just someone who was always around and made me feel safe. I didn't tell anyone about the horrible nightmares I was having, where ugly, dirty men broke into my bedroom and did unspeakable things to me. I'd wake up in a sweat, shaking and crying. I don't think I realized it at the time, but I was too traumatized by what had happened to me to consider a relationship that might include intimacy.

Luke and I were both busy that spring, and he spent more time in Jean Ville than I did because he was often in court for motions, hearings, and orders. He filed for a trial continuance to give Rodney time to recuperate further. Luke said Rodney's testimony was vital to the case and that Rod needed to be able to speak clearly enough to be understood by the jurors.

I worried that my apartment in Jean Ville would be vandalized by whoever had beat me up, so I asked Luke to stay there when he was in town and gave him a key.

The trial was set for June 12, and could no longer be delayed. The timing was perfect for me because Lilly could go to New Orleans during the week and I could stay in Jean Ville. I wanted to attend every day of the trial—from jury selection, to witness interrogation, to the verdict.

Lilly went to Bobby's senior prom and had a date with him graduation night. She floated on a cloud all through May, and I wondered whether she would pass her finals, but she finished her first year at LSU with good grades and registered for her second year. She wasn't happy about spending the summer in New Orleans away from Bobby, but our compromise was that I would meet her in Baton Rouge every Friday evening and stay with her on weekends so she could see him. That seemed the perfect solution because she could be with her parents during the week and with Bobby, Jessie, and their family on the weekends.

It worked for me, too. During the trial and for weeks prior, Luke stayed with me in Jean Ville, sleeping in the study at my apartment during the week. He worked late most weeknights, often until after nine o'clock, so I'd have a TV dinner and was usually in bed when he got in. Sometimes we had coffee together in the mornings, but mostly he was gone by the time I was up.

*

I sat in the gallery behind the long wooden table where Luke's team was positioned. A wood-spindled partition separated me and the other spectators in the gallery from the courtroom. There was a swinging gate in the center of the railing and on the right side of the gate was the defense table, identical to the prosecution's. Thevenot sat between his two attorneys, and most of his family sat on the pew behind the partition.

The jury box was perpendicular to Luke's table, facing the judge, who sat on a raised platform behind a high desk called, "the bench," set at an angle in the front corner of the courtroom.

The first week was all about jury selection, and the gallery was filled with reporters, family members, friends, and curiosity seekers. The lawyers on both sides asked potential jurors questions to weed out those who might already have their minds made up or be prejudiced in one way or another.

A young black woman got on the witness stand and answered the basic questions clearly and with astute understanding. When Luke asked her whether she'd read any of the news articles about the case, she said, "Yes. And I think he's guilty as sin!" She was excused.

A white woman dressed in jeans and a tight, pink T-shirt with silver, glittered writing that said, "I'm all yours," took the stand and said it didn't matter who did it because, "It was just a black man who got shot." Excused.

A white man from the north side of Toussaint Parish said he knew Thevenot and had hunted with him in the past. Luke asked the potential juror if they had hunted animals or humans. "Both," the man said. Excused.

A well dressed black man with a shaved head, a starched oxford shirt, and khaki slacks who identified himself as Larry Smith said he'd heard someone shot "a brother," on his wedding day. "Whoever would do something like that should be hung." He scratched his slick head and ran his hand down his forehead to his chin. "Man, I'd like to get my hands on whoever did that." Excused.

Several potential jurors knew the defendant. Some were hunting buddies. Some went to high school with Thevenot. When those guys were asked about Thevenot's character, one of them said, "Questionable," another said, "Renegade," a third one said, "He's a badass, that's for sure."

*

By the end of the first day, only two jurors had made the cut. Judge DeYoung was frustrated by the attorneys' questions, which he said were more geared towards exclusion than selection. During a bench conference, Judge DeYoung emphatically told the attorneys that a jury would be selected even if a "tales" or emergency jury call would have to be issued. Neither attorney was interested in that plan, which would call for emergency notices to be delivered to people in the middle of the night or early in the morning, requiring them to appear at the courthouse to be questioned. For the next few days, the lawyers tried to overlook some of the obvious signs of prejudice in order to seat jurors.

On day two, a woman who was recently married was chosen, even though she said she couldn't imagine how she'd feel if her husband had been shot when they walked out of the church on their wedding day. She stared at Thevenot with a look that could kill, but, in the end, she convinced the defense attorneys she would keep an open mind.

An older man who walked with a limp and said he was a Vietnam veteran took the stand. His stated that his name as Nathan Moore, he was from Oregon, and had moved to Toussaint Parish two years before because he was tired of rain.

"There was a hurricane the first week I moved here. It rained for days, maybe weeks. I wanted to go back to Oregon, but I couldn't afford the trip." He stared at Luke without blinking.

"Do you know the defendant?" Luke asked.

"No, sir. Never saw him in my life." The man shifted in the witness chair.

"Do you have an opinion about whether he's guilty or innocent?"

"Of what?"

"Of shooting Rodney Thibault. Almost killing him."

"Why'd he do that?"

"That's the sixty-four million dollar question." Luke made a note on his legal pad that sat on the podium in the middle of the courtroom.

"He got paid to do it?"

"No, sir. I'm sorry. That was a euphemism."

"He's a foreigner?"

"No, sir." Luke tried not to laugh, but everyone in the gallery had broken the silence. The judge banged his gavel and said he'd throw the entire gallery out if we erupted again. After that, I couldn't control my giggles and used a Kleenex to cover my mouth.

Mr. Moore was accepted. By Tuesday afternoon, a total of five jurors had been seated.

*

Luke came to my apartment at about eight o'clock that night. I didn't expect him until later and was watching TV in my pajamas, which consisted of sleeping shorts and a cut-off T-shirt.

"What are you doing here?" I crossed my arms over my chest to hide my untethered breasts.

"Damn. You are the sexiest thing I've ever seen." He smiled at me from the doorway.

"Luke. Don't embarrass me. Turn your head so I can go into my bedroom and get decent." I drew my knees up under my chin and wrapped my arms around my legs. I saw his eyes wander to the tops of my thighs where my shorts rode up. I put my legs down with a jerk, and my breasts bounced. I covered them again. "Please, Luke."

He turned around slowly, still holding his briefcase, his tie loosened and the top button of his shirt undone. When I returned to the living room in my terry cloth robe, he was rooting around in the fridge.

"Are you hungry? I have TV dinners." I walked up behind him, and the timing worked out that when he turned around his face was a smidgen away from mine. I could smell the chewing gum his breath: spearmint. He was still bent forward, which made us eye-level. At first, we just stared at each other, his blue eyes twinkling, dots of lime green flickering just inside the whites. It was a moment, and I was a deer in the headlights. Something washed over me in that brief connection, and I burst out crying. He wrapped his arms around me and steered me to the sofa.

I cried for a long time while he held me. I tried to work through the pent-up feelings that made me have such a breakdown. I pictured Warren, the beating, the bloody pillowcase, the burning pain between my legs, the IVs and catheters, the stitches and casts, Luke's face that morning, the red truck, the note on my windshield that said *Stay out of this investigation or you'll end up like your sister,* my doubts and suspicions, my guilt and disgust. When I finally stopped crying, I asked him if he'd like a drink.

"I need one. You?" He got up and went to the kitchen, turned on the oven, poured a couple inches of Crown Royal over ice, and brought me a glass of wine. "You want to tell me about these tears?"

"I think I'm having a delayed reaction." I was still sniffling. I put the glass of wine on the coffee table.

"I wondered when it would hit you. You breezed through the emotional part way too quickly, as though it never happened." He took a long sip of his whiskey and put his glass on the table. He wrapped both of his arms around me and pulled me close to him, my head on his chest where I could hear the thump, thump, thump of his heart.

"I suspected you," I whispered it.

"You what? Me?" He pulled back so he could look at me but didn't take his arms away. I folded my arms over my breasts and drew my knees up.

"I'm sorry. I couldn't imagine who would have done that to me. I didn't know you very well at the time." I whimpered and curled into a ball.

"Sissy. I'm so sorry. I had no idea you were afraid of me." He sat next to me. I was rolled up, and put my head on his thigh.

"I know now," I whimpered, and sniffled so much I didn't know if he heard me. He let go of me and knelt on the floor in front of the sofa so we were eye-level. By this time, I was in a fetal position.

"You don't have to move, but please open your eyes." He put his hand under my chin. I opened my eyes and stared at him through the teary glare. "Tell me you know it wasn't me."

"I know." I sniffled. I thought about how he had been with me almost every day since the incident, which I referred to as "the break-in," because I couldn't say words that were so much bigger.

I thought about how Luke had never tried to touch me inappropriately, never tried to sleep with me. But he'd taken care of me, protected me, made me feel safe. He didn't push me to come to grips with my fears; he let me do it in my own time.

"It couldn't be you, Luke. I know that now, but, I didn't know then…" For the first time, I knew in my soul that he didn't do it. All those months I'd wondered. But I'd come to know him, and something in my instinct knew he would never hurt me.

"I understand, baby. You have every right to wonder, to be afraid." He was sitting on the floor, his chin on the sofa, his face so close to mine I tasted bourbon in his exhales.

"I'm not afraid of you, Luke." My eyes felt as big as oranges, and they were so full of tears, it was like opening them underwater in a swimming pool.

"I'm glad, baby. You should never be afraid of me. I want to take care of you." He kissed my cheek, then each of my eyes, then my mouth, gently. He took his handkerchief out of his back pocket, and dabbed at my tears, then wiped my chin where they had accumulated. "Who are you afraid of?"

"I'm not sure, but the list has dwindled down to only a few." I loosened the grip on my legs and stretched out some, my knees still bent, but no longer under my chin.

"A few? I mean more than one person could despise you that much? Who, baby? Who do you think did it?" he whispered and planted several little kisses on my cheeks.

"I can't say. Not yet." I started to sit up, and he helped me, then handed me my glass of wine and took a long slug of his drink.

"Okay. I'm in no hurry. You can tell me your suspicions when you're ready." He got off the floor and sat on the sofa, his legs stretched out in front of him, holding his drink in both hands. I sat up slowly, drank some wine, and put my head on his shoulder.

"Luke?"

"Yes, sweetie."

"Why are you calling me baby and sweetie?"

"Is that what you wanted to ask me?"

"No." I giggled, and he laughed.

"That's my girl. What, then?"

"Could you sleep with me, but that's all?" I whispered into his shoulder, and I felt his chest lift and recede as though laughing at me.

"Are you asking whether I can hold you all night and not try to have sex with you?" He laughed aloud now.

"Don't laugh at me." I started to giggle, but I didn't want to. I wanted to be serious. "Yes. That's what I'm asking."

He sat up straight, put his drink on the coffee table, leaned forward with his elbows on his knees, his hands folded together between his legs, and was very still. He remained in that position for what seemed a long time. I was afraid I'd said something wrong, and I held my breath. Finally, he stood up and looked down at me with the most tender expression.

"I've known you since September. This is almost July. What's that? Ten months, almost a year. Right?" He leaned towards me, his hands on either side of my face, his mouth close to mine.

"I guess so." I was feeling more relaxed and loosened the grip around my knees.

"Have I ever tried anything?"

"No."

"It's not that I haven't wanted to. I'm crazy about you, and you turn me on like—well, I can't describe it, but trust me. I'm attracted to you." He smiled at me, and I felt such affection for this man that I thought my heart might burst. "But you've needed space and time after what happened."

"How did you know? I didn't even know." I put my legs down, my feet on the floor, an actual sitting position. His face was very close to mine.

"You changed." He didn't blink or look away.

"How?"

"More serious." He knelt on the floor and put his hands on my knees. "Sometimes your mind was a million miles away. You haven't played the piano, you don't break out and sing along with the radio, you stare into space often."

"Oh. I didn't know." I felt my brow wrinkle. Why had he stuck with me, even when I shut down?

"I've been afraid to leave you alone in your apartment." He took both my hands in his. "I think I've felt your fear along with you."

212

"How can you be so patient? I might have given up on you."

"You're worth it."

"How do you know?"

"I know." He kissed me on the cheek and stood up. He stared at me a few seconds then went to the kitchen and took his TV dinner out of the oven. He sat at the island with a glass of milk and his Salisbury steak. I watched him for the longest time, then I got up and walked up behind him and put my arms around his waist. He lowered his chin, and I could feel him shiver, like he was crying. I put my face against his back and cried with him.

*

Day three of jury selection was a red-letter day.

A man in a Superman hoodie sat in the witness chair. The judge said men were not allowed to cover their heads in the courtroom. His bald head shined under the lights when he pushed the hood to the back of his sweatshirt. He said his name was Joe Bourbon. "Like the whiskey." He said he didn't drink, though, because he was a pastor. He had a church called the Sovereign Independent Church of Souls of the Lord. The judge asked him whether it was a particular denomination and he said, "No, sir. It's Baptist."

I looked at the lady sitting next to me, and she lifted her black eyebrows that were dyed as dark as her cotton candy hair, like shoe polish, and frizzy. It was all I could do to control myself.

"Do you know the defendant?" Luke asked Mr. Bourbon.

"He's never been to my church, sir." Bourbon looked directly at Luke, never even glanced at Thevenot.

"Please look at the defendant. He's the one sitting in the middle of that table, the one who isn't wearing a suit. Have you ever seen him?"

"Not in my church, no." Bourbon looked at Thevenot then back at Luke.

"Mr. Bourbon. Try to focus. Have you ever seen this man anywhere? In the grocery store? At the movie theatre? At a friend's house? At a bar?"

"I told you I don't drink."

"Mr. Bourbon, please answer the question."

"What's the question?"

"Have you ever seen this man?" Luke walked over to the defense table and pointed at Thevenot. Perkins, the defense lawyer, stood up and objected. The judge asked the lawyers to approach the bench. Four men in suits leaned over the DeYoung's desk, their arms folded on top of it, and listened to the judge, who spoke softly so the jury couldn't hear him. The lawyers went back to their tables, except for Luke, who returned to the podium in the middle of the courtroom. I stared at his back as he faced Mr. Bourbon on the witness stand.

"I have no more questions for the prospective juror." Luke sat down.

John Perkins, the lawyer from James's firm who represented Thevenot, went to the podium. He faced Mr. Bourbon, who sat on the stand in his sweatshirt with a picture of Superman plastered across the front, the hood hanging down his back, his bald head shiny and slick.

"Mr. Bourbon, do you know Mr. Thevenot, the defendant?"

"I'm not sure. He looks familiar." He glanced at Thevenot then at the judge. "Hard to say, Judge." He looked back at Perkins.

"What would it take for you to know for sure?"

"I don't know. Maybe I seen him somewhere before. Maybe not."

"Let's just say you know Mr. Thevenot." Perkins paused and looked at Thevenot, then back at Bourbon. "What is your opinion of him?"

"Seems okay to me." Bourbon licked his lips and stared at Perkins.

"Do you think he could have shot a man in cold blood?" Perkins put his hands behind his back. He was holding a Fanta orange soda.

"Oh, no. I don't think he could do that. Not a white man, at least." Perkins froze, then looked at the judge who shrugged as if to say, "You asked the question."

"Okay. Do you think he could shoot a black man?"

"You mean a nigger? Sure, Thevenot could shoot a nigger, but I don't think he could shoot a white man." Bourbon licked his lips again.

Luke jumped up. "Your Honor, I move that this juror be dismissed."

"We accept this juror, Your Honor." Perkins looked at Luke then back at the judge.

"You have one more peremptory challenge remaining, Mr. McMath. Do you want to use it now?" Judge DeYoung looked at Luke, then turned his glare towards Perkins as though he wanted to hit him. Everyone knew Perkins wanted as many prejudiced jurors as he could seat. The defense and the prosecution each had twelve peremptory challenges. If Luke used his last one on Mr. Bourbon, the Defense could railroad another six prejudiced jurors onto the panel.

"May I have a few minutes to confer with my team, Judge?"

"I'll call a ten-minute recess." The judge banged his gavel and walked out the private door behind the bench. Luke sat at the prosecution's table with his head bent towards the others, who were in a semicircle.

The Judge returned in precisely ten minutes.

"You decision, Mr. McMath?" The Judge sat in his tall, leather chair and addressed the defense table. Luke stood up behind his table.

"We accept Mr. Bourbon, Your Honor." Luke sat down. There was a collective gasp from the gallery, and the Judge banged his gavel but didn't speak. Everyone shifted around, looking at each other, eyebrows lifted, then we all tried to settle down. Mr. Bourbon went to sit in the jury box with the other five jurors.

One additional juror was selected by the end of the day on Wednesday, a total of seven.

When the judge adjourned at five thirty, Luke turned around and motioned for me to wait a few minutes. The courtroom cleared out, except for the lawyers. Thevenot left with his parents, following them through the door to the hallway. I sat with my purse on my lap, and

Luke came through the gate and sat next to me.

"I'm going across the street to Charlie's Cafe with my team." He patted my knee then pulled his hand away as though he was afraid someone would see him being affectionate with me. "We are going to meet for about an hour. Would you wait to have dinner with me?"

"Sure. Are we going out or eating in?" I tilted my head and tried to look at him sideways because he was sitting next to me, and it was hard to look him in the eye.

"I'll bring something from Charlie's." He patted me again then went back to his table.

*

I stopped by my dad's house on my way home. James's car was in the driveway. I walked up the steps onto the front porch where they sat in rockers facing the street. I kissed Daddy on the top of his head and James on the cheek, and I sat on the swing.

"What are you guys talking about?" I noticed that James had a beer, and Daddy was drinking something that looked like lemonade. He was under doctor's orders not to drink alcohol because he had cirrhosis and had almost died. He was back on his feet after years of recovery and hadn't worked as a CPA since I was fifteen.

"Just shooting the breeze." James took a long swig of beer.

"Oh. I was wondering whether you've heard whether the investigators have turned up anything related to what happened to me." I pushed myself gently on the swing and looked directly at James.

"How would I know that?" His voice sounded gruff.

"Because you're my brother, and you're a lawyer, and you see Reggie Borders every day, and you should want to find out who did such horrible things to me." I took a deep breath and let it out slowly.

"Borders told me you refused to give the investigators any leads." He stood up to leave.

"What kind of leads would I have?" I got off the swing and faced him. Daddy was between us sitting in his rocker. "My head was in a pillowcase. My hands were tied behind my back. I don't know if it was a man, woman, or beast; I'm not sure whether I was beaten with a bat, a fist, or a shovel."

"Well, if you can't help the investigators, how do you expect them to find the guys?" He squeezed his empty can until it caved in at the center, then he bent it in half. The sound of crushed aluminum pierced the air and made me angry.

"Surely they found fingerprints or hair samples or something." I took a step in front of Daddy's chair, so I could be closer to James.

"Why don't you talk to Borders yourself?" He turned and walked towards the door to the house. "It's not my case. Maybe you should get a lawyer." He slammed the door when he went through it.

"You'd think my brother would be more sympathetic about what happened to me." I sat back on the swing and looked at Daddy.

"James has a lot on his mind." Daddy looked straight ahead and rocked hard in his chair. "Give him a break."

"What kinds of things does James have on his mind?" I raised my voice. I felt angry and confused.

"You'll have to ask him." Daddy kept rocking, and I knew our conversation was going nowhere, so I walked down the front steps and never said goodbye.

*

I went to the store and bought some candles, a nice bottle of red wine, and canapés. When I got home, I inserted a tape of classical music in my stereo and set the candles out: two on the island, one on the coffee table, and one on the piano. I turned on two lamps and waited to light the candles just before seven o'clock.

I'd gotten a couple of Sam Massey's sons to move the upright Steinway my dad had bought me when I was six from his house to my apartment. I sat at the keyboard for the first time since the beating on October 30 and played Fur Elise, my dad's favorite. Then I played my own favorite, *The Emperor's Concerto* by Beethoven, sometimes referred to as, *Emperor,* that I had played for my recital the end of my freshman year at Centenary College.

I felt tears stream down my cheeks as I leaned into the piano and played the riffs, then the opening cords. I could almost hear the violins in the background as I played forte for the first half of the piece, then softened to mezzo forte, then back to forte, almost banging the keys as though they made me angry. After the first half, I started to slip into pianissimo. The quieter the music sounded, the more I cried. I was playing so softly that I barely touched the keys. My eyes were closed, and I thought about the previous night.

*

Luke had spooned me in my bed. He'd worn gym shorts and a T-shirt, and I'd slept like a baby for the first time in months. He slipped out of bed early, and I turned over and snuggled in the warmth he left on the sheets, inhaling his scent, so masculine, so Luke. I could hear him in the kitchen, then in the bathroom, and I continued to savor the incredible feeling of peace and serenity. I tried to remember how long it had been since I'd awakened without first thinking of the beating and expecting the villain to be standing over my bed with a pillowcase and a rope.

Luke came back into the bedroom in his suit slacks and dress shirt. I smelled coffee and opened my eyes to see him standing next to the bed with two steaming mugs. He sat on the side of the bed and put one cup on the bedside table. I stretched and sat up.

"I showered and dressed. I was afraid if I didn't, I'd crawl back into bed with you." He ran his hand through my tangled hair.

"Hmm. Is that coffee?" I yawned.

"Yep."

"Coffee in bed. You could spoil me."

"I hope so." He kissed me on the forehead, took a sip of his coffee, then handed the other mug to me. He'd stroked my cheek, kissed my forehead again, and left for the courthouse. I sat up in the bed, drank my coffee, and tried to keep feeling that feeling.

*

My mind returned to the present, and I finished playing *Emperor* and left my fingers on the keys, my head bent, tears falling freely on the tops of my hands. When I opened my eyes, Luke was standing with his hands on the back of the piano, tears streaming down his cheeks. We stared at each other through what looked like raindrops.

"You didn't give me time to light the candles," I whispered, lifted my hands off the keyboard, and put them in my lap, as though I'd just completed a performance.

"Don't need them. You light up the room." He leaned on the back of the piano.

"How long have you been here?" I felt vulnerable and didn't like being out of control.

"Long enough to hear your soul sing through this piano." He smiled at me, and I blushed.

"I was thinking about us. About last night." I felt the heat rise from my chest to my neck, and my cheeks began to burn.

"I love it when you blush." He stared at me with a huge smile across his face, the dimple in his cheek sunk in so deep I wanted to put my finger in it to see if it ended somewhere. "And I loved sleeping with you."

"Me, too. I slept like a baby." I took a deep breath and considered whether I should complete my sentence. "And I didn't wake up feeling afraid."

"I'm glad." He didn't move, nor did I. We were both afraid to break the spell. There was a special aura around us, like angels singing softly and a cool breeze blowing rose scents through the air. I wanted to ask him about his day. I wanted to tell him about my visit with Daddy. I wanted to get up and light the candles, and open the wine and set the table, but I sat there and basked in whatever I was feeling that I didn't want to go away.

*

Day four of jury selection was productive, and everyone was hopeful there would be a full jury by Friday afternoon.

A beautiful black woman, about Tootsie's age, sat in the witness chair wearing a black, silk dress with a red blazer and three-inch red heels. Her hair was cut in a bob just below her ears, and I was sure it was a wig because it was smooth and an auburn color. She crossed her legs and let her red shoe bob up and down while she waited for Luke to begin questioning her.

"Good morning, Mrs. Jones." Luke placed his legal pad on the podium and leaned forward, one hand on either edge.

"Good morning." Mrs. Jones smiled and looked directly at Luke. He asked her the basic questions, then asked about her occupation, and she said she worked in the lunchroom at Jean Ville High School.

"How long have you worked there?" Luke's shoulders lifted, and I recognized it as a sign that a light went on in his brain.

"Twenty-four years." She nodded as though she were agreeing with herself.

"Do you recognize Mr. Thevenot?"

"Yes, sir. He was a student at the high school some years back. He looks much older now." She looked at Thevenot and grinned.

"Have you ever had a conversation with Mr. Thevenot?" Luke walked to the side of the podium and stood between it and the jury box. All seven of the jurors had their eyes glued to Mrs. Jones.

"No sir, I never spoke to him, not once." She shook her head to emphasize "No."

"Thank you, Mrs. Jones." Luke picked up his pad and returned to his table.

I noticed Thevenot and Perkins had their heads together. Perkins walked to the podium. He had a plastic bottle of Dr. Pepper in one hand and put it on the platform. Judge DeYoung frowned at Perkins and eyed the soda. Perkins removed it from the rostrum and held it behind his back in both hands.

"Mrs. Jones," Perkins's back was to the gallery, but I could tell he was feeling cocky by the swagger he used when he strolled to the jury box and leaned against it with one hip stuck out. "Has Mr. Thevenot ever spoken to you?"

"Oh, yes, sir. A number of times." Mrs. Jones uncrossed her legs and put both her spike heels on the platform in front of her.

"What did he say?" Perkins took a couple of steps towards the witness box, and DeYoung glared at him as though there was an imaginary line Perkins might cross.

"He said lots of things when he come through the line to get his food." She leaned forward and put both her hands on the railing in front of her.

"Like what?" Perkins looked at the judge, who gave him the evil eye.

"He'd say, 'Give me some of that, nigga,' or 'Don't touch my food, mammy.' Or 'Why they let a nigga-woman like you serve me?' Stuff like that." She glared at Thevenot while she spoke.

"How did that make you feel?" Perkins saw DeYoung's evil-eye and stepped back a few feet.

"I just prayed for his soul. That's how it made me feel. Like praying for his soul." She sat back in her chair abruptly and folded her arms across her chest, like she was done.

"The defense rejects this witness, your honor." Perkins backed up to the podium, holding his Dr. Pepper behind his back with both hands.

"Are you sure, Mr. Perkins? This will be your final peremptory." DeYoung looked down and wrote something on a pad.

"I thought that was number eleven, Your Honor." Perkins turned around and lifted his shoulders. His law partner turned pages on his legal pad.

"We'll recess for ten minutes to give you time to recount." The judge banged his gavel and left through the back door. When he returned, the defense decided to accept Mrs. Jones, and she sat with the other seven jurors. By the end of Thursday, there were eleven jurors, several should have been rejected, but the attorneys each had one peremptory challenge which they were saving for the extreme person who might sneak onto the jury.

Judge DeYoung reiterated that the attorneys needed to choose one more juror and two alternate jurors the next day, then he adjourned. It was six o'clock.

*

Luke got to my apartment at seven thirty. I'd had time to light the candles, open the bottle of red wine, and marinate the steaks. The potatoes were in the oven and the salad made. I sat at the piano to play. When he walked in, I was playing *My Girl*. He grinned at me, put his briefcase on the bar, took his coat off, hung it on the back of a bar stool, and came to sit next to me on the piano bench. I finished the piece and took my hands off the keys.

"You're coming back." He said it softly and took one of my hands in his.

"I hope so." I squeezed his hand and turned towards him. "Want a drink? You deserve one. Long, hard day."

"Yes. Jury selection is always hard, but I can't remember it ever being this difficult." He kissed me on the cheek, stood, and pulled me up.

"You've never selected a jury in Toussaint Parish. It's a foreign country." I faced him and noticed how tired he looked.

"You mean like a euphemism?" He laughed and the bottom of his eyes lifted, making them look like a bird's wings.

"That was hilarious!"

"That's what I mean by it being so much more difficult." He took my hand and walked me to the island where he poured red wine into the two glasses next to the bottle. "It smells good in here."

"A mixture of baked potatoes and scented candles." I took a sip of wine and smiled at him over my glass.

"You're too much." He pushed the cassette tape into the stereo, and we sat on the sofa for a while and enjoyed our wine.

"You want to grill the steaks or do you want me to cook them on the stove?"

"I'll grill." He got up and walked out on the deck to light the coals. I took the steaks out of the marinade and put them on a platter, then put the bread in the oven with the potatoes. After dinner, we cleaned up and finished the bottle of wine.

"Can I sleep with you again?" He stood at the sink with a dishtowel in his hands.

"Can you keep your hands off me again?" I was wiping off the countertops and turned to look at him.

"Do you want me to?" He looked hopeful.

"I'm still not ready, Luke. I'm sorry." I felt like something was wrong with me. Why didn't I want this gorgeous, smart, devoted guy to kiss me and make love to me?

"Will you ever be? Ready, I mean?" He stood a few feet away from me and didn't attempt to get closer.

"I don't know." I could tell the energy in the room had changed. He was asking me to commit, something I wasn't ready to do.

"After almost a year and you still don't know?" Lines deepened on his forehead, and his eyes squinted.

"I don't know what to say, Luke." I looked at my hands that were shaking. "I was raped."

"I know. I'm sorry. Sorrier than you can know. I'm not asking you to have sex with me. I'm asking you for a commitment, a future together." He hugged me for a long time.

"Luke, I'm sorry. I can't. Not yet." I looked at him through a film of tears. He walked out of the kitchen, and I heard him in the bathroom, then in the study where he kept his clothes. I turned off the lights in the living area, washed my face, brushed my teeth, and put on long pajama pants and a big T-shirt. I got in bed and waited, wondering whether he'd come.

*

When I woke up Friday morning, Luke was gone. I went to the

kitchen, and the coffee was hot in the coffee maker. There was a note next to it.

Sissy,
I'm leaving for Baton Rouge after the trial adjourns today. See you in court
next week.
Yours,
Luke

What did he mean, that I wouldn't see him over the weekend? We always got together in Baton Rouge at the house that Lilly and I shared. On Friday nights we'd go out to dinner and he'd grill steaks at his house on Saturdays. He'd go with me to mass on Sunday, and we'd pack up and head back to Jean Ville. Had all of that changed?

I sat in the courtroom Friday and Luke never looked at me. At lunchtime, I tried to get his attention, but he stayed huddled with his team. That afternoon there were twelve jurors in the box.

A girl about my age took the stand. She had bleached-blonde hair and red lipstick. She wore a denim jacket over a purple T-shirt that said 'LSU,' and purple and gold sneakers.

Luke asked her name, and she said, "Maggie Flores."

"Are you married, Miss Flores?" Luke shifted his weight from left to right.

"Divorced." She crossed one leg over the other and folded her hands in her lap.

"Is Flores your married name or maiden?" Luke wrote something on his legal pad.

"It's my given name. I didn't keep that creep's last name." She folded her arms across her chest.

"Okay." Luke took a deep, exhausted breath. "Would you tell me whether you know the defendant, Mr. Thevenot?"

"I don't know him, but my ex does." She stared at Thevenot with eyes that could kill.

"What is your ex's name, Miss Flores?"

"Keith Rousseau."

"Judge?" Luke looked at DeYoung, then at Peter Swan, Luke's partner, who stood up. Perkins and his partner jumped from their chairs, but no one said anything. I looked over at Thevenot, who was laughing.

"You are dismissed, Miss Flores." DeYoung watched Miss Flores until she was out of the courtroom. Luke went to the defense table and said something to Detective Sherman, who left the courtroom in a hurry. Once Miss Flores was out of the room, the judge looked at the lawyers and said, "That one slipped through the cracks. Sorry." The judge could dismiss as many prospective jurors as he thought might not be fair and impartial, and had dismissed a number of them during the course of the week, but none had been as obvious as Maggie Flores Rousseau.

The judge called the next prospective juror, and a young man who looked like Jesus walked in wearing a dirty, once-white T-shirt, blue jeans, and flip flops. His brown hair hung in strings to his shoulders and looked as though it hadn't been shampooed in a week. He had a five-day beard and dirty fingernails. He said he worked on the pipeline and that jury duty didn't pay as much per day as he made on the job. He didn't want to serve. He didn't know Thevenot. He didn't know Rousseau. He hadn't heard about the shooting.

"How do you feel about a black man being shot in cold blood?" Luke was wrapping up his questioning of Jeremy Blanchard.

"I work with black men. They pull their weight. I don't see no difference." Jesus, aka Jeremy Blanchard, pursed his lips, which revealed two dimples on his unshaven face.

"I'll accept, Your Honor." Luke sat down. Perkins had no questions, and the first alternate was seated. It was obvious that Mr. Blanchard was unhappy he'd been picked, and didn't understand what he'd said to make him a winner.

Several potential jurors followed Blanchard, but DeYoung rejected them because they had their minds made up one way or the other or they were blatantly prejudiced. At five fifteen, the jury was missing one alternate. The judge called the lawyers to his chambers, and I later learned that DeYoung went over some of the Jurors who'd been rejected by either side and asked if they would reconsider seating one of them as an alternate.

At six o'clock, the lawyers returned through the main door, and the judge entered through his back door.

"We've seated our second alternate from the pool who'd been rejected, agreed to by both teams of attorneys. We have our jury. The trial of the State of Louisiana vs. Tucker Thevenot will begin at eight o'clock Monday morning. This court is adjourned." He banged the gavel on his desk and left the courtroom.

*

I remained in my seat behind the defense table until everyone left but Luke, Detective Sherman, and Peter Swan. They talked for a long time, bent over the desk, taking notes. Finally, they stood up and began to pack their briefcases. Swan left first, followed by Sherman. When Luke stood up and headed for the door, I cleared my throat. He turned around and saw me holding my purse in both hands across my chest. He froze.

"Can we talk?" I whispered. I didn't want any of the ghosts of the people who'd once been in the gallery to hear me.

"Nothing to talk about, Sissy." He looked at his shoes while his briefcase swung a few inches back and forth.

"Please, Luke. I deserve an explanation." I stared at his blonde hair that hung over his forehead, his head tilted down.

"I don't know what to say." He finally lifted his head and looked at me, holding back tears.

"Are you breaking up with me?" I wanted to cry, too, but I couldn't let him see how much I cared about him, something I didn't know myself until I realized I could lose him.

"Is there anything to break up?" He shifted his briefcase from his right hand to his left and looked from me to his feet, then back at me.

"I thought there was. Was I mistaken?" I took a couple of steps towards him, and he put his briefcase on the floor. He loosened his tie and unbuttoned the top button of his shirt. "Please don't be stubborn, Luke. You're exhausted. You don't need to drive to Baton Rouge tonight. I'll call Lilly and ask her to stay with the Morrises until I get there tomorrow." He grinned, and I thought he was about to agree with me, then he picked up his briefcase and turned around. "Luke?" He walked out the door, and I heard him take the stairs two at a time, then the sound disappeared into nothingness.

I sat in the pew in the empty courtroom with my purse in my lap and started to cry. A woman deputy came in to turn out the lights and saw me. She paused for a moment, then sat next to me and put her arm over my shoulder. Her empathy made me cry harder. She let me sob for a long time and patted my shoulder every now and then. I wondered if I would have been a more well-adjusted person if my mother had ever done that for me.

~ Chapter Thirteen ~

Trial

SUSIE AND RODNEY MET with Luke and his team in a private room across from the courtroom at seven o'clock Monday morning. I arrived at about seven thirty and took a seat on the pew behind the defense table, saving seats for Rodney, Susie, and Lilly. Susie told me that Marianne and Dr. Warner were coming Wednesday night because Luke thought they would testify on Thursday.

At seven fifty-five, Susie rolled Rodney into the courtroom, which was filled with spectators. She parked his wheelchair in the aisle next to the first pew and sat on the end next to him. Lilly sat next to her, then Mr. and Mrs. Thibault, then me. Rodney was dressed in a dark suit, white starched shirt, navy, red, white, and pink tie, and gold cufflinks. He looked handsome and sophisticated. Susie was her ever-beautiful, classy self in a navy suit with a white silk blouse and multi-colored scarf. I wondered what the jury would think of them, whether Susie and Rodney would garner sympathy or make those who were prejudiced more apt to want to let Thevenot off with a slap on the wrist.

Luke ignored me when he walked into the courtroom behind Peter Swan, and they joined the rest of their team seated at the prosecution's table. My eyes bored a hole in Luke's back when he sat down and faced the judge's bench. It had only been a few days, but I was miserable without him. I had to think of a way to get him to talk to me.

The bailiff cried out, "All rise. Hear ye, hear ye! The Judicial District Court in and for the Parish of Toussaint is now opened according to law; the Honorable Edward DeYoung, presiding. Silence and order are commanded. Please be seated."

Judge DeYoung entered through the door behind the bench with some files under one arm.

"You don't have to stand every time I enter the courtroom." The judge stood behind the bench and smiled at the gallery, then at the lawyers. The fourteen jurors came through the main door and walked in single file down the aisle, through the swinging gate, between the prosecution and defense tables, and into the jury box, which had seven seats on the bottom row and seven on the top. The judge told them that they were to sit in the same seats at all times as they would be numbered—Juror #1, Juror #2, and so on.

The judge took his time giving the jury instructions. He told them that the prosecution, which was called, 'The State,' was represented by the attorney general and that The State would make an opening statement to outline their case and the evidence they expected to present.

"After The State gives their opening statement, the defense may give an opening statement, too, but they are under no obligation to do so." DeYoung explained that the opening statements were not evidence, only what the lawyers expected the evidence would be. He reiterated that it was up to the prosecution to prove that Mr. Thevenot was guilty and that the defense was not required to call witnesses because Thevenot was already considered innocent until proven guilty beyond a reasonable doubt.

"As jurors, you are the sole judges of the facts of this case." He paused and looked each of the fourteen jurors in the eye. "You must rely on your memory, you may not take notes. It is very important that you give this case your close attention."

I watched the faces of some of the jurors. Mr. Bourbon kept nodding his head as though he understood what the judge was saying.

Jesus, aka Blanchard, looked fidgety and anxious, as though he needed a cigarette. Mrs. Jones's eyes were closed, and her hands folded in her lap as though praying. Mr. Moore from Oregon looked confused.

"From this point on, during breaks and any other time until the trial is over, I'm going to ask you to refrain from reading any newspapers, watching any TV, or listening to any radio stations." He looked down at his notes and back up at the jurors. "Also, do your best not to discuss this trial when you go home, not with your significant others or friends or family members."

After the Judge completed his introduction, Tucker Thevenot's attorney, John Perkins, called for a bench conference and asked that the witnesses be sequestered. The Judge ordered all witnesses to leave the courtroom. Susie and Rodney were not required to leave since they were the victims in the case, but Susie took the opportunity to push Rodney in his wheelchair into the hallway, and Lilly followed them. Susie later told me that they didn't want to hear all of the testimony, and that sitting through the trial would be physically difficult for Rodney. He and Susie both wanted to save their strength for their own testimonies later in the week. I had not been subpoenaed, so I remained in the gallery with Rodney's parents.

*

Luke walked to the podium and put his legal pad on top.

"On June 30, 1984, a retired army major, a JAG officer who served our country for ten years, who did a tour in Vietnam and returned to Louisiana to marry the girl he had loved since he was sixteen years old, was shot and almost killed." Luke paused and looked at the jury. "When the couple walked out of the church on their wedding day at one ten in the afternoon, shots rang out, and a blue truck with license plate 37L402 sped north on Jefferson Street.

"Major Thibault, who is military trained, used his quick reflexes when he saw the shooter. The major immediately turned to protect his wife, shaving a split second off the time it took for the bullets to reach the couple, thereby taking both bullets himself. The first bullet went through the major's arm, exited and entered his back, lodging near his right lung. That bullet was meant for his wife, Susanna. The bullet meant to strike the major between his eyes, entered above his right ear.

"Major Thibault's quick thinking took Susie to the ground, which was a concrete platform in front of the church. He landed on top of her. The back of Susie's head split open when she hit the pavement, and she suffered a severe brain injury. She was first taken to Jean Ville Hospital, where doctors took her to surgery and placed a drain in her head to minimize the fluid build up.

"Major Thibault was taken by ambulance to Alexandria Regional Hospital, but due to the severity of his injuries was immediately airlifted to Ochsner Medical Center in New Orleans where he lay in a coma, hovering between life and death for weeks. He spent months in the hospital, having to learn all of the basic things we learn as children: how to make words, how to hold a fork, how to button a shirt and tie a shoe.

"Sadly, Major Thibault is still unable to walk. You will see him when he testifies. His speech is slow and sometimes slurred. He is in a wheelchair.

"Maybe African Americans are raised to believe it is their lot in life to be brutalized by white people. Maybe you believe that, too. If you do, I ask you to open your minds. This is 1984, not 1864. We have a Constitution that says, 'All men are created equal and are entitled to certain unalienable rights.' Remember this when you hear the testimony. If any of you believes that a person who does such an atrocious thing to a white man ought to be punished, but if he does this to a black man he deserves a pass, you should tell the judge of your prejudices now and be excused. If you cannot sit in that jury box and see all of these people, witnesses, defendant, and victims as God's children, people who deserve the same things that all American citizens deserve, you should not be on this jury.

"Mr. Thevenot shot the major and his wife with intent to kill them. He planned the shooting in advance—premeditated. Mr.

Thevenot never served in the military, never went to Vietnam, he didn't fight for you. He...never...fought...for...you." Luke said the last five words very slowly and emphasized the word, never.

"Remember that as you listen to the evidence and hear the witnesses. Thank you." Luke nodded at the jurors, and I presume he smiled at them with his charming grin, the one that had captured my heart. He went back to his table and sat down, his shoulders slumped ever so slightly as though what he'd said had taken a great deal of energy. I wanted to hug him.

*

John Perkins strolled to the podium with a swagger and the arrogance of someone who believes he is right and everyone else is wrong. I wondered whether the jurors would respect him, fear him, hate him, or love him.

"Ladies and gentlemen. Thank you for your service." He put his legal pad down, took a pen from his pocket, and clicked the top a few times. "Once The State has presented its evidence, I think you will agree that it is inconclusive. They cannot prove that the bullets that hit Mr. Thibault came from my client's gun, nor can they prove that my client pulled the trigger. All they can prove is that a blue truck stopped in front of St. Alphonse's Catholic Church and someone in the cab, maybe the driver, maybe a passenger, shot twice and the truck sped off. There will be no eyewitnesses who can say with 100% accuracy and assurance, that my client shot a gun from that truck.

"The State will tell you that the truck belongs to a man named Keith Rousseau, who is a friend of my client. They will tell you that Rousseau and my client have been known to terrorize black folks. The State will try to make you believe that my client and Mr. Rousseau have used violence against black folks in the past. Don't be fooled by The State's spin on things—even if they are able to convince you that my client terrorized black people in the past, they will not be able to convince you, beyond a reasonable doubt, that my client shot a gun at Rodney Thibault.

"Yes, they will show you evidence that my client has a gun like the one the bullets came from that injured Mr. Thibault. They will bring witnesses who will say they have seen my client in Mr. Rousseau's truck from time to time." John Perkins paused. I thought about how I had seen Tucker Thevenot riding in Keith Rousseau's truck and that they had been at my brother's house together. I felt a dark cloud of gloom settle over me and wrap around me like a rough blanket.

"The State will call witnesses who will tell you awful things that Mr. Thevenot has done in the past in hopes of showing you that my client has violent tendencies towards black people. None of this...I repeat, none of this is evidence that proves, beyond a reasonable doubt, that my client was the one who shot Mr. Thibault.

"Thank you." John Perkins sauntered back to his seat and sat down hard. He stared at the jurors without blinking.

*

"Ladies and gentlemen, that concludes the opening statements." Judge DeYoung leaned forward on his desk to get closer to the jurors. "We will now begin with the presentation of evidence, first by The State. Mr. McMath?"

Luke strolled to the podium. "The state calls Catherine Saucier."

A young white woman about my age, with dark, curly hair came through the door and walked up to the witness chair. I recognized her from somewhere but couldn't place her. I tried to think of her ten years younger without the dark, frizzy hair, but rather with long, shiny black hair that hung down her back. I finally remembered her as Callie Smith. She was from an area outside of Jean Ville known as Bayou Boeuf.

My skin began to burn as I remembered being with Warren and his friends one night at a football game. We were drinking beer in the parking lot when we heard a ruckus and ran through the gate in time to see Tucker Thevenot and Keith Rousseau grab a girl who I later realized was Callie. They pulled her under the bleachers, and I watched, statue-like, as Keith held her down and Tucker pulled a gun out of his pocket and got in her face, yelling, "You better keep away from that nigga-boy, you hear? Or you'll be sorry." He pulled at her clothes, and I thought he was going to rape her, but instead, he rammed his pistol between her bare legs and said, "The next time won't be a warning. We don't accept our white girls fooling around with no black boys, you hear?" Then he hit her across her forehead with the gun.

She cried for help, but none of us lifted a finger.

She had been a beautiful girl, slim with big boobs and a gregarious personality. When I realized the woman in the witness box was Callie, I felt sick to my stomach. What kind of person had I been back then?

I barely heard her testimony as she described being fourteen years old when Tucker and Keith grabbed her. "They pulled me under the bleachers and that guy over there," she pointed at Thevenot, "He pulled my shorts off and stuck his gun between my legs and threatened to blow up my private parts if I ever so much as spoke to a black guy." She spat the words out quickly, like tearing a Band-Aid off with one swift pull—acute but short-lived pain. She must have held her breath because her face was red, and her lips were pursed together. I held mine too, and after she said, "gun between my legs," I shut down and barely heard the rest until Luke asked her whether she was married now and she said she was divorced and had three children.

"I'm a nurse at the Baptist Hospital in Alexandria," she said, and I thought that, if she could survive what she'd been through, maybe I could, too. But would I survive being a witness to something so cruel without trying to help her when she needed it?

"What he did, well it changed me. It has haunted me all these years, and I've been to counseling and tried to move on, but the trauma, the way he did it and left me there under the bleachers, half-naked, bleeding, humiliated. There was a crowd that had gathered to watch. They saw it all." She looked up and I felt as though she stared at me, accusing me of being in that crowd and not helping her. She had every reason to hate me. I hated myself for what I'd done, or hadn't done.

She started to cry, and the judge made a sign to his clerk, who left the bench and took a box of Kleenex to the witness. Callie pulled three tissues out of the box, blew her nose, and dabbed at her eyes.

"Ms. Saucier, you said something that I'd like to follow up on." Luke resumed his professional tone. "You said you were bleeding. Can you tell me why?"

She took a deep breath and, once again, spoke as though ripping off a Band-Aid. "He hit me in the eye with his gun. It split my cheek open."

*

"Does the defense have any questions for Ms. Saucier?" Judge DeYoung made a note on a pad then lifted his chin and looked at John Perkins.

"Yes, Your Honor." Perkins got up and went to the podium. "Good morning Ms. Saucier. I'm John Perkins, and I represent Mr. Tucker Thevenot. You said that your encounter with Mr. Thevenot took place ten years ago. Is that right?"

"Yes, sir." Callie looked confused.

"Are you the same person you were ten years ago, Ms. Saucier?"

"I'm not sure what you mean, sir."

"Well, have you changed over the past ten years? Matured? Grown wiser? Become more empathetic, less self-centered, since you had children. Stuff like that?" Perkins had his hands in the pockets of his slacks, his suit coat pushed back behind his arms.

"Yes. Of course." Her look of confusion was replaced with a defiant expression.

"Do you think that happens to most people? That they grow up and mature after they are out of high school?" Perkins had a lilt in his voice as though he'd won a prize.

"I suppose so." Her forehead wrinkled, and her eyes squinted as though she were trying to bring Perkins into focus.

"No more questions, Your Honor." Perkins walked back to his

table.

"Any redirect, Mr. McMath?" Judge DeYoung asked.

"No, Your Honor." Luke seemed satisfied with whatever had just happened. He returned to his table, sat down, and leaned back in his chair, the back of it extended like a recliner.

"Ms. Saucier, you are free to go, but make sure somebody has your number in case you're called back." Judge DeYoung smiled at the witness.

*

Luke and his team stood and stretched. Detective Sherman left the room, and Luke and Peter Swan talked to each other. I hoped he would look my way so I could wink at him, but he never did. I reminded myself that this was the biggest case he'd ever been assigned as lead attorney and he needed to stay focused.

"The State calls Rella Moran." Luke stood behind the prosecution's table and spoke loudly. A young black girl, probably eighteen or ninteteen years old, entered the courtroom and stood next to the witness box. The bailiff swore her in.

"Do you know the defendant, Mr. Thevenot?" Luke asked Miss Moran.

"I don't know him, but I've seen him before." She looked afraid and glanced into the gallery as though looking for someone. I followed her eyes and saw a woman about thirty-five or forty years old, who was probably the witness's mother. The older woman nodded and smiled at the witness.

"Can you tell me where you saw him and what happened?" Luke stood on the side of the podium with one arm resting on the surface, the other hand in his pocket, looking casual and non-threatening.

"Well, it was at a football game five years ago. I was thirteen, in the eighth grade. I was walking to the concession stand during half-time, and that man right there," Rella Moran pointed at Tucker Thevenot, "He grabbed me and pulled me way up under the bleachers and pulled a pistol out of his pocket. There was another guy who held me down while that man started yelling at me to stay away from the white guys on the football team. He called me a nigga and said girls like me ended up dead. He hit me with his fist and beat my head with his gun. I guess I was knocked out, because when I came to, my mama was bending over me, pouring water over my face. The game was over, and everybody was gone."

"Did you report this crime to the police?"

"No, sir. My mama took me to the hospital, and they examined me." She looked down at her hands that were folded in her lap. She spoke so softly, I could barely hear her, and twice the judge asked her to speak up. "Then the doctor called the police, and they came to interview me. My mama went to meet with the district attorney. He recommended we drop it."

"Was there another reason you didn't file charges?" Luke asked.

"Yes, sir. I was scared of what Tucker Thevenot would do to me. He threatened to shoot me if I went to the police."

"Did you believe him?" Luke took one step back towards the podium and looked at the judge, who grinned. "Did you believe that he would shoot you?"

"Oh yes." She looked up at Luke with a furrowed brow. "He held a gun to the side of my head and clicked back the trigger. It scared me to death."

"Do you know what kind of gun it was?"

"Yes, sir." She nodded her head as if to emphasize that she, indeed, knew about guns. "My dad has one. It was exactly like my dad's. A 45-caliber Smith and Wesson."

Luke said he had no more questions, and the judge asked Perkins whether he had questions for this witness.

*

Perkins strolled to the podium and introduced himself.

"You said that your encounter with Mr. Thevenot took place five years ago. Is that right?"

"Yes, sir." Rella inhaled. "I was thirteen."

"Do you remember if Mr. Thevenot said anything to you?" Perkins put his hands behind his back and cupped them together.

"Yes, sir. He told me he would shoot me."

"Anything else?" He stood with his legs apart, cocky.

"Let me think." Her nose lifted, and her brow wrinkled. "He told me I was pretty."

"Do you remember what you were wearing that night? At the football game?" Perkins was going somewhere with his line of questioning, and I was interested in how he would make it look like beating and tormenting a thirteen-year-old child with a gun was okay.

"It was hot. I think I was wearing shorts and a T-shirt." She kept glancing into the gallery at her parents.

"Would they have been very short shorts and a cropped T-shirt?"

"I don't think so, no." She talked slower, as though she had to think about what she said before she said it.

"Are you known to dress indecently?" Perkins said it quickly because he knew there would be an objection. Luke was on his feet before Perkins completed his question, then said he was done with the witness.

"Any redirect?" The judge looked at Luke.

*

"Briefly." Luke stood up behind the table, didn't go to the podium. "Just for the record. Do you remember what you were wearing that night, Miss Moran?"

"I don't remember exactly, but I think it was shorts and a T-shirt." She was much more relaxed with Luke's questions than with Perkins's.

"Were you at the game alone or with friends, and what were they wearing?"

"I went with my parents and little brother. Some of my friends were there, and two of them went with me to the concession stand. We were all dressed the same. I remember we called each other before the game to talk about what we would wear, so we all dressed alike, uh, not the same colors, but we were all in shorts and T-shirts."

"Would your parents have taken you to a public place if you were dressed indecently?" Luke was still standing behind the table. He had a pen in one hand that he was tapping on the palm of his other hand.

"Oh, no, sir. My daddy is very strict about that stuff." She shook her head side to side and looked into the gallery and smiled. "He makes sure I dress like a lady."

"So you don't remember how you were dressed, but you are sure your dad wouldn't have taken you to the ball game in short shorts and a cropped shirt, right?"

"That's right, yes."

"No more questions, Your Honor."

The judge told Rella Moran she could leave, but to make sure the court knew how to contact her if they needed for her to return.

"Next witness." He looked at Luke and nodded.

*

"The State calls Billy Buras."

Billy Buras was a big, burly man with a potbelly and a full beard. I wouldn't have wanted to be caught in a dark alley with a woolybooger like him; he gave me the spooks. He stated his full name as Billy Bob Buras. Who'd name a kid that? I mean, at one time he was a kid, right?

He said he was thirty-five, divorced, and had four children, "That I know of." He laughed at his own joke as though everyone caught it. He said he knew Thevenot—that they used to go in the woods hunting together.

"There would be a crew, like maybe six or seven fellows." He put his hand in the air, palms towards Luke, and raised six fingers, then seven. "Sometimes a couple off them would go off with Tucker and Keith. They said they were going to chase women, but I didn't go with them, except one time."

"Can you tell me about that one time?"

"Me and Tucker went to this nigger joint in the Quarters near the Indian Park." He scratched his beard and pulled on it, like a caveman.

"We waited until a couple of those jiggaboos came out of the bar and got in their car and we followed them. Tucker was driving Keith's old truck, and when we got down that dark road, he got close up behind the niggas and started hitting the back of their car with his front bumper. At first, it was kind of fun, but then he took out his pistol and started shooting at the car. He shot out a tire and their car peeled off to the side and went in the ditch. Tucker put the truck in park and jumped out. I watched because it was like a movie, and I was like the audience."

"What did you see?" Luke stepped to the side of the podium as though he was very interested in the story Buras told.

"Well the niggas got out of their car and said, 'What the hell,' and Tucker, well, he started shooting at their feet and yelling at them to dance." Buras took a deep breath and stared at Luke. "And they did. Man, I couldn't believe he could shoot that many bullets at their feet and not hit one of them."

"Did he?"

"Well, at first he didn't, but after a while, one of them fell down screaming and holding his leg." Buras scrunched his mouth as though he remembered something distasteful. "I saw blood, but Tucker, well he jumped in the truck and peeled out. I didn't get to see how bad they was injured."

"Did Mr. Thevenot say anything to you after that incident?" Luke took a step backwards, towards the podium. The judge smiled.

"He said, 'That was fun.'" Buras took a breath. "I asked him if he'd ever done that kind of thing before and he said, 'All the time. Where you been?'"

"Do you know what he meant by that?"

"The next day I asked a couple of my friends who went with Tucker on chases, and they said where did I get the idea they was chasing girls when they was chasing darkies."

Perkins said he had no questions for Billy Bob Buras and the judge excused the witness, then called for a recess. The clock on the back wall said twelve thirty. I wondered whether I would be able to convince Luke to have lunch with me. I walked into the hall and followed Lilly into a private conference room where Detective Sherman and Lt. Schiller were talking to Susie and Rodney. He looked tired, and they were trying to decide whether they could let him go home for the afternoon. Luke walked in with his team, and they sat around the conference table. He ignored me, as though I were invisible standing next to Susie.

Luke told Susie that she and Rodney could go home, that he wouldn't call them until later in the week, and he would give them advance notice so they would be ready. Luke sat in a chair he'd pulled in front of Rodney's wheelchair and leaned forward. Susie sat next to her husband with her hand on his knee. "I want to call you closer to the end when you'll have the most impact, Rodney."

"Thanks, Luke." Susie patted Rodney's knee. "He's very tired. He hasn't been up this long."

"I understand." Luke shook Rodney's hand, then held the door open while Susie pushed Rodney through it. Lilly followed them out, and I followed Lilly.

*

After lunch, a black man named Wade Dolan took the stand. He said he was twenty-one years old, and testified that just last year Tucker Thevenot and Keith Rousseau chased him through the outskirts of town in an old blue truck. He said Keith drove and Tucker hung out the window and swung a rope, like a lasso.

"He throwed the rope over me, and they sped up, and the rope was tied around my waist, and I couldn't keep up with the speed of the truck. I fell, and they dragged me a ways. I was all scratched up, and the seat of my blue jeans was worn through." Wade Dolan had a high forehead and wide-set eyes. He had large lips, and a wide nose with big nostrils that flared when he talked. His hair was cropped short, almost in a crew cut, and his ears stuck out like Dumbo. He was tall and skinny and didn't look like he was strong enough to fight a two-year-old, much less two strong Cajun boys.

"What happened next?" Luke stood behind the podium and shifted his weight from one foot to the other.

"They stopped the truck and that guy over there," Dolan pointed to Thevenot. "He got out and had a board in his two hands, like a piece of lumber you use to build a barn. And he come after me with it, but as soon as that truck had stopped, I wiggled out of the rope and took off running. That guy there started to run after me, then he stopped, and when I turned around I didn't see him or the blue truck no more. So I slowed down and walked through the alley between Mr. Joe Coulon's store and the Feed and Seed. When I come out on Chenevert Street, soon as I walked out of the alley, I felt something hit me across the face, and I seed stars. I fell flat on my back, and when I squinted my eyes open, I saw that man over there holding that board and laughing. He threw the board in the bed of that old blue pickup, and they sped off, tires squealing on the blacktop road."

I marveled that these kinds of things could still happen in 1984, and there were no repercussions. It was a small wonder that bigots like Thevenot and Rousseau went on the rampage. They could get away with anything they did to black people. I was disgusted as I sat there and listened to the brutal things white people did to African Americans, and recalled witnessing similar events and thinking nothing of them. I hated myself, and I hated the town I grew up in.

*

Another black man, named Ron Bevy, said that the same two guys ran him down only a few weeks ago. The judge asked Mr. Bevy if he remembered the date.

"Yes, sir. I sure do because it was my little girl's birthday." He smiled and had large white teeth that seemed to catch the light and shimmer like snow in sunshine. "She turned four, and I'd gone to town to buy her a doll for her birthday present."

"What was that date, Mr. Bevy?" Judge DeYoung wrote something down and motioned for one of the deputies to come to the bench.

"It was May 15, sir." Mr. Bevy had light skin, with big freckles on his nose and cheeks. His eyes were small, and he had thick eyebrows. His nose wasn't overly large, nor were his eyes, but they were wide-set, and he had frizzy hair and a large forehead.

Judge DeYoung looked from the defense table to the prosecution, and I could tell that something was amiss. All four lawyers went to the tall desk in the front corner of the room. They bent their heads together for about five minutes. Perkins banged his fist on the Judge's desk once, and the Judge pointed a finger at him. My lip reading wasn't very good, but I could swear the Judge told Perkins he would hold him in contempt if he pulled another stunt like that. Perkins backed away from the bench a few steps. A few minutes later, the lawyers returned to their places.

"Proceed, Mr. McMath." The judge bent to the side and said something to his clerk, who nodded and wrote on the legal pad in front of her.

"Tell the jury what happened."

"Well, sir. That man over there," Bevy pointed to Thevenot. I wished I could have seen the defendant's expression because Bevy didn't seem the least bit afraid of Thevenot. "He come after me that day when I was walking home from town. I had my little girl's present with me. I'd even paid the lady at the Five and Dime to gift wrap it."

"You say he went after you." Luke looked up from the podium at Mr. Bevy. "Was he on foot, on a bicycle, in a car? And where exactly were you?"

"I was on Roy Street headed to my house near the Indian Park when I heard a motor come up behind me and I could hear it idle like it was going real slow, following me. I moved into the ditch so they wouldn't run over me, but I didn't look back. Before I know it, there's a rope around my waist and the vehicle, now I know it was an old blue truck, it takes off in front of me and starts to pull me along. That man over there, he was holding the end of the rope out the window on the passenger side and was laughing so hard I couldn't see his eyes." Bevy took a breath and said something to the judge. The judge said something to the clerk, and she left the room.

"Go on, Mr. Bevy." Luke took a couple of steps to the side of the podium and glanced at the Judge, who was writing something on his pad.

"Well they start to speed up, and I couldn't keep up, so I fell in the ditch, and the present that was under my arm came a-loose, and I started screaming, not because I was being dragged, but because of the present. You understand?"

"Yes, sir," Luke said. "I understand."

"Well, they was dragging me through the mud and dirt, and it had rained the night before, and I was filthy, and there was mud and stuff in my mouth and nose, and it got to where I couldn't breathe. Then the truck stopped, right in the middle of the road, and that man jumped out holding the end of the rope. But by the time he got to me, I had gotten loose and was on the run. I'm little, and I'm fast." Bevy laughed at himself. He was short and slim, and could probably run like lightning.

The bailiff appeared with a paper cup and handed it to Mr. Bevy. He drank almost all of whatever was in the cup. He wiped his mouth with the back of his sleeve.

"Did you get away?"

"I thought I did, but when I was almost to my house, that blue truck caught up with me, and that man was swinging a long board out the window, trying to hit me upside the head." He put his hand on the side of his head and shook it back and forth as though he couldn't believe what he was saying. "But I ducked like a boxer, and when he swung it again I caught hold of it and pulled and it out of his hand, and I dropped it and ran the rest of the way to my house."

"What did you do next?"

"I went inside and locked the door, and I called the police." The way he said police sounded like 'PO-lease' with an accent on 'po.' I wanted to laugh, but I knew I'd cause a scene.

"Did the police come to your house?"

"Shore did." He nodded his head to emphasize he'd actually called the cops and they'd actually showed up. "They come to my house, and I tole them what happened, and I got in their car, and we went back and looked through the ditch for my little girl's present. It was all torn up and muddy, but we cleaned up the doll, and it was okay, except one arm was missing."

"What did the police do?"

"They took me down to the station and took down my story." He grinned as though he'd just won the lottery. "They believed me because of the doll. They said they would go looking for the blue truck, but I never heard from them again."

"So there's a police report?"

"Shore is."

"And were you able to identify the men who attacked you?"

"I didn't know their names, but I gave some good descriptions." He nodded again. "And I memorized the license plate while I was being pulled behind that truck through the mud. 37L402. So, I know the police could locate it somehow."

"Thank you, Mr. Bevy." Luke went back to his seat. "No more questions, judge."

"Any redirect?"

"No, Your Honor, but I reserve the right to recall Mr. Bevy if necessary." Perkins stood up behind his table and addressed the judge.

"Of course." The judge dismissed Mr. Bevy with his regular instructions about being available. "We'll adjourn for the day."

The jury left the courtroom, followed by everyone in the gallery.

I waited for Luke outside the courtroom, and when he came through the door, he was talking to Peter Swan and walked right past me as though he didn't see me. He didn't nod or smile or acknowledge me.

⁓ Chapter Fourteen ⁓

Witnesses

THE FIRST WITNESS ON Tuesday was a white man named Daniel Tyler. He said he saw Tucker Thevenot in Keith Rousseau's truck at about noon on June 30.

"Do you know Mr. Thevenot?" Luke asked Mr. Tyler.

"Yes, sir." Tyler's blonde hair was cut in layers, like a girl's shag, short over his ears and long in the back. His eyes were light brown, and he had a mustache that made his face look dirty. He was pudgy, but not fat, about 5'10", with a barrel chest and skinny legs. He talked like a redneck from across the river. "We went to high school together. He didn't play football with me, but I knew him, and sometimes we'd go out together in a group."

Luke asked him when he graduated from high school, and he said 1969, which made him close to Susie's age. Luke asked Tyler whether he'd seen Thevenot since graduation.

"Oh, yes. I see him a lot." Daniel Tyler looked at Thevenot and nodded. Thevenot nodded, too, but I could only see the back of his head and one side of his face. "He's a regular at the bar where I bartend. I'm off on Mondays and Tuesdays, so I don't know if he goes on those nights, but the rest of the nights he comes in. Sometimes he grabs a beer and leaves, sometimes he hangs around and plays pool with some of the other guys who hang out there."

"So you see him on a regular basis." Luke's statement caused Perkins to object. The judge sustained, and Luke apologized. "So would you say you'd recognize Mr. Thevenot if you saw him outside of the bar?"

"Of course." Tyler nodded. "I see him around town, and we always speak. I wouldn't consider him a friend, just an acquaintance."

"And do you know Keith Rousseau, too?"

"Sure do. He and Tucker are best buddies. They're always together, usually in Keith's old blue Chevy truck."

"When was the last time you saw them together in that truck?"

"Oh, last weekend, at the bar." Tyler nodded, and the judge bent to the side and said something to his clerk.

"Did you see them together last summer, on June 30?" Luke walked to the table and picked up a typed piece of paper.

"Yes, I remember that date because I typically drive in front of St. Alphonse's Catholic Church on my way to work, and I go in early on Saturdays because it's very busy." He grinned at Luke. "I remember seeing lots of cars there at noon, and a bride in a white dress got out of a car. There were three girls in long pink dresses, so I figured it was a wedding. I drove past the church, maybe a hundred yards, and Keith Rousseau went by going the other way. I waved to him and saw Tucker sitting shotgun with his arm hanging out the opened window. Keith stopped his truck, and I stopped too, rolled down my window, and we talked right there in the street in front of the priest's house, next door to the church. I went on to work, and I don't know where they went."

"Did you see them again that day?" Luke clicked his ballpoint pen behind his back.

"Yes, they came to the bar at about one fifteen or one thirty. I know because I opened up at one o'clock and they came in soon after that. They were my first customers and, for a while, the only customers in the bar. They sat on bar stools and ordered beers, and I chatted with them for a while."

"Did they say anything unusual?"

"Not really, but they were laughing a lot, like they had an inside joke. When I asked them what was so funny, they said, 'You ever kill a nigger?' I said, no, of course not."

"Did they say anything else?"

"Not to me, but later I overheard them telling another customer that they killed a nigger." Tyler started to say something else, but Perkins jumped up.

"Objection, Your Honor. Hearsay." Perkins shouted.

"Sustained." The judge bent towards Daniel Tyler and said something I couldn't hear. Daniel nodded, and Luke said he was done with the witness.

"Redirect, Mr. Perkins?" DeYoung asked.

"Just a couple of questions, Your Honor." Perkins stood with his legs spread, his hands on the podium. "You said you aren't friends with the defendant that you consider him an 'acquaintance,' is that right?"

"Yes, sir." Tyler ran his hand through his hair and blinked a couple of times, like he had a tic. "I mean, I see him a lot, but we don't socialize. I've never been to his house and he ain't been to mine."

"Have you ever been in the woods with him?"

"A few times. There were lots of us, and he was there, yes."

"Did you ever go with him to chase women?"

"I wasn't going to talk about that because I didn't want to get him in more trouble than he's already in." Tyler licked his lips and looked at Thevenot, then back at Perkins.

"No more questions, Your Honor." Perkins sat down quickly as though he knew he'd opened a door he shouldn't have. I think he had expected the questioning to go a different way, maybe he was trying to prove that Daniel Tyler and Tucker Thevenot were closer friends than they were, but somehow Tyler's answer surprised Perkins.

"Redirect?" Judge DeYoung looked at the prosecution table. Luke and Peter Swan were huddled together, their heads almost touching the table.

"Can you give me two minutes, please, Your Honor?" Luke looked up at the judge but kept his shoulders crouched over the table.

"I'll give you one minute." Judge DeYoung looked at his watch. I noticed he wore it on his right arm, so I figured he was left-handed, like Rodney. I'd read that left-handed people, on average, are smarter than right-handers and that lefties are more likely to become doctors, lawyers, and professional baseball players. I wondered whether that was true. I made a mental note to notice lefties and whether they seemed smarter than the average bear.

"May we approach, Your Honor?" Luke stood up. The judge motioned to the attorneys to gather around his bench. They huddled together, and the judge said he and the lawyers were going to have a brief meeting in his chambers and would return shortly.

"Y'all come this way, counsel." He motioned for them to follow him through the door behind the bench, which was directly across the hall from his offices. They were gone about ten minutes.

The judge returned through his back door the lawyers through the main door into the courtroom.

"Alright, Mr. McMath, if you want to resume your questioning of Mr. Tyler, please, at the appropriate time, we'll hear an objection, and then we'll take care of it."

"Mr. Tyler, when you went with Mr. Thevenot and others in the woods, did some of the men leave to go chase women?" Luke stood straight, his tailored grey suit falling perfectly from his broad shoulders to his narrow hips. I wished I could see his face, but his backside looked pretty good, too.

"Well, that's what I thought it was, at first." Tyler sat on the edge of his chair, and the microphone picked up his voice loud and clear. "But it wasn't women they was chasing, it was Negroes."

"Objection, Your Honor." Perkins stood up, but there was no anger in his voice, almost resignation. I wondered what they had discussed in the judge's chambers that caused Perkins to look defeated.

The judge asked the jury and Daniel Tyler to step out of the courtroom. Blanchard, alternate juror, aka Jesus, looked relieved and I could picture him running down the stairs to get outside so he could smoke. The judge heard Perkins's objection and denied it. The judge and lawyers had another bench conference, off the record. After the jury returned, and Luke asked Tyler, again, about chasing women, Perkins stood up and objected again. The judge asked what grounds and Perkins stuttered. The jury and Daniel Tyler had to leave the courtroom two more times while Perkins and the judge argued about the objection.

Luke said that Perkins opened the door for the questioning, and the Judge agreed. Luke sounded confident, no stuttering or stammering from him, no sir! "If they had stayed with establishing the relationship between Mr. Tyler and Mr. Thevenot, that would have been fine, but Mr. Perkins insisted on bringing up the trips to the woods. And if that wasn't enough, he asked about the 'chasing' thing that we've already heard about from other witnesses."

"Any response, Mr. Perkins?" The judge looked from Luke to Perkins.

"Your Honor. This testimony…to The State…" Perkins tried to find words but was fighting a losing battle. The judge finally made Perkins understand that the objection was overruled. The jury returned, and Luke continued his questioning.

"Mr. Tyler, I'm going to repeat the question, and the judge agrees that you can answer it," Luke spoke slowly, his voice was clear and strong. "Mr. Tyler, when you went with Mr. Thevenot and others in the woods, did some of the men leave to go 'chase women'?"

"Your Honor," Perkins stood up, red in the face "I'm going to call for a mistrial."

"Hold up. Wait a minute. Repeat that, Mr. Perkins." The judge looked at the defense table as though he was unsure of what he'd heard. Everyone in the courtroom inhaled.

"We'd like to motion this court at this time for a mistrial." Perkins and his law partner were both on their feet behind the defense table.

"Alright, ladies and gentlemen." The judge looked at the jurors and motioned to the door. "You'll have to get back outside."

The jury and the witness left the room

The judge was aggravated. Perkins argued that the line of questioning was inadmissible and not pertinent to the case. Luke argued that Perkins opened the door. The judge reminded the lawyers that, in his chambers, he had decided in favor of the prosecution on the issue. Perkins agreed that the judge had overruled his objection, but this was a motion for a mistrial.

Perkins and his partner were still on their feet.

The judge cited two cases that had similar testimony where one side or the other had opened the door to questions that the court had tried to keep minimal. He got very technical, and I quit listening until he said, "The motion for mistrial is denied. Objection to the ruling by the court is noted, and error is assigned." Whatever that meant. "Bring back the jury."

*

"Mr. Tyler, before the recess I'd asked you about going with Mr. Thevenot to chase women." Luke's voice was even and confident.

"Like I said, that's what I thought they did, but I hadn't gone with them because I had a wife and kid. Then I got a divorce, and one night we were in the woods and we were drinking a good bit, and Rousseau and Thevenot said it was time to load up for the 'chase.' I got in the back of Rousseau's truck with three other guys. Thevenot rode in the front seat, shotgun."

"And do you remember where you went that night?"

"Yes, sir." Tyler licked his lips and took a sip of water from the now ever-present paper cup the bailiff made sure was on the witness stand. "We went to town and headed down one of the streets towards the Indian Park. About halfway down those three or four streets is what they call the Park Quarters."

"What happened when you went on this 'chase'?"

"Well, it was dark and, there's no street lights down there." Tyler said there were two black men walking down the street and that they must have heard the truck because they turned around and saw the truck and took off running. "They ran through the ditch and between houses. It was like they knew that blue truck."

"Objection. The witness doesn't know that for sure." Perkins was on his feet again.

"Sustained." The judge noted something then turned to the witness. "Continue, Mr. Tyler. Just don't say something you don't know to be true."

Tyler looked at Luke. "Well the two men disappeared, but Keith, well he drove around the block just as those two appeared on the next street. Tucker, he had a rope, and he lassoed one of the guys, and Keith stepped on the gas pedal and started dragging that guy down the road while the other one ran after us trying to catch up."

"What did you do?" Luke's arm went up in the air, and I knew he was pushing his hair back off his forehead.

"At first, I froze. I couldn't believe what was happening." Tyler took a deep breath and looked at the judge, who nodded to encourage him. "I couldn't believe what they were doing."

"Why were you in disbelief?"

"Well, I never seen anyone treat another human being that way." Tyler looked confused.

"Do you believe black people are human beings?"

"Object." Perkins was on his feet.

"Overruled, Mr. Perkins." Judge DeYoung looked aggravated. "Please sit down and let Mr. McMath continue his questioning. I'll stop him if it gets off track."

"Thank you, Your Honor." Luke looked from DeYoung to the witness. "You may answer the question, Mr. Tyler. Do you believe black people are human beings?"

"Yes, sir." Tyler paused, thinking of how to phrase his words. "Back in high school, I went to school before integration, you see. Well, back then I didn't think much about black people one way or the other. They'd do the jobs white people didn't want to do, and as long as they stayed away from us, I didn't think much about them."

"Did your opinion change? And if so, why?"

"Your Honor, can we agree that this line of questioning is...?" Perkins was on his feet again.

"Mr. Perkins, I asked you to remain seated." DeYoung's face was red. "I said I would stop Mr. McMath if he gets out of line. Please, Mr. McMath, continue." Perkins sat down, and Luke took a deep breath.

"You can answer the question, Mr. Tyler. Did your opinion about black people change after high school, and if so, why?"

"Yes, sir." He took a sip of his water. "You see, I can't read real good. They say it's dyslexia, or something like that but I can do numbers, so that's why I'm good at taking money, making change, memorizing drink recipes, stuff like that. So, after high school, I couldn't go to college, then I got this job as a helper in the bar. I was just a clean-up person at first." Tyler went on to explain how he'd bussed tables and washed dishes and that the cook took Tyler under his wings and taught him how to make a few things, like burgers and fries.

"That man, L'Roy, was kind to me. And as I moved up to bartender, then manager, he stayed with me. He works harder than three men, he's always happy, he loves his wife and two girls, he sings all the time, and he lifts my spirits when I'm down. He's black as the ace of spades, but I don't see that no more. I see him as a friend and a good person. He made me a better person."

"So what happened the night you went on the 'chase' with Mr. Thevenot?" Luke stood on the side of the podium and leaned against it on one elbow, his other hand in the pocket of his slacks.

"I jumped out of the truck and tried to stop it, but they just kept going." Tyler looked like he wanted to cry. You could hear a fly buzzing around in the gallery, it was so quiet. "When they finally stopped, that poor man was all bloody, his face was ripped up, one of his legs looked to be broken. I ran to him and removed to rope from his waist. Thevenot thought I was helping him out by retrieving his rope, but I was disturbed. I wanted to help the man. His friend got there just as Keith started to drive away. One of the guys in the back of the truck yelled, 'Wait up, Tyler's not in the truck,' and Keith backed up so I could get in.

"I still feel bad that I got in that truck and didn't stay to help that man." Tyler took a deep breath and said something to the judge.

I sat still, my hands shaking because I was trying to forget about the time I rode in the back of Keith's truck with Warren and a bunch of people, and Tucker roped a black teenager and Keith dragged the poor boy behind the truck until he looked like ground meat. I'd sat on the railing of that truck and watched as though it were a movie, not real life. Listening to Daniel Tyler talk about the incident he witnessed, I felt a sheet of shame cover me. I wanted to hide... from myself. In that instant, I hated Warren for subjecting me to such evil. And I hated myself as much.

I didn't hear the rest of Tyler's testimony. I spaced out until the judge called for a recess.

*

That afternoon, one witness after another testified to seeing Keith Rousseau and Tucker Thevenot in the blue truck in front of the Church.

The neighbor across the street from the Church sat on her front porch because she heard a black man and white woman were getting married and she wanted to see the couple when they came out. She told how the blue truck pulled up in front of the rectory at about ten minutes before one o'clock and waited.

"The truck was idling," she said as she rocked back and forth in the witness chair. "I could tell because there was smoke coming out the tailpipe." She said she could see the driver clearly and would be able to identify him because the truck was parked facing town. "I could see the other guy, too. He looked shaggy and blondish." She said the couple came out of the church at ten after one. "The man sitting shotgun stuck something out of his window, and I heard two shots. Then the truck took off, and I looked up at the couple, and I couldn't see them no more. Some people made a circle and crowded around something on the concrete porch on the front of the Church. Pretty soon the ambulances and police and firemen all came."

A man who lived next door to the rectory said he saw the blue truck and he could identify Tucker Thevenot, "Clear as day. They drove slow in front of my house, and his window was down, and he had his arm resting in the opened window. I stood on my porch so I could see what was happening because it seemed awful strange, an old truck like that with two scraggly looking fellers, parked outside the Church when there was a big wedding going on inside.

"That man right there," Mr. Tim Laborde pointed at Thevenot. "He sticks his other arm out the window, and I hear two shots. Then the truck peels out on the blacktop road and heads towards town."

"Are you sure you saw this man, the defendant, Mr. Thevenot?" Luke seemed amazed at Laborde's testimony.

"Yes, sir. I never seed nothing like it before. I'll never forget it."

Perkins crossed examined Mr. Laborde with questions meant to trick him into saying that maybe it wasn't Thevenot, maybe a green truck, maybe not June 30; but Mr. Laborde stood his ground, and by four o'clock evidence against Thevenot was mounting.

Luke did not redirect; there was no need.

*

The last witness of the day was the man who called himself the maintenance person at the church. He said he kept up the grounds, including the cemetery and the priest's house, that he fixed things when they broke and he cleaned up after weddings and funerals and the like. His name was Everett McCann, and he said he'd been working for the church since he was an altar boy. "It's the only job I ever had," he told Luke.

"Where were you on June 30 at about one o'clock in the afternoon?" Luke had one leg bent, and his right hip cocked out a little. He leaned on the podium for support.

"I was at the church, of course." Mr. McCann was short and squatty with a little hump in his shoulders that made him bend forward a bit. He had a straw hat in his lap that he'd taken off when he entered the courtroom, and his head was completely bald. "We had a big wedding that day, the ex-senator's daughter. And he's a member of St. Alphonse's. He gives generous donations to the church, so we wanted to make sure everything went off perfect."

"Where exactly were you standing when the couple came out of the church, and what did you see?"

"I stood on the side of the front steps so I could go in the church as soon as everyone came out. I saw an old blue truck. It stopped in front of the rectory. I watched it for about ten minutes or so and waited for it to leave. When it didn't, I started to walk towards it, so I could tell the driver to move on. Just then, the church bells started ringing, which meant the wedding was over. The truck moved forward about fifty yards and stopped in front of the church. I saw that man sitting in the passenger seat." McCann pointed at Tucker Thevenot. "Just as I came up on the truck from behind, he stuck something out the window. I heard two shots; actually they sounded like firecrackers, then the truck took off. I turned and looked at the front of the church, and there was people coming out and rushing to where the newly married couple should have been. I ran over there and saw the bride and groom on the concrete slab that spans the front of the church. They were bleeding."

Perkins got up to cross-examine McCann. He looked as tired as Luke.

"Mr. McCann, you said that you came up on the truck from behind, right?"

"Yes, sir. They didn't see me coming, I don't imagine." McCann nodded and ran his hand over his bald head.

"If you approached from the back of the truck, how are you so sure the person who shot the gun was my client, Mr. Thevenot?"

"Oh, I saw him for ten or fifteen minutes sitting there in that truck, parked in front of the rectory. I watched and saw him real clear. I didn't start to walk over to the truck to tell them to leave 'til the church bells rang. I should have gone sooner."

"How did it happen that you could see him so clearly, but the truck was in front of where you were standing?" Perkins was trying to disqualify the witness, but Mr. McCann didn't seem the type to make things up.

"Oh, no sir, you don't understand. They was parked directly in front of me, then when the church bells rang out, they pulled up from the rectory about fifty feet to in front of the church, so that's when they got in front of me. For ten or so minutes, I stared at the two of them. I could identify the driver, too, if he was here. But I don't see him in the courtroom."

"I tender this witness, Your Honor." Perkins went to his seat and slid down in his chair as though he'd been beaten at his own game.

"Redirect, Mr. McMath?"

"No, Your Honor." Luke stood up behind his table, then sat back down. He, too, slid down in his chair.

The judge dismissed Mr. McCann then adjourned for the day. "We'll start at nine in the morning rather than eight. See you then."

*

Luke was the last one in the courtroom and didn't see me behind the prosecution's table, sitting on the bench in the corner.

"Luke?" I spoke softly, and he jumped, as though he'd heard a ghost. He turned around holding his briefcase, and was about to walk towards the door.

"Sissy?" He looked at me with an expression of utter amazement. "What are you doing here?"

"Waiting to talk to you." I didn't move. Had he turned and walked out, I wouldn't have tried to stop him.

"I'm really beat." He let both his arms fall by his sides, one holding the briefcase.

"I know." I stood up and took a couple of steps towards the railing that separated us. "Could we have a drink? You look like you could use one." He looked at his shoes, then back at me. His eyes said that he still cared about me, but he was trying to move on. I still didn't know what I'd done to run him off. Just when I thought our relationship was going somewhere, he'd walked out. Go figure.

"Sissy, this is a bad week." He looked so tired I wanted to back off and leave him alone, but I needed to know why he had walked out on me so abruptly.

"I just want to know why." I could hear him breathe, in and out, but there was that damn fence between us, so I couldn't put my arms around him like I wanted to.

"I'm surprised you don't know the answer to that question." He looked down at me from his towering height to my five-foot-two frame, taller because of my two-inch heels.

"I don't. Help me understand."

"It's simple. I love you, and you don't love me." He turned and walked out of the courtroom, and I stood glued to the floor, like a dummy, trying to understand what he'd just said. I heard him run down the stairs, as though he couldn't get away fast enough, but I couldn't move from my spot to go after him.

All night I thought about his words: "I love you, and you don't love me." What did that mean? The next morning I was at Susie's kitchen table at seven o'clock, dressed and ready for court. I'd made a pot of coffee, and she came into the kitchen at about seven ten. She saw me sitting there, poured herself a cup, and sat down next to me.

"Spill it, Sissy. What's wrong?" She bent forward so she could look me in the eye. Her face was very close to mine, and I wanted to hug her. I thought about all she'd been through, what she was still going through, and I felt selfish for dumping my problem on her.

"Luke walked out on me last week." I was determined not to cry and ruin my mascara, so I spoke as though I were detached from my own feelings. "He just left and refused to see me. Yesterday, after court, I waited for him and asked him, why. He said, 'Because I love you and you don't love me.' What does that mean?"

"Do you?" She squeezed my hand, which made me lift my eyes to hers. "Do you love him?"

"How would I know?" I'd never been in love. I had no idea how love felt.

"You just know." She let go of my hand and took a sip of her coffee. "Sometimes it happens immediately. Sometimes it grows over time. But you know that you're in love with a man if you are miserable without him, if you think about him all the time, and if you feel as though your life would be destroyed if he fell for another girl. I mean, Sissy, you just know."

"Oh, God, Susie." I put my hands on my cheeks because I could feel the heat rise from my neck. "If I thought he was with someone else, it would kill me. And I do think about him all the time. I'm happiest when I'm with him and miserable when I'm not."

"You need to tell him that." She patted my hand and smiled at me. "Now that he's confessed that he loves you, the next move is yours. But you have to be honest. None of that, give me time stuff. Just go for it, or you'll lose him."

I went back to my garage apartment and gathered my purse and car keys. All the way downtown, I thought about what Susie said.

~ Chapter Fifteen ~

~

Victims

T HE FIRST WITNESSES WEDNESDAY morning were the three cops who had been at the scene.

The first one on the stand was Mike Richard who said that he never thought the shooting was a crime because it was just a black boy who'd been shot. He said, "Now, if that white girl had got shot, we'd probably had to file a police report." Even the jury saw the fallacy in his testimony.

Grady Baudin was the second cop called. He said that he had talked to some of the folks who'd attended the wedding and, "No one saw nothing. You can't put, 'nothing,' in a police report."

The most surprising witness was Joey LeBlanc. He testified that he was the third cop to arrive at the church and that he saw the two people lying on the concrete bleeding. He said by the time he got there, the paramedics were putting them on stretchers. "I saw a lot of blood, but it looked to me like they fell and busted their heads. I couldn't see no crime." Then he laughed a coarse, wet laugh.

The judge called for a short recess, and I tore out of the courtroom looking for Joey. When I didn't find him in the hall, I headed down the stairs, out of the courthouse. He was standing near a city police car, smoking and talking to the other two cops who'd testified. I recognized them as having been at the scene, but I was sure Joey had not been there. In fact, I remembered that the third cop was Dennis Smith, a redheaded guy who'd been one year behind me in high school. I wondered why he hadn't testified and how Joey could have replaced Dennis. Was that legal?

"Hey, Joey, got a sec?" I walked towards the car, and all three cops looked at me with shocked expressions. Joey took a step backwards, as though he was afraid of me. I almost burst out laughing, but instead, I walked right up to him and slapped him across the face, then, for good measure, I slapped him again. I'll admit my palm burned like I'd set it on my stove's electric burner, but I didn't let on. The shocked look on his face was worth any amount of pain.

He reared back his fist and was about to slug me, but Grady caught his arm. "Hey, man! There are witnesses all over the place. Careful."

"You think I care about witnesses? I'm a cop, and she just slapped me. That's a crime—hitting an officer of the law." He reached back and pulled a pair of handcuffs from his belt loop and attempted to place them on me, saying, "You are under arrest."

"Just try that, Joey LeBlanc." My words were sharp, and my voice loud, which stopped him for a nanosecond. "I'll turn you in to the attorney general for assault, rape, and perjury. Did you truly think you could get away with testifying that you were at the church when you were never there? Where's Dennis? Did he pay you to take his place because he's a decent guy and would admit that someone should have filed a police report?"

"What the hell?" He waved the handcuffs in the air.

"I'm not done with you." I turned around and ran up the steps into the courthouse as fast as a bunny skipping across my backyard. I dared him to try to put his hands or his cuffs on me inside the courthouse.

*

When I got to the courtroom, it was half empty. I went right through that swinging gate and up to the prosecution's table. Luke was standing up, bent over a legal pad that was on the table. I tapped him on the back.

"I need to talk to you."

"Not now Sissy."

"Yes, now!" I motioned with my finger for him to follow me out of the courtroom to Judge DeYoung's office. Something about my determined walk must have told him he should follow me. I pressed the beige button on the wall beside the door to the judge's chambers and heard the click. When I opened the door, the judge was standing in front of his secretary's desk.

"Judge, I need to tell you something, and I want Mr. McMath to hear it, too. It's important." I stepped towards the opened door to his inner office, and the two men followed me. The judge shut the door, and we stood in a semicircle in front of his desk. "It's about Joey LeBlanc."

"The police officer who testified this morning?" DeYoung looked from me to Luke and back at me.

"Yes. First of all, he was not at the church. The third city cop was Dennis Smith. I'm sure of it. I saw all three of them clearly. I'm not sure why Joey testified. He was not there. Ever."

"Well, that's certainly unusual. I'll call the chief and tell him to pick LeBlanc up for questioning." The judge walked around his desk and sat in his chair. He picked up the phone and asked Lydia to get Winn Marchand on the phone.

"That's not all," I said when he hung up. Luke and I were standing in front of the judge's desk. "He was one of the two guys who assaulted me. I'm one hundred percent sure he's the one who raped me."

"Sissy, there's something you need to know," Luke took my elbow and guided me into one of the two chairs in front of the desk. "I haven't known how to tell you."

"Don't you dare keep anything from me, Lucas McMath." I could feel the warmth start on my neck begin to crawl up to my cheeks. I was so angry I could have spat.

"The semen samples gathered at the hospital." Luke sat down and took my hand. I pulled it away and crossed my arms over my chest. "There were two."

"Two what?"

"Two different sets of DNA."

"So both of those bastards raped me? I was only awake for the first one. The second creep must have raped me after I blacked out. Wait until I get my hands on that asshole." I stood up and started for the door.

"You know who the other guy was?" Luke stood up and tried to follow me, but I was already out of the judge's chambers and walking in front of Lydia's desk when he caught me by the arm and turned me around. "Do you?"

"Yes, and I'm going to find him now." I could see the judge standing in his doorway as though he were watching a movie.

"Sissy." Judge DeYoung took a few steps towards us. "That's not a good idea. Give me his name, and I'll have Marchand pick him up, too. Mr. McMath can question him."

"I have to do this, judge. I want to get in his face." I turned and walked out of the office, into the hall, and was down the stairs before Luke caught up with me.

"Let me go with you, Sissy." He was breathing hard; so was I. "It's too dangerous for you to go alone to confront an assailant. I can't imagine what he might do to you."

"Luke, you have to let me do this. I know how to take care of myself." I ran across the street, got in my car, and drove off. I knew Luke couldn't follow me. He had to get back to the courtroom before the recess was over.

*

I found Warren on Highway One. His red truck was parked next to a new Dodge Ram truck on the side of the highway that went from Jean Ville to Alexandria. An older man was standing behind something that looked like a camera on a tripod. Warren was across the road, holding something in the air. I pulled up on the shoulder in front of Warren and jumped out of my car.

My short legs never took such long strides, and in a few seconds,

I was facing him. I pulled my elbow back as far as I could and threw my arm forward. My fist caught him under the chin, and he grabbed his face. His shocked expression made my bleeding knuckles tickle as I socked him again, this time catching the side of his eye. He grabbed me by the shoulders and started to shake me. I kicked him in the crotch, and he let go of me and grabbed himself.

The older man must have crossed the street because he had an arm around my waist and was pulling me off Warren. He lifted me in the air and started to back away.

"Let me go. I'm going to kill him." I was kicking my feet, which were off the ground.

Warren started to come at me, and the man dropped me to my feet and caught Warren. "No way, Warren. You are not going to hit a woman."

"What about what she just did to me?" His chin and eye were bleeding, but not as much as my fingers and knuckles. The man said something to Warren, but his voice was drowned out by sirens. Two state troopers pulled up on the shoulder and jumped from their cars. Before I knew what happened, Warren was sitting in the back seat of one of the cruisers and the two troopers made U-turns in the highway and headed back to Jean Ville.

I drove home and nursed my hand all afternoon. I hated missing the trial, but I was in no shape to sit on a church pew in that crowded courtroom. My phone rang at five o'clock. I was on my second glass of wine.

"Sissy, I'm going to the parish jail to interview LeBlanc and Morrow." Luke's voice was tender, and he spoke as though afraid he might upset me.

"Can I go with you?"

"Yes. We need your testimony, too."

In his car, on the way to the sheriff's office, I asked Luke how the trial went that afternoon. He said the four paramedics testified that they triaged Susie and Rodney and put them in the two ambulances.

Luke said the volunteer firemen took the stand one at a time and, although it took almost an hour to interview each of them, they didn't have much to say, mostly they said that they "watched the police and the paramedics and talked to some of our friends who had attended the wedding."

Luke said that Dr. Cappel and Dr. Switzer both took the witness stand and were asked about the injuries Susie and Rodney suffered. It took most of the afternoon to hear about their approach to the injuries and the types of treatments they administered. "Dr. Switzer talked about how Rodney was taken to Alexandria then airlifted to Ochsner and that he, Switzer, went with Rod and returned the next morning." He looked straight ahead as he drove.

"Marianne and Dr. Warner showed up at noon," Luke said. "I guess they are at Susie's house."

"I wondered who that strange car belonged to." I muttered that I'd seen several cars next door at Susie's house, but was in no shape to visit.

"You really didn't miss much," Luke said. "Tomorrow we'll question Dr. Warner."

*

There were two interrogation rooms at the parish sheriff's department. Joey was in one of them, Warren in the other. They sat behind tables and had Styrofoam cups in front of them. Joey looked angry, Warren, worried. I watched them through the one-way windows. Luke went into the room with Joey, first. He introduced himself and sat at the table. Joey started ranting and raving about how someone should arrest me for assaulting a cop. "That bitch slapped me, twice. I told her she was under arrest and she ran away. She should be charged with fleeing the scene, resisting arrest, battery of a police officer…" Luke let him carry on until he ran out of words.

"You've been accused of a number of crimes, including simple burglary of an inhabited dwelling, sexual battery, simple battery, second degree battery," Luke spoke slowly and looked Joey directly in the eye and explained how much trouble Joey was in, and that I had identified him as one of the two assailants. "You could go to prison for a very long time."

"How does she know who did it?"

"What do you mean, Mr. LeBlanc. Do you think Miss Burton didn't recognize you?"

"She never saw me..." Joey realized what he'd said and shut up. *Dumbass*, I thought, and laughed aloud. Then he said something that took my breath away. "What about her brother?" Luke got up and pulled the curtain across the window and turned off the microphone so I was shut out of the rest of the interview. I sat on a sofa in the waiting room and wondered what Joey meant by that comment.

It was dark outside when Luke came into the waiting room and sat next to me.

"Sorry, I had to shut you out. I felt LeBlanc had information about another investigation, which is confidential." He tried to hold my hand, but I pulled away.

"What about Warren?"

"Both guys will be in lockup overnight." Luke took a deep breath and let out a sigh. "The attorney general is sending a couple of state investigators here to interview Morrow and LeBlanc tomorrow."

"Don't let them out of jail. They'll come after me again, for sure."

"The judge signed warrants and will hold a bond hearing tomorrow during the noon recess. If they bail out, we'll put a couple of troopers on them."

"Why don't you assign the Troopers to me?"

"Same thing, only this way you'll have some privacy, and we'll know who they talk to, where they go. It's part of a broader investigation."

*

Day four of the trial seemed longer than all the other days, combined. Donato Warner was the first witness. Luke questioned him about Rodney's injuries, his recovery, how it was touch-and-go. Warner stated that without Susie and Lilly, Rodney wouldn't have survived.

"I watched love actually heal a person who should have died." Dr. Warner's statement brought a group sigh from the gallery, followed by dead silence as he continued. "While his wife was in ICU in the Jean Ville Hospital, his daughter came to see him. We'd put him on Propofol, a drug that induces coma, to give his brain time to heal after the extensive surgery to remove the projectile."

"Dr. Warner, for those who don't know, what is a projectile?" Luke stood behind the podium, and I couldn't take my eyes off him. When he walked into the courtroom that morning, I was sitting in my regular place: first pew behind the prosecution's table, at the end, near the wall. He wore a dark gray suit, light blue shirt, and a purple, pink, white, and blue tie. He looked exceptionally gorgeous, or maybe I thought so because I saw him with new eyes, eyes that knew he loved me.

"A projectile is, technically, a bullet." Don Warner was direct and deliberate, but he was warm and composed. "So we had to remove the bullet that had entered his brain above his right ear."

Luke had set up an easel that had a poster with a diagram of a brain. He asked Dr. Warner to step down and show the jury where the bullet was lodged and what he had to do to remove it without causing further brain damage. Don Warner stepped down from the witness box and used a pointer to show the location of the bullet. He said it was up against the temporal lobe.

"The temporal lobe is the part of the brain associated with understanding language, also with memory, hearing, and sequencing, or organization which is, basically, the ability to make sense of things." Warner said there was no way to know how much damage Rodney's brain had incurred until he came out of his coma.

"We took him off of the Propofol, but he was totally unresponsive for several days. Then his daughter came into his room, took his hand, and began to talk to him. He responded when she said she loved him and told him that Susie, his wife, was okay. He actually turned his head towards her, then tried to open his eyes. Lilly, his daughter, said he squeezed her hand. But the most significant thing was, when she began to cry and put her head on his chest, he reached his left arm over and began to stroke her hair.

"That's the power of love." Warner testified for almost two hours with Luke prompting him to describe Rodney's difficult and painful recovery, and explain that he still couldn't walk.

"But if you could see him with Susie and Lilly, you'd know that if anyone can overcome such dire conditions, it's Rodney Thibault. He and his family are the most amazing people I've ever known. I hope I have a family like his one day."

Luke asked Warner questions about Susie's recovery, and he explained all the obstacles she had overcome. He talked about how Lilly was there every day, going from Susie's room to Rodney's, and how, according to Warner's opinion, Susie made herself recover so she could work with Rodney and bring him back to some type of normal life.

"'Miraculous,' is all I can say." He took a deep breath and let it out. "In all my years as a neurosurgeon, I've never seen anything like it. Rodney should be dead, and Susie should be an invalid." Warner looked at the jurors then at the judge.

On cross-examination, John Perkins tried to make Warner say that other patients with similar injuries had recovered. Perkins tried several angles to make Warner agree that the bullets were meant to injure, not kill; but Don Warner did not fall into the trap. In the end, Perkins's Perkins' cross-examination, in my opinion, helped the prosecution.

"I'm convinced one bullet was meant to hit Rodney between the eyes, and the other Susie, right in the center of the brain where it would cause certain death, or, at minimal, severe brain damage." Warner stared at Perkins as though he were an imbecile.

"How can you determine motive? You're a doctor, not an investigator." Perkins barked his questions in anger.

"If you compare Susie's height to the location of the bullet that entered Rodney's right arm, you would come to that conclusion." Don Warner spoke while Perkins tried to interrupt him and get him to stop. It was as though Warner didn't hear Perkins barking at him. "And the bullet that hit Rodney above the right ear would have hit him in the forehead had he not turned to protect his wife."

"Your Honor, I object to the witness's testimony." Perkins walked towards the bench, and the judge put his hand in the air like a stop sign. "He's not qualified to discuss trajectory and the intention of a shooter."

"Who is qualified, Mr. Perkins?" The judge glared at Perkins, and he began to take a few steps back when he realized he had crossed an invisible line. "If not a doctor, a neurosurgeon, the one who removed the projectiles?"

"There are qualified investigators who are trained to make those determinations." Perkins walked backwards and returned to the podium.

"I'll sustain your objection, but I will not instruct the jury to disregard." DeYoung looked at the jury then at his clerk.

"Your, Honor, that's completely unfair." Perkins' voice rose again.

"This is my courtroom, and I'll say what's fair and unfair." DeYoung was visibly angry but did a great job of remaining composed. He actually smiled at Perkins, but it was a sideways grin, more like a sneer. "Are you finished with your questions?"

"Yes, Your Honor. I tender." Perkins walked back to his table and sat down.

*

Luke called a ballistics expert who said she worked in the State Crime Lab. Luke went through all of her credentials and asked that she be entered as an expert witness. The judge approved, and the defense did not object.

The woman stepped down from the witness stand and approached the easel with a poster that showed a diagram of two people, exactly the height of Rodney and Susie, standing outside the church doors, facing the street. She drew a line from the blue truck in front of the church to Rodney's forehead and one to Susie's. Then she took that poster down, and there was another one behind it that showed the same two figures with the taller figure turned to the left, his right arm over the shorter figure, just as Rodney's was when he wrapped his arm around Susie to protect her. The trajectory of the bullets was the same, but one entered the taller figure above the right ear, the other bullet entered the taller figure in the right arm.

"The conclusion from this study is that one bullet was aimed at the forehead of each of the victims, but because the taller victim turned and threw his arm over the shorter one, the bullets missed their targets." The investigator returned to the witness stand.

Perkins chose not to cross-examine and looked defeated.

*

"It's lunchtime. We'll take a one-and-a-half hour break and return at one forty-five." The judge looked at his watch and told the jury for the fourth day in a row about the conference room and their lunches. He banged his gavel, and the jury filed out. When I got into the hall, the woman deputy who had been kind to me asked me to follow her. We went to the judge's office and Lydia buzzed us in. The judge was standing near her desk.

"Sissy, please...come in." He led the way into his chamber and closed the door. Luke was sitting in one of the chairs in front of the judge's desk. I nodded at him and tried to be as professional as possible. "I am going over to the sheriff's department to hold a bond hearing for Morrow and LeBlanc. Is there anything you want to tell me before I go?"

"They did it. I'm sure of it. I thought it was Thevenot and Rousseau, but I'm convinced it was Warren and Joey."

"Can you explain how you know this, since you admitted not seeing the assailants?'

"When Joey was on the witness stand yesterday, he laughed that wet, coarse laugh, and I remembered hearing it that night." I looked at Luke and back at the judge. "Luke, I mean Mr. McMath, said that I should try to remember smells, sounds, tastes, anything that would help me know who did it. When I heard Joey laugh, I knew it was him. Then I thought about smelling beer breath and body odor and knew the other guy was Warren. He and I used to be…well, let's just say I know his odor and how he smells when he drinks beer. And he was belching. I'd know that belch anywhere."

The judge suppressed a grin and looked at Luke. "Will this be enough to convict?"

"We have the DNA, judge." Luke took a deep breath and looked sympathetically at me. "And these two guys are part of a larger investigation, so maybe we have a bargaining chip with Sissy's testimony."

"Okay, I'm going to arrange for a high bond, seeing as how this was rape." The judge stood up and took a suit coat off a coat rack behind him and put it on. "Let's see whether they've lawyered up."

"I'll request a search warrant from the state police to collect the DNA samples from Morrow and LeBlanc, Your Honor." Luke put his hand on my shoulder, which sent chills down my arm.

"I'll need an affidavit of probable cause signed by the officer." Judge DeYoung looked at Luke intently. "If probable cause exists, I'll order that Morrow and LeBlanc submit for DNA testing."

"Thank you, Your Honor. Once that's done I'll have swabs done and send them to the state lab with the DNA collected from Sissy at the hospital." Luke squeezed my hand, and we watched the Judge walk towards the private elevator down the hall.

*

I followed Luke into the conference room where Susie was crying on Rodney's shoulder. I could count on one hand the number of times I'd seen my big sister cry, so I figured it was serious. Warner, Marianne, and Lilly were sitting around a table, sandwiches in Styrofoam containers in front of them and a stack of similar containers on the countertop across the back wall. Luke grabbed a container and sat down. I stood behind Lilly and watched, but I felt dis-attached as they all talked about what a shock it was for Susie to hear that the gunman had actually meant to kill her, too.

I felt numb. Too much was happening at one time and I couldn't sort through it all. I squeezed Susie's shoulder and kissed her on the cheek then slipped out the door.

*

I found my dad in his kitchen, eating lunch.

"Hey, little girl. What are you doing there? I thought you were at the trial."

"Lunch recess." I sat across from him and folded my hands together on the table.

"Need something?" He took a bite of salad and didn't look at me.

"Information."

"Shoot."

"What do you know about Warren and Joey LeBlanc beating and raping me?" I didn't take my eyes off him.

He looked like he'd been gut punched and started choking on his food. "Who?" He drank a half glass of water to stop choking.

"You know who. They've been arrested for what they did to me."

"That's good. How did they find out who did it? You said your head was covered and you had no idea who it was." He began to regain his composure and tried to act unaffected.

"Evidence. Did you know they both raped me? Now I know why I hurt too much down there. My vagina burned for weeks. I bled. I was raw."

"I don't need to know all the details."

We stared at each other, and after what seemed several minutes, he looked down. "Someone tried to scare me so I'd leave the case alone. Which begs the question: why didn't James want Thevenot and Rousseau arrested for trying to kill Susie and Rodney?"

He pushed his chair back from the table, stood up straight, and said, "You should continue to leave things alone, young lady." He walked out of the kitchen, and I heard the door to the Lion's den slam shut and the deadbolt click.

I drove to James's office and walked past his receptionist, who followed me saying, "You can't go back there." I threw his office door opened and saw Keith Rousseau and Mr. Borders, the DA, sitting across the desk from James. They all looked at me like I was a ghost. I just stared at them, then turned and walked out. I felt as though the walls were closing in on me, and I could barely catch my breath as I drove back to the courthouse.

*

Marianne was the first witness called that afternoon. Luke asked her what she saw when she came out of the church, and she described the blue truck speeding away. She explained how she rode in the ambulance with Susie and said that Lilly was with them. She described Susie's injuries, and how she'd stayed with her half-sister day and night except for the two days she went to New Orleans so they could see Rodney.

"His condition was the most important thing to Susie, and I was afraid she wouldn't recover if he died." Marianne started to say something else, but John Perkins stood up and objected.

"She can't know that. No one could know." Perkins was adamant.

"She's a nurse." Luke turned to look at Perkins then back at the judge. "And she's Susie Burton's sister. Of course she can make that determination."

The judge called a bench conference. They met for a few minutes, then the lawyers returned to their places, and Luke asked Marianne how she was related to Susie. He probed her until she admitted that they had the same *biological.*

"Ex-Senator Bob Burton." Marianne glared at Luke as though she could kill him, and no matter how hard he tried to get her to say it again, she waltzed around it, not repeating our dad's name.

Regardless of Marianne's unwillingness to plunge deeper into her biological background, there was an impact on the jury when they realized Marianne was half white, the daughter of a senator, the venerable ex-mayor of Jean Ville. She was educated, intelligent, beautiful, and her features were more Caucasian than African American. I watched her charm the jury, and if Luke's goal was to make the jurors who were prejudiced against blacks rethink their stance, it worked.

*

The bailiff announced Lilly's name, and she walked into the courtroom, down the aisle of the gallery, through the swinging gate, and to the witness box with the air of confidence and sophistication. She had Susie's long, auburn hair, but it was curly, not wavy like Susie's. She wore it in a high ponytail and tendrils of curls popped out around her face. Her green eyes were huge, shaped like almonds, and she had beautiful lips that were full without being overly large. She had Susie's nose, although it could have been Rodney's, too because his was narrow and regal.

Luke asked Lilly all the typical questions about name, age, where she lived, what she majored in at LSU. She answered clearly and looked at the jury when she told them she was going to be a doctor so she could save people who were shot, like her parents.

Luke set up the wedding and how Lilly was the first one out of the church behind her parents.

"What did you see?" Luke scratched the side of his face and ran his hand through his hair.

"When I walked out, I saw a flash out of the window of an old blue truck. I saw the truck speed off, and my parents fall to the ground, which was actually a concrete porch."

"What else did you see?"

"There was blood everywhere. On Susie's face, on the concrete. I didn't know who was bleeding, whether both of them had been shot." Her eyes grew to the size of silver dollars, but she held back her tears.

"How did you know someone had been shot?" Luke put his hands behind his back to act casual and help Lilly to relax.

"I heard the shots and saw my parents fall."

"You heard shots? How many?"

"Two."

"Did you see anyone in the truck?"

"Not clear enough to identify them, but there was a man with sandy blonde hair and a goatee." She glanced at the defense table, and I watched a shadow fall over her eyes, then it disappeared when she looked back at Luke. "His hair looked shaggy and unkempt. The driver had dark hair, but I only saw the side of his head."

After a few more questions, Luke tendered the witness, and Perkins walked to the podium. He made small talk with Lilly and asked her simple question, then he got serious.

"How could you see a flash and a blue truck if your parents were in front of you." Perkins stood on the side of the podium with his feet about a yard apart, hands on his hips. "Didn't they block your view?"

"I can't tell you exactly; you'll have to ask my dad, but it seems like they moved, and I had a clear view of the truck."

"Have you seen pictures of my client in newspapers or on television?" Perkins spoke softly and respectfully. I had heard Luke warn Lilly that Perkins would do that to set her up, build her trust then go for the kill.

"Yes, when they were first arrested." She sat with her hands in her lap. "Do you think you might believe the person you saw that day looked like my client because you saw the pictures, not because you actually saw him?" Perkins's voice raised a little.

"That's possible, except that I have continued dreams, you could call them nightmares, and I can see the guy." She looked directly at Perkins as though he didn't intimidate her in the least.

"Is it possible that the dreams are clear because of the pictures in the newspapers?"

"Actually the person in my dreams is not clear." Lilly paused and thought for a few seconds. "I can't see the man's face or make out features in my dreams. And I can't look at your client and say, with complete certainty, that he is the person I saw that day, although he has similar features." Lilly's last sentence threw Perkins off, and I watched Luke bend down and say something to Peter Swan.

*

The State called Susie Burton Thibault to the stand. Susie looked like a beauty pageant contestant: exceptionally stunning and regal, with long strawberry blonde hair that leaned towards red, huge blue-gray eyes, and alabaster skin. Her eyelashes were so long and thick that they touched her eyebrows when she looked up. Besides her face, her best assets are her legs, long and shapely with thin ankles, which contribute to her five-foot-eight-inch height.

When she walked into the courtroom, there was a gasp in the gallery. She was dressed in a royal blue, two-piece suit with a skirt that touched the tops of her knees and a white silk blouse that had a cravat type front. She wore nude low heels and carried a matching leather bag. She followed the bailiff, took the oath, and sat in the witness stand. The courtroom was so quiet I could hear some sort of insect buzzing near the ceiling.

Luke asked Susie all the set-up questions and dove into what she saw on her wedding day. She said almost the same thing Lilly had testified to: an old blue truck, a guy with a goatee and sandy blonde hair, a driver with dark hair.

"I saw a flash in the passenger's window as though the sun glanced off a metal object. Then there were popping sounds, and I heard Lilly scream." Susie did not blink or shift her eyes from Luke as she spoke. The jurors were riveted.

"What else do you remember?" Luke knew what she would say because they had practiced several times.

"I remember feeling Rodney on top of me." She closed her eyes as though the memory was difficult to talk about. Lilly squeezed my hand, and I put my arm over her shoulder. "I remember a warm liquid running down my face and into my hair, and I opened my eyes and saw that it was blood, and that it came from Rodney. I thought he was dead, but when I closed my eyes and concentrated, I felt his heartbeat against my chest. It wasn't very strong, but I knew he was alive. Then everything went black."

"What's the next thing you remember?"

"I sort of remember lying on my back with seat belts around me and feeling my head pound as I was pushed on something that dipped and plunged into holes. I heard the crunching of gravel and footsteps." Her voice was clear but riddled with emotions. I looked at the defense table, and even Thevenot and his two lawyers were captivated by Susie's testimony. "I remember trying to scream, but no sounds came out of my mouth. Lilly was begging someone to let her inside the place they'd put me. I later discovered it was an ambulance. She held my hand, and everything went black again."

"Do you remember anything else?"

"Pain." She automatically put her hand to the back of her head, her eyebrows raised, and furrows appeared across her forehead. "So much pain; I could feel my eyes bulge and fill with tears. Pounding pain." She put her hands back in her lap and looked up at Luke, her expression back to normal.

Luke asked her about her transfer to Ochsner, her recovery, physical and occupational therapy. She talked about being in a wheelchair, then a walker. She explained about how wonderful it was to be in the same hospital as Rodney because as soon as she got into a wheelchair, she could go to visit him twice a day. She looked happy and grateful to be alive and to have Rodney and Lilly with her.

"Are you angry with whoever did this?" Luke had been building up to this question, and I knew he and Susie had talked about it.

"Yes, I was plenty angry at first; especially when I thought I would lose Rod." She looked serious and contemplative, then she began to smile, slowly, at first. "And I wanted someone to find out who did it. Thankfully, my younger sister took that on, and here we are. Once we have some closure, and now that I know Rodney will survive, we will all be grateful and ready to move on with our lives."

"I tender this witness, Your Honor."

"Mr. Perkins?" The judge looked at John Perkins, who leaned back in his chair, engrossed in Susie's testimony. He temporarily got lost in her charm and generous spirit and was stymied. I wanted to laugh because I was amazed that he had lost his composure after being such a hard-ass through the entire trial.

Perkins sat up, looked at the judge, glanced at his partner, and rose.

"Judge, would you give us a few minutes?"

The judge called for a ten-minute recess and told Susie she could remain in the witness chair or leave the room for ten minutes. She chose to leave so she could check on Rodney. Luke followed her out of the room, and I was sure he would go over some of the questions Perkins might ask her.

When the trial resumed, Perkins walked to the podium and placed his legal pad on the surface. He asked Susie if she was sure of the description of the person she saw and she said almost the same things Lilly had said.

"But you saw a gun; your daughter didn't mention seeing a gun." Perkins was grasping at anything to discredit Susie, but he didn't know he was up against a brilliant, composed, thoughtful woman.

"No sir, I didn't say I saw a gun." She sat back in the chair, her legs crossed, her hands in her lap. "I said I saw sunlight glance off metal. I couldn't say what the object was."

"Would the clerk read back Mrs. Thibault's statement about what she saw?" Perkins looked at the judge and he nodded to his stenographer, who pulled up a ream of paper that looked like a wide roll of adding machine tape. She found the section and read.

"I saw a flash in the passenger's window as if the sun glanced off a metal object. Then there were popping sounds, and I heard Lilly scream."

"Thank you." Perkins wrote something on his pad and paused. Susie never took her eyes off him. "I have no further questions, Your Honor."

"Redirect, Mr. McMath."

"No, Your Honor."

"Thank you, Mrs. Thibault." The judge looked at Susie and smiled a wide smile as though to communicate how much he admired her testimony as well as her beauty. I'd seen untold numbers of men look at Susie that way through the years, but she never noticed. "You will not be called again, and you are free to remain in the courtroom if you like."

"Thank you, Your Honor." She stepped down from the witness stand, smiled at the jurors, and walked towards the gallery. She nodded and smiled at Perkins, then at Luke. She saw Lilly sitting with me and winked, then she walked out of the courtroom.

*

"The State calls Major Rodney Thibault." Luke stood up and looked towards the courtroom door. The bailiff repeated Rodney's announcement, the courtroom door opened, and Susie pushed Rodney's wheelchair into the gallery, through the gate, and parked it in front of the witness stand. The bailiff brought a stand-up microphone and put it on the side of Rodney's chair. Susie secured the brakes on the wheelchair, kissed him on the cheek, and came to sit with Lilly and me.

Luke was respectful of Rodney, called him Major, thanked him for his service to his country, and asked whether he was comfortable. Rodney smiled constantly, his eyes a-twinkle, almost like Santa Claus, and his demeanor was calm and respectful. He was a gorgeous man— huge, hazel eyes with green specks that danced in the light's reflection. He wore his hair short, but it wasn't nappy, more curly like Lilly's. His skin was light; people in Louisiana referred to his race as Mulatto, a mixture of white French and African American. Both of Rodney's grandfathers were white and Rodney's dad, Ray, was very light skinned.

Rodney wore a dark suit, white shirt, and red tie with tiny white dots. He had an American flag pinned on his lapel.

Luke went through Rodney's service in the army, and his retirement in May, 1984, just before his wedding. He asked Rodney how he and Susie had met, how long they'd known each other, and some of their history.

"The first time I met Susie was at my dad's gas station." He looked into the gallery at Susie and smiled. "She was in her father's car when he pulled in to get gas. He went into the office to talk to my dad, and I filled his car up. When I washed the windshield, I talked to her. I was only sixteen, but I think I fell in love with her then. I knew there was no hope for me to have a relationship with Susie Burton, but through the years we became friends, and fell in love. We tried everything to be together, but it was hopeless."

I watched the jury. Every one of them stared at Rodney without blinking. They were mesmerized by his story and his delivery. He was soft spoken but intelligent and had a gentle masculinity about him. There's something humbling about a man who will admit to the whole world how much he loves a woman.

Luke asked Rodney probing questions, and he explained how the Klan had tried the kill his dad and burned down their family home when Rodney was seventeen. He said that, ten years later, they hung his brother in a tree, that Jeffrey almost died, and that it took two years for him to recover completely. Rodney described how a group of men he called a "posse" had kidnapped him in Baton Rouge, but he was saved by state troopers who stopped the kidnappers for speeding. He described the weeks he spent hiding in Jackson, Mississippi, unable to call Susie, who waited for him to show up in Washington DC to marry her. He said he finally gave up and went home and was drafted into the army.

"How much time passed before you and Susie got back together again?" Luke asked.

"Another ten years." He looked at Susie again and smiled. Several of the jurors followed his gaze. "That was when I found out about Lilly, our daughter."

Luke let Rodney explain how he'd visited Susie in New York after she turned eighteen and how it was the first and only time they'd made love. He told how Susie didn't tell him about the baby, how she allowed a mixed-race couple to adopt Lilly, and how he'd met his daughter when she was fourteen.

"It was the most amazing day of my life to that point." He looked at Lilly and winked. Again, the jurors followed his glance and saw Lilly break into a smile and wink back at her dad. I had chill bumps and presumed everyone else did, too.

Luke finally moved on to the shooting and asked Rodney if he knew the defendant.

"Sure," Rodney looked at Thevenot, nodded and looked back at Luke. "Know Tucker... since high school."

"Would you say you two are friends?" Luke asked.

"No. Tucker ... not the kind ...person ...friends with, uh, colored person." Rodney looked at Thevenot again.

"Object, Your Honor." Perkins stood up. "How would the witness know what kind of person the defendant is, especially after admitting they aren't friends?"

"Mr. McMath?"

"Your Honor, I'll ask the defendant how he would know that." Luke looked at Perkins, and then at the judge.

"Okay, but tread lightly, Mr. McMath." DeYoung looked at Perkins. "Overruled at this time."

"How do you know how the defendant feels about black people, Major?"

"Well, he was part of ... posse tried to keep me... get to... Susie, uh, New York." Rodney spoke clearly but stopped every now and then to choose his words. His brain was still a bit slow in telling his mouth what his mind was thinking. "I saw him on train to... Memphis. The one I jumped from."

"Where else have you seen Mr. Thevenot?"

"He came to my dad's gas station, uh, a lot... in high school and college." Rodney picked up his knee by putting both hands under it and lifted, then moved it a few inches so his foot could land in a different place on the footrest of the wheelchair. He repeated it with the other leg.

"Your Honor, this witness is tired. It's six o'clock, and he's been testifying for three hours." Luke looked from Rodney to the judge. "I wonder whether we could stop now and pick this up in the morning."

"Do you have any objections, Mr. Perkins?"

"No, Your Honor." Perkins didn't stand up. He looked more exhausted than Rodney.

"Then we will adjourn until, uhm, let's say eight thirty in the morning." DeYoung banged his gavel and left the room.

⌒ Chapter Sixteen ⌒

Testify

L UKE SHOOK ROD'S HAND and was talking to him where he sat in his wheelchair in front of the witness stand. I caught Luke's arm as he turned to walk towards his table.

"Can we please talk? I won't take much of your time." I looked up at him, and I knew, for the first time, that I loved this man.

He let out a deep breath of resignation. "Okay. I guess." He didn't move. "Where to?"

"My place?" I looked up at him, and our eyes finally met. There was a magnetism and an electricity in that stare.

He grinned, and I saw the old Luke in his eyes, the one who was not so caught up in the trial, the one who loved and protected me. I stood still, as though by moving towards the door, it might give him a reason to change his mind.

He led me out of the courtroom with his hand on the small of my back, which made goose bumps gather on the back of my neck and the tops of my legs. I went down the stairs in front of him and felt his body heat behind me. He took my hand as we crossed the street and continued to hold it when he opened my car door for me. He was standing so close that I couldn't get to the door, so I stood still until he moved aside. I got the impression he was playing with me, or trying to remind himself why he had agreed to go home with me.

The driveway at Susie's house was full of cars, and I knew Rodney's family and Tootsie, and some of her family were at Susie's for dinner. I was invited, too. Luke followed me up the stairs on the outside of the garage to my apartment. He stood near the island and took off his suit coat and tie, unbuttoned a couple of buttons at the neck of his shirt, and sat on one of the bar stools.

"Wouldn't you be more comfortable in the club chair or on the sofa?" I poured bourbon into a glass of ice and set it in front of him, then poured myself some white wine.

"Let me get this first one down, then maybe I can move." He took a long pull on his drink. "It's been a long day, a long week; actually it's been a grueling month."

"I'm going to call Susie and tell her I won't be there for dinner." I went to the phone on the kitchen wall and called next door. Lilly answered, and when I told her I wasn't coming, she sounded disappointed. When I hung up, Luke asked me to play the piano for him.

"Anything special?" I got up and went to the piano, which faced the living room, and I sat on the bench where he couldn't see me unless he stood up.

"How about that Beethoven piece?" He sighed, and I played *Beethoven's Emperor* as though I were playing for a huge audience. I got lost in the music and didn't notice that he had gotten up and was standing at the back of the piano, looking at me. I stared at him while I finished the piece, then I patted the bench, and he came to sit next to me. I started to play *My Girl*, and he put his arm around my waist and sat very close to me, our thighs glued together.

I took my hands off the keys and put one on his thigh, the other in my lap. When I turned to face him, we were so close I could breathe in his exhales.

"Please kiss me, then I'll know." I moved my face as close to him as I could without touching. He kissed me, long and hard, then he pulled back.

"What will you know?" His words slid into my mouth, and I swallowed them.

"How I feel about you. How you feel about me." I opened my eyes wide.

"How could you *not* know. All these months…?"

"Luke, I've never been in love. I don't think anyone has ever been in love with me. Let's just say I don't really know what love is." He pulled his head back and looked at me. "Come with me."

He led me to the bar, poured himself another drink, and refilled my wine glass. I sat on a stool, and he stood in front of me, my knees between his long legs. He put his hands on my shoulders and stared at me as though he were looking for something behind my eyes, in my soul.

"I happen to know that something is coming down the pike, something terrible for you, something that you will blame me for…that you *should* blame me for because I instigated it. You will hate me." Luke twisted his legs to the side so he could turn his body towards the bar and away from me. "It's better if we say goodbye now. The longer this goes on, the more hurt we will both be."

He put his head in his hands, and I thought he was crying, although there were no sobs, no tears. Finally, after what seemed like a very long silence, he looked at me. "Would you mind driving me to my motel? I'm really tired, and I have a big day tomorrow."

"If that's what you want." I was too bewildered to speak. We didn't talk all the way to the Ranch House, which was about a mile from my house. I parked in front of his room, put my car in park, and turned to look at him. His hand was on the door handle. "So, is this it? I mean, are we through?"

"We have to be, Sissy." His expression was sad and tender at the same time. "Look, I'm crazy about you, but in a couple of weeks, maybe sooner, you'll understand why this had to end. You will hate me, and that will make it easier for you to forget we ever had this relationship, as wonderful as it's been." He kissed me on the cheek, got out of the car, and was behind the door that said #24 before I could catch my breath.

*

Luke called Rodney back to the stand Friday morning. Lilly sat between Susie and me while we listened to Rodney explain how he had seen Tucker Thevenot several times a week from the time he was in high school until he went off to the army.

"I'd know him... anywhere," Rodney told Luke. "Keith Rousseau, too." He talked about how Tucker had terrorized black boys since they were in high school. He told about an incident when he and a friend, Milton Jones, were walking home after a football game and Keith and Tucker started chasing them in the truck. Rodney said he was faster than his friend, so he got to the end of the block, turned around, and saw Tucker throw a rope over Milton, and then Keith took off in his truck.

"They dragged... Milton through... the ditch." Rodney said he backtracked as the truck was coming towards him and he had to jump in the ditch to keep from getting plowed over by Keith.

I was horrified hearing the story, and I could tell it was the first time Susie and Lilly had heard it. There were tears streaming down Susie's face, and Lilly squeezed my arm so hard I thought she would bruise me.

"And you are sure it was the defendant?" Luke asked Rodney.

"Oh, yes." Rodney looked at Tucker but didn't change his expression. "I'm... sure."

"So would you know Tucker Thevenot if you saw him anywhere?"

"Without... a doubt."

"When is the last time you saw him, the defendant?"

"On my... wedding day... last year. June 30, 1984." Rodney did not stumble as he said the date, which was unusual because numbers tripped him up more often than words.

"Tell the jury, once again, what you saw that day."

"When we walked... out of the... uh, I saw... Keith's old blue... truck parked in... front of the church. I saw... Tucker clear as day. I... started moving to... cover Susie as soon as... I saw the truck...

because, somewhere in my, uh… psyche I knew what… they were there for. Tucker pulled… a, uh, gun… out of the window."

"And you're sure it was the defendant."

"I'm certain." Rodney did not blink.

"Major Thibault, are you angry with Tucker Thevenot?" Luke's voice lowered an octave and softened.

"I'm so happy to… be alive, to be… uh, married to the… only girl I've ever… loved, to, uh… have the most… wonderful daughter… in the world. And, uh… I guess I… resigned myself… that people like… Tucker and Keith… can terrorize black folks and, uh… get away with it… in this… parish. But, yes… I'm… angry." He looked at Susie and Lilly and smiled. "But, uh… I learned… a long time ago that… un-forgiveness eats at the person who harbors it… not the one it's aimed at."

Susie pulled a tissue from her purse and wiped the tears off her face. All fourteen jurors looked at Susie and Lilly, some smiling, some wiping away tears. Somehow, Luke had done his magic, and it was obvious that the jurors had forgotten that Rodney was black, Susie, white, and Lilly, mixed. It had been amazing to watch the transformation.

Rodney testified until noon, then Perkins did his cross-examination in the afternoon. There wasn't much Perkins could do to trip Rodney up or make him change his testimony. Perkins finally gave up at about two thirty, and the prosecution rested.

The judge decided to adjourn court early since it was Friday and it had been a long week. I was in my car headed to Baton Rouge before most of the people had filed out of the courtroom.

*

Miss Millie was thrilled to see me, as always. She stared at me over the rims of her cat-eyed glasses and didn't bother to ask what I wanted.

"Is Mr. Morris in?"

"Is he expecting you?" She barely opened the sliding glass window.

"No, ma'am. But I really need to speak with him."

She shut the window and picked up the phone. When she put the receiver down, she pointed her chin towards the sofa behind me, so I sat and waited for about thirty minutes. When I walked into Robert's office, he came around his desk, hugged me, and pointed to one of the chairs at the round table. His brow was furrowed, and his frown was pronounced as though worried.

"What can I do for you, Sissy?"

"Robert, there's something very wrong happening in Jean Ville and, as much as I hate to admit it, I believe my brother might be involved."

"Wait! Do you have specific information? Let me get Sherman in here." He went to his desk and picked up the phone. "Oh, that's right. Well, have him and McMath come into my office as soon as they arrive."

"I left Jean Ville before anyone else. The judge shut down the trial early today."

"Millie said that Luke and Chris are on their way back now. Meanwhile, tell me what you know."

For the next thirty minutes, I explained to Robert how, at first, I had believed that Thevenot and Rousseau were the ones who'd accosted me, but that I was wrong.

"When they realized they were being followed by the state police, they passed the job off to Warren and Joey." I hugged my purse to my chest. Just thinking about that night made me feel sick in the stomach.

"What does this have to do with your brother?" Robert asked me in a soft voice.

"I went to the bar that Daniel Tyler runs. When I told him I was interested in who might have been in his bar the night I was accosted, he told me he remembered that night well, because Thevenot, Rousseau, Warren, and Joey LeBlanc were shooting pool together and they got really drunk." I explained to Robert that Daniel said he had to stop selling them beer and was worried when they left because they would be driving intoxicated.

"Daniel said that Thevenot gave Warren a wad of money and that he overheard them talking about passing a job off. He said that Thevenot said, 'Her brother said to scare her. Make sure she understands that she needs to leave this whole shooting thing alone.'" My throat was dry, and I felt squeamish, so I asked Robert for a glass of water. He called Miss Millie, and she appeared with a couple of glasses filled with water.

Luke and Detective Sherman came in and sat down. Robert repeated everything I'd told him, and Chris Sherman asked me questions I didn't know the answers to. He stood up, shook hands with each of us, and left the room.

*

"Hey, you two want to follow me home and have a drink with Brenda and me?" Robert Morris looked from me to Luke. "She wants to meet you, Luke." We were both a bit shocked but nodded, and I rode with Luke to the house in Spanish Town.

"Are you going to rat out your brother?" Luke was driving very slowly.

"I'd rather not, but if I have to, I will."

"What exactly do you think he did?"

"I believe he paid someone to beat me up. Maybe he was the bag man, maybe he instigated it himself."

"If he was the bag man, who would he have been working for?" Luke parked across the street from the Morrises' house and turned towards me. His expression said, "Think about this carefully."

"I'm not sure." I turned towards Luke with a jerk, but didn't say the words. I think he knew that I knew.

"Warren and Joey probably went farther than they were supposed to because they were so drunk, but *still*." I was suddenly angry, just thinking about my brother sending lunatics to beat me up. "Why would he want to protect Thevenot and Rousseau?" My mind couldn't go any further than the fact that my brother might have had me attacked. I couldn't wrap my brain around him having anything to do with the shooting. "This feels awfully sick to me."

Luke nodded, and we were both quiet while all those thoughts ran through my mind. When he spoke, it brought me back to the present. "If this goes even deeper, I mean, if your family members are implicated in something very serious, will you hate me?"

"If this is why you think I would hate you, you're wrong, Luke." I felt sad, but resigned. "I'm the one who started this investigation. If my brother is involved, that's not your fault. I want justice for Susie and Rodney. And for ME!" He squeezed my shoulder and kissed me on the cheek before we went into the house for dinner and drinks.

I was quiet all evening. I felt sad and angry, and the combination was frightening. Luke was charming, and Brenda fell in love with him. After dinner, when they all pressed me to play the piano, I played *All By Myself*, by Eric Carmen and *Diary* by Bread, before Brenda asked me to play something more upbeat. All I could come up with was *I've Gotta Get a Message to You*, by the Bee Gees, which Brenda said wasn't very upbeat. Luke sat beside me on the bench and whispered, "Try *Bennie and the Jets*." I played the Elton John song, but couldn't bring myself to sing along with everyone. Then I got up from the piano and went to the bathroom. I knew I was putting a damper on the party, but my heart wasn't in it.

Luke took me to my car, parked across from the AG's office.

"Let me take you home, Sissy. I'll bring you back in the morning to get your car." He held my hand on the console.

"I don't think so, Luke. I'd feel trapped without my car... just in case... I mean... what if...?" I tried to put into words how afraid I'd felt ever since I had been assaulted and raped. I didn't think he'd understand.

"Okay, then let me follow you home and see you inside, safe and sound." He grinned at me, as though maybe he did understand.

When we got to the house on Lee Circle, it was dark. He took my keys from me, unlocked the door, went inside, and turned on all the lights while I stood inside the front door and waited.

"I looked under the beds, in the closets, on the back porch... no boogie men." He took both my hands in his.

"I hate to be such a baby, but I've never stayed in this house at night alone." I trembled when I thought of him leaving. "Can you stay with me?"

"Sissy, what you need is a bodyguard." He laughed, but there was something serious in that statement.

"You're right. It's too much to ask of you." I felt my cheeks burn, and my eyes were wet with the beginning of tears that I held in check. "I don't know when I'll be ready to have an intimate relationship, Luke. I'm damaged goods, and I have nightmares about sex."

"Rightfully so." He led me to my bedroom door by the hand. "Have you thought about getting some professional help?"

"Yes. I'm going to, as soon as this trial is over."

"That's enough for me." He kissed me on the mouth.

"Does this mean we aren't breaking up?"

"Not if you won't hate me if it turns out your family is implicated in a crime." He kissed me again.

I wasn't sure how I would feel if my brother were arrested, but I knew I wouldn't blame Luke.

"Goodnight, baby. Sleep well. I'll be in the next room if you need me." He walked down the hall to one of the guest rooms. He left his door open, so did I.

*

Monday morning, we were back in court.

Several of Tucker's friends testified to his character, but they did not garner much respect. They were dressed in jeans and T-shirts, unshaven, dirt under their fingernails, filthy boots; and they talked as though they had no education whatsoever. It was almost laughable.

They told what a great guy Tucker Thevenot was, a loyal friend, a solid citizen. Each of them spoke at length about what an excellent marksman Tucker was, "The best in the parish, maybe the state," said Barry Guillory, who worked for the state penal system but "had to go on disability last year."

At four o'clock, John Perkins called Tucker Thevenot to the stand. Someone had cleaned him up, and he wore a starched white dress shirt, a solid navy tie that was too short, and cowboy boots that had been polished. His hair was clean but shaggy, and his goatee had been trimmed, yet his face still looked dirty.

He sat slouched in the witness chair, his legs extended in front of him, ankles crossed. Perkins tried to motion to him to sit up straight, but Tucker didn't get the message. Perkins asked him what he did for a living, and he said he worked at Keith Rousseau's mechanic shop. Perkins asked if he was married and he said, no, but he had two kids, a boy and a girl, six and eight. Perkins asked if he paid child support and Thevenot squared his shoulder with pride and said, "Yep. Sure do."

"Mr. Thevenot, do you hate black people?" Perkins had one hand on his hip, the other on the podium.

"No, not really. I don't hate anyone I can think of. I'm a pretty fun-loving guy." He laughed at his own comment, but none of the jurors smiled.

"Would you shoot an innocent man?"

"Of course not." He slid down in the chair and put his hands behind his head, his elbows out to the side. The judge told him to sit up straight, and some of the jurors snickered.

"Would you shoot a woman?"

"Not a good woman." Thevenot laughed aloud, as though his comment was hilarious.

"What about a white woman?"

"No. I like women." He winked at Susie, which caused her to shiver. Rodney reached his hand over the side of the bench and took her hand in his. She looked at him, and he smiled and nodded as if to say, "It's alright, we're together, and that's all that counts." She smiled and turned her attention to the witness.

"What did you think about the testimony from the expert who

said you aimed at Susie Burton's head and meant to shoot her between the eyes?"

"I'm the best marksman in the parish, so if it had been me, and if I had aimed to put a bullet between her eyes, that's where it would have landed. In fact, it couldn't have been me who done it because they'd both be dead if it had been me." He slouched in his chair again, and the judge cleared his throat and motioned for Thevenot to sit up straight. "Anyway, no one proved it was me who shot that Mulatto she married.

"Help me understand." Perkins stood to the side of the podium, as close to the witness chair as possible without getting the stop sign from DeYoung. "You and others have stated that you are a superb marksman, is that right?"

"Yep. That's right. You heard it from some witnesses. I have a reputation."

"So is it your testimony that you are such a good shot that you would not have missed, therefore it couldn't have been you?" Perkins was almost as perplexed as the rest of us. I later learned that he didn't want to put on a defense and hoped the prosecution hadn't convinced the jury, beyond a reasonable doubt, that Thevenot had been the shooter.

"That's exactly what I'm saying." Thevenot sat up in the chair and leaned forward, his elbows on his knees. "If it was me shot that man, he'd be dead. And if I had meant to shoot that woman, which I would never shoot a woman, specially a beauty like her; well if I had meant to, she'd be dead, too."

Perkins was done, and sat down heavily.

*

"Cross, Mr. McMath?"

"Yes, Your Honor." Luke walked to the podium and put his legal pad down. "Have you ever shot a person?"

"I'm not sure what you mean." Thevenot looked confused. "I never killed no one."

"That's not what I asked, Mr. Thevenot. I asked you whether you ever shot a person with a gun." Luke put both his hands on the podium and leaned forward slightly.

"Well, I don't really remember." Thevenot started to perspire and reached for his handkerchief to mop his forehead.

"Maybe I can refresh your memory. There was testimony that you shot at a man's feet to make him dance and one of the bullets hit his ankle and crippled him. Do you remember that?"

"Can't say as I do. If I was shooting at someone's feet to make him dance, I wouldn't have intended to hit him. And if one of those bullets hit him, it couldn't have been mine, cause I'm a perfect shot. If I weren't aiming for an ankle, it wouldn't get shot." He seemed satisfied with his answer and sat back in his chair again, more relaxed.

"Mr. Thevenot, several people saw you in the truck with Keith Rousseau, and two of those witnesses actually saw you shoot the gun at Rodney and Susie Thibault."

"Object, Your Honor. I'm waiting for a question." Perkins was on his feet.

"Sustained." Judge DeYoung looked at Luke. "A question, Mr. McMath?"

"Did you hear the testimony of people who claimed they saw you shoot Rodney Thibault?"

"I heard it, but they was old people who can't see good, nohow." Thevenot grinned at Luke.

"Mr. Thevenot, under oath, I want to ask you whether someone paid you to shoot Rodney Thibault?"

Thevenot looked at the judge, at Perkins, at Luke, and shifted his eyes all over the courtroom. "I don't gotta say nothin'."

"Your Honor, would you remind the witness that he's under oath and explain what that means. I have a couple of questions that I'd like to solicit truthful answers." Luke looked at DeYoung, who was looking at something on his desk.

"Mr. Thevenot." Judge DeYoung's clerk handed him a piece of paper, and he read it to Tucker. "You are under oath, which means that if you don't tell the truth while you are on the witness stand, you commit perjury. Perjury is a felony which carries a prison sentence of up to five years, plus fines and probation, after which you would be classified as a convicted felon for the rest of your life."

"Judge, if I'm convicted of shooting that man, I'll go down for longer than that."

"The jury might find you innocent, but you could still go to prison for five years if you lie." DeYoung's face got red, and he bent forward as though trying to get closer to Thevenot—in his face, so to speak. "I'm warning you, tell the truth, or I'll make sure you spend a lot of years in jail."

"Thank you, Your Honor." Luke wrote something on his pad and walked around the podium. "Mr. Thevenot, under oath, I want to ask you again: did anyone hire you to shoot Rodney and Susie Thibault?"

"I object, Your Honor." Perkins was on his feet. "There has been no testimony to open the door to that line of questioning."

"It goes to motive, Your Honor." Luke's voice was louder.

"I'll allow it." DeYoung nodded at Luke as though he wanted to hear the answer to that question himself.

"Mr. Thevenot, did someone hire you to shoot Rodney Thibault?"

"Where would you get that?" He squirmed in his seat.

"Answer the question." DeYoung glared at Thevenot.

"Do I have to?" Thevenot looked at his lawyer.

"May we approach the bench, Your Honor?" Perkins walked around his table, followed by his partner, whose name was Joseph Barton. All four lawyers leaned on DeYoung's bench and conferred for about five minutes. The lawyers returned to their tables, and the judge called for a ten-minute recess.

Perkins waited until the jury had filed out of the courtroom, and went to talk to his client who was still on the witness stand. We couldn't hear their conversation, but every now and then Thevenot nodded like he understood what Perkins said.

Perkins went to Luke's table. They bent their heads together and talked for a minute or two. The jury filed back in, the judge entered through the back door, and Luke returned to the podium.

"Mr. Thevenot, did you shoot Major Rodney Thibault?" Luke spoke in a deliberate and even voice.

"No." Thevenot crossed his arms over his chest and sat straight up with his legs spread and looked past Luke with a blank stare.

"Were you paid to shoot Mr. and/or Mrs. Thibault?"

"I plead the fifth."

"You can't plead the fifth, because you agreed to testify." Luke looked at Judge DeYoung, who told Thevenot he had to answer the question.

"What was the question?" Thevenot stared at Luke.

"I asked whether you were hired to shoot Mr. and/or Mrs. Thibault." Luke took a step towards the witness stand.

After a long pause, Thevenot said, "No." He seemed more agitated than ever, and I couldn't tell whether he was mad at Luke or contemplating what to say. After a delay that seemed pregnantly long, Thevenot lowered his head and almost in a whisper said, "I didn't shoot nobody, and that means no one hired me to shoot nobody."

The courtroom was deathly quiet. Luke didn't move, and although I couldn't see his face, I knew he was staring at Thevenot as though challenging him to change his last statement. I wondered what Luke meant when he asked Thevenot whether he was hired to shoot Susie and Rodney, but I tossed it up to legalese, and Luke's way of trying to trap Thevenot into admitting guilt.

"No more questions, Your Honor." Luke addressed DeYoung as though they were the only two people in the room.

"Do you have any redirect, Mr. Perkins?"

"No, Your Honor." Perkins looked confused.

"Does The State have any rebuttal evidence, Mr. McMath?" Judge DeYoung looked at Luke with a questioning expression.

"No, Your Honor, not at this time. No more questions." Luke remained standing.

"Mr. Perkins?" DeYoung almost looked sympathetic as he gazed at John Perkins.

"No, Your Honor. Not at this time." Perkins stood with his hands on the table, leaning forward as though the only thing keeping him from falling down was that table.

"Let's see. It's five thirty." The judge looked at his watch, then at the jurors. "All evidence has been presented, so the only things left are closing arguments and instructions tomorrow. Then you will begin deliberations. We'll adjourn until tomorrow morning at eight o'clock to begin those processes. Have a good evening, and remember not to discuss the case. You are not to repeat any of the testimony you heard."

The jury filed out, followed by the crowd of at least one hundred people who were packed into the small area of church pews behind the spindled partition.

Later, Luke told me that once the courtroom was cleared, Judge DeYoung looked directly at Thevenot and said, "Mr. Thevenot, you will be taken into custody, pending the outcome of this trial."

Two sheriff deputies walked toward the witness stand. One of them pulled Thevenot out of his seat, and the other handcuffed his hands behind his back. Thevenot hollered, "What the hell?" but the deputies ignored him.

"We've obtained the police report on the assault of Mr. Ron Bevy," the judge told Thevenot. "You violated the rules of your bond and will be placed in the parish jail, pending the outcome of this trial. I have taken great pain to have this arrest done away from the public, because I would not want to influence the jury as to your presumption of innocence. Your transportation to and from the jail for this trial will be done away from the public, and you will be allowed to wear street clothes in the courtroom."

DeYoung banged his gavel and motioned for the lawyers to follow him out of the Courtroom through his private door, while the deputies hauled Thevenot to the parish jail, kicking and screaming.

⁓ Chapter Seventeen ⁓

The Verdict

LUKE SLEPT IN THE study at my garage apartment Monday night and was gone when I woke up the next morning. I arrived at the courthouse at seven thirty, worried I wouldn't get my regular seat, but the female deputy whom I'd befriended had saved the entire first pew for our family. I hugged and thanked her, and told her I wasn't sure if anyone else would be there. Just before eight o'clock, Tootsie walked in, followed by Tom and Sam's wives, Gloria and Josie. Tootsie sat right next to me and held my hand. I'd never been so happy to see a familiar face in my life. I felt frightened and alone, and I had an overwhelming sense that my life was about to change forever.

The judge entered, the jury filed in, and the lawyers took their places. Luke glanced at me and winked, which made me smile.

The judge and bailiff went through all the regular routines, which had become as familiar as brushing my teeth. The State and defense both waved polling, which meant the bailiff did not have to do roll call to make sure every juror was present and in their correct seat. Tucker sat in the witness chair.

"The court records say that when we adjourned yesterday you were questioning the defendant." The judge looked at John Perkins, who stood behind his table.

"Thank you, Your Honor." Perkins did not approach the podium. "The defense rests."

"Does the prosecution wish to cross?"

"No, Your Honor." Luke half-stood behind his table. "The prosecution rests."

"Mr. Thevenot, you may step down and return to the table with your lawyers." DeYoung's chest rose as though he'd inhaled a ton of air. "Ladies and gentlemen of the jury, the case is concluded for taking evidence. Now the state will present closing arguments. Mr. McMath?"

*

Luke stood behind his table, wearing a black suit with a white shirt and multi-colored Tabasco tie. He looked gorgeous.

"Thank you, Your Honor, and thank you, ladies and gentlemen, for your patience in listening so attentively." Luke walked back and forth in front of the jury box and looked each juror in the eye as he talked. Every now and then, he'd return to the podium to look at his notes, then he'd go back to face the jury.

"This will be a summation, a reminder of the evidence we presented all last week. I'll try to make it short, but I'm going to cover everything so we can all be reminded about what we heard." Luke went through Thevenot's character flaws by reminding the jury about the women who said he held them at gunpoint when they were only thirteen and fourteen years old. "He beat them and threatened to kill them if they so much as spoke to a boy of the opposite race."

Luke also explained that several witnesses made it clear that Thevenot was prejudiced against black folks and spearheaded regular outings he called "the chase" where innocent young black men were lassoed with a rope, and pulled behind a truck until they were bleeding and half dead, and that some were beaten with a two-by-four.

"One witness described how he was hit across the face with a board, and another how he lost his daughter's birthday gift in the ditch he was dragged through—a doll, who lost an arm in the process." Luke looked at each juror and dropped his voice almost to a whisper. "I wonder how you would feel if someone of any race did those things to you." He paused for a long time.

"And no one ever charged Mr. Thevenot with a crime, not for assault or attempted murder. They didn't charge him because they didn't think it was worth the trouble. Think about that a minute..." Luke paused and looked at each juror, then continued.

"We also heard from eyewitnesses—people who saw Mr. Thevenot parked in front of the church in the famous blue truck from before one o'clock in the afternoon until after the shooting, when the blue truck sped away from the crime scene." Luke walked back to the jury box from the podium. "Remember Daniel Tyler, the bartender, who stopped to speak to Mr. Thevenot and the driver of the truck, Keith Rousseau, in front of the church just before one o'clock. Then, fifteen minutes later the two showed up in his bar and asked him if he'd ever killed a black man, although he used a term I won't repeat. Did that leave you with any doubt?"

"What about the neighbor, Mrs. Lee, who lives across the street from the church and actually saw the shooting? Or Mr. Tim Laborde who lives next door to the rectory who positively identified Thevenot? Do you remember when Mr. Laborde pointed at Mr. Thevenot and said, "That man right there, he points something out the window, two shots are fired, and the truck peels out?"

Luke reminded them about Mr. Everett McCann, the church's caretaker who had the best view of the crime, and watched the blue truck, identified both men, saw the truck pull up in front of the church, saw Thevenot aim something out of the window, heard two shots, then turned to see the two victims on the ground, bleeding.

"Mr. Perkins might say you should have reasonable doubt, but do you?" Luke walked slowly back and forth in front of the jury box. "Can you, in your conscience, say there is any doubt whatsoever that Tucker Thevenot shot Rodney Thibault and intended not only to kill the major, but to also kill his wife?"

Luke went back to the podium and flipped through a couple of pages of his legal pad. He reminded the jury about the testimony of the police officers and firemen and said he presented that testimony so that the jury would be outraged that so many law enforcement officers were at the scene, but there was no police report, no investigation, no charges.

"It was like all the other crimes Mr. Thevenot and others have committed against African Americans in this parish." Luke took a deep breath. "Swept under the rug. How would you like it if your daughter was beaten and threatened with a gun, your father dragged through a ditch behind a truck, your brother made to dance in the street under the firing of bullets? Do you think because you're white it can't happen to you?

"And, what if those things happened to you or someone you loved and nothing... I mean *nothing*... was done about it? How would you feel?" Luke took a deep breath and closed his eyes. Every juror watched him and listened intently. Two of the women had tears running down their faces. The bailiff took a box of tissues and placed it on the ledge that ran across the front of the jury box.

Luke reminded the jury of the testimony of the doctors, all of whom said that Rodney should have died and Susie should be an invalid. Luke talked about Marianne, Lilly, Susie, and Rodney. He spoke about their character and the way they carried themselves. He said that they had class, they were educated, that they contributed to society.

"Listening to Major Thibault's testimony, did you think of him as a black man? Or did you think of him as a good man?" Luke looked at each juror in the face as though he could read their minds and figure out how to reach them. "If you cannot see Major Thibault as an example of the man you'd like to be, or you'd like your son to be, then I ask you, 'Why or why not?' If it's because he is African American, then I ask you to search your soul and ask yourself whether you and Major Thibault have the same God. And if you do, why is it that you were not born with darker skin? How can you not put yourself in his shoes?"

Luke told the jury that the defense's only witness was the

defendant himself, who was not convincing when he said he didn't shoot Major Thibault and would not answer when he was asked if he was hired to do the job. Luke said that if the jury could not listen to Mr. Thevenot and see a difference between him and Major Thibault, they were blind, or they were brainwashed, in which case they should not serve on a jury.

"If you've been brainwashed to believe that there are different rules for black folks than there are for white folks, then you should have told the judge that so he could have disqualified you from serving." Luke walked slowly from the podium to the jury box. "I believe in you, ladies and gentlemen. I believe that each of you is an honest person who is serving on this jury because you can be fair and just; because you do not see color when there is a crime as serious and heinous as this one.

"You have to find the defendant guilty on both counts of attempted first degree murder of a beautiful woman and her husband, who served your country with honor. There are two reasons they are alive. First, Major Thibault had been trained to use his reflexes against an enemy, and he knew immediately that Mr. Thevenot, who was sitting in that blue truck in front of the church, was the enemy.

"The second reason the major survived is what experts— physicians, surgeons, doctors called a *miracle*. These experts said that Major and Mrs. Thibault should both be dead and Mr. Thevenot should be facing the death penalty. But by the grace of God, they lived. Should Mr. Thevenot be let off the hook because of the major's reflexes and a miracle from heaven?

"No. You must search your conscience and find the defendant guilty... Thank you." Luke took a deep breath. There was the silence of death in the courtroom while he looked at each juror individually, smiled, turned to tell the judge thank you, and returned to his table.

Finally, the judge spoke. "All right." He cleared his throat, and sat up straight in his chair. "Mr. Perkins, does the defense wish to make a closing argument?"

*

"Yes, Your Honor." John Perkins gathered his tablets and almost stumbled to the podium. He shuffled his notes as though he didn't know where to begin. "I know you're tired. I'm tired, too. And I don't do lectures, so I asked myself what I'm doing up here because I don't like to lecture people, but there are some facts I'd like to talk about."

Perkins went through every witness the prosecution brought before the court and attempted to discredit each of them. He said the two girls who said they'd been brutalized were too young to distinguish between violence and a boy's affection for them. He said that the black men who said they'd been stalked, lassoed, and terrorized by his client were disgruntled victims of a long line of people who thought every white man who joked with them and intimidated them were trying to hurt them. Perkins said that the cops didn't file a police report on the shooting at the church because there was nothing to report and that the firemen agreed, after speaking to lots of guests at the wedding—that no one saw anything.

"When it came to the doctors, I can't say for sure those doctors didn't get together and decide they would all say that Mr. Thibault should have died, and that a miracle saved him. When's the last time you heard a doctor deviate from scientific facts?" Perkins put the posters on the easel from the ballistics expert that showed the bullets were meant to hit Susie and Rodney between the eyes. He tried to make the jury believe that the lines from the truck to the images of the victims were incorrect.

"The prosecutor tried to wow you by parading the Thibaults and their daughter in here so you would feel sympathy for them." Perkins grinned at the jurors and paced in front of the jury box. "Don't let them pull that stunt on you. You're too smart to be swayed by some showboat stunt like that. Just because that white woman is pretty and her husband was in the army, should not make you see them as innocent victims who didn't deserve what happened to them. They had been warned for twenty years not to get married in Jean Ville.

What did they expect? They are not innocent, nor are they victims."

I watched Luke scribble something on his legal pad and push his elbow into Peter's side. They nodded at each other, and Luke continued to write.

"But that is not the point. The point is there is no substantial evidence that proves my client shot Mr. Thibault, not enough evidence that showed he or anyone intended to shoot Mrs. Thibault." He walked back to the podium and flipped through several pages in his legal pad.

"I'm not going to take up any more of your time. Ladies and gentlemen, you must find my client not guilty on all charges. Thank you." Perkins picked up all his papers and walked towards his table. Several papers slipped from under his arm to the floor, and he bent to pick them up. His face was red, and he looked flustered.

"Does The State wish to make a rebuttal argument?" Judge DeYoung looked at Luke.

*

"Yes, Your Honor. A short rebuttal if it pleases the court." Luke walked up to the podium without notes—no pen or pad. "Ladies and gentlemen, I'd like to remind you that the reason The State is prosecuting this case is because the local DA performed a bogus investigation and closed the case. The State reopened it because of all the evidence gathered by the state investigators.

"It's been a long two-and-a-half weeks for me, and I'm certain for you, and I think you're probably tired of listening to arguments and evidence, but I'd like to clarify a few things. The State does not represent Major and Mrs. Thibault. They are aligned with The State's case, which was brought by a bill of information signed by Judge DeYoung." Luke spoke slowly and softly, then he left the podium and walked to the jury box.

"I was struck by something the defense attorney, Mr. Perkins, said in his closing argument about the Thibaults. In fact, I'm shocked and appalled, and I hope you are, too, by what he said.

"Mr. Perkins said that the Thibaults are not victims because, let me quote him, 'They had been warned for twenty years not to get married in Jean Ville.' The defense attorney asked you, 'What did they expect?'

"The defense continues to open doors for me." Luke turned and smiled at Perkins as if to say, 'Thank you.' "This is exactly the kind of talk that prompted our detectives to investigate the possibility that Mr. Thevenot had been hired to murder Susie and Rodney Thibault—'They had been warned for twenty years.'

"Who warned them? That's a question for another trial, other defendants, people who arranged posses to try to kill Major Thibault ten years ago. People who hung Major Thibault's dad, Ray, in the tree in his front yard and burned his house to the ground back in the 1960s because Rodney had the nerve to speak to Susie in public. People who hogtied and hung Major Thibault's brother, Jeffrey, in a tree in the 1970s and left him for dead. Both Ray and Jeffrey survived—more miracles.

"None of the people who did these things have been charged, indicted, or brought to trial, yet. And I say 'yet' because we are closing in on them and we believe that justice will finally be done in this parish. We intend to clean up Toussaint Parish, to rid it of crooked politicians and a network of white men with money who actually run this parish from an underground network, and who aim to keep African Americans, like Major Thibault, Marianne Massey, Lilly Franklin, and others, in a place of inferior station.

"Ladies and gentlemen, don't let that happen. The rest of the world is moving forward. There are mixed-race marriages everywhere, even in Mississippi and Alabama, and in Louisiana, cities like New Orleans and Baton Rouge. And there are black people who live next door to white people, who rise up through the ranks and become educated and serve in the military and are nurses and doctors and school teachers.

"Do you want to know why Toussaint Parish is behind the times and is still so bigoted and prejudiced? It's *not* because of good people like you. It's because of a few powerful white men who are controlling your parish, your politics, your money. Men who are actually telling you how to think, what to believe. Don't let them do that to you anymore. Stand up to them by doing what's right. By finding the defendant guilty.

"And trust our team in Baton Rouge to clean up the mess in this parish and in Jean Ville, so all of you can live in peace and harmony, as God intended for all of us. Thank you." Luke's voice had risen two octaves, and he was almost screaming at the end. He threw his shoulders back and walked to his seat as though he had never been more proud of himself in his life.

I was proud of him. It was all I could do to keep from applauding when he finished, and I think others felt the same, except we were all intimidated by Judge DeYoung's glare when we so much as whispered to each other, so we all kept quiet and clapped to ourselves.

*

Judge DeYoung took a deep breath and read a list of instructions to the jury. He said that ten of the twelve jurors had to agree on a verdict. He said that if any of the jurors had reason to believe that he, the judge, had given the impression that he had any opinion concerning the guilt or innocence of the defendant, they were to disregard that impression.

"Tucker Thevenot is presumed innocent until each element of the crime necessary to constitute his guilt is proven beyond a reasonable doubt." The judge read, then looked up and cited from memory. "Remember, the defendant is not required to prove that he is innocent, and he began this trial with a clean slate. The burden of proof is upon The State, and they must prove the defendant's guilt beyond a reasonable doubt." DeYoung explained that Thevenot had been charged with two counts of attempted first degree murder, and a number of other crimes. "Attempted first degree murder means that it was premeditated, planned in advance," he said.

"If you are convinced, beyond a reasonable doubt, that Mr. Thevenot is guilty of one count, but not of the other, you must find him guilty on one and innocent on the other. If you feel The State did not prove first degree, but you're convinced that a lesser offense of attempted second degree, or attempted manslaughter, or aggravated battery should apply, then you are to find in that manner." The judge continued to instruct the jury, and they listened intently.

Superman nodded constantly, and I had begun to believe that maybe he had Parkinson's, not that he was agreeing, because he had done that nodding thing when Luke spoke and when Perkins spoke, too. The Vietnam veteran from Oregon had a wrinkled forehead as though his mind could not wrap itself around what the judge said. Blanchard, aka Jesus, had settled in over the past two weeks and looked contemplative, almost like he understood what was being said. As for the woman who was a newlywed, I thought she would shoot Thevenot if you gave her half a chance, and every now and then she'd glance at him and shake her head side-to-side. The cafeteria worker, Mrs. Jones, continued to pray.

*

The jury filed out to deliberate, and the judge told the lawyers to stay close, that if they'd like to get something to eat, he'd send someone to Charlie's Cafe to tell them when the jury was done with their deliberations.

Luke and his team packed their papers and things and followed the defense team out of the courtroom. I hugged Tootsie and the others, and they all went home. I promised to call them as soon as I knew the verdict. Once everyone was gone, two deputies handcuffed Thevenot and walked him out a side door.

I was alone in the courtroom and realized I would be alone when I heard the verdict. I sat in my seat in the gallery at the end of the first pew, up against the wall, and thought how I would feel if the jury returned a verdict of not guilty, or if they found on a lesser charge.

I didn't notice the courtroom door open as I sat hugging my

purse, wide-eyed, contemplative.

"I don't want you to be alone." Luke's voice was soft and beautiful from across the room near the door. "You shouldn't be alone, Sissy." He walked a little closer, but was still a pew's length away. I didn't look up.

I had been thinking how I would feel if James were arrested. Would I be angry with Luke? Would I think it was all his fault? I thought about what he had said at the end of his closing arguments. Did I want Toussaint Parish to remain in the dark ages? Corrupt, unlawful, discriminatory? If I had to choose between my brother and the safety and happiness of everyone else in the parish, where was my heart?

"I don't want to be alone, but everyone's gone." I stared at the purse in my lap, arms still folded around it. I could feel him come closer, but I didn't want to look at him because what he'd said at the end of his closing statement haunted me. "It's because of a few powerful white men who are controlling your parish, your politics, your money...And trust our team in Baton Rouge to clean up the mess in this parish and in Jean Ville, so all of you can live in peace and harmony, as God intended for all of us." It occurred to me that this was more serious than I'd thought. Maybe James had something to do with my assault, maybe he was also involved in covering up the shooting, but was it more? And what about Daddy? Was he trying to protect James?

Luke sat on the end of the pew with enough room between us for six people. "Do you mind if I sit with you." He sounded tired and sad.

"Would you sit closer?" He got up and came to sit next to me.

"I am so sorry, Sissy. I never wanted things to happen this way. For you to hear what you heard in this way."

"It's not your fault, Luke." I felt a tear behind my left eyelid but refused to let it escape. "I'm just sad."

He didn't say anything, and we sat there for about thirty minutes without speaking.

"Do you want to go across the street and get a drink, made have something to eat?" He moved closer to me and put his hand on my knee, the heat penetrated my skin all the way to my feet. I felt him turn his head to look at me. "It would take your mind off of things for a little while."

"Okay." I stood up. I had still not looked at him. If I hadn't been so familiar with his voice, it could have been a perfect stranger, but when I faced him, it was Luke, and I felt safe, and not quite so sad.

*

Charlie's Cafe was full and bustling—people at tables, people on bar stools, people standing behind the people on bar stools, there were even people outside the cafe standing on the sidewalk watching the third floor of the courthouse, drinks and wine glasses in their hands.

I sat at a long table with about ten people from the state attorney general's office, including the detectives, several state troopers, two female paralegals, Peter Swan, and Luke. The defense team, and what looked like the two lawyers' wives or girlfriends had been joined by Keith Rousseau and some of the guys who had testified about Tucker's character. They were all drinking beer and laughing.

Twice someone came running across the street and whispered to Luke. He and Peter, as well as Perkins and his partner, rushed across the street and up the two long flights of stairs to reconvene in the courtroom. They returned each time to tell us the jury had sent questions for the judge to answer.

The first time the jury asked about the difference between attempted first degree murder and attempted second degree murder. They asked the judge whether it was considered premeditated if the defendant had been hired by someone else to do the job. DeYoung explained that each case stood on its own merits, and that even though there was only one shooter identified in this case, several people could be found guilty of this crime, including the driver of the vehicle and any and all persons who might have encouraged the shooter to fire the gun. Judge DeYoung said these other people were referred to in the law as "principals."

The second time the jury wanted to see the evidence presented by Detective Rachel Fields from the State Crime Laboratory that analyzed the ballistics and trajectory. The judge showed them the posters again and asked if they needed to take them back to the deliberation room. They said, yes. Luke and Peter agreed that the jury was being deliberate and that could be a good sign for either the prosecution or the defense.

It was almost nine o'clock at night, and the jury had been in deliberation for about four hours when someone burst into the restaurant and said, "They've reached a verdict." Luke squeezed my hand and took off towards the courthouse in a lope, followed by Peter. I watched them climb the stairs as I made my way across the street.

Luke had been right—sitting next to him and being with all the people at Charlie's Cafe had, indeed, taken my mind off things for a while.

*

We all took our places in the courtroom, and the jury filed back in and took their assigned seats.

"Alright, we're back on the record in the State versus Tucker Thevenot." Judge DeYoung thanked the jury and told them he was proud of their service. "Okay, have you reached a verdict, ladies and gentlemen?"

"Yes, Your Honor, we have." A tall man in the middle of the top row stood. I looked at the roster of jurors I had made the first week and saw that his name was Richard Vanderslick. He had been selected as foreman.

"Let me take a look at it; don't unfold it, Mr. Vanderslick." The judge held out his hand, and the bailiff took the slip of folded paper from the foreman and handed it to DeYoung. He opened it, read it without a change in expression, and returned it to the bailiff, who gave it back to Vanderslick. "Would you like to read the verdict or would you like Madam Clerk to read it?"

"I'll read it, if that's okay." Vanderslick stood and faced the judge.

"In count one, charge that the defendant committed attempted first degree murder in the case of Major Rodney Russell Thibault, we find the defendant, guilty."

A collective gasp went through the crowd, and I stared at Luke's back in an effort to notice any change in his posture that might indicate how he felt about the verdict.

"In the second count of attempted first degree murder in the case of Susanna Burton Thibault, we find the defendant, guilty."

This time the gasp from the gallery was an audible, "Ohhhhh." Judge DeYoung banged his gavel and demanded order. The foreman continued with the other charges of resisting arrest, aggravated flight from an officer, and two counts of first degree felony assault and battery with intent to commit murder and said the jury found the defendant guilty on all counts.

The judge asked the clerk to poll the jury and ask each juror what his or her verdict was on each count. "Okay, she will call your name, and you say yes or no." The judge handed a sheet of paper to the clerk who sat next to him.

"Count one, guilty of attempted first degree murder in the case of Rodney Russell Thibault." The clerk stood behind the bench and spoke up loudly. "On this count, is this your verdict? Juror One?

"Yes." By Juror One.

"Juror Two?"

"No."

"Juror Three?"

"Yes."

All the other jurors, with the exception of juror eleven, said, "Yes." The verdict was 10 - 2." A tight win, but a win, just the same.

"I have two 'nos' and ten 'yeses,'" the clerk announced.

The second count of attempted first degree murder in the case of Susie was identical. On all the other charges, the jury voted guilty, unanimously.

The judge announced, "Proper verdict has been returned and will become the verdict of the court. Ladies and gentlemen, that concludes your service." The judge then told everyone to hold their places while the jury made their way out of the courtroom.

Once the door closed behind the last juror, aka Jesus, John Perkins stood up.

"Your Honor, we would like to move for an appeal bond, and *not* have our client remain in custody at this time."

"You would like a post a conviction bond, Mr. Perkins?"

"Yes, Your Honor, if it pleases the court." Perkins and his partner were both standing. Thevenot sat in his seat, looking confused. There were two deputies standing behind him, inside the fence that separated the main part of the courtroom from the spectators.

"You may file your motion, and it will be considered, Mr. Perkins." The judge looked at the defendant. "Due to the severity of the verdicts that have been returned, Mr. Thevenot is now to remain in custody with a formal motion for post conviction bond to be filed, which will be heard at the appropriate time. We will set the sentencing date for two weeks from today, at one thirty in the afternoon."

The two deputies handcuffed Thevenot's arms behind his back and led him out of a third door that was hidden by a set of curtains on the side of the prosecution's table, near the jury box. Thevenot kept looking over his shoulder at his lawyers as though he thought they should do something.

⌒ Chapter Eighteen ⌒

Justice

THE LOUISIANA HEAT PRESSED in from every corner of the earth. I was miserable and at loose ends. Luke and his team left for Baton Rouge Wednesday morning, and he said that they would be working the rest of the week and probably through the weekend on a huge case.

Susie, Rodney, and Lilly had returned to New Orleans after Rodney's testimony on Friday and said that unless they were needed in court, they were not planning to come back to Jean Ville. The day after the verdict, I decided to drive down to be with them. When I walked into the house on Jules Avenue, Susie and Marianne were sitting at the kitchen table, laughing and talking a mile a minute.

"Hey sisters, what's up?" I dropped my overnight bag on the floor, and they jumped up to hug me. Marianne flashed her left hand at me. On her ring finger was a sparkling diamond, about three carats. "When did you get this rock?"

"Last night." She was beaming. "It was a surprise, although we'd talked about getting married one day."

"The last time we talked about your relationship with Warner, you said you weren't sure whether you loved him." I looked from Marianne to Susie and back to Marianne. They were both still laughing.

"I guess I found out somewhere along the way." She hugged me again. "Will you be my maid of honor? Susie said she'd be my matron of honor. And I'm going to ask Lilly to be my bridesmaid."

"I'm honored." I hugged her again, and we all sat at the table.

Susie told us that she and Rodney had decided to leave Jean Ville, "For good. I'm going to put the house up for sale, Sissy. I hope you understand. You can have all the furniture from your apartment moved to the house in Baton Rouge. What you can't use from the house, we'll store here until Rod and I find a permanent home."

"I guess that means I'm leaving Jean Ville, too. I mean, unless I move back in with Dad." I suddenly felt sad again, and burdened, as though there were too many things happening at once.

"Are you okay?" Marianne took my hand and squeezed it.

"Lots going on." I looked at our hands: one white, one brown, and thought that we were not so different. Marianne and I were both in love with great guys, only I hadn't told Luke, yet. Susie loved Rodney, and Lilly loved Bobby. We should all be one, happy family; but there was a cloud that loomed over my head and, as hard as I tried to be happy for them, I was sad. "I'm really happy for you, Mari. So happy." I smiled, but I knew it wasn't my best, Sissy-smile.

"Then what's the sadness about?" Marianne stared at me the way she always did, which made me feel important and equal, even though I was so much younger and a whole lot less experienced.

"Something's wrong. I can't put my finger on it, but I'm sure James is in trouble." I looked down at the table, feeling confused. "And Daddy, I'm not sure what's going on with him. Maybe he's trying to protect James, but I'm afraid for him, too."

"Couldn't happen to a more deserving man," Marianne pushed her chair back from the table and went to the sink to rinse her coffee cup. The abrupt change in her demeanor caught me off-guard, and I let out a gasp, almost a choke.

"Sissy, are you okay?" Susie moved her chair closer to me and put her arm over my shoulder.

"I understand why you and Marianne don't like Daddy, but if something happens to him, it will be hard for me. I mean, I love my Daddy; you know how close we are." I stared at Susie for a second.

"I'm sorry, Sissy," Marianne was leaning against the counter across the room. "I don't mean to be insensitive."

"I'm sorry, too, Mari." I looked at her over Susie's shoulder. "I'm sorry he wasn't a Dad to you. I'm sorry he was an awful Dad to you, Susie." I looked at Susie and tried to grin. "But it was different for me. I was always Daddy's little girl. He made me feel loved, safe, protected."

The room was as silent as a church during Communion. I could hear the drip-drip of the faucet in the sink and my breaths coming out in short, jagged spurts of air.

Then I told my sisters that I'd thought I was in love with Luke. "But I don't feel like anyone could love me after what happened." I paused and looked down at my hands in my lap. "And I'm not sure I can really love anyone, either."

"You need to get some counseling, Sissy." Susie squeezed my shoulder.

"I know. I'm going to find a counselor in Baton Rouge, now that the trial is over."

"Sissy, don't let what happened to you stop you from living, the way it did me." Marianne looked me in the eye. "I lost twenty years of my life to harboring hatred for the guys who attacked me. I didn't know how to grieve and get past it. That incident was so life-changing that I quantified my life in terms of *before the rape* and *after the rape.* I thought that if I could go back to before, maybe I could be happy again. Don't do that to yourself. You can't undo what happened, you can't go back."

Marianne took a deep breath and walked over to the table. She put her hands on my shoulders. "Move forward. Your life will be different, but it doesn't have to be bad. Don't suffer for something you had no choice in." Mari had tears in her eyes.

I stared at her and thought about her words. "I know you're right, Mari. Maybe counseling will help." I thought about how, since my assault, I had been unable to even kiss Luke, and had still not told him how I felt about him. In fact, I didn't feel anything, except when I thought I might lose him. Then I panicked. That was as close as I could come to feeling love.

"What you said about James and Daddy being in some kind of trouble. What did you mean?" Susie's voice cut through the silence and brought me back to the present.

"I'm not sure. Why didn't they want anyone to know that Thevenot and Rousseau shot Rodney?"

"Why do you think that?" Susie looked confused.

"Just a feekung, It's baffling." I folded my arms on the table and put my forehead on top.

"I could probably guess why." Susie rubbed my back. "Daddy probably put those two no-accounts up to shooting Rodney and me."

I sat up with a jerk. "Daddy? He'd never hurt you."

"Oh, no?" Susie took her hand away from me and scooted back in her chair. "Have you forgotten how often he beat me when I was growing up. Have you forgotten that he tried to have Rodney killed ten years ago?"

"I guess I'm slow, or ADD, but I just can't wrap my brain around the Daddy I know doing anything violent." I felt my mind retreating from the kitchen to my happy place: a beach with waves rolling in, sunshine all around, the smell of suntan oil and salt hanging in the air. I could hear Susie and Marianne talking, but even though they were right next to me, their voices sounded like far away murmurs.

*

On Thursday and Friday, I went with Susie, Rodney, and Lilly to look at houses in New Orleans. Their realtor showed them several beauties, and on Friday they decided on a two-story stone house in Audubon Place, an exclusive, gated, neighborhood off St. Charles Avenue, near Tulane and Loyola Universities. Marianne and Dr. Warner were at the house on Jules Avenue for dinner that evening, and we kept things light and festive, celebrating their engagement and teasing them about how they looked at each other with goo-goo eyes. They said they were going to live in Warner's house for about a year, then they might try to find a home near Susie and Rodney's new place.

That night, Lilly and I stayed up and talked for a long time, facing each other in the twin beds in her room. I told her I was going to Baton Rouge for the weekend and asked if she'd like to come with me so she could see Bobby.

"I think Bobby has a new girlfriend." She didn't sound like it was the end of the world for her.

"What makes you think that?"

"He's been 'busy' the past few weekends, and he hardly calls me anymore." She turned on her back, put her hands behind her head, and stared at the ceiling.

"How does that make you feel?"

"Sad, I guess, but I'll get over him. It's been a hard year. I'm just glad to have Susie and Dad back." She was quiet for a while, then said, "I'm going to transfer to Tulane in the fall so I can live at home with them. I want to focus on making good grades and get into medical school in three years."

I went to sit on the side of her bed. "I thought you two were in love." I rubbed her arm and patted her cheek.

"We don't know what love is. I'm not ready for sex, and Bobby is. I think he equates love with sex; I don't agree." She seemed resigned and unaffected by the breakup, but I knew there would be a huge hole in her life where Bobby had existed, and she would be lonely until she filled that hole with other relationships. We talked into the early morning hours, then I got back in my bed, eyes wide opened.

The next morning, I told Susie I needed to be in Jean Ville in case something happened to James and Daddy.

"Sissy, let whatever is going to happen, happen. Don't get involved. I don't want to see you hurt."

"I need to take care of the furniture at the house and apartment on Gravier Road and get a realtor to list it for you. I'll be too busy to obsess about it."

*

I got to Baton Rouge late Saturday morning and called Luke. He didn't answer at his house, so I called the AG's office and dialed 3-2-3. He answered and said he'd be working all weekend, but he wanted me to come by his office that afternoon.

I pushed the beige button on the wall next to the entrance door of the AG's building at about four o'clock, and Luke came right away. He took my hand and led me to a small conference room.

"A bunch of guys are in my office." He kissed me and smiled. "I don't want to share you. What are you doing in Baton Rouge today?"

"I just wanted to see you, even if it's for a minute. If you're too busy to see me tonight, I think I'll go on to Jean Ville."

"That's not a good idea. You should have stayed in New Orleans." He pulled out a chair for me, and I sat in it.

"I have things to do. Susie wants to put the house on Gravier up for sale. I need to get a listing agent and arrange to have furniture moved to my house on Lee Circle and to Susie's in New Orleans.

"So are you going to move away from Jean Ville permanently?"

"Yes. I'm leaving Jean Ville. Everyone's leaving Jean Ville: Susie, Rodney, Marianne, Lilly." I looked up at him. He sat on the edge of the table in front of me. I thought about James, that maybe he'd be going off to jail. "There might be others leaving Jean Ville, too."

"I'm sorry, Sissy."

"I'm not. It's time for me to move on, cut ties, grow up." I told him I was going to live in Baton Rouge, even though Lilly would be staying in New Orleans. "I need to be on my own, not depend on Susie and Rodney to replace my parents. "I'm going to get a counselor, and I'm going back to school. That's another reason why I'm in Baton Rouge to register for the fall semester at LSU."

"This makes me happy. I'll have you close."

"Do you want me near you?"

"How can you ask me that? You know how I feel." He took both my hands and bent to kiss me.

"I don't know when, or if, I'll be able to give you what you need from me."

"I have lots of time. I'm a patient man, and you are worth waiting for." He pulled me to my feet and wrapped his long arms around me. It was like being bound up by an octopus, but it made me feel warm and safe.

We had dinner at my house that night, and Luke stayed over in the guest room. He worked Sunday and came back to be my bodyguard again that night. I registered at LSU on Monday, declaring myself a music major. Luke gave me a list of counselors that the state employees used, and I called to make an appointment with a lady named Rebecca Flynn for the following week. I felt I was gaining a little control of my life.

*

When I got to my garage apartment in Jean Ville, I felt panicky, like the walls had ears, and even my exhales bounced off them and settled above me like a cloud. I knew I couldn't stay there alone. In fact, I didn't think I could ever stay in that apartment alone again.

I packed an overnight bag and went to see Tootsie in the Quarters. She told me I could stay in Marianne's cabin, which was still empty because Tootsie continued to believe that Marianne would come home once Susie didn't need her anymore. Little did she know that Donato Warner had a much tighter hold on Marianne than did Susie.

I settled into the little cabin and went to sit with Tootsie on her porch next door. She didn't ask questions, and I didn't offer an explanation, but she told me I could stay all week if I wanted to.

I went home Wednesday morning to wash my clothes and pack some extra things since I planned to stay in the Quarters all week. If nothing happened by the end of the day Friday, I would drive to Baton Rouge for the weekend, where I could relax and, hopefully, spend time with Luke.

I threw my keys on the kitchen counter and noticed the red light blinking on the answering machine I had purchased in March. People rarely left messages because home answering machines were a rarity in Jean Ville. They didn't become affordable until recently with the restructuring of AT&T, so they were not widely used, and most people were afraid to talk to a machine. I found it funny that Jean Ville was so slow to catch on with the rest of the world. Another reason to leave.

I pressed the 'Play' button, and Dr. David Switzer's booming voice came through the speaker.

"Sissy, this is Doctor David." He paused and said, 'uhm' a few times. "Look, give me a call. I'd like for you to come over to the hospital to have lunch with me today, if you can." He hung up, and I tried to figure out when he'd called. My machine didn't have the feature that told the day and time, and he didn't say.

After Dr. David's message, there was one from Luke: "Sissy, I don't know where you are. I'm worried. Please call me." He breathed into the receiver for a long time as though he hoped I'd pick up. I guess I should have told him I would be staying in the Quarters.

I called Luke back right away. When the robot answered, I dialed 3-2-3, and he picked up.

"It's me. Sorry I worried you."

"Where have you been?" He sounded out of breath.

"I'm staying in the Quarters with Tootsie this week. I didn't want to be alone in my apartment."

"Why don't you come back to Baton Rouge?"

"When?"

"Well, can you leave soon? I think Robert wants to meet with you."

"Robert wants to see me?" I felt disappointed that Luke didn't want me with him.

"Well, I do, too."

"I'll come tomorrow, okay? I need to wash some clothes and tie up some loose ends." I started to click off in my head the things I needed to do: Call Dr. David, wash clothes, clean apartment, put stickers on the furniture that would be delivered to Baton Rouge, call the realtor to tell her I'd be gone for a few days. The list was long, and I had to dis-attach myself from it so I could concentrate on what Luke was saying.

"Tomorrow will be fine. Come to the AG's office, okay. Maybe about four o'clock?"

"Sure. Okay." I took a breath. "Luke?"

"Yes."

"This sounds official." I felt my cheeks getting red. "Is there something you need to tell me, so I'll be prepared."

"Not really." He paused, and I heard him swallow. "You want to have dinner with me tomorrow night?"

"Sure. But, Luke?" I thought about that empty house in Baton Rouge because Lilly, Susie, and everyone else was in New Orleans. "I'll need a bodyguard if I'm going to stay in that house alone."

"I think I know someone who will volunteer. See you tomorrow." When he hung up, I had a feeling of dread, but I wasn't sure why. Was he going to break up with me? Again?

I put a load of clothes in the washer and took a long shower. Once I was dressed, and the clothes were in the dryer, I remembered I needed to return Dr. David's call.

"Dr. Switzer's office," It was Miss Mamie, Dr. David's long-time receptionist, secretary, Girl Friday and, sometimes, nurse.

"Hi, Miss Mamie." I tried to sound chipper and upbeat. "It's Sissy Burton. I think Dr. Switzer has been trying to reach me."

"Oh, yes, Sissy, he's had me call your phone number every hour since Monday afternoon. He even had me call your dad to see if he knew where you were." She took a breath that sounded like relief. "I'll get him. You hold on, now."

"Sissy!" Dr. David's voice came barreling through my receiver, and I had to hold it away from my ear. "There you are. I've been looking for you."

"Hi, Dr. David. Sorry, I haven't been staying at my apartment. I don't like being here alone at night... ever since... well, you know." I hoped I still sounded upbeat.

"Yes, well, I'm sorry about that. You should feel safe in your own place." He took a breath and started to say something, thought better of it, then started again. "Listen. Can you come over to the hospital and we'll have lunch. Free sandwiches and sodas, you know." He laughed at himself.

"Sure. I can come. What time?"

"How about now? Let's say we meet in the doctors' lounge in about fifteen minutes. You remember where it is?"

"Yes, sir. I'm almost on my way." I couldn't remember Dr. David ever calling me, much less looking for me for a couple of days. I checked on my clothes, but they weren't dry, so I left them tumbling, grabbed my purse and car keys, and drove downtown to Jean Ville Hospital.

It was only about a five or six-minute drive, but by the time I parked, used the memorized code—4863—to enter through the back door and made my way to the doctors' lounge, I was a few minutes late. Dr. Switzer was sitting at the table we'd shared a year before, eating a sandwich and chugging a Coca Cola. I put my purse and keys on the table, kissed him on the cheek, and helped myself to half of a turkey sandwich and a Sprite.

We ate in silence for a few minutes, and when he finished his last sandwich, he wiped his mouth and put his hands on the table.

"I'm thinking we should walk over to Judge DeYoung's office." He looked over my head as though watching someone out the window behind me, and I wondered if he was trying to act casual for some reason.

"Now?" I swallowed the bite I'd just chewed and drank some Sprite to wash it down.

"Well, when you've finished eating." He got up and put his paper plate and soda cans in the trash and came back to the table. He stood behind his chair, impatient for me to finish so we could get going. I got up, dumped the rest of my lunch in the trash, grabbed my purse, and followed him out of the front door of the hospital. We retraced our steps from the previous summer, and I raced to keep up with him, again, dragging my purse behind me and counting the thirty-one cracks in the sidewalk before we turned toward the courthouse, then another twenty-two cracks to the concrete steps—ten, then a landing, then another ten.

He took the stairs two and a time, and I struggled to get my short legs to take the twenty outside steps and twenty inside stairs one at a time without putting both feet on each one. When we got to the judge's chambers, I was out of breath. Dr. David had already buzzed us in and was holding the door open for me. Judge DeYoung stood in the doorway to his inner office and his secretary, Lydia, was typing on her typewriter with earphones in her ears. She nodded at us, and the judge ushered us into his office and closed the door. It must have been soundproofed because I couldn't hear Lydia's typewriter once the door was closed.

"I'm glad you could come." The judge pointed to the two chairs in front of his desk. "Have a seat."

"Ed, I'm just going to sit here and listen while you tell Sissy what's going on." Dr. David turned his attention from the judge to me. "I'm here for you, Sissy. Consider me family... if you need me. Well, you know what I mean."

I was confused as to why I was there, but I sat on the edge of my seat and listened to Judge DeYoung. He spoke directly to me, almost in a fatherly tone, with his eyes fixed on mine. I was afraid to blink, much less look away.

"Sissy, I had to sign a warrant yesterday—to arrest someone close to you." He looked at Dr. Switzer and back at me. I had the distinct feeling that Dr. David nodded at the judge to continue, but I didn't shift my eyes and DeYoung immediately reestablished the magnetic field between our lines of vision.

"In order for me to sign a warrant, police officers, in this case, state investigators with the CID and a number of state troopers, have to present evidence to me that is compelling. In fact, I have to be very convinced a person has committed a crime worth being arrested for, before I sign a warrant. Once I sign a warrant, the person is asked to turn himself in at the parish jail, or the commander dispatches a police unit to find him and bring him in."

He paused and asked whether I understood, and I nodded.

"What does this have to do with me?" I could hear the fear in my voice, and I tightened my clench on the arms of the chair.

"Well, you are here as a courtesy, really. I think the world of you. This is going to hit you hard; that's why I wanted Dr. David here."

"Is it James?" I felt my eyes grow in size as though I'd seen a diving airplane and knew immediately I shouldn't have blurted James's name.

"Why would you think that?"

I looked at Dr. Switzer, and he shrugged his shoulders as if to ask, "Well, why would you think James might be arrested?"

"I'm not sure, just a feeling." I felt the rash start on my chest, and the familiar heat began to crawl up my neck.

"Yes, it's James." His glare was fatherly and sympathetic and confirmed my worse suspicions.

"What did he do?"

"James paid Tucker Thevenot and Keith Rousseau to kill Rodney and Susie." He put his chin down and slumped his shoulders but didn't take his eyes off me. I felt Dr. David's hand pat mine on the armrest.

"So, they were really going to kill Susie, too? Not just Rodney?" I thought about the posters with the bullet trajectories that showed the shooter aimed for both Susie and Rodney's heads, but I didn't want to believe that piece of evidence, so I let the information go in one ear and out the other.

"Yes. I'm sorry. The attorney general's office worked out a plea bargain with Rousseau, and he exposed the whole thing. Once he sang, Thevenot backed up his story."

"I figured the Klan was behind the shooting." My words

evaporated into the air, unanswered, maybe unheard.

For a while, I watched the judge's mouth move but didn't hear anything he said. I sort of spaced out, something I had trained myself to do as a child—I would go to my happy place to avoid hearing the screaming when Daddy beat Susie, or James, or Mama. Only this time, when I blocked out everything, I couldn't find the beach and sunshine in my head.

When my hearing returned, Dr. David was kneeling beside my chair, taking my pulse. I felt a cold chill run up my spine, and I shuddered. I looked from Dr. David to Judge DeYoung.

"She's okay, Ed." Dr. David removed his hands from my wrist. "Sissy, you need to be brave and mature. The judge has more to tell you, and I can't have you fainting or going into trances. You did that when you were a little girl, but you are a grown woman, and you need to step up and be strong."

"There's more? More than my brother paying to have my sister killed?" I heard my voice rise two octaves like I was singing soprano in the choir. I tried to calm myself.

"Yes, the second case is your case—the beating and double rape." DeYoung glanced at Dr. David, who was still kneeling beside my chair. "It's been solved."

"Really?" I wasn't expecting what came next.

"You were correct. It was Warren Morrow and Joey LeBlanc. We have DNA proof." Judge DeYoung spoke slowly and leaned forward on his desk with his hands folded in a praying position. "Their goal was to scare you away from the case and warn you to keep quiet."

"Oh, my, God!" all I could think of was Joey LeBlanc's penis inside me, and I wanted to vomit. I stood up and asked for the bathroom. The judge pointed to his left, my right, at a door I'd never noticed, his own private john. I went in and stared at myself for a few minutes and thought about how to gain control, to act mature. I didn't need to fall apart now. At least not here, not in the judge's office.

I opened the door to Judge DeYoung's office, and the two men were talking quietly. They stopped when they saw me, and both watched me walk to the chair and sit down.

"Okay, I'm sorry." I smoothed out my skirt and crossed my legs. "Please, Judge. Is there anything else?"

"Yes. What I was about to tell you is that Morrow and LeBlanc were paid to scare you,"

"Was that James, too?"

"Yes, he paid Thevenot and Rousseau, and they passed the job on."

*

I ran out of the Courthouse without saying goodbye to Dr. Switzer or Judge DeYoung. I pulled into James's driveway and parked behind a state trooper's unit. I jumped from my car before it was fully stopped. I ran up the steps and through the front door screaming, "James! James!" I could see through the back door where two state troopers were speaking with James. I barreled through the door still hollering, "James!" He was standing at the top of his back steps, as though about to run. His eyes met mine and a sadness passed between us.

"Why? James? Why would you do what you did to me? You paid those creeps to rape me!"

"That was never supposed to happen." He smashed the empty beer can he was holding, threw it in the trashcan, and stared at me. The two troopers took a few steps back and watched us.

"What was supposed to happen, James?" My voice sounded high-pitched and strange, even to my own ears. "They almost killed me, and those filthy, nasty guys rammed their penises inside of me. I'm your sister, for God's sake."

"Look, Sissy." He looked so sad; there were tears under his bottom lids, making his eyes blurry. "They went overboard. They were supposed to slap you around and warn you to leave the case alone. They were never supposed to blindfold you, beat, or rape you."

"Well, maybe you didn't make it clear. And what about Susie? You paid to have her murdered."

"No, that was not my intention, either." He sat down in one of the rockers, bent forward with his elbows on his knees and put his face in his hands. "All I did was deliver the money. I said, 'shoot Rodney.' I never said to shoot Susie. I told them to scare you, not to hurt you."

"So what do you think happened? Why did things get so out of whack?"

"Either they took it upon themselves to go to the extreme, or someone gave them alternative instructions."

"Why would you agree to be involved in something so horrible against your own sisters?" I stood in front of him with my hands on my hips.

"I thought it was what Dad wanted." His look was pleading.

"Daddy?"

"You don't know what I've been through with Dad, how he beat me until I left for college, then he berated me every time I came home. He's never let me forget that he paid for me to go to law school and that I owe him." James took a deep breath and sat back in his rocker as though something had just occurred to him for the first time. "I think I was willing to do anything I could to get his approval, to make him proud of me."

"You mean to make him love you, right?"

"Probably." He looked at me as though it was the first time he'd ever seen me. "Yes, you're probably right. And look where it got me."

"Can we agree to hate him?"

"I don't know, Sissy. I've always thought of him as the smartest, most successful, most educated man in the world. I've looked up to him, spent thirty-seven years trying to be just like him."

"I'm happy to say that you've failed miserably, James." I tried to let my anger wash away. I'd gone to James's house to beat him up emotionally for what he'd done, but now I actually felt sorry for him. "You'll never be like him. Thank God."

*

I drove to Baton Rouge after lunch the next day and went directly to the AG's office. Miss Millie actually seemed happy to see me and immediately called Robert to tell him I was in the reception area. He and Luke both came into the waiting room before I could open a magazine.

"Sissy!" Robert's big, hoarse voice was pitched an octave higher than usual. He hugged me, and Luke held the door open to the hallway. I followed Robert through the door and walked in front of Luke. He patted me on the back as I went by.

When we went by the opened door to Luke's office, I glanced in and saw the sketch of me that the Jackson Square street artist had done the night we went to the French Quarters for dinner. I stopped dead in my tracks and looked at Luke, who followed my stare to the framed rendering hanging on the wall over his desk. A chill went through me as though I'd seen a ghost, but Luke's smile reassured me that the presence of that artwork was a sign of his love for me.

When we got to Robert's office, we exchanged niceties about Brenda, Jessica, Bobby, Lilly, Susie, et al. Then the room got very quiet.

"Have a seat." Robert loosened his tie and sat at the round table. I sat across from him, and Luke sat between us. "I have some news that will be pretty unpleasant for you."

"Is it something I don't know about? I mean, I thought finding out that James was involved in… well, you know." I took a deep breath and listened to my voice trail off into the abyss.

"Let's see. How can I explain this all to you?" Robert unbuttoned the top two buttons on his shirt and took a deep breath.

"It's about James, right?"

"Yes, and others." He tried to smile at me and looked at Luke as though he wanted to be bailed out of something.

"I know about James. He was arrested yesterday." Suddenly I felt a layer of dread, like wet fleece, cover my brain, and my heart began to beat so hard I thought it would come blowing out of my chest.

I told Robert I'd had hints all along but didn't put them together until Judge DeYoung told me that James had paid those goons to shut me up. I told him about seeing Thevenot and Rousseau at James's house, about Warren pulling in and out of my driveway several times, about seeing my Dad and James together and having a feeling they were hiding something from me.

I pulled the note out of my purse that had been on my windshield. I handed it to Robert.

"When did you get this?" He read the note and looked at me with alarm. *"Stay out of this investigation or you'll end up like your sister!"*

"Just after you went to Jean Ville and met with my Dad, James, Borders, DeYoung, and the others." I took a long slug of water.

Robert showed Luke the note.

"Why didn't you tell me about this? Where did you find it?" Luke was breathless and grabbed my hand, a little too tightly.

"It was on my windshield at the Capitol House Hotel."

"Who knew you were staying there?"

"My Dad knew because I charged the room to his credit card. I hadn't met you at that time, so I knew it wasn't you."

Luke and Robert exchanged looks that said they knew something I didn't know. I let it slip past me because I already had too much on my mind.

"I'll send the note to the crime lab to have the handwriting analyzed," Robert said.

"I don't think that's necessary. I know who wrote it." I took a deep breath. "I know his handwriting."

"Who?"

"James." I exhaled and realized I'd been holding my breath, trying to decide whether to rat James out.

"Oh, Sissy, I'm sorry." Robert stared at me, unblinking. The air in the room felt stale, like it was just sitting still, not circulating. We were silent for a long time, my mind wandering to the night I was raped. I had cold chills on my neck and felt the redness climb up to my cheeks.

"What others?" I sat on the edge of my seat as Robert began to speak to me, almost in a fatherly tone, with his eyes fixed on mine. I was afraid to blink or look away. "You said there were others, not just James."

"Sissy, we've wrapped up an investigation on corruption, assault, and a number of crimes against some folks in Toussaint Parish. Some of these people, well, you are fond of." He looked at Luke and back at me. I had the distinct feeling that Luke nodded at Robert to continue, but I didn't shift my eyes from Robert.

"James wouldn't have anything to do with corruption or criminal activity." I felt my eyes grow in size and knew immediately I shouldn't have said what I did. "James was the bagman for someone. What else did he do?"

His glare was fatherly and sympathetic and confirmed my worse suspicions.

"There are three cases. A number of the men are involved in all three, James was involved in two."

"I'm lost. What two or three cases. How many men?" My cheeks were red now, and I felt flushed all over.

"Seven men, including James. The others will be arrested for various levels of participation. Maybe I should tell you that one of the cases has to do with the shooting."

"Of Rodney?"

"Yes. James paid Tucker Thevenot and Keith Rousseau to kill Rodney and Susie."

"I know. I figured the Klan was behind the shooting, that they gave James the money to pass on."

I felt Luke's hand pat mine on the armrest. I went into a trance. All the air was sucked out of the room, and there was no sound: no one breathed, the fan didn't whirl, the air conditioning didn't hiss, horns didn't blow outside the window. It was as though all those soft noises stopped, as though life itself stopped. Robert's lips were moving, but I didn't hear a sound. Nothing. Nada.

Luke removed his hand from my arm. "Sissy, are you listening? Do you want to hear this in slow dribbles or should we tell you everything at once? Like pulling a Band-Aid off in one swipe?"

"There's more? More than my brother paying to have my sister killed and me beaten up to within an inch of my life?" I heard my voice rise and I tried to calm myself.

"It's about who hired James to pay people to commit crimes. And it's about a network of political corruption in Toussaint Parish that kept people like Thevenot and Rousseau from being arrested for horrible crimes, for decades." Robert searched my face to make sure I was listening and had not zoned out, so I nodded as though I followed him just fine.

I took a deep breath and thought about that: why Mr. Borders closed the case, why all the things Thevenot and Rousseau did to black people were never prosecuted.

"The CID has been investigating complaints of corrupt politicians in the parish for the past year, powerful men who have been covering up crimes against black people for years." Robert spoke slowly and looked directly in my eyes. "Crimes like the ones you heard about in court last week. For instance, when Thevenot and Rousseau chased black folks, lassoed them, pulled them behind that truck, brutalized young girls, shot people in the leg, burned down black people's houses—and there were lots of other crimes you didn't hear about, not only by Thevenot and Rousseau, but others, too.

"The evidence states that city or parish cops would show up at the scene of a crime, but the mayor, chief of police, sheriff, fire chief, and DA swept things under the rug. In most of the cases, no police reports were written, and in the few cases where they were, there was no investigation, and the cases were closed.

"That's what was supposed to happen with the shooting on June 30 of last year. Do you recall that there was no police report? And once the mayor was forced by the judge to produced one, the DA said he did an investigation and closed the case? That's how things have been handled for years, even before Sheriff Desiré was elected, who, by the way, I believe started out a good, honest man, but Sheriff Guidry had set things up, and Desiré had no choice but to go along with the system, or quit—in which case Guidry would step back in." Robert scratched the back of his neck and leaned back in his chair.

"Judge DeYoung signed warrants this morning to arrest six more men who have been behind a number of crimes in the parish for almost thirty years, including the shooting and your assault."

"It wasn't just James?"

"No, Sissy. This is much bigger than James."

"So are you going to arrest Mr. Borders for not prosecuting cases?"

"Yes, Borders is being arrested. And Red Wallace. And Pierre Desiré. And Winn Marchand. And Gerald Brazille."

I counted arrests in my head: Borders the DA, Wallace the mayor, Desiré the sheriff, Marchand the chief of police, Brazille the fire chief. That was five. Did Robert say six? I looked at Luke, who looked away as soon as our eyes met. I reached out and squeezed his hand, and he glanced at me, a sad, sad look on his face.

"Okay." I sat up straight in my chair, squared my shoulders, and looked at Robert. "I can count. There's one more. Who?"

"The ring leader of all three crimes: the shooting, your beating, and the political cover-up. The person who spearheaded the criminal activity and political corruption in the parish since the 1960s. The Grand Wizard of the Klan in Toussaint Parish." Robert looked at his watch, and I glanced at the clock on the wall behind his desk: 5:30 PM.

There was a bus-stop sort of pause, and everything I'd been hiding from myself, everything I'd denied, all the things I refused to hear from Susie or Marianne, or Tootsie or Luke, or anyone; all of those ideas, conversations, intuitions flooded into my brain.

"My Dad!" It wasn't a question. It was a statement of knowledge. I sat back in my chair and heard a whoosh, like water rushing over a dam. Neither Robert nor Luke confirmed my statement, and I didn't expect them to. We all sat back in our chairs and breathed sighs, and the air that had been sucked out of the room began to return, and the tick-tock of the clock started back up, and the wind whirled from the ceiling fan and rushed out of the air conditioning vents, and I heard air brakes on a diesel bus outside on Third Street.

Life started to flow again. The world moved. People went about their business. And although I'd just heard news that no one should ever hear, I knew that I, too, would learn to move forward and go about my business; that my life would flow again.

I looked at Luke and smiled. He squeezed my hand, and I felt I was already taking a step into the future. I didn't have to go into a trance to feel sunshine on my face and hear the waves of the Gulf of Mexico rolling towards the hot sand. I was in my happy place.

Acknowledgements

Thank you to:

My husband, Gene who read every chapter as it came off the printer, every time, before revisions, after revisions, and after more revisions.

Judge William Joseph "Billy" Bennett (my brother) who painstakingly went through the entire manuscript and gave me invaluable direction, instruction, and changes to the legal parts. Not only an awesome brother, but a dedicated judge, loving husband and devoted dad, step-dad, and grand dad.

For my sister, Sally, who reads my first drafts, as horrible as they are.

For my step-daughter, Anna Gay, who believes in me and brought me to Charlotte for signings, readings, book club meetings.

JT Hill, editor extraordinaire.
Lori Hill, web master extraordinaire.
Mark and Lorna Reid of Author Packages for cover and interior

design, line editing and all the extras that got this book to print.

For Mark Dodson, master stylist with Jyl Craven Hair Design in Canton, Georgia, who gave me a new look.

For those who hosted book signings and launches, especially: Mike Dempsey, Laura Hope-Gill, Lenoir Rhyne University in Asheville, NC for launching "Lilly" at Wordfest, 2019.

For all of the book clubs who read *Catfish* and *Lilly* and those who invited me to meetings in person and via skype and facetime.

My family: children and step children: Lulie, David, Paul, Gretchen, Anna, Sean, Christopher, Kristine, Lee; my other brother, Johnny and my other sister, Angela; my cousin Letty, special friends, Beverly, Tanya, Clare, Jane, Karen, Laurie, Heather, Taryn, and so many more . . .

For Benny and Bobby, our brothers who preceded us, and for our parents, Ben and Mary Bennett. You are all together in heaven waiting for us.

For those of you who posted reviews on Amazon, emailed me, friends and strangers alike, to tell me that my stories and characters meant something to you, that you could see, feel, smell, taste, and touch the things I put on the page.

For everyone who reads my blogs and comments and for those who shared my posts on Facebook, Twitter, and Instagram. Thank you. You keep me writing.

Send your email address to Maddy at madelynedwardsauthor@gmail.com to be included on the list of readers who receive advance notice of new releases.

Pronunciation of French/Cajun names

A note: So many of you in Book Clubs I've attended, asked me how to pronounce the Cajun names in my books. Since I grew up with these names, it never occurred to me they were unique.

Baudin—Bow-dan
Brazille—Bra-zeel
Breaux—Broh
Chenevert—Shin-ver
Comeaux—Co-mo
Desiré—Dez-er-ay
Galatoie's—Gal-a-twahz
Goudeaux—Goo-dough
Guillory—Gill-oh-ree
Lamoré—Lah-more-ay
Marchand—Mar-shon
Michel—Me-shell
Ochsner—Ahk-sner
Richard—Ree-shard

Rousseau—Roo-so
Saucier—So-shay
Thevenot—Tiv-in-oh
Thibault—Tee-bow
Toussaint—Two-sant

Other terms
Bayou Boeuf—Bye-you buff

Reading Group

Discussion Questions

1. Sissy calls Susie and Rodney's wedding, "The wedding that never should have happened?" Does she still feel this way at the end of the book? What was most surprising about the wedding itself?

2. Is it realistic to believe that this level of discrimination existed in the 1980s? What about today? How has discrimination changed over the past thirty years?

3. Who do you believe should pay for the crime? Thevenot? Rousseaau? Burton? Borders? James? Others?

4. How did Sissy's relationship with her father differ from that of Susie's and Marianne's? How did those differences blind Sissy to the truth?

5. Did Dr. Switzer's role in helping Sissy make up for his complicities in Bob Burton's abuse of Susie? How important was Switzer's role in this story?

6. What did you think of Sissy's reaction to Warren and Joey when she realized they were the ones who attacked her?

7. "That's the power of love," Dr. Warner testified about Rodney and Susie's recovery. Why do you think they survived?

8. Rodney said, "un-forgiveness eats at the person who harbors it… not the one it's aimed at." What do you think of this statement?

9. At the end of the book Sissy says "I didn't have to go into a trance to feel sunshine on my face and hear the waves of the Gulf of Mexico rolling towards the hot sand. I was in my happy place." How could she be happy after all that she had learned? And all that had happened to her?

Biography

Madelyn Bennett Edwards is a Louisiana native who lives in Canton, Georgia with her architect husband, Gene. *Sissy* is her third novel, the final book in the Catfish-Lilly Trilogy.

"Maddy," as her friends and grandchildren call her, went to beauty school to put herself through college, graduating from Louisiana College with a BA in journalism and English at 38—a single mom with two children. She earned an MA in writing from Lenoir Rhyne University in North Carolina after age 60. The former television health journalist started MBC, a television production company, in Alexandria, Louisiana in the 1980s, moved it to Nashville, Tennessee in the 1990s, and sold it in 2003.

Maddy is presently working on a fourth novel, also set in Jean Ville, Louisiana, from 1990-2010. She also continues to plow through painstaking work on her memoir with the help of Jessica Jacobs, a poet-writer in Asheville, NC.

You can read more about Maddy and her upcoming releases on her website, www.madelynedwardsauthor.com

CPSIA information can be obtained
at www.ICGtesting.com
Printed in the USA
LVHW031630071119
636673LV00004B/695/P